About the author

R. F. Delderfield was born in South London in 1912. On leaving school he joined the *Exmouth Chronicle* newspaper as a junior reporter, where he went on to become Editor. From there he began to write stage plays and then became a highly successful novelist, renowned for brilliantly portraying slices of English life.

With the publication of his first saga, *A Horseman Riding By*, he became one of Britain's most popular authors and his novels have been bestsellers ever since. He died in 1972.

Praise for R. F. Delderfield

'He built an imposing artistic social history that promises to join those of his great forebears in the long, noble line of the English novel. His narratives belong in a tradition that goes back to John Galsworthy and Arnold Bennett'
Life Magazine

Also by R. F. Delderfield

A Horseman Riding By
Long Summer Day
Post of Honour
The Green Gauntlet

The Swann Saga
God is an Englishman
Theirs was the Kingdom
Give Us This Day

The Avenue Story
The Avenue Goes to War

Diana
To Serve Them All My Days
Come Home, Charlie, and Face Them
Too Few For Drums
Cheap Day Return

R. F. DELDERFIELD

The Dreaming Suburb

HODDER

First published in Great Britain in 1964 by Hodder & Stoughton Ltd
An Hachette Livre Company

This paperback edition published in 2008

6

A CIP catalogue record for this title
is available from the British Library

ISBN 978 0 340 96376 0

Typeset in Hewer Text UK Ltd, Edinburgh

Printed and bound by CPI Group (UK) Ltd, Croydon, CR0 4YY

Hodder & Stoughton policy is to use papers that are natural, renewable
and recyclable products and made from wood grown in sustainable
forests. The logging and manufacturing processes are expected to
conform to the environmental regulations of the country of origin.

Hodder & Stoughton Ltd
338 Euston Road
London NW1 3BH

www.hodder.co.uk

To my three old friends
Frank Gentry
Alan Walbank
Vic Whitworth
each of whom, in their several ways,
helped to father this book
The Dreaming Suburb is dedicated.
R.F.D.

Although, here and there in this book, the names of actual localities have been employed, Manor Park Avenue is not any particular Avenue, and neither are the Carvers, Friths, Frasers or Cleggs any particular families, residing in or around this area. They might be any people, of any South London suburb, indeed, their lives throughout the period 1919–40 might be the lives of any suburban dwellers, on the outskirts of any large city in Britain.

These people are, for the most part, unsung, and that even though they represent the greater part of Britain's population. The story of the country-dwellers, and the city sophisticates, has been told often enough; it is time somebody spoke of the suburbs, for therein, I have sometimes felt, lies the history of our race.

R.F.D.

Contents

INTRODUCTION: IX

CHAPTER I: THE AVENUE 1

CHAPTER II: HOME-COMING 5

CHAPTER III: PRINCE WAKES BEAUTY 13

CHAPTER IV: MISS CLEGG TAKES A LODGER 26

CHAPTER V: CARVERS, AT WORK AND PLAY 39

CHAPTER VI: MUTINY AT HAVELOCK PARK 56

CHAPTER VII: ARCHIE TAKES A HOLIDAY 71

CHAPTER VIII: NEW WORLDS FOR EDITH 81

CHAPTER IX: ELAINE FRITH AND THE
                FACTS OF LIFE 93

CHAPTER X: ALIBI FOR ARCHIE 108

CHAPTER XI: HAROLD AS GIANT-KILLER 117

CHAPTER XII: JIM BURNS A 'BUS 130

CHAPTER XIII: EDITH IN MOURNING 141

CHAPTER XIV: SCHOOLDAYS FOR THREE 150

CHAPTER XV: THE ICE CRACKS AT
                NUMBER SEVENTEEN 164

CHAPTER XVI: LADY IN A TOWER 183

CHAPTER XVII: CARVER ROUNDABOUT. I 205

CHAPTER XVIII: CHANGES AT NUMBER FOUR 235

CHAPTER XIX: ESME 248

CHAPTER XX: JIM HEARS RUMBLINGS

CHAPTER XXI: ABDICATION AND USURPATION 284

CHAPTER XXII: PROGRESS FOR TWO 310

CHAPTER XXIII: CARVER ROUNDABOUT. II 318

CHAPTER XXIV: EDITH AND THE HOUSE
                  OF WINDSOR 336
CHAPTER XXV: ESME'S ODYSSEY 342
CHAPTER XXVI: JIM CLOSES THE DOOR 356
CHAPTER XXVII: ARCHIE UNDER AN
                  UMBRELLA 361
CHAPTER XXVIII: ELAINE COMES IN OUT
                  OF THE RAIN 369
CHAPTER XXIX: ESME AND THE PROMISED
                  LAND 385
CHAPTER XXX: CARVER ROUNDABOUT, III 410
CHAPTER XXXI: HEROICS STRICTLY
                  RATIONED 428
CHAPTER XXXII: A LAST LOOK AT THE
                  AVENUE 445

INTRODUCTION

I have never been persuaded that history was made in the tents of the mighty. Social development, that most of us recognize as progress, together with the trends of thought and emotion that ultimately become the policy of a nation, have their origin in far less exalted places, the towns and villages of the governed whence they filter through to leaders standing in the spotlight. This, I think, is particularly true of the Western democracies, at least during the present century. The newspapers and the television screen record the outfall but they seldom penetrate to the sources, high up in the headwaters of the bedsitters, the sparsely populated rural areas of market towns and villages and, above all, the suburbs. Two-thirds of Britain's population live in suburbs of one sort or another, in long streets and terraces that have crusted round our cities. In The Dreaming Suburb *and* The Avenue Goes to War *I have tried to tell the story of the British thought-developers and policy-makers from 1919 to 1947 and here, for the first time since the first of these books was published, the story is presented as a continuous saga, in a single volume spanning a period of twenty-eight years. A great deal of history was made in that half-generation, more perhaps than in any century that preceded it. Some of the older characters in this book, people like Jim Carver, Harold Godbeer and Miss Clegg, were closer to the England of the Stuarts in, say, 1910, than we today are within reach of the Boer War period. Life has moved at a terrifying tempo since the trench veterans came home to a land fit for heroes to live in after the 1918 Armistice, the real starting point of the story, and in the decades that follow after the story ends Western Europe is still catching its breath in an attempt to keep up with the pace of events. I like to think of this*

*book as a modest attempt to photograph the mood of the
suburbs in the period between the break up of the old
world and the perambulator days of an entirely new
civilisation ushered in by the bleat of Russia's first sput-
nik in the 'fifties. In the main, of course, the story concerns the personal lives of the twenty odd men and
women who spent these years in the terrace houses of
Manor Park Avenue but in a wider sense the main-spring
of the book is the time in which they grew up, loved,
laughed, despaired and had their being.*

                                        R. F. DELDERFIELD

CHAPTER I

The Avenue

IN the Spring of 1947 the bull-dozers moved down the cart-track beside Number Seventeen and deployed across the meadow to the fringe of Manor Wood.

The grabs and the bull-dozers ravaged the Avenue and despoiled its memories. In the first week they clawed down the tiny greenhouse, where Esme first kissed Elaine, and Elaine's father, Edgar, had tended his hyacinths, and planned to abandon his family; it was not long before concrete-mixers were set up on the very spot where Judy Carver had pledged her soul to Esme Fraser and later, when the first Dorniers droned overhead, Elaine Frith had lain with her Polish lover in the long, parched grass. The Clerk of Works himself set up his office in the abandoned sitting-room of Edith Clegg, where, long before, she and her sister Becky had played *Horsey, Keep Your Tail Up* on the cottage piano during the evening soirées with their lodger, Ted Hartnell. Workmen flung their tools into the half-ruined hall of Number Twenty-Two, scratching the primrose paint that Harold Godbeer had lovingly spread at the behest of the pretty Mrs. Fraser. These, and many other desecrations were performed briskly and cheerfully, for everyone was shouting for houses, more and more houses, and the Manor Estate was wide. It was merciful that the families whose homes these had been for so long were dispersed when all this took place.

This was the first movement in the south-easterly assault on the suburb's surviving area of wild wood. Soon the axes

1

rang, and the double-handed saws whined among the aged beeches and oaks, and huge piles of scythed brambles made a pyre of the suburb's salient along the Kent-Surrey border. By late autumn the last clump of manor beeches had been thrown, and the salient, of which the Avenue had been the advanced line for so long, existed no more. Soon the Avenue itself was swallowed up in a tangle of new roads, new crescents, new avenues, each lined with semi-detached houses, quite unlike the terraced houses of the original curve. The odd numbers still looked across at the even numbers, but for the even numbers the old outlook was entirely altered, for they could see, through gaps torn by bombs, acres of new-looking houses, and pegged-out sites stretching to the horizon.

*   *   *   *   *

This is the tale of an Avenue in a suburb and of some of the people who lived in that Avenue between the long, dry summers of 1919, when one war had just ended, and 1940 when another had just begun, a tale of what they did, and what they dreamed.

About the time the story starts the word 'suburban' was beginning to acquire the meaning it has today. It is never said without a sneer or a hint of patronage. This is curious, for three-quarters of our population continue to reside in suburbs of one sort or another; they are not unlike other folk, and quite capable of extending their dreams beyond the realms of the 8:25 out and the 5:48 in. They dream, in fact, as consistently, and as extravagantly as anyone else.

This story is an account of the lives and the dreams of five families of the Avenue, four on the even side, one on the odd. The Avenue is not any particular Avenue, and might exist in any suburb of Greater London. The time is important, not the place, for every decade has its own fads, fashions, hopes, and fears, just as it has its own dance-tunes and screen favourites, its own terms of approval and condemnation. That is why this is a story of boom, slump, full employment, unemployment, new freedoms, new restrictions, hope, faith, and despair; a tale of the Charleston, the General Strike, the hunger-marchers, the amateur Blackshirts, the

Peace Ballot; of Amy Johnson, Al Jolson, and a strident Austrian comedian, who was said to gnaw carpets but wasn't so screamingly funny after all.

The Avenue's real name was "Manor Park Avenue" but nobody who lived in it ever used the words "Manor Park". They simply called it the Avenue, taking the Manor Park, which they could see across the buttercup meadow, for granted.

The Avenue ran in a scimitar curve from Shirley Rise, off the Lower Road leading to London, to the eastern entrance of the Recreation Ground, known as "The Rec", and was thus the southernmost rim of the most southerly suburb. It remained so for a long time because nobody could build on the Rec at one end, or the golf-links in Shirley Rise at the end. Behind it lay the older, more sedate section of the suburb, a dozen or so roads built in the eighteen-sixties, and named after generals and incidents of the Indian Mutiny. In front of it lay the Old Manor, and its surrounding woodland, that held out against the developers (no one ever discovered why) for more than a quarter of a century. Because of this the odd numbers had open views at the back but, by another happy accident, the even numbers enjoyed a similar previlege, for between their gardens and the Mutiny roads lay an abandoned Nursery, long since given over to briar, thistle, and dock.

This is not a complete story of the Avenue or anything like it. There were over a hundred houses in the crescent and approximately four hundred dwellers therein, so we shall hear only of the Pirettas, the Cleggs, the Carvers, the Frasers, and the Friths, respectively, of Numbers Two, Four, Twenty, Twenty-Two, and Seventeen.

The tale of these twenty-odd people as a group may be said to have commenced in the middle of the First World War, when the last of them settled in the Avenue; it ended, again as a group, when the sun was high over the beaches of Dunkirk, and dreams were cast out by stark incredulity and fear.

I did not know the Avenue until the Spring of 1918, so my story begins shortly after that season, when men like Jim Carver were drifting home from hell to look for work.

Some of the people I have writen about I understood. All of them I knew, and knew well. Most of them I loved much more than I knew, and when I left the Avenue I missed and remembered them.

CHAPTER II

Home-Coming

MORE than a dozen people in the Avenue caught Spanish 'flu in the Spring of 1919, but only Ada Carver died of it.

Four years' struggle on a low diet, stints of charring between pregnancies, and, on Christmas Eve, the news that her quiet, loose-limbed husband, instead of being demobbed within weeks of the Armistice, had now been posted off to Germany with the Army of Occupation, had combined to rob Ada of the will to combat the virus. She collapsed at the copper, and died within three days of tottering to bed, a few hours before Jim Carver could get home from Coblenz.

Jim came as quickly as he could, standing nine hours in the corridor on the Monday leave train, and another seven in the Ostend boat queue. The appalling discomfort of the journey did not worry him. Three years on the Western Front had made him indifferent to the lack of sleep, and extreme temperatures. His long, lean, slightly-stooping frame, on which his new uniform hung loosely and awkwardly, had been thumped by innumerable army doctors since that day in the autumn of 1914 when he walked into the Hammersmith recruiting office; but his category was still A.1, despite odd whiffs of gas, and several pieces of shrapnel, one of which was still "travelling" between knee-cap and thigh.

He did not know what to expect when he turned in at the gate of Number Twenty. Louise, his eldest daughter, had wired "Mother critically ill. Asking for you", but this was a pre-arranged exaggeration on Louise's part, and was written in obedience to Jim's instructions during his last leave. Ada Carver had not asked for him, or for anyone or anything except, perhaps, to lie still, and float away from muddle, and backache, and the eternal washing of nappies, and amateur endeavours to repair children's shoes. The Doctor had paid her but one visit. Doctors were grossly overworked in the Spring of 1919.

On the morning of the fourth day Louise had gone into the porch bedroom (the large front bedroom was occupied by the three boys) and found that Ada had died during the night. Jim arrived the following afternoon.

Sergeant Carver had never been to the Avenue. The Carvers, Ada, Louise, Archie, Judith, and "Berni" and Boxer, the elder twins, had moved into Number Twenty of necessity during the previous August, when Ada was quite certain that she was pregnant again. The rent was fifteen shillings a week, inclusive of rates, and although three of them were earning, the money was very difficult to find, particularly when Ada ceased to work, and the second twins were born on New Year's Day.

All through the war the Carvers had been a bare inch or two above subsistence level. Soldiers' wives, and 'teenage girls like Louise, could earn good money in munitions, but if they had gone into factories there would have been no one to care for the younger children, and Archie, now turned seventeen, was himself at work all day as a shop assistant.

So Louise and Ada took shifts of part-time domestic work, office-cleaning, milk deliveries, and long hours at the camouflage-net yard. The war seemed to go on for ever and the children, apart from Archie, seemed never to grow beyond the jam-smearing stage. The moment Ada returned from her stints Louise began hers, and she took over the cooking and housework. Usually, her day began at dawn, and ended around midnight.

Under these conditions it was not surprising that she succumbed so swiftly to the epidemic. What was surprising was that she had held out for more than four years. Even the veterans of the front-line trench system were pulled out every now and again, and sent into rest billets. There were no rest billets available to women like Ada Carver in 1918—just Spanish influenza, at the end of the line.

Jim Carver, having no key, had to ring the front bell. While he was waiting for one of the children to let him in, his eye took in the house that Ada had written so much about. Its general appearance surprised him. The Carvers had never yet lived in a house with a front garden, or a festoon of dropping chains between front door and the pavement. They had never occupied a house with three bedrooms and a bathroom, or a house that was within easy reach of open country, and they had never expected to move into a neigh-bourhood where some of the houses had names as well as numbers.

Studying the multi-coloured panes in the upper half of the front door, Jim thought he could appreciate Ada's references in her letters to the cost of living back home. He found it difficult to understand why she had moved the family right out here, and into a neighbourhood so obviously superior to the one they had left behind in Bermondsey.

Louise let him in, her plain, pale face pinched with anx-iety, and lack of sleep; Louise, the patient, the stand-by, the uncomplaining, her protruding blue eyes clouded with grief, her loose mouth, as always, slightly open, and her big, un-gainly feet planted at a near-Chaplin angle, as though better to take the weight of family cares that had been piled on her shoulders since Jim went to war so long ago.

He smiled at her absent-mindedly, for everyone was ab-sent-minded towards Louise, and dumping his kit-bag beside the hallstand, said:

"How is she, Lou? I'll go right up, shall I?"

She called out to him before his long legs had covered three stairs.

"*Wait*, Dad!"

He turned then, and knew on the instant. At all times Louise found difficulty in expressing herself. Now, she was hopelessly out of her depth.

He came back to her, and stood holding the newel-post of the banisters. He made no outcry. He was very familiar with death.

"When did it happen?" he asked, very quietly.

Louise moistened her lips but said nothing. At that moment Archie came out of the kitchen.

"Yesterday," he said, and left it at that.

Jim went slowly upstairs, his clumsy boots skidding on the polished linoleum. Dear God, he thought, over here the people still polish floors, even while they're dying.

He went in, and lifted the patched sheet from his wife's face, wondering as he did so if her angular features would touch him, as the dead boy's face had touched him, opposite the machine-gun nest outside Mons last November. When he found it did not, a tiny spasm of guilt gripped him, and then went away again. After all, Ada had lived over half the normal span, and that boy, sprawled on the clay bank, had hardly lived at all.

He replaced the sheet and went over to pull up the blinds. It occurred to him then that the customs of a dead world, the world of Victorian and Edwardian England, were still practised here—blinds drawn for death, sheets laid across the faces of the newly-dead. It seemed to him incredible that people still did this sort of thing, almost as though they had never heard of places like Passchendaele and Messines Ridge, where the bones of the dead were welcome landmarks to the ration parties, and stretcher-bearers coming up from supports.

He went back to the bed, and sat beside it, touching his dead wife's hand through the thin blanket. The vague sense of guilt returned, demanding that he should experience grief, but he felt none. Instead, his mind returned again to the dead boy at Mons, perhaps the last casualty of the war—and if not the last, then certainly the most pointless, for when the bullets cut him down, German emissaries were already driving to a rendezvous, with the white flag flying on the car bonnet.

Perhaps it was this knowledge, acquired by Sergeant Carver during a call on Signals, the previous evening, that made the memory of the boy's death so poignant and bitter. The order to attack that particular post had been an act of murder. The two gaunt Bavarians manning it would have retired, Armistice or no Armistice, long before dawn. Yet, despite Carver's protest, despite his pointing this out to the pot-bellied Major, fresh from base, and thirsting for blood, the attack had been ordered. A few grenades had been thrown, there was a thin spatter of fire from the gun, and the section had crossed the bank with a single casualty—the kid.

When the gun had been dismantled Carver went back over the captured ground. It was fortunate for the Major that he had returned to battalion headquarters immediately prior to the skirmish. If he had come upon "B" platoon sergeant when he was engaged in removing the kid's identity disc he might have been the final British casualty of the war.

Carver never saw the Major again but he remembered what was inscribed on the disc—*"Private Barnes, J. T. Number 2727650. C. of E."*. He remembered his face, too, and would always remember it, as a symbol of crass stupidity, and of a scheme of things that made such sacrifices possible.

For more than four years Sergeant Carver, tanner, meat salesman, and trench veteran, had fought the German Kaiser. On the final day of the war he changed sides. From now on he was to fight his own people.

The wail of a cornet from the road brought him out of his reverie. From the bay window he saw one of the ex-Serviceman's street bands moving slowly along the Avenue. The cornet player, and a one-armed banjoist, his instrument buckled to his chest, were playing *Tipperary*, while a third member of the the team knocking on the doors, and jingling a cap in front of anyone who passed.

He saw young Archie go out and point upwards, towards the porch window. The man with the cap looked confused and hurried away. The music stopped, to start again further down the Avenue.

The incident helped Jim to concentrate on the present. The habit of discipline, of the will to survive, reasserted itself, and he began to grapple with immediate problems. Had anyone done anything about the funeral? How soon could he get demobilised? What kind of job could be found in a strange district? How were the eight of them going to fit into a three-bedroomed house, and what had happened to the latest twins, the girls he had never seen?

He kissed Ada on the brow and went out, locking the door. Before going downstairs he toured the upper floor, noting that a reshuffle of bedrooms would be necessary, now that there were four of either sex living in the house.

Louise called him from the kitchen.

"I've made a stew, Dad. You must be hungry!"

He clumped into the tiled kitchen, and found the children crowded round three sides of the table, with Louise already ladling from the saucepan.

He sat down, and for a moment nobody spoke. He realised they were waiting for a lead, and the awkward silence embarrassed him. He tried to think of something to say, but the utter inadequacy of family small talk kept him silent. Louise concentrated on the plates, and even Archie avoided his eye.

Suddenly Judith, the eight-year-old, burst into tears, and pushed her plate away. The odd tension broke as Louise's arm shot round her.

"Try, Judy—please *try*," she pleaded. "Daddy won't like it if you don't; Daddy wants you to try!"

The child's puffy face, framed in dark curls, touched Carver. He got up, and lifting Judith from her chair sat down in her place, putting the child on his knee. He spooned a slice of dumpling into her mouth and was absurdly gratified when she swallowed it, and smiled suddenly, nestling closer to him. He noticed then that she had brown eyes, like his own, and that her hair was deep chestnut, like his mother's. His contact with her melted something, far down in his breast, and he felt his eyelids twitch. Unable to speak, he twisted his mouth into a smile and immediately, to his intense relief, a ripple of smiles answered him from all sides of the table.

He cleared his throat and spooned up a mash of carrot and onion—there was barely a shred of meat on the plate.

"It's all right now," he told them; "I'll be home very soon and everything's going to be all right."

"Will we move again?" Boxer, the bull-headed twin, wanted to know.

Jim shook his head.

"I'm glad," Boxer went on. "Me an' Berni like it here, don't we, Berni?"

Berni grinned, and Carver recalled then that Ada had written telling him that the six-year-olds, Boxer and Berni, although utterly unlike in appearance, had behaved as though they were a single individual from the moment they could crawl. Other fragments of her letters came back to him— Judith, the one on his knee, kissed his photograph every night before she was tucked up; Archie, the eldest boy, had taken to wearing coloured socks and going out with girls; Louise was such a help, and had been having trouble with her teeth —a mass of uncorrelated family gossip that he had read, primarily as a duty, in dugout and billet and base hospital over the years. Out there he seemed to have lost all touch with the children and if he thought of them at all it was as a group, not as individuals.

He went back to his own chair, and under cover of spoonfuls of stew he took a cautious look at them, noting that they were doing the same to him. Poor little devils, he thought; how much simpler it would have been if Ada had survived, and he had died out there. At least they would have had the pension.

Suddenly his eye met Boxer's and Boxer winked. It was a solemn, man-to-man, "this-is-a-bit-of-a-fiasco" wink. Jim grinned, and Berni, watching Boxer, outgrinned the pair of them.

All at once a curious sense of well-being possessed Carver and, with it, a ready acceptance of responsibility. So he had felt when a new draft of recruits had been handed over to him, before going up the line during the uneventful nights before the March push, but this time it was without the accompanying knowledge that, in a matter of weeks, days even, most of the youngsters would be dead, blinded, or maimed. These children would not be called upon to face a creeping barrage, and none of them would lie out on a clay bank, with machine-gun bullets embedded in their bodies. It was all over, and he had survived. There was some sort of future. He, and all the other survivors, would make quite sure there was a future, and that Private Barnes, No. 2727650, would be the last youth to throw away his life at the behest of a pot-bellied base Major. Without doubt, the very last one.

"Where are the babies?" he suddenly demanded. "Why aren't they here? Who's looking after them?"

"The District Nurse took them down to the Settlement, and said they could stay," faltered Louise. "When Mum was so ill I couldn't manage . . . they kept crying. . . ."

He reached across the table and squeezed her hand.

"You've been fine . . . fine, Lou. I'll get somebody before I go back. I don't know where or how, but I'll get somebody. Here, I expect you'll need this," and he pulled two folded pound notes out of his breeches pocket, and laid them beside her.

Boxer's eyes widened, and he nudged the steadily gulping Berni.

"Look, Berni . . . it's money!"

Jim's mouth twitched, this time involuntarily. There was something irresistibly comic about Boxer's bullet-head, and the way his pink ears stood out, reminding Jim of a ditched ammunition lorry with both doors swinging free.

"That's housekeeping," said Jim; "this is for you—new ones!" And his hand emerged once more from his breeches pocket, holding a pile of new sixpences. Ceremoniously he placed a coin in front of each twin, and a third in Judith's free hand.

Archie, who had said nothing so far, put his hand in his pocket and jerked it to and fro. He drew it out and scattered a pile of coppers on the cloth.

"Share 'em out, kids," he said, getting up suddenly. He winked, heavily, in Jim's direction, and at that moment yet another fragment of one of Ada's letters came back to Carver. "*Archie's earning, and never seems to be short. He's saving for a motor-cycle. He helps me sometimes.*"

Archie got up, stretched, and lit a cigarette from a packet of Goldflake. He performed these movements with studied nonchalance. Watching him out of the corner of his eye, Jim marked the challenge in the way the boy blew smoke through his nose. There was something aloof and vaguely contemptuous in Archie's attitude, almost as though, after four years' reign as the man about the house, he resented his father's return, and was by no means ready to abdicate. "He helps me sometimes"—Jim wondered grimly how often, and quietly prepared for battle.

CHAPTER III

Prince Wakes Beauty

1

THE Frasers, mother and son, moved into Number Twenty-Two the week Mrs. Carver died, and Esme, from his mother's bedroom, watched the funeral party leave for Shirley churchyard.

Although only eight years old, Esme was no stranger to death, and a funeral was not a new experience.

Less than a month ago they had buried Grannie Fraser, and Esme himself had ridden with his mother in the first carriage that had set out from the tall house in Kensington, where he had grown up, to Waterloo Station, and thence to Woking.

A few days later the Kensington house was sold, and they came to the Avenue, the house having been found, and purchased on their behalf, by Mr. Harold Godbeer, managing clerk to Stillman and Vickers, the solicitors who administered the estate of Grannie Fraser, and that of her son, the late Lieutenant Guy Fraser, sometime of the London Scottish Regiment.

Guy Fraser had been killed on the Marne, in 1914, and ever since, his pretty widow and their only child had lived with the Lieutenant's mother.

There was enough money, from the two estates, to have kept the Kensington house going, but Mr. Harold, who seemed to be taking rather more than a professional interest in the affairs of pretty Eunice Fraser, had persuaded her that this would be both uneconomical and inconvenient, and that a far more sensible course would be to find a little house in a pleasant outer suburb, somewhere not too far from his own bachelor lodging in Lucknow Road, Addiscombe.

Eunice had let herself be persuaded. Bewildered by the abrupt demise of her husband, who seemed to be beside her in a fetching new uniform one moment, and nothing more than a photograph on the piano the next, she had promptly moored herself to the ample bosom of her formidable Scots mother-in-law, and weathered out the remaining years of the war in Mrs. Fraser's well-staffed, well-ordered, town house, emerging only to tend a stationery stall at a war charities bazaar, or take little Esme to see Peter Pan's statue in Kensington Gardens.

Eunice was quite unused to fending for herself and floated through the days pleasantly enough, occupying herself, and such mind as she possessed, in looking pretty, playing simple pieces on the piano, gazing into shop-windows, and reading the novels of Mrs. Henry Wood, particularly *East Lynne*, in which she saw herself as Lady Isobel, prior to that heroine's elopement with the wicked Captain Levison.

She was, indeed, rather like a mid-nineteenth-century wife from the leisured classes; there had always been a Mr. Carlyle to cosset her, pay her bills, and encourage her belief that life, for all but the collarless manual workers, was a gentle, downstream drift in an Arthurian barge.

The only girl in a large family, she had been spoiled by her father and brothers. At seventeen she had met Lieutenant (then plain "Mr.") Fraser, and at eighteen she had married him, and shared his modest private income in a small country house his mother had owned near Ascot.

She was petite, flaxen-haired, blue-eyed, utterly trusting, and quite stupid. Understandably her husband had adored her, for she possessed, in generous measure, that characteristic feminine helplessness sought after by the chivalrous.

Lieutenant Guy was chivalrous to a fault, so chivalrous in fact that he was blown to pieces by a grenade, whilst kneeling to hold a water-bottle to the mouth of a wounded enemy. In the autumn of 1914 there were still a number of men who saw war in terms of Rupert Brooke's poetry, and the Battle of Zutphen. Even so, Lieutenant Fraser's action, in the midst of a precipitate scramble for cover, so amazed his Company

Sergeant Major that he too stopped dead in his tracks, and
was shot through the knee by a sniper.

At eight-and-a-half little Esme was beginning to look like
his father. He had the same narrow, sensitive face, large and
serious grey eyes, and excessively romantic disposition, part
inherited, and part cultivated by the bedtime stories of his
gentle mother, and the nineteenth-century romances he pored
over in his grandmother's house, from the moment he could
tackle three-syllabled words.

Like his mother Esme was never really aware of the
present, but unlike her his mind was not a comfortable vacuum. On the contrary it seethed with action, ranging from
single-handed captures of Spanish settlements, to participa-
tion in thundering cavalry charges, alongside Rupert of the
Rhine, and Warwick the King-maker.

Gertrude, the old Nannie who had charge of him throughout the Kensington part of his childhood, had been put to
some pains to bring him out of these engagements in time
for his meals, and his passion for dressing up as a Cavalier,
or the right-hand man of the Scarlet Pimpernel, played havoc
with his mother's extensive wardrobe.

He was fond of his mother in the way one is fond of an
attractive spaniel bitch wont to curl up cosily out of range of
one's feet in front of the fire, but his romantic idealisation of
his soldier father claimed a larger share of his thoughts,
ousting even Rupert, Jack Shepherd, and the Nevilles. He
saw Lieutenant Fraser, not as a quixotic Territorial, whose
life was untidily snuffed out in a muddy French turnip field,
but as the embodiment of Arthurian manhood who went
singing into battle, was killed opposing fantastic odds, and
was subsequently borne away by mourning queens to a Flanders Avalon.

Without even knowing it, his mother gave positive encouragement to the colourful illusion, and consequently Esme
was spared, throughout his entire childhood, the bewilderment of a child who has no recollection of his father. Not
until he was in his late 'teens, and had read books like
Aldington's *Death of a Hero*, did Esme see Guy Fraser as he
actually was at the moment of his death.

From the time of their settling in Number Twenty-Two,

Esme had disliked Harold Godbeer, the over-solicitous solicitor's clerk, and as time went on, and Harold became a daily visitor to the house, the boy's resentment grew into a repugnance that was altogether disporportionate to the earnest little man's shortcomings.

Harold was spare, eager, bespectacled, and physically frail. He was also fussy, pedantic, and inclined to be pompous. His pomposity was that of a man who had always been unsure of himself, and was at an additional disadvantage when dealing with a woman whose china-blue eyes, and tiny rosebud mouth, caused him to stammer every time he began to speak to her.

Basically, Harold was kind, amiable, and genuinely sympathetic towards a woman whose abysmal ignorance of money matters, he sensed, was certain to lead her to penury if somebody with a business training was not on hand with good advice.

Harold was very conscious of Esme's sour dislike, and did what he could do combat it, even bringing him little gifts from time to time, and going so far as to read two chapters of *Huckleberry Finn* to the boy the night that he and his mother moved in, and Esme had to sleep on cushions in the back bedroom.

It was no use, however, and after a time Harold resigned himself to seeing Eunice alone, in his office in St. Paul's Churchyard, or in an ABC teashop during her bi-weekly excursions up West.

That first summer he made some sort of progress with her. He knew that she trusted and respected him, that she thought he had a wonderful head for figures, and limitless capacity to serve, but somehow these things were not what one wanted from a twenty-seven-year-old client, who had a disturbing habit of laying her tiny hand on the back of your own, of looking right into one's eyes and whispering: "I do *envy* you, Harold! You have such a wonderful *grasp* of things!"

At times like these poor Harold Godbeer, thirty-five and still virginal, longed to grasp something less crackly than a bundle of share certificates and a mortgage deed.

For Esme, however, the move brought vast compensations. Within a fortnight of moving into the Avenue he had explored far afield, and was delighted with his discoveries. Hitherto his experience of the countryside was limited to Green Park, Kensington Gardens, part of Hyde Park, and the Serpentine. Now, within a few minutes of his front gate, he had the Manor fields, the Manor Woods, the vast plough-land along the Kent border, and, in other directions, the "Rec", the Lane, the Links, and the mysterious adandoned Nursery on which his bedroom window looked.

The summer of 1919 was very hot, one of the hottest and longest on record. Week after week the sun beat down on brown grass and drooping, dust-laden hedgerows. In the early mornings the thrushes and blackbirds sang for joy in the thickets, and a riot of daisies, buttercups, speedwell, and viper's bugloss rolled away from the very pavement-edges of the Avenue, towards the cool rhododendron clumps on the fringe of the Manor woods.

Inside the woods it was solemn and mysterious, and so quiet, in the long, hazy afternoons, that Esme could some-times hear the woodpecker hammering away at a trunk on the far side of the reed-grown fishpond. There were always dead leaves here, that rustled pleasantly as he scuffled along the bramble-grown paths, and sometimes, when a light breath of air struck the top of the woods, the huge boughs quivered and sighed, and the filtered sunbeams danced across the thickets and were suddenly still again.

There were hundreds of brilliant butterflies out here, but-terflies Esme had so far only peered at in fly-blown cases in shop-windows, Red Admirals, Peacocks, Tortoiseshells, and common Blues. By June the bluebells were nearly over, but their scent lingered, and every now and again he came upon great clumps of nodding foxgloves, or a low, ivy-matted bank, starred with periwinkles.

The smell of the countryside became for Esme almost tangible that summer, a smell of cut grass, and crushed hyacinth; of turned earth, and distant wood fires; of cottages, farm manure, boiling tar, and a thousand things growing under the fierce sun, and towards evening, when he came out of the woods, and crossed the buttercup meadow to the Avenue, he heard, for the first time, the summer evening orchestra of the suburbs, the low, pleasant whine of lawn-mowers, the chink of watering-can and spade, the scuffle of unlaced garden boots on cinder path and concrete, and the metallic snick-snack of hand-shears, hard at work on unruly privet. He opened his heart to it all and was happy, happy to look, to sniff, to sense, to absorb. It almost spoiled his pleasure when he reflected that he owed his presence here to Mr. Godbeer, who had now, alas, become "Uncle Harold".

2

It had been late May when the Frasers first came to Number Twenty-Two, and Eunice decided to take Mr. Godbeer's advice, and enter Esme at Elstone College, in the main road. The College was by no means as important an establishment as it sounds, being a small private school of some eighty boys, who were housed, with four or five unqualified staff, in a large three-storey house occupying an enclosed garden at the corner of Hayseed Road.

The summer term was well advanced by late May, and by the time Eunice had visited the school, and signed the entrance forms made out by Mr. Godbeer, it was mid-June, and Esme easily persuaded her to delay his commencement until the September term. In the meantime he explored further and further afield, pushing along the paths that led through the heart of Manor Woods until, one airless noon, he came within sight of the Manor itself.

He stopped short against the crumbling stone balustrade that bordered the overgrown lawn. As he came upon it suddenly, from the deep shade of the woods, its impact was considerable, for it was huge, rambling, and awesomely empty. Once white, its porticoed façade was now a dirty grey. Plaster was falling away from the cornices, and the woodwork of the window-panes was rotting. Some of its first-floor windows were broken, and all were cob-webbed, and thick with grime. The outhouses were beginning to fall in, and some of the garden ornaments that bordered the terrace had been overturned and chipped. Broken flower-pots littered the weed-sprouting drive, and festoons of ivy, honeysuckle, and red creeper were climbing right across its face, in some cases half obscuring the shattered, upstairs windows.

There was a small lake within a stone's throw of the porch, its surface thick with water-lilies. In the middle of the lake was a tiny islet, studded with silver birches, and through them Esme could just glimpse the roof of a summer-house.

What struck him most forcibly about the ruin was the quiet that surrounded it, a quiet so different from that of the woods, a quiet that seemed to have endured for a century, as though the last carriage wheels to crunch that weed-grown forecourt, were those in the days of the Prince Regent and Beau Brummel. It was an eerie, man-made quiet; sad, deliberate, and very frightening to an imaginative child of eight.

He was standing there wondering if he could ever have the courage to climb the balustrade, and peep through the windows, when he heard a twig crack immediately behind him. He wheeled around poised to flee, back through the woods, across the field, and into the Avenue, away from this eerie stillness to the safety of people and houses.

Then he relaxed, for it was only a child, a girl about his own age, and as she picked her way over the straggling briars towards him, he recognised her as the girl from next door, the girl whose mother's funeral he had watched a week or two ago.

She was wearing a neat, cotton frock, of red checks, with little puffy sleeves that bunched out above her elbows. She had no stockings but wore a pair of open sandals, and he saw that her legs were scratched, and that one long scratch had been bleeding.

She did not appear to share his awe of the great blind house, for she smiled, and in smiling showed fleeting dimples. She obviously recognised him, and took it for granted that he would be glad of her company, for she said, by way of an introduction:

"I followed you. I've been meaning to ever since I got the holiday. You come here every day, don't you? I see you across the field. I can see from our bedroom. Once I saw you go early, while I was dressing. I've never been this far before, but Berni and Boxer have; it was them who broke some of the windows."

A sudden shyness fell upon him, induced, perhaps, by the shamelessness of her admission regarding her brothers' vandalism. He looked down at his shoes and kicked hard at a beech root that had bored under the wall, and was making a wide crack in which dandelions had seeded.

Her air of assurance suddenly left her, and she became anxious.

"You don't *mind* me following you, do you? You see, you've only just come, haven't you, and I knew you wouldn't know anyone. You don't hate girls, do you?"

His silence restored her confidence.

"Berni and Boxer do," she went on; "they hardly ever let me play, except when they want a squaw, but I don't mind really. They always play rough games, not 'house', and things like that. I like 'house', don't you?"

"I don't know," said Esme, at last, glad to be able to answer one question without committing himself.

"You don't?" She seemed very surprised. Then she smiled reassuringly. "Oh, but you wouldn't, would you? You're an 'only'."

"An 'only'?" he queried.

"An only child. There's seven of us. Mum had twins just before she died. Louise says that's partly what killed her. I don't seen why, but that's what Louise says. Louise is my sister. She looks after us. They're home now—the twins, I mean—and Dad's coming soon. I'm going to take them out in the pram when we get one; Louise said I could."

She looked speculatively at the tangled path behind her. "They'd be wonderful for 'house', *real* babies, but I don't suppose we could get them here, the pram would get all tangled up. I could bring dolls, tho'; I've got all my dolls, right back to 'Inky'. 'Inky's' the nigger boy I had years and years ago. I've got nine altogether."

"I come here exploring," said Esme, very firmly. He thought it essential to establish, once and for all, that a dispatch-rider for Prince Rupert, or a missionary in search of a lost tribe to convert, could not reasonably be expected to waste his valuable time playing dolls with a strange girl. He began to suspect; moreover, that a game of 'house'—

whatever it was—would involve dolls as its principal stage properties.

The girl was not put out by the implied rebuff.

"What's your name? Mine's Judith. I know yours is Fraser, but what else? Is it David?"

"No," said Esme heavily. "It's Esme. Why should it be David?"

"Esme." She savoured it and nodded. "It's nice, but not as nice as David. David's my favourite boy's name, because David is my favourite Bible person. You know about David, don't you?"

"Of course," said Esme, a little shocked that she should be so ready to put him among the heathen. "I like David too, because he could sling. Can *you* sling?"

"No," said the girl; "show me."

Delighted at the prospect of proving his manhood so easily, and so promptly, he took out the unused handkerchief that his mother had placed in his pocket that morning, folded it like a bandage, found and placed a heavy pebble in the crease, and whirled the sling three times round his head, before suddenly releasing the shorter fold.

The pebble went straight over his shoulder and struck a beech tree immediately behind them. He began to flush before it hit the ground, but Judith had brothers and knew enough about the male to refrain from comment.

"That's spiffing," she commented; "I bet that would have sunk into Goliath's head if he'd been standing there."

Esme felt himself warming towards her.

He nodded towards the silent house. "Shall we go in?" he said, surprised at his own recklessness.

She was a realist. Vigorously she shook her head, and her chestnut curls bobbed.

"It's too creepy. Even Berni and Boxer have never gone inside. Besides," she added more comfortably, "it's all locked up."

"Damnation!" said Esme very deliberately. Sir Eustace, swash-buckling exiled Royalist in the book he was now reading invariably exclaimed "Damnation!" when thwarted, and for almost a week Esme had been longing to use the expression in front of a safe audience. The audience-reaction was not remarkable. He was not to know that Boxer, the girl's bullet-headed brother, habitually used a somewhat stronger expletive.

"We'll have a look around, anyway," he compromised, adding: "and you needn't be afraid when we do go in, because then I'll be armed. When we get home," he promised, "I'll take you into our back lavatory and show you." When Judy did not respond to this unconventional invitation, he gave her a sidelong look and added, "The back lavatory is my armoury. Mum said I could use it; it's far too dirty to go in!"

They moved around to where the coping was broken, and whilst she still hesitated he jumped down into the forecourt, and turning, held out his arms as an encouragement to her to follow.

She jumped immediately, and her expression, when he caught and steadied her, intoxicated him. In her unwavering eyes and parted lips he read her complete acceptance of him, not merely as a protective male, but as a hero, straight out of the pages of one of his books. He began to swagger, and as they crossed the court to the margin of the lake, he made sudden darts and thrusts with his left hand, sometimes turning aside to do it, but more often keeping his stern gaze immediately ahead.

"Why do you do that?" she asked presently.

"Do what?" he asked, with mock surprise.

"Jab at things ... like that—" and she made an inexpert attempt to imitate him.

"Oh *that!*" His tone implied that the movement should not have had to be explained. "That's sword-play, just to get you used to sudden ambuscades!"

Her dark brows met, and she made no immediate reply, but when they reached the dilapidated gazebo, opposite the island, she asked:

"Is an ambuscade an illness?"

He stopped short, and regarded her with genuine pity. Then he laughed outright. After all, she was only a girl, who didn't know enough to avoid getting her legs clawed by blackberry shoots.

"An ambuscade," he explained patiently, "is a sudden at-

tack from an alley. They come at you all the time, 'specially
after dark, and always," he added with dark emphasis, "always when you're carrying dispatches!"

"Oh," said the girl, and was content to leave it at that.
Something in the studied patience of his voice warned her
not to enquire further into the nature of this exciting creature's present mission, and the risks she obviously ran in
accompanying him.

She stood silently beside him, and looked across the shallow lake to the islet.

"That," he pronounced, "would be a wonderful place to
get wrecked on!"

She gave him a quick, nervous glance. She had heard
Boxer tell of a boathouse, and a punt on the lake shore, and
Esme was obviously the sort of boy who, once he was aware
of this fact, would insist on her joining him in a journey
across open water. She had never been on water, and never
wanted to; it was enough, for the moment, to be alone with
him, in the huge, brooding presence of the eyeless Manor.

He kept his eyes fixed on the islet so hungrily that she
decided to divert his thoughts into a safe backwater.

"I always thought," she said, "that this place must be like
the Sleeping Beauty's palace and now I've seen it it is."

The word "palace" interested him. He knew about the
Sleeping Beauty, but could not, for the moment, recall her
connection with a deserted palace.

"Tell me about the palace," he demanded.

She sat down on the last of the terrace steps and hugged
her knees.

"They all went to sleep in a place like this. They slept for a
hundred years before the Prince came, and cut his way
through to them. He woke her up," she went on, appreciably
lowering her voice, "with a kiss!"

"What," he wanted to know, "did he cut his way through?
Was it Guards?"

"No, just briars and things, like here," she said, pointing to
the red scratches on her bare legs.

He remembered now, but still vaguely. "Did they *all* wake
up?" he wanted to know.

She nodded. "We could play that," she went on, but without much hope.

She was astonished by his enthusiasm. "It would mean getting inside," he said and then, noting the look of fear in her eyes, "but I'm unarmed!" He was able to dismiss his own fears with such a cast-iron excuse. "We could play it in the summer-house, though. I'll tell you what; you go in there and lie down, and I'll go into the thicket and then fight my way out."

There seemed no help for it. With dragging steps she left the sunny safety of the lakeside, and crossed the terrace to the ramshackle gazebo. Its windows were still glazed, and thick with cobwebs. The floor was sagging, and grass sprouted between the boards.

The sun had not yet passed beyond the beechwood, and in here there was deep shadow, and the smell of mildew, and mouldering woodwork. As she entered she looked back, and was horrified to discover that he was nowhere in sight. She would have run out, and fled back to the terrace, but she suddenly recalled that, without his help, she could never climb the wall, so she stood trembling, on the very edge of the threshold, her feet planted on the rim of sunlight.

"Esme!" she cried out, "Esme, where are you?"

There was a long, heavy silence in which she was able to fight down her panic. He was not the boy to leave a game half-finished. He would come for her, so long as she played her part.

She retreated further into the shadow and curled herself against the damp wall. She lay still for a moment, listening to her wildly beating heart, then, turning over on her back, she screwed up her eyes so tightly that she saw brilliant sun-patterns. Suddenly, something brushed her lips, and she opened her eyes to find him kneeling immediately above her. A small crooked branch was stuck in his belt, and in his left hand he held a length of hazel twig, with a cross-piece tied to it with his handkerchief.

"It's all right," he told her; "I found a pistol, and made this. I'm not sure they *had* pistols," he said doubtfully; "I should have to look it up. Have you got the book at home?"

She said nothing, but continued to stare up at him with

shining eyes. In kissing her he had transformed her into a real Princess. She knew now that she would marry him, would never contemplate marrying anyone else and she knew with an intuitiveness beyond her years, that this was not the time to tell him, but the time to tread warily, and let him realise he had a ready-made audience for any venture he might pursue in the future. How lucky it was that he lived next door, and because of today, no one else should ever have him, no one, boy or girl, never, never, never. That was to be her reward for not running away.

Soon afterwards they took the path home. On the way, once the mansion was safely beyond the trees, she asked him who could have lived there.

"Why, the Squire," he said; "Squires always lived in manors. They had hundreds of scullions, and heaps of horses. They had big dogs that bit poachers, and when they grew old, they put great, thick bandages on their feet, and cursed people who banged against them."

"Do you mean they cut their feet purposely?" she asked, immensely impressed by his vast store of knowledge, and assuming that the bandaged feet were part of a strange, manorial ritual.

For the first time since their meeting he confessed to half-ignorance.

"I don't know what the bandages were *for*," he admitted, "but they always had them. It was a sign of being a squire. Perhaps it was chilblains."

And then, as they emerged from the wood, and into the meadow, "*I'm* going to be a Squire when I grow up, and perhaps I'll live there."

She said nothing, but it occurred to her how wonderful it would have been if he had said "*We'll* live there", instead of "*I'll* live there". On reflection, however, this struck her as ungrateful to God, for giving her such a wonderful morning, and the courage not to run screaming when she had found herself alone in the gazebo. Perhaps, in time, he would invite her to join him on an estate. In the meantime, she must say nothing to anybody, not even Louise, and strive only to please him.

They reached the Avenue and crossed it.

"This is my house." he told her, pausing outside Number Twenty-Two.

"I know," she said, and with singing heart turned into Number Twenty.

CHAPTER IV

Miss Clegg Takes A Lodger

1

THE Misses Clegg. Edith, and Becky, qualified as the Avenue's oldest inhabitants. This was not on account of their age, for in 1919 Edith was forty-six and Becky forty-three, and the doyen of the Avenue was Grandpa Barnmeade, of Number One Hundred and Two, who had served at Omdurman, but because the Misses Clegg had moved into the Avenue as long ago as 1911, when the "Rec" end of the Crescent was still unbuilt.

The Cleggs came from a tiny parish in North Devon, where their father, the Rev. Hugh Clegg, D.D., had been vicar for over forty years. When he died, they had good reasons for moving far away from the area in which they had been born and brought up, and Edith chose the Avenue because it was the most rurally situated terrace house offered her by the London house-agents.

At first she had been very homesick for the open skies of Exmoor, and the thin, misty rain that fell so persistently throughout eight months of the year, but as time went on she found herself preferring the casual neighbourliness of the suburb, and the undoubted convenience of the shops, to the stifling intimacy of the Devon village, and the wretched isolation of the grim old parsonage in which they had lived so long.

Moreover, the Avenue seemed to suit Becky, whose "spells" had become far less frequent in the last few years, and were now limited to less than one a month, not counting those brought on by the spring air-raids of 1917.

All along the Avenue Becky was known as "the dippy sister." This was chiefly on account of her occasional appearances, in the garden of Number Four, in a flannel nightdress, with her thick chestnut hair hanging down her back, but Becky's immodesty in this respect had nothing to do with her "spells"; they were occasioned by genuine anxiety for her cat, Lickapaw.

Lickapaw was a huge, sullen-faced Tom, who repaid his mistress's frantic devotion by disappearing for long periods, in search of fresh wives. He sometimes stayed away a week, but he always came home in the end, to nurse his damaged whiskers and renew his spent vitality, on heaped-up platefuls of fresh fish and saucer after saucer of milk, spooned from the top of the can.

Under Becky's ministrations Lickapaw quickly recovered from the effects of his sporadic debauchery, putting on flesh again, and sleeping, for days at a stretch, in the best armchair. Sometimes he slept for more than a week, occupying the chair all day, and the foot of Becky's bed at night, and on these nights she sometimes stayed awake until the small hours, delighting in his weight on her feet, and hardly daring to move for fear of disturbing his recuperative slumbers.

Ultimately, however, he always went off into the nursery garden again, and then, night after night, Becky would "fish" for him, standing on a box placed against the fence that divided the Avenue gardens from the nursery, and dangling a piece of hake, or a kipper, from the end of a long string.

These moonlit matinées were a source of great delight to the Carver boys, and to other children living lower down the Avenue. They would stay out late, risking good hidings on their return, solely for the pleasure of seeing Miss Clegg, looking a little like Lady Macbeth, jerk her kipper over the six-foot fence and call: "Lickapaw! Lickapaw! Come away from those nasty strays!"

Edith, Becky's sister, jeopardised the popularity her natural warmth and generosity had earned among the children, by seeking to cut these entertainments short, and by tugging gently at Becky's nightdress, until she reluctantly stepped down from the box, and went disconsolately to bed.

Poor Edith spent most of her life tugging her sister's garments, in one way or another, but she would not have had it otherwise, for her loving care of Becky, besides being a sisterly obligation, was part of a lifelong penance, imposed by the conviction that it was she, in large measure, who was responsible for Becky's periodical lapses.

On nights like these, and those during Becky's "spells", Edith's memory reconstructed every detail of that soft June night nearly twenty years ago, when Becky, a radiant young girl madly in love, had been compelled to confide in her sister because she needed money to elope with Saul Cooper, the painter who had bewitched her.

Parson Clegg's wife had died when Becky was born, and the tubby little man had resisted all the efforts of his parishioners to get him married again. Instead, he had sunk into a morose half-life, content to perform the barest minimum of his parochial duties, and devoting the greater part of his time to building model ships.

His study, where he should have been writing sermons, became his workshop, and dozens of calf-bound theological works were pulled from the shelves to make room for the exquisitely-made galleons, and carracks, and clippers, he fashioned. He seldom addressed more than a word or two to his daughters, and throughout her adolescence Edith had been obsessed by the fear that the Church Authorities would dismiss him for neglect of duty, and throw them all into the street.

They never did, however, and she came to believe that he must have had some influence with them, of which she was unaware.

One winter morning, on his way back from a funeral, he staggered and fell as he passed through the lych gate, dying an hour or so later of coronary thrombosis.

That was in 1909, years after the Saul Cooper scandal, and Edith had had the two of them on her hands ever since she found Becky abandoned in London, and had successfully fought her father, and parish busybodies, on the issue of bringing Becky home again, and not sending her to an institution.

Edith was never able to discover anything of importance about the man who had shattered Becky's health, and had reduced her, in the space of a few months, to a semi-imbecile. Nor, for that matter, was she ever able to learn much of what happened after the night Becky stole into her room, kissed her, took the wash-leather bag containing fifteen gold sovereigns, and said: "I'm going now, Edie darling!"

In the morning there was the terrible scene with her father, the meeting with the vicar's warden and, later, with the Bishop; the futile visits of Parson Clegg to the police in Barnstaple, and ultimately, the ill-spelled letter from a stranger, who kept a boarding-house in Lambeth.

Even now Edith shuddered when she recalled her arrival outside that boarding-house. It was a shabby stucco villa, in a sunless street off the Embankment. Inside the narrow entrance passage there was a strong smell of cabbage, and rancid cooking fat. The stairs were so dark that Edith had to grope her way up, despite the services of the elderly slut who admitted her, and on the uncarpeted landing, where the pervading stench suggested something more unpleasant than cabbage water, the landlady had wheezed her version of events.

"She's in there now. Can't get nothing out of her. Been bashed about, she has. *He's* gone, owing three weeks. Never saw much of 'im when he was here. Heard 'em 'avin' a fight or two, but never took much note. Get used to it in my line o' business. Learn not to stick your nose in too far!"

"How did you find my address?" Edith had asked, fighting her nausea, and trying hard to control her trembling limbs. "Did my sister tell you about me?"

"Not her," said the slut, with a mirthless chuckle. "*She* ain't in no state to tell nothing. See for yourself!" And she flung open the door of a back bedroom and, marching in, flipped up the blind and let daylight into the hideous little room.

Becky was sitting on the bed, naked except for a short cotton chemise. Her beautiful chestnut hair was loose, obscuring the greater part of her face. Her brown eyes, eyes that had always been so full of laughter, were fixed on the distempered wall immediately opposite, in a stare so blank that Edith knew at once it would be hopeless to expect recognition.

She made a supreme physical effort, and turned back to the landlady.

"Has she had a doctor?"

The woman snorted, "Doctor? I told you, he went off owing three weeks!"

"What about food?"

"She 'asn't touched nothing, not fer days; I tried to feed her once, but she knocked the bowl out of me 'and. Look, you c'n see, if you don't believe me!"

The woman pointed to a large stain on the edge of the filthy blanket. Edith noted, too, that there were faint traces of what appeared to be porridge on Becky's chin. She opened her chain purse, and took out three half-sovereigns.

"Will this pay what she owes? It's all I can spare; I've got to leave enough to get home."

The sight of the money eased the strain from the woman's face. Truculence gave way to coarse amiability as she reached for the money.

"That'll about cover it. I did right to tell you, didn't I? He must have served her crool. Still, that's men all over, ain't it? I'll get her things together, while you wash an' dress her. There's no trunk. He took that, I reckon."

Saul had indeed "served her crool", as Edith discovered the moment she began to wash her sister's limp body. There were long greenish bruises on both thighs, and more recent bruises over the whole area from left shoulder to elbow. One eye was slightly discoloured, and the back of her right hand was puffed and mottled, as though it had been struck with something flat and heavy, in warding off a blow aimed at the head.

Together they did what they could. Becky was dressed and led downstairs. A scrubby-haired youth, the son of the slut, went along the Embankment to fetch a cab, and as Edith was settling her sister inside, and preparing to enter herself, the landlady imparted one final piece of information.

"There was a kid, you know. Born dead, so I 'eard, a bit before time!"

That was all Edith was ever able to learn about Becky's brief absence from the vicarage. She never discovered whether Saul had actually married the girl, or whether the child had been still-born, or had died within days. When Becky made a partial recovery her mind resisted all attempts to probe into the immediate past. This could only be guessed at through her behaviour during her "spells", the "getting-ready" spell, the "layette" spell, and, most upsetting of all, the "getting-supper-for-Saul" spell.

Apart from these flashbacks Becky's mind dwelt exclusively in the more distant past, in her childhood and girlhood days, up to shortly before the time she had met Saul during a tramp across the Doone Valley.

After a few half-hearted attempts to get at the facts Edith was content to let her sister remain there, chattering happily of half-forgotten croquet tournaments, and Sunday School picnics, and talking of long-dead parishioners as though, at any moment, they might call at the Vicarage to put up banns, or discuss a forthcoming bazaar. Even Lickapaw the cat did not really belong to the present, but was identified with a cat the sisters had owned, jointly, as children.

Edith had long since adjusted herself to moving in and out of this shadow world. She would converse with her sister gravely about an epidemic of scarlet fever in Devon, in 1890, as though it was a current topic and, a moment later, walk to the back door and deal with a tradesman, or hawker. Physically, her sister could do almost everything for herself, having relearned the habits of every-day life under her sister's patient tuition, during the long period they spent together in the rented bungalow at Simonsbath, soon after Becky's initial stay in hospital had ended.

Becky's mental age was now about seven, and it was only during a "spell" that Edith had to watch her closely. Sometimes a "spell" lasted all day, more often only an hour or so. They invariably followed the same pattern: a frenzied packing of clothes, an equally frenzied "spell" of knitting, and a tearful appeal to visit the shops in order to buy baby's clothes. A "getting supper spell" involved a general upheaval in the kitchen, where Becky would solemnly pour everything she could lay hands on into a large bowl and, after a long stir, tip the mixture into a frying-pan, "because Saul will have everything, fried"!

Edith coped very well with the "spells", but not quite so efficiently with the family finances. In one of his rare communicative moods, shortly before his death, Parson Clegg had said to her: "There'll be enough, Edie—not much, mind you, but enough, providing you're careful." And then, a few moments before his death, he said a strange thing. Catching Edith by the hand he spoke slowly and clearly, straight into her ear.

"Look after *Edie*," he said; and came as near to winking as matters. He must have meant to say "Becky", of course, and Edith was relieved to hear him say it, for it implied forgiveness on his part, but she had never understood the solemn wink. In all the years they had lived together, she never recalled seeing her father wink and, even allowing for the circumstances, and the fact that he had only just emerged from a coma, the wink upset Edith more than his sudden death, and remained vividly in mind long after the pattern of the final scene had become blurred.

About the time Jim Carver came home, and Esme bewitched Judith in the gazebo of the old Manor, Edith Clegg received her first letter from the Barnstaple solicitors, who were executors for Parson Clegg's modest fortune.

She had to put on her steel-rimmed spectacles, and read the letter at least three times before she perceived, behind a number of finely-turned legal phrases, that the communication was a piece of well-meant advice to take stock of her financial position.

Parson Clegg had left uninvested capital of about £2,500 (to her dying day Edith never discovered its source: it could never have been saved from his stipend), and each Friday, since the old man's death, Edith had drawn a cheque on the local bank for fifty shillings. Only on rare occasions was she left with more than a copper or two when the week ended, and in her simple, uncomplicated mind she put this down to careful housekeeping on her part. She made no allowances for the rising costs of living after 1914; indeed, it is doubtful if she was more than half aware of them, for she never bought a newspaper. All her war news came through the agency of Mr. Piretta, the rosy-faced, ever-smiling grocer, in the corner shop.

Occasionally, however, there were lump-sum expenditures— a tweed costume, a chair-cover, settlement of rates and, every quarter, the rent. To cover these contingencies Edith drew a monthly cheque of ten pounds, so that her expenditure ran into something under three hundred a year. Parson Clegg died in 1909, so that his capital had now dwindled to just over £1,000. It was pointed out to Edith that if she continued spending at the present rate, she would be penniless in less than five years.

The letter, once she had thoroughly understood it, brought her up with a severe jolt. She was not a fool, and realised immediately that she must invest the remaining money, and then set about earning some more. Never having earned a penny in her entire life, she sought advice from the nearest source, the local bank manager.

This gentleman, who had that sound common-sense proverbial among managers of small banks, promptly invested her £1,000 in gilt-edged and, after questioning her for over an hour on the limited possibilities, advised her to set up as a music-teacher, and let one of her bedrooms.

Once she got used to the idea the prospect of earning her living delighted her, and she went about the preliminaries with a promptness that took the bank manager (convinced until then that he was dealing with an impoverished aristocrat) by surprise. She advertised for pupils in the local paper, and for lodgers in the drawing-room window. The results were immediate and gratifying. In less than a month she had twelve music pupils at two guineas a quarter, and had let her back bedroom to Ted Hartnell.

Edith had chosen a propitious time to advertise for music pupils. All over the suburb mothers were dragging their children to the piano-stool. There was a boom in scales and short pieces. Tin-Pan Alley was cock-a-hoop. More sheet-music was being sold than at any time in history and, of all musical instruments, the piano far outstripped all others in suburban popularity. At any time between the hours of 4 and

7 p.m. a passer-by, pausing outside almost any of the detached, semi-detached, or terrace houses between the Lower Road and Shirley Rise, could hear a cacophony of blundered scales issuing from the open windows of the drawing-rooms (as parlours were now known) for every other house possessed a cottage piano, at which two or more of the family took turns to pick their way through the shorter and simpler excerpts of Schubert, or the inevitable *Down on the Farm* jingles. On a summer evening in 1919 one might have heard half a dozen renderings of *A Merry Peasant Returning from Work*, *L'Orage*, or *Autumn Ride* in the Avenue alone, and the leather music-case, in the hands of sullen-faced boys or their pig-tailed sisters, became as familiar in the street as the school satchel.

Edith, who had been soundly taught as a child, divided her hour-long lessons into thirty minutes theory and thirty minutes practice, and was thus able to cope with two pupils at once. She relied almost exclusively on a fat book of scales, and a *Down on the Farm* for beginners, for the latter tinklings possessed for her, an exiled country-woman, a strong nostalgic flavour, and she never grew weary of hearing *In a Quiet Wood* or *Now All is Sleeping*.

She quickly learned to distinguish between those of her flock who would never progress beyond the musical farmyard, even when anxious mothers guaranteed regular practice with the help of twopenny canes, sold in bunches at all ironmongers along the Lower Road, and those who, with a little patience, would soon master elementary theory, and absorb as much as she could teach them.

Among her first dozen there were only two who did not regard the weekly lesson, and its accompanying obligation of at least half-an-hour's daily practice, as a monstrous inroad into their playtime. Of these two, Esme Fraser, of Number Twenty-Two, was one. The other, little Sandra Geering of Lucknow Road, subsequently obtained her L.R.A.M., but that was years later, when she had far outgrown Edith's methodical "One-two-three, one-two-three's a straight back dear, and don't, oh *don't* encourage lazy fingers!"

Edith found a curious sense of fulfilment in these music lessons and, as time went on, they came to mean more and more to her, for they brought her out of the tiny world in which she and Becky had been living since they left Devon, a world in which the only breaks in the routine of getting up, housekeeping, shopping, reading, and going to bed, were Becky's occasional spells, and the migrations, and prodigal homecomings of Lickapaw, the cat.

The arrival of Ted Hartnell, the lodger, provided a sharper and more permanent break with the past.

2

It might be said that, through Ted Hartnell, Edith found, and grasped, the thread of purpose that she had lost the day she left the Vicarage to fetch Becky home. Perhaps she realised this. Perhaps that was why she came to love him. . . .

Ted knocked on the door of Number Four one evening in early autumn and Becky, who answered the knock, looked him over, shuffled back into the kitchen, where Edith was making loganberry jam, and said: "It's a man! I think it's Mr. Fosdyke's boy!"

Edith wiped her hands very carefully. She knew, of course, that it was not Mr. Fosdyke's boy; Mr. Fosdyke's boy, George, had been killed on the Somme, in 1916, but she remembered him well enough—he had sung in the choir for years, and was once very sick in the middle of *For All the Saints*. Edith's long habit of translating Becky's curiously accurate recollections from past to present told her, at least approximately, what the man on the doorstep would look like. He would be dark, sleek, and probably about nineteen, for that would be George Fosdyke's age when Becky ran off with her painter.

This was indeed a physical approximation of Ted Hartnell in the autumn of 1919. He was short, narrow-shouldered, pink-cheeked and brown-eyed, with lavishly brilliantined hair, and well-cared for off-the-peg clothes. Edith's first impression of him was that he was rather like a young rook. His dapper jauntiness sat upon him rather nervously, as though, at any moment, he would spread his neatly-folded wings, and soar across to the next elm, where he would sit, head thrown back, chest puffed out, swaying slightly in a high wind.

He was hatless, and carried a large canvas hold-all in one hand, and a short black music-case in the other. At first glance Edith mistook him for a new and adult pupil, who was under the mistaken impression that she gave violin lessons as well as pianoforte lessons. His hands, she noticed, were the only part of his person that looked uncared for, being rough and seamed, like the hands of a bricklayer, or pick-wielder.

"It's about that room, Miss," he began; "they said you got one."

Now that it had actually come to the point of inviting a young man into the house, not to drink tea, like the plumber's appentice, but to live with them, a spasm of nervousness shook poor Edith. She hesitated and, noticing as much, a clouded, almost hunted look showed in his brown eyes.

"There's the card ..." he began, and stopped when she smiled.

"Of course; come in, *do*," replied Edith, consciously pulling herself together. She spread her hands and added incongruously, "I was making jam. We had lots of loganberries this year."

She slipped across the hall, and shut the kitchen door on Becky. He walked upstairs behind her, still gripping his hold-all and instrument case, still not too sure of his welcome, and neither of them said anything more until she had displayed the back bedroom, overlooking the old nursery.

He was obviously impressed with its spotlessness, and its unexpectedly open view. Edith had laid out nine pounds to get the room ready, and she had purchased wisely. There was a mahogany chest of drawers, wanting three drawer handles, an oak washstand, carefully draped cretonne curtains, a narrow but solid-looking bed, a bamboo night-table, new linoleum, and a strip of patterned carpet beside the bed.

Everything in the room was second-hand, but Edith, in her new role as business-woman, had not been fobbed off with rubbish. Over the bed Edith hung her own contribution—a framed sampler she had worked when she was ten. Its message was simple and direct. "God," it said in royal blue, "is Love" in faded crimson.

"How much all in?" he wanted to know, as soon as a decent interval had elapsed. She bit her lip. Her stomach was making low but very distinct rumbling noises, and making them so persistently that she was sure he could hear them. He came to her rescue immediately, and she decided there and then that he must be a kind and very sensitive young man.

"I take sandwiches mid-day. I'm a stonemason at Kidd's, in Shirley," he volunteered.

"A stonemason? That must account for the hands. He didn't *look* like a stonemason. A clerk or a shop assistant, but certainly not a stonemason.

"I . . . we . . . decided a pound, bed and breakfast . . . we didn't expect to cater," she said, suddenly quite nervous of frightening him away. "I . . . I suppose I *could* do an evening meal. We have ours about seven, not dinner, you know . . . just . . . just something warmed up or . . . or . . . an egg."

She saw in his surprised expression the grim necessity of making a clean breast of her utter inexperience.

"We've never had anyone before: perhaps you could tell me what is usual?"

He was genuinely touched by her naiveté. In the three years since he had left school, and been out to work, he had encountered a dozen or more landladies. Some had been unpleasantly off-hand, showing him round with a studied take-it-or-leave-it air; others, the majority, had looked him over very thoroughly, and asked him a number of questions about the sort of hours and company he kept. One had even told him: "No women, definitely no women!" Edith was his first experience of a landlady who consulted him on the amount she should charge for bed and board. He began to relax and congratulate himself on his good fortune.

"Place where I was," he said, with a wide engaging grin, "charged me twenty-five bob, but the grub was shop stuff; nothing really cooked, if you see what I mean."

She saw, nodding sympathetically. Poor young man! No wonder he was thin and undersized. He must have been living for years on soggy, pieshop pastry, stewed tea, and kippers. He probably had severe indigestion, took powders.

"I like cooking," she told him; "I always have, ever since . . ." She was going to say ever since she had taken full charge of Becky, after the Vicarage housekeeper walked out during

one of Becky's "getting-supper-for-Saul spells," but she realised that these sort of confidences would have to come later,
if indeed they came at all. She completed the sentence rather
lamely with·"ever since I was a girl".

They finally fixed on twenty-five shillings, to include a
packed lunch five days a week, and Edith left him sitting on
the bed, to savour his miraculous good fortune.

When he was sure Edith was downstairs, and could hear
her talking to the blank, good-looking one who had answered
the door, he bounced about on the bed, prowled around the
room fingering the curtains and the washstand, its dainty jug,
bowl, and flower-decked soap-dish, and finally opened his
music-case, and took out his banjolele, striking a single, soft
chord—the opening chord of *Coal-black Mammy*. Having
done this he decided that he must not strain his luck at this
early stage, and resolutely replaced the instrument in its
case.

He wondered if she would object to smoking, and decided
to take the chance, sitting on the cane-bottom chair beside
the window and inhaling, deeply. He gurgled to himself with
sheer delight. Ted, old sport, he told himself, Ted boy, you've
struck oil! Take it easy and you've struck oil! A room like
this, fifteen minutes from work, and home cooking! Boy!
You're in clover—clover!

Ted Hartnell talked to himself more than most people,
partly from natural exuberance, and partly because he had
made no real friends since the uncle, with whom he had lived
after his parents' death, had presented him with the "chuck-it-
or-else" ultimatum involving his banjolele and his gramophone.

Ted Hartnell had no real interest in the job that provided
him with a bare livelihood. He was a stonemason simply
because a post at a stonemason's yard had presented itself the
week he left school, more than four years ago. His mission in
life was to play jazz tunes in public, or, if no such opportunity presented itself, to listen to them, hum them, beat them
out with his chisel as he chipped marble gravestones, tap
them with his feet as he munched lunchtime sandwiches, pick
them out, chord by chord, on his wire-strung banjolele, or
follow them, beat by beat, on his portable gramophone—now,

alas, in a Hammersmith pawnbroker's window, and likely to remain there until he could save enough out of his thirty-two-and-sixpence a week to redeem it.

The gramophone and banjolele had been responsible for frequent shifts of lodging on the part of Ted Hartnell. No landlady could endure one or the other for long and, once the initial impact of his cheerful personality was spent, out he went, neck and crop, to look for a fresh lodge. The woman in Catford had helped him to establish his record, a mere nine weeks in one bed, but that was because she was stone deaf. He was asked to leave two nights after her married daughter came to live with her.

Ted did not much mind moving about. Once his gramophone was going, or he became absorbed in strumming, he was as oblivious of his immediate surroundings as a Montparnasse painter. The trouble lay in the limited number of stonemason's yards available, and the vast distances that stretched between them. Every time he moved he seemed to go further and further from work, and the fares were a great strain on his pocket. What he was searching for was a room within easy reach of a stonemason's, let by a landlady who was either stone-deaf, or excessively partial to New Orleans rhythm. It seemed an unending quest. Even now, having met a landlady who taught music, liked cooking, and asked what she should charge, he lacked the confidence to unpack, and contented himself with extracting pyjamas and sponge-bag. He would have been immensely cheered if he could have heard Edith discussing him as she stood by the gas-stove, stirring jam, for Edith was saying:

"He's a lodger, dear; no, *not* Mr. Fosdyke's boy, but a friend of his, I expect. I don't *know* whether he'll stay, Becky dear. I think not. I expect he'll find us *old-fashioned*. Young men like that like a bit of life, dear."

Nobody would have been more surprised than Edith Clegg if somebody had whispered in her ear that evening: "Stay, Miss Clegg? Why, bless you, he'll stay nearly twenty years!"

National Railcards

Get 1/3 off rail fares

Find out more at **railcard.co.uk**

Advance Single 1st

From London Kings Cross
To Edinburgh

Valid on 11-AUG-19   Adult 1st Class

On specified LNER trains & connections

10:30 London North Eastern Railway
Coach L Seat 33
From London Kings Cross
To Edinburgh

Not refundable. Exchangeable for a fee before travel

£105.00 X

Mrs A Weir

Snc Ref *9SXK8YTUT

92906 92907 8021 808 11 03 01

1416 280519A

1–12

CHAPTER V

Carvers, At Work And Play

1

THE four male Carvers were products of the pre-war era, the war itself, and the Charleston, or vo-deo-do era.

The forces that moulded the character of James Carver, and made him what he was, and what he was to become, were those familiar to the great majority of European males, born during the late 'seventies, and early 'eighties, men who had endured the horrors of trench warfare, yet survived to taste the full bitterness of victory.

Jim was discharged in the late summer of 1919, when the drought went on and on, and the leaves hung, dust-bowed, along the parched hedgerows. It seemed, that summer, as if the sun would never stop shining, as though it had made up its mind to burn away the memories of the long, hard frosts of wartime winters, and make the veterans forget the days and nights under the weeping skies of Artois and Picardy.

It was not the sort of weather in which one would have chosen to go looking for work, but Jim had no choice but to set out on the quest day after day, and with increasing desperation, for Louise was needed to keep house, and mother the new twins Felicity and Caroline, now referred to by the Carvers as "Fetch" and "Carrie", and of his remaining children only Archie was earning.

More than a million ex-servicemen, many of them much younger than Jim, and some with pre-war trade training behind them, joined him in his search for limited security.

Jim was not long in discovering his handicap. Prior to 1914 he had never followed a regular trade, preferring to earn his money by piecework, as various jobs presented themselves. Because he was strong, honest, clever with his big, red hands, and very conscientious in his dealings with those who employed him, he had never been idle for more than a day or two between spells. He liked it that way. It flattered his strong sense of independence, so damaging to him during his army career, and in days when two pounds a week was a good wage for an untrained man, he had often brought his wife three, withholding but a shilling or two for tobacco and tram-fares.

He had been a leather-dresser, drayman, market porter at both Smithfield and Covent Garden, omnibus driver, groom, coach-builder, and even clerk, for he wrote an exceptionally neat, legible hand, and was quick at mental arithmetic.

He entered the post-war labour-market with confidence but it was soon evident that either his qualifications, or the economic system in which he was trying to market them, was at fault. He could find temporary jobs, but he lost them when the younger men joined the queue.

He was astonished at the number of young men who had managed to survive the successive slaughters of the Somme, Passchendaele, and the final German offensive. He had sometimes imagined, during the last months of the war, that he was one of the few Englishmen alive and whole, but at the local Labour Exchange his impression was soon corrected, for here they were, by the thousand; young, hefty, strident-voiced men, some of whom looked blank when the Marne and Ypres were mentioned, and many of whom, he was informed by sardonic ex-infantrymen, had managed to avoid active service for years on end.

Yet Jim did not at first take refuge in the general bitterness that had soured the easy comradeship of the trenches by the time the first anniversary of the Armistice came round. He was an obstinate man and prided himself on being a fair-minded, level-headed, unemotional sort of chap. It was 1920 before he began to relate his personal problems to those of Society. The victorious Empire, it seemed, would never find its way back to the highway it had been swinging down so blithely, when the fateful shots were fired at Sarajevo.

Jim, however, was inclined to blame his bad luck on his own fecklessness in the closing years of the century, when he could have learned a trade years ago, and made a niche for himself. Had he done so, he reasoned, he could now claim re-entry into industry, even if those who had performed his job during his absence were disinclined to step down, and make way for a veteran.

He was not alone in his bewilderment. Up and down the queues, and in and out the transport yards where he presented himself every day, he ran across plenty of other ex-servicemen as unfortunately situated as himself. They were not all as fair-minded. The majority were inclined to blame the women, who had taken their places at lower rates of pay while they were serving abroad, but this seemed unfair to Jim, who recalled seeing young girls perched on the topmost girders of Charing Cross Station when he came home on leave, and doing a man's work very efficiently if his short experience as a painter had taught him anything. Others blamed the politicians. They had always been fair game in the trenches. "The Pilot who weathered the Storm!" grunted one hard-bitten Cockney, as he turned away from beneath a poster of Lloyd George in sailor-rig at the wheel—"Blimey, thinker that! We're still in the bloody middle of it, an' he don't even know it!"

Everybody blamed somebody else, and what made the struggle so wretched for men like Jim Carver was the collapse of that solid-scaffolding of trench comradeship, that had kept the morale of units intact through years of unmitigated hell. That, to Jim at all events, was the most disappointing aspect of the situation. It made him feel mean and small to see men scratch and snarl at one another, when one had secured a temporary advantage over the others. He found it difficult to witness, unmoved, this one undoubted spiritual gain of four years' struggle, being dissipated in a sordid wrangle over a two-pound-ten-a-week job.

In March, 1920, he retired from the fray, and took stock of himself. The result was rewarding. He successfully applied for training as a motor-transport driver, under a minute Government Grant. At the end of three months he passed out as a heavy-van driver, with 87%, and thus qualified for an ex-service vacancy at Burtol and Twyford's Removal and Storage Mart, in the Crystal Palace Road, Anerley.

Here, at least, he found his niche, and not a moment too soon. He had been more frightened than he cared to admit,

and donned the leather apron they gave him with an over-
whelming sense of relief. The job, driving a removal van, and
helping with the loading and unloading, suited his taste for
roving, acquired long before the war, and developed during
his overseas service. He was thirty-nine, and exceptionally fit.
He felt that, given luck, he had a better chance of survival
than most.

2

Archie Carver was typical of those males in the Avenue
who belonged to the age group too young to serve in the
war, yet old enough, when it began, to be men about a
house.

Archie was nearly fourteen when his father enlisted, and
had just started as errand boy at Coolridge's, the multiple
grocer's in the Lower Road. There were, as he quickly
learned, certain advantages in belonging to the provisioning
trade at that particular time, and perhaps it was this circum-
stance, more than his own natural shrewdness, that encouraged him to begin thinking as a man while he was still little
more than a child.

His thoughts, as he pushed his heavy carrier cycle up the
steep drives of the larger houses on his extensive round, were
not by any means original, but they were certainly precocious
in a pink-cheeked lad of fourteen. They were concerned, in
the main, with the odd relationship between commerce and
patriotism, with the preoccupation of the few with profits,
and of the many with the fate of "the boys out there."

In his trapesings about the suburb he became aware of
many social contrasts, and the conclusions he drew from
them were docketed, and filed away in his memory for future
use. Archie was that sort of boy. He wasted nothing, least of
all experience.

He noted, for instance, that some people were getting rich
very quickly, and after pondering this in general for a month
or two he began to study it in relation to the people he
worked among, notably Mr. Cole, the senior hand.

Mr. Cole, his immediate superior at the shop, and the man
responsible for making up the cardboard boxes containing the

week's shopping list for the Lucknow Road district, underwent a mysterious change of heart about January, 1915.
Almost overnight he stopped nagging Archie and went out of
his way to be helpful to the boy, even going so far as to offer
to relieve him of all those heavy boxes, still awaiting delivery
after closing time.

The first time this happened Archie gladly skipped off
within five minutes of completing shutter-drill. The second
time, being curious, he concealed himself in the smoking-
nest, made up of crates in the yard, and from here, through
a convenient embrasure made for the observation of seniors,
he watched Mr. Cole add various packages to certain of the
boxes. He knew where the boxes were going and it was a
simple matter to slip out of the yard, and settle himself in a
new ambush, this time a rhododendron screen, abutting the
tradesman's door of Number Five A, Outram Crescent.

His observations from this second vantage-point satisfied
his curiosity regarding Mr. Cole's sudden kindliness, and
within forty-eight hours the astonished Mr. Cole found his
thoughtfulness repaid by the prompt offer of an alliance. He
was not in need of an ally but succumbed, quite readily, to
Archie's persuasive offers of co-operation. It was not right,
Archie pointed out, that Mr. Cole, asthmatic and nearing
sixty, should add to a tiring day's work by lugging all those
heavy boxes up steep, gravelled drives in winter weather.
From now on, he insisted, Mr. Cole should stay in the warm,
and make up the lists, while he, Archie, should come back
after shutter-drill, and do all the deliveries. There was, of
course, an alternative to this happy arrangement. Failing Mr.
Cole's immediate acceptance of the plan he would, in Mr.
Cole's own interests, have to tell the manager about the chief
storeman's excessive zeal. Mr. Cole accepted.

The system worked quite well until poor Mr. Cole was
taken seriously ill, in the autumn of 1917, and died quite
suddenly. Archie went to the funeral, and patted Mrs. Cole
sympathetically on the shoulder, saying nothing about the
patriotic over-time endeavours he had shared with the deceased, but contributing generously to the large cross of
chrysanthemums sent by the staff of Coolridge's.

As the war dragged into its final year all the counter hands and storemen at Coolridge's who had managed, on one pretext or another, to avoid conscription, left the shop and went into munitions. Some of them looked in from time to time, wearing new suits, and looking very prosperous. They chaffed Archie for his failure to seize the opportunity of making good money, four or five times as much money they told him, as they had been getting a year ago at Coolridge's, but not once did Archie consider taking their well-meant advice. He liked the grocery trade he told them and, because of the serious staff shortage, he had obtained rapid promotion, and was now occupying the late Mr. Cole's position as senior storeman. Munition-making, he warned them, would cease one day, and they would soon be seeking re-entry into the provisioning trade. They would then, perhaps, see the wisdom of Archie's loyalty to the firm of Coolridge, notwithstanding the scandalously low basic wage it paid its suburban counter hands. Archie had a wry sense of humour. He particularly stressed the word "basic".

Archie stayed on at Coolridge's until some time after the Armistice. By then he had so consolidated his position that he had been moved to a larger branch in Lewisham. With the return of the trench veterans, however, he grew strangely restless and dissatisfied. Perhaps he missed his evening sessions with customers in the big houses, like Number Five A, Outram Crescent, or perhaps the end of rationing had something to do with it. At all events, he was quite ready to leave when the Rita Ramage episode occurred, and made it necessary for the manager of his new branch, a strict Baptist, to inform him that he would be most obliged if Archie would "begin to look for other employment". This enigmatic phrase was already becoming familiar to ex-servicemen, returning from their earnest endeavours to make the world safe for democracy, but it had few terrors for Archie. He had done very well out of rationing. His cash-box, which reposed in the locked suitcase under his bed, now held a floating reserve of nearly a hundred pounds, and he felt that his nest-egg was an adequate buffer between himself and the dole queue. He surprised everyone, including his family, by leaving, then and there, without even serving out his notice, and, far from economising, walked into a garage and bought the Douglas motor-cycle he had been promising himself for so long.

No one at home, of course, knew anything about Archie's nest-egg, or about Rita Ramage, and the part she had played in Archie's dismissal after six, outwardly blameless years, with Coolridge Ltd.

Rita was one of those favoured wartime customers who occupied the lower half of a detached house in Outram Crescent. She was the wife of an ex-officer in the Tank Corps, who spent most of his time in hospitals, undergoing a series of operations designed to make him walk again. So far, they had not succeeded, and his' wife Rita had ceased to pretend to herself that they ever would. Being a realist, not much given to sentimentalising, she had come to terms with herself emotionally, and had decided that she was too young, at thirty-three, to enter the purdah reserved for the young wives of totally disabled veterans. She was a full-blooded, buxom woman, and she needed a whole man, not two-thirds of one.

She had money of her own, so that a man to support as well as solace her was not a necessity, unless the right one showed up, in which case she could think about a divorce. In the meantime Reggie could have the whole of his disability pension, but a substitute must be found who could perform those functions that a direct hit on Reggie's tank had effectually prevented its commander from performing.

It was only a day or two after she had arrived at this decision that Archie Carver let himself into her kitchen, and whistled for Letty, the Belgian refugee maid whom Rita had employed throughout the war. As it was Letty's night out Rita herself answered the whistle.

She had just emerged from a hot bath, and had helped herself to a large double-whisky. Perhaps these two factors had something to do with the impact upon her of Archie's aggressive masculinity. At seventeen-and-a-half, Archie was six foot, broad-shouldered, and extremely well-muscled. He had, moreover, an exceptionally clear complexion, lacking those rashes and pimples that trouble adolescence. To these physical advantages he added a studied affability, a judicious mixture (reserved for this type of after-hours customer) of mild jocularity and moderate respect. This approach, he had found, paid off handsomely. Customers who knew they were breaking the law resented easy familiarity and distrusted servility. What was needed, on these occasions, was something in between, and Archie had good reason to believe upon the compound.

"The groceries, Ma'am, plus the usual," he told her, with the ghost of a wink.

Rita gave her kimono cord a hitch, and glanced at the box he placed on the table. She knew nothing of Letty's private arrangements with the provision merchants, but simply that the girl was marvellous at getting everything they needed, notwithstanding all this paper talk about shortages, and U-Boat blockades. Archie's manner, however, and the slight smile that lurked at the corner of his wide mouth, informed her that there was something more in his whistle and wink than a desire to see the provisions checked. She picked up the bill, crossed to the dresser, found her purse and added half-a-crown to the total, putting the money on the kitchen table.

"Is that what Letty usually gives you?" she asked him.

Archie toyed with the idea of earning an extra shilling or two but decided, almost immediately, that the ultimate risk was not worth the immediate gain. This woman looked hard-bitten and he did not want to upset the sound business-like relationship he had established with her maid.

"That's about usual," he told her, pocketing the half-crown, and slipping the rest of the money into his leather satchel.

On impulse she took out the bottle of hock that stood among the packages.

"Did Letty ever give you anything else ... a drink, for instance?"

"Never," said Archie, truthfully. Letty was a wooden sort of girl and he had never made much impression on her.

"I was just going to get myself a snack. Are you hungry?" she asked him.

He was surprised and flattered. The woman was too old and too classy for a frolic, of course, even if she wanted one, which he could hardly believe, but she had a well-stocked

larder, as he was well aware, and a change from Louise's
eternal, warmed-up suppers would be welcome.

"It's very kind of you," he said, taking a chair. "Do you
mind if I smoke?"

"Not at all," said Rita, promptly; "have one of these," and
she took a small silver case from her kimono pocket, and
gave him a flat Turkish cigarette.

"How old are you?" she asked him, as she busied herself at
the gas stove, and the smell of fried eggs, bacon, and tomatoes (what a business it had been to get those tomatoes)
began to fill the cosy room.

"Nineteen," he replied, promptly. His age jumped about
between sixteen and twenty-one; according to possible advantages in the offing. She did not suspect a lie. He looked
nineteen.

"How have you managed to dodge call-up?"

He considered for a moment. She was obviously not a
flag-flapper, none of his special customers were, and he did
not want to say anything that might spoil the good impression his physique had obviously made upon her.

"I don't believe in it," he said, finally.

She laughed outright, and crossed over with the grill.

"Shall I tell you something . . . what's your name?"

"Archie, Archie Carver, Ma'am!"

"Shall I tell you something I've never told anyone else?
Don't call me ma'am; it makes me feel *my* age. *I* don't
believe in it either, and what's more, I never have, not even
in poor little Belgium!"

After that they both relaxed. She told him about Reggie,
and he told her about his father, more than three years in the
line, and still only a sergeant. He told her some of the things
he had noticed on his rounds and, once the hock had been
finished and she had poured him a whisky, he spoke frankly
of his dealings with the late Mr. Cole.

She listened attentively. He was a refreshing change from
the men Reggie had brought from the Officers' Training
Unit—men who invariably referred to the German as "the
Hun", and flirted with her cautiously, much as they might
have flirted at an Edwardian soirée. And as she noted his
clumsy handling of the knife and fork, and his strong white

teeth, and the movement of his powerful shoulders, she yearned for him with the unreasoning desire of a strong woman who has outgrown modesty, but is a long way from resignation.

When he had finished, and had risen, wiping his mouth, she suddenly experienced panic. Her reason told her that he was far too young to be rushed, that forwardness on her part might easily frighten him off, that the way to handle this situation was to throw out a casual invitation for a repetition on their cosy supper, say, this day next week. But as he stood by the kitchen door, his big limbs relaxed, and a rather shy smile on his full lips, she realised that she could not wait a week, or even an hour, and she made up her mind to accept the risks, whatever they were. She was judging on appearances at this stage, and had no means of knowing that the risk was very slight indeed.

She moved quickly round the table, amazed at the violence with which her heart was beating. Looking straight at him, and forcing a smile, she said:

"Well, Big Boy, aren't you going to say 'thank you' properly?"

He knew what was expected of him. Up to that moment he had felt flattered, and amused. His experience with women was more limited than he would have cared to admit, a few fumblings in the stock-rooms, and on the windswept links, nothing real, nothing like this. He was conscious of a swift spasm of fear, of being trapped, and although merely momentary the quirk was strong enough to prompt him to turn and run. Then his egotism flooded in, and he felt uplifted. He reached out like a vigorous young bear, and gripped her, kissing her full on the mouth, and thrilling to her responsive shudder.

He was not, however, prepared for her next move.

She wriggled out of his embrace, reached swiftly behind him, and locked the kitchen door.

"Wait here," she said, a little breathlessly; "the girl doesn't come back until ten."

She almost ran out of the room, leaving the door to the hall half open. He moved over and stood by the hissing gas-fire, conscious of the inadequacy of his seventeen years.

His throat was dry, and his eye caught the whisky battle on the littered table. He slopped a measure into a used glass and gulped it down, gasping as the unfamiliar spirit struck his palate. The loud ticking of the clock on the mantel-shelf seemed to fill the stuffy room.

Presently, he heard her call and went slowly into the hall. He remembered then that this was a flat, not a house, and that there were people living upstairs. He moved quietly, like a big cat, fighting down another spasm of fear and forcing himself to savour, in advance, the obvious delights of this gloriously unexpected encounter.

She had made her bedroom out of the old dining-room, and the door was open. He saw the light go out as he crossed the hall, but a warm red glow remained, and when he reached the threshold he saw to his surprise that there was a bright coal-fire in the grate.

She was standing, quite naked, beside the heavily curtained window. Her mass of thick, dark hair reached to her broad buttocks, and he noted with satisfaction that she did not appear nearly as old as when he had faced her, a few moments ago, over the kitchen table.

He stood there, just inside the door, staring at her in quiet wonderment. A subtle change revealed itself in her manner, as though the forced smile, and incongruous coyness of her original invitation, had been scornfully discarded with her clothes, now stacked neatly on the big armchair beside the fire.

"All right, shut and lock the door!" she said briskly.

He was disconcerted by her directness, and a sense of bewilderment took possession of him. He kept reminding himself that she was a married woman, married to an officer, and that he was just Archie Carver, a glorified errand-boy. Nevertheless she wanted him, far more urgently than any girl his own age had ever wanted him. It was hard to understand.

She stood with one plump arm on the low mantelpiece, bathing her body in the dancing firelight. Outside, the wind whipped up, and January sleet slashed across the window-pane.

"Come over here, Big Boy," she said, in the same authoritative voice.

He moved across the room and put out his hand tentatively, as though to stroke a strange cat. She smiled then, and he noticed her white teeth, and heavy pink underlip. In after years, whenever he thought of Rita Ramage, he always remembered her excessively heavy underlip, and came to judge the accessibility of women accordingly. If they had fleshy lower lips, like those of Rita, they were all right. If their lips were balanced, they were not. He found this was a very reliable criterion.

"You're not shy are you, Big Boy?"

She suddenly seized his hand, and pressed it to her breast. Then Archie did a strange thing, something he was never to repeat in the presence of any woman he met in the future. He fell on his knees before her in a sort of obeisance. She looked startled for a moment and then, reaching out, she drew him closer to her and gently stroked his hair.

3

Rita remained Archie's mistress until the Spring of 1922. During that period she was completely faithful to him.

He, for his part, might have been married to her. Measured against Rita, the bobbed, tune-humming, flat-chested flappers of the Avenue were like strident children; and Rita, on her side, could never erase from her memory the mysterious gentleness he had shown her that first evening.

She soon came to know his shortcomings, his ridiculous confidence in himself as a millionaire in the making, his callowness, his silly, persistent lying about his age, his humiliating habit of taking her for granted, after the first month or so of their association, his thin Cockney accent, his general air of suburban vulgarity. All these things, however, meant less than nothing weighed against his slow, heavy strength, and his unbounded virility.

Their relationship was purely physical. He delivered himself, as it were, with the groceries, and after the maid had gone home to Belgium and had been replaced by a daily who left at five, he let himself in the back door two or three

times a week. They never went out together. It never occurred to them to go, for the pattern of their association
quickly resolved itself into a sort of three-part-ritual, half-
hour at a meal, half-hour in bed, and two or three hours
pottering about the house, exchanging small talk. Then he
went home, and let himself in with the key he had carried
since he was fourteen. He never mentioned her to anyone,
and nobody at Number Twenty dreamed of questioning Archie about his movements. Louise was somewhat surprised at
his loss of appetite, but she concluded that he was finding
plenty to eat at work, and during Jim Carver's long spell of
unemployment, she was very glad of the reduced demands on
the family larder. To Archie, there was soon no, excitement
in his visits to the house in Outram Crescent. Rita became a
habit, like eating and shaving, and getting up and going to
bed. It was much better this way, for it left his mind free to
range on a more important matter, the acquisition, somehow,
of a shop of his own. He accepted her gifts of clothes, and
cuff-links, and cigarettes, in the spirit in which he picked up
his wages on Fridays. They were part-payment for services,
faithfully rendered, and when he made love to her he was
neither demanding nor grateful, simply acquiescent, and dutiful, like the feminine partner of a mid-Victorian marriage.
She made no emotional demands on him at all, and he never
once paused to consider how this odd relationship might end,
or indeed, if it would end.

This pleasant state of affairs might have continued indefinitely, had not Reggie Ramage died under his twelfth operation. He was buried in the North, and Rita was away making
arrangements for more than a week.

On her return she made a proposal that was to upset the
rhythm of their lives. She suggested that, from now on,
Archie might as well move in, and live with her openly.
There would be no scandal with her neighbours. The house
was her own, and in view of the acute housing shortage, the
people in the upper half were very unlikely to object. Such an
arrangement, she pointed out, would relieve Archie of the
necessity of contributing fifteen shillings a week to Louise's
house-keeping purse.

Without being able fully to explain why, Archie felt violently opposed to the idea. Somehow it made him feel cornered. He was, he explained, very well satisfied with the present arrangement, and much preferred that it should continue.

"We might as well be married," he told her, "and that's never going to happen to me."

She said little at the time, but his rejection of the offer rankled, and a note of strain crept into their partnership. One night they had an argument over what Archie claimed to be a lack of variety in the supper fare.

"Always fried, never nothing but fried," he complained.

She hit back at him with uncharacteristic harshness.

"Never *anything* but fried!" she corrected. "When will you cease to talk like an errand boy?"

He chose to interpret this as a piece of possessive nagging. Getting up, he walked out of the house, and stayed away three days in succession.

He was surprised at the sense of freedom the break gave him, and the following week he stretched the interval to five days.

On the fifth day she was frantic. She bought him a sportscoat, and took it along to the shop. She had never called on him at his work before, and her presence there embarrassed him, even though she was careful to give the impression that she was a relative who had called with a birthday present.

That night he warned her:

"Don't you ever come for me again. I don't like it! I don't like being chased!"

Rita fought down her panic. Her pride, as far as he was concerned, had long since disappeared.

"All right, Archie, let's not get edgy; let's go to bed."

But they did get edgy, in spite of going to bed, and soon their edginess began to display itself in the bedroom. He would remain for ten minutes, staring moodily out of the window after she had undressed, and what frightened her even more was that he began to show a disposition to go home earlier, sometimes as early as ten o'clock.

One night, unable to stand the strain any longer, she challenged him:

"You don't like coming here any more, do you?"

Although she felt that she knew everything about him, she was shocked by the brutality of his reply.

"No," he said bluntly, "I haven't liked coming for months. It's not the same any more."

She felt sick with fear. With a great effort, she forced herself to sound reasonable.

"Don't come for a month. Then maybe you'll want me again. I'll go away, I'll close up the house and go abroad for a month. When I come back it will be like it used to be."

"All right, Rita," he said amiably, and it was agreed. She left that week-end, and at the end of a week he found that his powers of concentration were weakening. At the end of a fortnight he was in such a state of nervous depression that he lost his temper, and struck a counter-hand in the face for taking his raincoat from the cloakroom in error. Before the third week-end had arrived he had decided he could stand it no longer, and would have telegraphed her had he known where she was to be found. He did not, and so he consoled himself with the red-haired cashier, Lorna, who had tried, throughout several months, to attract his attention in and out of shop hours.

Lorna was only nineteen, and grossly inexperienced, but she was an attractive, warm-hearted girl, and after a few evenings in her company Archie decided that one woman was very like another, and that Lorna had the undeniable advantage of being there to be dropped and picked up again at will. He made up his mind at once. He was never going back to Rita, never in this world. He was not going to be cornered, certainly not by a woman old enough to be his mother.

Rita, however, did not surrender without a struggle, and for Archie the next two or three months were full of anxiety.

First of all, she wrote to him, her letters growing more and more hysterical until he took to dropping them, unopened, into the store-yard incinerator. Then she began to ring him up on the cash-desk telephone, and he had to persuade Lorna, the cashier, to stall for him. Lorna, the redhead, was an enthusiastic ally, but there came a time when even she was unable to resist the telephone siege without the manager, Mr. Brooks, discovering something of what was going on.

After Archie had been warned that incoming private calls must cease he wrote her a note, but he could scarcely have done anything more calculated to complicate the situation, for his blunt message brought Rita round to the shop, and after he had avoided her two or three times at the counter, she took to picketing the staff entrance.

It was here, in the unfortunate presence of Mr. Brooks, most of the staff, and several customers, that the first scene of the tragi-comedy was played out. Rita caught him, late one afternoon, as he came out into the yard, carrying a crate of soda-water syphons. She took full advantage of this, and when he backed away, hugging the crate, she followed him into the stock-room behind the shop.

"Archie, we've got to talk, we've *got* to! ..." she pleaded.

Archie set down the crate and regarded her with desperation. He was appalled at the change in her. Her eyes were red and her face puffy and infinitely strained. He could not imagine how he had ever found her desirable, and was quite unable to conceal his disgust.

"Not here, Rita, for Christ's sake!"

"Then where? When?"

"Tonight. I'll come round!"

"But you won't, you won't come! I know you won't!"

His voice rose, hysterically. "I will—for Pete's sake, leave me *alone*; why can't you leave me *alone*? I'm going with someone me own age, blast you!"

The taunt caused Rita to lose all control. The communicating door, between stock-room and shop, was wide open, and customers stood along each counter, not five yards away.

"Why, you bloody little whippersnapper!" she screamed, lashing out at him across the crate with a heavy shoulder-bag; "you have all you want month after month and then you walk out! I'll show you, you saucer-sucking little swine! When I picked you up you'd never laid hands on a woman. You didn't know what to do with one when you had one. ..."

At this point Mr. Brooks leaped into the stock-room, and slammed the shop door, to the intense irritation of counter-hands and customers alike.

Mr. Brooks was a religious man, and the situation appalled

him. Never, in his wide experience as a branch manager, had he encountered its like, and because his knowledge of such matters was extremely slight, he immediately concluded that this violent, vulgar woman was a common prostitute.

"Leave these premises immediately!" he sputtered. "Get out, before I ..." he paused, his mind groping for a threat sufficiently strong to frighten a prostitute—"... before I fetch a policeman!" he concluded triumphantly.

Rita calmed a little, just enough to turn aside and swear at him. Rita had an extensive gutter vocabulary, acquired in her obscure youth, and she made full use of it now. The words she used, and the venom with which she spat them at him, took the manager's breath away. Until that moment, he had never heard a man use them, much less a well-dressed woman, and that in his own stockroom, within hearing of at least eight suburban housewives. Having silenced him, Rita turned back to Archie, who was perspiring freely, his back to the wall.

"All right!" she screamed at him. "This is it! This is the finish! But I wonder if this poor little bastard knows how much you've had out of the till during the years you've been working here?"

Their expressions told her there was absolutely no need to amplify the statement, and she tasted, for a brief moment at least, the full flavour of revenge. It had the effect of steadying her, and she was able to collect herself sufficiently to walk into the yard, and out into the side-street that led to Lewisham Road.

Archie was the first to recover. When she had passed beyond the big gates, he turned desperately to the trembling manager.

"It's just a woman who's been chasing me, Mr. Brooks. She's ... she's just barmy with jealousy ... she just *said* that. I've not had anything out of the till; honest to God, I haven't!"

It took Mr. Brooks a full minute to regain a little of his branch-managerial poise.

"Come into the office, Carver," he said hoarsely.

CHAPTER VI

Mutiny At Havelock Park

1

OF all the children of the Avenue throughout the 'twenties, the eldest pair of Carver twins, Boxer and Bernard, were the most popular.

This was partly because of their marked dissimilarity, and partly because they were almost never seen apart. It also had a little to do with the varied and zestful ways they had of entertaining themselves.

No one ever took them for twins, just as, once they had emerged from the pram, no one ever mistook the girl twins, Fetch and Carry, for anything but twins. Boxer and Bernard were not even recognisable as brothers. Boxer, senior by twenty-five minutes, was broad-chested, and bullet-headed, with dark brown hair, like all the other Carvers, and a low fringe that gave him a faintly mediæval look. One always felt that Boxer should have issued from Number Twenty wearing a pointed cap, and pied hose, and shuffled along, one foot in the gutter, whistling hey-nonny-nonny staves instead of *Everybody's Doing It*, which was the twins' signature tune, and a warning to householders in the Avenue to be prepared for a little jollying-up of one sort or another. It also warned the patient Mr. Piretta, proprietor of the corner shop, that it was time for one of the twins' facetious demands on his stock.

These demands ranged from poker-faced requests for glasshammers, to appeals for sticks of liquid glue, or pots of elbow-grease.

Boxer—whose original name Maurice had been conveniently forgotten by everyone—possessed a cheerful aggressiveness that adults found at once irritating and amusing. To those who knew the twins by sight and reputation, Boxer appeared the dominant partner, but his family and their few intimates knew that this was not so, that it was Bernard who led the way both in and out of trouble.

Bernard was thin, narrow-faced, and wiry. His hair, as yellow as new straw, stuck up in short, sawn-off tufts, accentuating the vivid blue of his eyes. He weighed nearly half-a-stone less than his twin but, like his father, concealed unsuspected strength in loose, shambling limbs. Acting as one, they were a formidable team, Boxer having the necessary solidity for defence, and Bernard the agility, and élan for darting attacks. They were on friendly (but never intimate) terms with the other children of the Avenue, finding all the companionship they needed in each other. They never joined a gang, or joined in the games played by Avenue children in the Lane, or the "Rec". Instead, they thought out, and engaged in, their own private diversions, such as knocking-down-ginger, allotment raids, and the string-and-parcel game, a pastime usually reserved for the early dusk of winter evenings.

They would often go for weeks without knocking at doors, or pulling up carrots and radishes from the allotments, but they never tired of the string-and-parcel game. As dusk fell on the suburb they would select a new house-brick from one of the building sites, and make it up into a neat brown-paper parcel, attach a thin piece of twine to one end, and lay it carefully in a pool of lamplight, just outside one of the boundary walls of the big, detached houses, in Outram Crescent, or Lucknow Road.

Then, from their ambush among the laurels, they would sometimes wait for as long as twenty minutes for a passer-by. Always the gullible pedestrian would pause, bend, reach out for the parcel. Then they would jerk the twine, and the parcel would slide out of the lamplight, and the pedestrain would either straighten up and sheepishly make off, or switch his attention to his bootlace, as though he had never seen the parcel in the first place.

Occasionally they would vary this routine by substituting a purse for bait. They would then pull hard at the line, and whisk the purse right out of sight. This was always more rewarding if the victim was a woman, for a woman usually screamed, and Boxer, almost inarticulate with mirth, would gurgle; "Set it again, set it again! Whad'ysay, Berni; whad'ysay?"

Bernard would always pretend to think before answering this question. Finally he would shake his yellow head, and propose a variation of the sport. "Let's do the criss-cross," he would suggest, and Boxer would bubble over at the prospect of fastening loose strings to letter-box knockers, on each side of the Avenue, in order to watch exasperated neighbours summon one another in rapid succession, as the string of Number Eighty-Four tugged the knocker of Number Seventy-Three immediately opposite, and the opening door of Number Seventy-Three rattled the knocker of Number Eighty-Two.

In spite of these and other routine annoyances, the Avenue folk were fond of the "Unlikes"—a name they acquired when their twin sisters were old enough to be labelled "The Likes". Perhaps the true secret of their popularity lay in the boys' unswerving devotion to one another. This appealed to the womenfolk, most of whom were resigned to violent squabbles between their children. Sometimes they would quote the twins as an example of how brothers ought to behave one to another.

This relationship had its origin in an incident dating back to the early childhood of the pair, an incident that came to have an almost religious significance to Bernard, the introvert of the pair. For Bernard, at the age of six, had saved Boxer's life, and had guarded the secret ever since.

It happened in the hard frost of February, 1920. The twins' favourite playground was "the Lane", that leafy left-over from the Old Manor's home farm, that now led to the golf-club headquarters.

The Lane was marked out by long lines of elms, and where it curved, about half-way down, there was a large duckpond, shallow in summer, but all of eight feet deep after winter rains.

During a short, sudden frost, the duckpond froze over, and the elder Carver twins were the first to discover this exciting fact. Louise was an early riser, and the Carver boys were

always abroad nearly an hour before the other children of
the Avenue had finished their Saturday breakfasts.

On this particular morning, they went out early to comb
through the long grass near Number Four green for lost
balls. They seemed to be much luckier than most children in
stumbling upon almost new Silver Kings in this particular
area. Possibly their good fortune had something to do with
their keen vision in following the flight of a ball, but more
probably it was related to the fact that a birch coppice ran
close to the green, and swift movement, in and out of this
coppice, was screened from the eye of approaching golfers by
the big bunker, hard by.

However, on this occasion the twin did not reach the
green, but paused at the bend of the Lane to test the strength
of the ice on the duckpond. Boxer hesitated on the edge of
the water, and looked across at Bernard, who had moved
round to the opposite bank.

"Whad'ysay, Berni?" he asked, as usual.

Berni gave a crossing his sanction.

"Try it, Boxer," he said, and watched tensely as his brother
inched across the frozen surface, arms outspread like a tight-
rope performer, mouth set in a tight, nervous grin. He was
exactly halfway across when the ice gave way. He staggered,
and then, urged on by Bernard, made a run for it, slithering
towards the high brick coping, here Bernard stood reaching
out to grab him.

The ice split in every direction. Boxer fell on his knees and
lurched down into the brown water, his hands flailing for
support, and grasping, in the final split second, a thin, tenuous twig, that hung low over the water from a hazel clump
on Bernard's immediate right. Miraculously, the twig held,
for a mere ten seconds, but this was time enough for Bernard
to act. With the speed and precision of a young baboon, he
flung himself at the elm branch immediately above him, and
swung out, hand over hand, to the spot where Boxer was
shoulder deep in jagged fragments of ice. He reached him
just as the twig gave way, and Boxer made a despairing grab
at his brother's ankles. They hung there, one below the other,
for the better part of a minute, and then Bernard, with a

strength he could never afterwards believe that he possessed, drew himself high enough to get his chin over the bough, and prevent his grasp being torn away.

An inch or less at a time Bernard edged himself towards the parapet, dragging the floundering Boxer in his wake. He had covered more than half the distance when his will could no longer command his fingers and he fell, the two of them rolling together in the soft, churned-up mud under three feet of water.

When Bernard got his head above it, he discovered that he was alone. Boxer was doubled up at his feet. With a sudden access of strength he bent under the water and grasped his twin by the collar of his overcoat, dragging him bodily with one hand towards the bank while, with the other, he smashed at the ice, clearing a passage.

Somehow, they won the firm mud crust, where Boxer opened his eyes and was promptly sick. They lay together gasping for a few minutes. Then Bernard got slowly to his feet.

"We got to make a fire, Boxer, and we got to keep this a secret."

They made their fire, dried themselves, and kept their secret. Very occasionally Boxer would refer to it, looking sideways at his twin as he did so:

"Remember the pond, Berni?" And Bernard would reply: "Shut up about it, Boxer." His own reaction to the few moments of drama, and its immediate aftermath, was something he was not even prepared to share with Boxer; and even had he wished he would have found it impossible, then or later, to put into everyday speech the curious sense of responsibility towards his twin that had been born during those few terrible moments, when Boxer's weight was dragging him down into the depths of the pond. For this, in a strange and final way, became Bernard's dream—to watch over Boxer, to look out for Boxer, to make sure Boxer survived by every means, by any means. Nothing else was of the smallest importance.

2

When the twins were nine they left the local kindergarten and crossed the Lower Road to attend Havelock Park Elementary School.

Havelock Park was a dull, red-brick Council School that stood, like a vast public convenience in about an acre of asphalted yard. The playground was surrounded by gaol-like railings.

It was a joyless place, with high-ceilinged classrooms ("septic tanks" one L.C.C. Inspector called them), each housing some sixty boys, and partitioned off from a central hall as vast, and as chilly, as a French cathedral.

The school served a tough neighbourhood, one of the outer ring of suburbs, where many of the houses were well on the way to becoming new slums. The overworked staff, faced with the hopeless task of teaching sixty children apiece, and keeping out of the way of a tyrannical headmaster, were a shambling, dispirited lot, who lived on only in the hope of drawing a pension.

Mr. Adam Little was one of those headmasters who had chosen headmastering as a profession because of the unrivalled opportunities it afforded him of getting his own back on healthy humanity. All his life he had been a chronic suffer from dyspepsia, and now that he was nearing retiring age he was constantly attacked by severe stomach cramps, that caught him mostly at night, and left his abdomen tender to the slightest pressure.

To guard against this tenderness he had developed a curious manner of walking, his body bent slightly forward, and his left arm crooked horizontally across his stomach, as though to ward off the agony that would result from a possible collision.

As he grew older, and the cramps became more frequent, Mr. Little changed from a sour nag into an active bully, and ultimately into the sort of man who, a few years later, would have qualified for a gas-chamber post under Heinrich Himmler.

Every day he had to have human sacrifices, boys or colleagues, either or both would do, and when victims did not present themselves he went out to look for them, or sat in his study framing new and complicated school rules that would be certain to snare one group or the other.

Boys and staff, particularly female staff, lived in terror of his sudden appearance, and one and all prayed nightly that he might be taken from them, by L.C.C. whim, by illness, by forced retirement, or by swift and bloody death, they cared not which.

Under the sway of Mr. Little, Havelock Park School became a latter-day Dotheboys Hall. The headmaster spent several hours of his working day prowling along the corridors, and taking sly peeps through the glass partitions and wainscot chinks. When he saw, or fancied he saw, an undetected misdemeanour within, he would spring into the room, haul the culprit on to the teacher's dais, and proceed to thrash him unmercifully with a short cane that he carried in his trouser leg, like a concealed swordstick.

This erratic behaviour on the part of a headmaster, who should have been safely insulated in his study at that hour of the day, enraged the pupils and terrified the staff, who were usually called to account for their poor supervision as soon as the punishment was over.

At the time Boxer and Berni joined Havelock Park School a stream of prayer was ascending from the district, beseeching the Almighty to put an end to the tyranny, and the news that Mr. Little had been pulped under a No. 93 'bus in the Lower Road would have resulted in genuine mafficking on the part of his boys and colleagues. Even Mrs. Little would have been consoled by the fact that now, at last, she would be relieved of her special cooking, and be able to enjoy an unbroken night's rest.

At length God answered their prayers, and His agents in the matter were none other than the Carver twins, who earned thereby a reputation in the district second only to Jack Cornwall, the boy hero of Jutland, whose gun could be seen any fine Saturday at the Crystal Palace War Exhibition.

During the ten-minute morning break at Havelock Park, hundreds of Head-haters were turned loose in the vast playground, and encouraged to stretch their little limbs, and air their little lungs, in the anticipation of another hour's spell in stuffy, overcrowded classrooms. They took full advantage of the interval. The scene in the playground at ten minutes to eleven each morning resembled an Asiatic revolution, and the din that rose from the enclosure could often be heard as far away as the Lower Road tramway depot.

For ten glorious minutes the boys fought and rolled, kicked and cavorted, without the smallest hindrance, whilst Mr. Little sat, as though carved in stone, in the porch of the main entrance, a gold watch in one hand, and a small, silver' whistle in the other.

On the stroke of eleven he would raise his whistle to his mouth, and blow three short, piercing blasts. This was the signal for the entire school to cease fighting, rolling, kicking, and cavorting, to cease, in fact, all movement whatever, even eye-rolling, on the very second that the first, shrill blast cut across the uproar.

The effect of this signal was very curious to behold. Housewives in their front bedroom, opposite the area railings, often paused in their window-cleaning to watch, for it was like nothing so much as the sudden shutting down of a boiler factory, staffed by midget maniacs. One moment there was nothing but sound, and frantic movement; the next, there was silence, and utter stillness. For anyone to move a finger was to earn a sound thrashing on the spot.

At the close of break on the historic morning, Bernard and Boxer were in the throes of ten-sided game of hi-cocko-lorum, played against the railings, and the twins' team was jumping when the whistle sounded.

Boxer had taken off about three seconds before Mr. Little's whistle touched his lips, and when the blast reached the railings he had just landed, a clear four backs from the point of take-off.

The boy on whom he landed collapsed under the impact, and fell forward on his knees, where, having heard the whistle, he remained like a small Mohammedan in prayer. Boxer rolled sideways, and then he too lay quite still, for this instantaneous transition from violent action to immobility tickled his humour, and Mr. Little's whistle always produced one of his harsh, inward chuckles.

Unfortunately for Boxer, Mr. Little's eye happened to be focused directly upon this group and it seemed to the headmaster that Boxer had not only flagrantly disobeyed his edict, by moving after the whistle, but was now actually laughing at him.

With a little grunt of fury, he jumped up, ploughed through the grotesquely frozen groups between his seat and the railings, dragged the grinning Boxer to his feet, and cuffed him across the side of the head with a vigour that sent Boxer staggering against the railings. Boxer immediately covered up, and this gave Mr. Little an opportunity to draw his cane. Whipping it from his trouser-leg he raised it above his shoulder and aimed a heavy cut at Boxer's knuckles.

The blow never fell. In a flash the cane was seized from behind, wrenched from the headmaster's grasp, and flung high over the railings into Cawnpore Road.

A long drawn-out gasp greeted this astounding action.

All over the yard the frozen groups relaxed. Raised arms were lowered, outstretched legs were slowly set down, and almost imperceptibly, boys began to converge on the group against the railings. With strained faces, and wildly beating hearts, the cowed five hundred waited breathlessly to see what would happen next.

Nothing did happen immediately. When Mr. Little discovered that he no longer held the cane it crossed his mind that the stick must have caught in something—he could not imagine what—as he raised it above his head. Instinctively he turned to see what inanimate object had cheated him of the first blow. It never occurred to him that the cane had been torn from his hand by a human being. He had been a schoolmaster nearly forty years, and during that period he must have raised his cane a hundred thousand times without anything like this happening. When he swung round, and met Bernard's unblinking stare, he still did not connect the boy standing there with the loss of the cane, and addressed him simply because he realised that this boy must have been the nearest eyewitness to the improbable occurrence.

"What . . . what happened to my cane?" he demanded, and

as he shaped the words something in the boy's sullen expression gave him an inkling of the incredible truth.

Bernard's gaze did not waver. "You can't do that," he said levelly. "Boxer wasn't moving. He stopped, soon as the whistle blew, soon as he could!"

Mr. Little stood stock still. There was a faint roaring sound in his ears, and the close-packed ranks of the boys swam a little before his eyes. It was an old, familiar warning. He was due for a cramp at any moment, but he mastered himself with great effort, pressing his left hand hard against the taut muscles of his stomach.

"You ... you *snatched* it!" he gibbered, "you ... you *snatched* it from me?"

"He wasn't moving, he stopped when the whistle blew," repeated Bernard, doggedly.

Boxer had now straightened up, and was massaging his crimson ear.

"I wasn't, neither," he corroborated flatly.

A strangled, inarticulate sound issued from Mr. Little's moist lips. It sounded vaguely like the word "snatch", but it might have been anything.

Suddenly, unexpected corroboration came from another source. The small boy whom Boxer had flattened decided to defend his own honour, and deny in advance any possible claim of "weak horses", a claim that would have undoubtedly been made by Boxer's team, had the whistle not sounded when it did.

"He fell off," said the small boy, adding grudgingly, "but he stopped falling, soon as the whistle blew, I *sore* it!"

For a moment it seemed to those watching that Mr. Little was considering the scientific aspect of this remarkable assertion, that he was, in effect, trying very hard to picture to himself a boy's body defying the laws of gravity in a praiseworthy attempt to obey his headmaster's injunction to the very letter.

Then two things happened simultaneously. Mr. Little's first spasm doubled him up like a jack-knife, and the ranks surrounding the group suddenly found courage in their numbers and anonymity.

They began to groan and hiss, first a few, well away at the

back, and then all of them, even those standing directly under Mr. Little's eye.

The sound of their own voices encouraged them. In a moment the groans became shouts and catcalls; then they stopped hissing, and began to laugh, and thump one another, to hop about exultantly, point directly at the gasping figure of Mr. Little in their midst, and vie with one another in the violence of the personal abuse they hurled at him.

Then, as the first wave of pain receded, and Mr. Little half-straightened himself, a tall boy, known as Lofty Gibson, recognised as one of the more daring spirits, sang out:

"Shorty's got the belly-ache! Shorty's got the belly-ache!", and the cry was immediately taken up on all sides, until every boy in the enclosure was hopping up and down to the rhythm of "Shorty's got the belly-ache!", shouted at the top of his voice.

For a period of about five minutes the entire school drank deeply of the wine of revolution. It was very intoxicating, and they savoured every sip. For all who were present it was to prove the high spot of their stay at Havelock Park School, and those that took part never forgot the incident. Years afterwards, when one Havelock Road old boy of this cadre encountered another he would always say: "Remember the revolution?" It became a kind of pass-word among them, and those who were too old or too young to have witnessed it regarded it as having established an epoch in the history of the school, so that Havelock Road events were always labelled "Before the Revolution", and "After the Revolution".

Yet it all ended rather lamely.

From the staff-room window, Mr. Porless, the second master, and deputy Head during Mr. Little's periodical spells of absence, put through a panic telephone call to one of the regular inspectors, with whom he had recently had a guarded conversation on the subject of Mr. Little's fitness to command. The inspector, who lived in the Lower Road, owned a motor-cycle, and arrived on the spot within ten minutes of the outbreak. He was an ex-regular officer in the Buffs, and his experienced eye took in the scene the moment he had parked his machine against the railings. The boys nearest the road ceased to chant as soon as the inspector appeared, and when he climbed upon the brick base of the iron gates, and roared "Shut up!", in a voice that had terrified recruits in a dozen base camps, and on hill-station parade-grounds, the chanting ceased altogether and there was a general scuttle for the classrooms. In less than a minute the yard was empty of everyone except Mr. Little, the inspector, and the twins, with a breathless Mr. Porless peeping from the main door.

Bernard stood his ground, his cool brain already grappling with the various repercussions he might expect, and Boxer remained because Bernard had given him no alternative lead. The inspector was an observant man, and noticed that the boy against the railings had a crimson ear. He looked from the ear to Mr. Little, now struggling with his third cramp.

"How did this idiotic business begin?" he demanded, and when Mr. Little seemed incapable of answering, he turned towards the fair-haired boy, who was still standing stiffly to attention, immediately behind the headmaster.

"He was bashing my brother for moving," said Bernard, in a curiously flat tone. "He never did move. He stopped, soon as the whistle blew!"

"That's right, sir," said Boxer; "then they all started shouting!"

At last Mr. Little found his voice. He straightened himself and began to speak in a gobbling, high-pitched voice: "He snatched the cane ... he snatched it ..." but the inspector now turned to Mr. Porless, who had at last nerved himself to leave the safety of the buildings.

"Did you see it begin, Mr. Porless?" he asked briefly.

Mr. Porless was perspiring freely. He looked even less in command of himself than the headmaster.

"Well, no, sir ... not exactly ... they ... they ... suddenly seemed to ... er ... get out of hand. I thought I'd better ring ... there was nobody else."

"You did perfectly right," said the inspector crisply. "We'd better all go to the study, and someone had better make arrangement to get Mr. Little home immediately."

He turned to Bernard, as Mr. Porless gingerly took hold of his chief's arm.

"I shall want you two. You'd better come along with me now."

"Yes, sir," said Bernard mildly. "Come on, Boxer."

Five hundred pairs of eyes watched the little procession trail across the playground, and disappear through the main door.

"Lumme!" said Lofty Gibson, climbing down from his observation post on the radiator of Standard Six. "It'll be bloody Borstal for them two, you see if it ain't!"

There was no reaction to this prophecy among Standard Six. Now that they were back in the classrooms, individualised by their desks, stripped of the security they had enjoyed when they were pressed closely against one another in the tumultuous circle about the groaning headmaster, they felt naked and defenceless. Hysterical elation had ebbed from all but Lofty Gibson, and would ebb from him after a few minutes' reflection.

They looked at one another and giggled nervously. Mr. Porless waddled in and rapped his ruler on the desk.

3

It was fortunate for the twins that Mr. Goreham, the ex-officer Schools Inspector, had had his eye on Havelock Road for some time past.

Having disposed of the incoherent Mr. Little, who was ultimately taken home by ambulance, and having on his own resonsibility installed Mr. Porless as deputy Head until further notice, he set about seeking corroboration of Bernard Carver's laconic account of the mutiny.

A conscientious and thoughtful man, he was tremendously impressed by Bernard's manner. The child showed no sense of contrition, or anxiety over reprisals, but simply reiterated his story without the slightest attempt to elaborate. Boxer had not moved. Boxer had been unjustly set upon. He, Bernard, had checked a renewed assault by quietly relieving Mr. Little of his cane, and throwing it into Cawnpore Road, where it was subsequently retrieved by the householder of Number Seventeen.

All Mr. Goreham could extract from Boxer was three words: "That's right, sir!" and these he repeated as often as Bernard repeated his modest outline of events.

Soon there was not the slightest doubt in Mr. Goreham's mind that the twins were speaking the plain truth, and his heart warmed towards them. Like the women of the Avenue, he was touched, deep down, by their mutual devotion, and it seemed to him that if he could confirm their story he might improve upon the occasion by disposing of Mr. Little once and for all.

This proved a good deal easier than he anticipated.

The housewife who returned the cane provided further corroboration, and so, with a little judicious prompting, did two of the oppressed female staff. Their statements opened the door to further investigations, and finally Mr. Porless was prevailed upon to put on paper a factual report of Mr. Little's behaviour during the past twelve months.

There was a certain limit, it seemed, to the powers that headmasters of Council Schools could exercise, and it was now very clear to the authorities that Mr. Little had exceeded that limit on numerous occasions. Mr. Porless was promoted, Mr. Little was promptly retired on grounds of ill-health; the changes were carried out with a minimum of fuss and, to Mr. Goreham's soldierly relief, without a whisper of newspaper publicity. He, in fact, was warmly congratulated by his superiors on the efficiency and dispatch he had exhibited in handling the affair; and with this commendation the incident was officially closed.

For the twins, however, there was a curious sequel. During investigations Mr. Goreham called upon their father, and discovered that he and Jim had served in the same sector during the Passchendaele offensive. Having established this, they were not disposed to go very deeply into the business which had brought Mr. Goreham into the sitting-room of Number Twenty. They had taken part in great events, and were thus able to get Mr. Little's stomach cramp into its correct perspective. Only when they were parting did Mr. Goreham refer once more to the mutiny, and give Jim Carver a final piece of friendly advice.

"Those lads of yours," he said, with apparent casualness; "it might be a good idea to shift them for their own good."

"But you said they weren't to be punished," protested Jim.

"That's true," replied Mr. Goreham; "but Little's name stank over there, and it isn't surprising that they are now regarded as heroes!"

"Well," said Jim, "that's understandable, isn't it?"

"Certainly it is," replied Mr. Goreham affably, "but it might go to their heads. Bernard isn't likely to get big-headed about all this nonsense, but the other one might. Why don't you try getting them in at the Grammar School, over at Godley? It's only a two-penny bus fare from the Lower Road depot, and they'd get a better start there."

"On three-fifteen a week?" replied Jim cynically. "Unless they win scholarships, I couldn't think of it. Isn't there some other school round here they could go to?"

"I'll see what I can do to get them shifted over to Sydenham Road," promised the Inspector. "It's not in my district, but I dare say I can manage it in the circumstances."

Mr. Goreham did manage it. Like almost everybody, he had succumbed to the unity of Bernard and Boxer. In a highly competitive world they became, for other people, a sort of symbol of co-operative bliss. Without either of them ever knowing it they were to reap the advantages of this all their lives.

They moved over to Sydenham Road School, where their fame as "the twins who got the Head sacked" preceded them, and made their settling-in easy, but they did not remain at a Council School much longer. Mr. Goreham continued to interest himself in them, and maintained his casual friendship with Jim Carver. The result was that he found their fees for the Grammar School from some mysterious ex-servicemen's fund. By their eleventh birthday they were bedded down at Godley, and were to be seen almost any morning in term-time, leaping on to the tail-boards of slow-moving lorries in the Lower Road, in order that they might arrive at school before second bell, and yet retain their twopenny fares for gob-stoppers.

Bernard and Boxer accounted for thousands of gobstoppers during their school-days. Whenever you saw them they appeared to be suffering from agonising toothache, and their speech was slurred and clumsy. There was the same element of share-and-share-alike even about their gobstopper-sucking, for Boxer crushed his to pieces within minutes of popping one into his mouth, whereas Bernard conserved his, in order that he might pass on the diminished globe to his twin, as soon as Boxer's cheeks ceased to bulge.

"Mine's gone, Bernie," Boxer would announce at length; "they don't last like they used to. How about you, Berni; you half-way yet?"

Berni would hesitate, as always, as though pondering the judicial aspect of a transfer. After a few moments, however, he would capitulate, quietly extract the bright blue ball, and hand it to Boxer. Boxer would put it straight into his mouth. He was untroubled by thoughts of hygiene. Bernard's digestive processes were also his, like all things that were Bernard's.

CHAPTER VII

Archie Takes A Holiday

1

BY the autumn of 1923 the families of the Avenue had shaken down and adjusted themselves to patterns they were to maintain, with little variation, throughout the decades between the wars.

The households that had lost menfolk on the battlefields and on the high seas, had ceased to mourn them. The injured had crept from the hospitals, to lick their wounds, and look for part-time employment. The unpensioned survivors, like Jim Carver, had joined in the struggle for a full-time job with a living wage. All along the Avenue the war dead had lost their individuality, and merged into a six-figure total, their photographs revered for an hour or two each November 11th, then put aside on occasional tables, and what-nots, to be taken down and dusted during a spring-clean, or when visitors in the drawing-rooms asked polite questions about the

bearded sailors, and bayonet-brandishing warriors in puttees
and field-service caps.

"Who was that, Florrie? Was it your husband?"

"No, my brother, Bert. He was drowned on the 'Creçy', at
the start of it. Ever such a nice chap Bert was. D'you take
sugar, dear?"

There were so many other things to worry over, and gossip
about—unemployment, the Sinn Fein outrages, the Thomp-
son-Bywaters crime, the rise of Rudolph Valentino.

Jim Carver was away on removal trips all day, and often
for two or three days at a stretch. He did not look around
for a second wife; for one thing he had Louise to care for
the family, and for another he was now wedded to politics,
and spent most of his spare time at political meetings.

One of the drivers at his depot was an active member of
the Labour Party, and had talked Jim, hitherto a lukewarm
Liberal, into joining his local branch.

Having once put his hand to politics, Jim applied himself
to them with the same quiet doggedness that characterised
everything he did. He never missed a committee meeting. He
was always at hand to distribute leaflets, and to support
speakers at street-corner gatherings. He took the trouble to
study facts and statistics and, although a shy, halting speaker
on the soap-box, he found he could usually silence hecklers
by quoting a string of figures in a quiet, authoritative tone.

By the noisier members of the group he soon came to be
regarded as a useful and highly dependable comrade. He had
the great merit of believing everything written down for him
in the party brochures and handouts. His sharp lesson in the
helplessness of the unorganised manual worker, during the
first post-war slump, was not easily forgotten, but the work
he carried out for the cause of Labour was done without any
expectation of reward, or personal aggrandisement, but simply because he had imagination, and a kind heart.

In addition, at the back of it all, was the memory of the
dead boy on the bank, for by this time the scrutiny of
countless pamphlets had convinced him that competitive capitalism could only mean another war, and any system of
government was preferable to one that made such a horror
remotely possible.

Inside the framework of his political work he was an active supporter of the League of Nations, and his main theme, in such speeches as he made in support of more spectacular demagogues, was always that of unquestioning support of the League, as the one means available to mankind for bringing about the Millennium.

He was happy enough, with his unexacting job, and his earnest, if woolly political outlook. His domestic worries were few, for Louise was a better housewife than his wife Ada had ever been, and his meals were always on the table when he wanted them, while the younger children seldom intruded into his thoughts.

Louise was always at hand, with a clean towel, and his neatly darned underwear. Archie, he hardly ever saw. Boxer and Bernard were in bed when he went out in the morning, and playing in the street when he returned to wash, and change for a meeting. Judith, he kissed absentmindedly now and again, or passed her the top of his boiled egg, when she stood expectantly beside him at high-tea. The girl-twins never came downstairs at all when he was at home, except on Sunday mornings, when Judith pushed their perambulator as far as the "Rec", and Jim was asked to manoeuvre it along the narrow hall and over the step to the front path.

For the rest he lived remote in his dream of the Brotherhood of Man, with his steady gaze fixed upon the day when Labour would obtain a majority at Westminster. Then, if at all, would be the time to sit back secure in the knowledge that Pandora's Box had been double-locked, and cast into the Atlantic depths. Then would be the time to enjoy life as it could be lived, and devote less of his energies to the conversion of theory into practice.

Archie, meantime, was fully occupied with his own dreams, and these were of a somewhat more practical nature.

Employment at various provision shops, from the time he was fourteen, had taught Archie Carver, a valuable commercial lesson. This was simply the conviction that, to make money *all* the time, one must deal in food. One could expect quick returns in many other spheres, but not one of them (with the possible exception of funeral furnishings) could be relied upon to yield steady profits come war come peace, come boom come slump, come glut come dearth. Food, only food, was the one commodity people could not go without, even if shortage of houses compelled them to live in home-made shacks, and shortage of money sent them scrambling to jumble-sale counters, and junk-shop marts for clothes to wear, and beds on which to sleep.

During the last two or three years of the war, Archie had been astounded at the lengths to which people would go for sugar, butter, and tinned meat, for sauces even, and other items down on the stock-lists as luxuries.

He was a young man who was determined to have money, yet there was sufficient of his father in him to make him prefer earning it honestly, and this despite his brief and successful essays in the making of money on the side, as at Coolridge's.

In short, he was determined to have a shop of his own. Once he had that, everything else would follow—car, comfortable flat, women, holidays abroad, security.

He did not crave money to buy power. Abstract power did not interest him, but what did, what interested him a great deal, was power to indulge his appetites, to go where he liked, to eat and drink what he fancied, to acquire, for as long as she amused him, any pretty girl who caught his eye.

His interlude with Rita Ramage had whetted his appetite for women, preferably sophisticated women, and it was a source of continual irritation to him that, as the employee of anyone else, he would never have the means to buy their company for long enough to make them need him for his own sake, the way Rita Ramage had needed him.

He was confident, however, that once he had a shop of his own, and its attendant source of steady profit, he could indulge himself to the full, not only in this respect, but in any other respect to which his fancy inclined him.

The thing to concentrate upon, therefore, was a small business, one that could be picked up for a hundred pounds or so. A year's hard work at his own counter, with no employees to raid the till, or lose a customer through inso-lence or incompetence, and his life's ambition could be real-ised before he was twenty-five.

Following his dismissal from the stores, immediately after the shameful business of Rita Ramage, Archie's dream looked a very long way from being realised. He had over ninety pounds put aside from his wartime tips at Coolridge's, but grocery-hands were notoriously ill-paid, employers had a help-less pool of unemployed to draw upon and, now that every-thing was in general supply, he was unable to supplement his thirty-two-and-sixpence a week by any sideline.

It would be folly, he reasoned, to sign on with another chain-store for the same sort of wage. By this time he had no illusions at all about the future a chain-store offered its counter-hands and storemen, even the cleverest among them. The managership of a small branch was the best he could hope for, and that meant hard work for forty years, on a salary rising slowly to something like four hundred a year. Archie at twenty-one had ceased to think in terms of any-thing under a thousand a year, and he had never heard of a branch manager earning that amount, or anything like it. Besides, a branch manager worked all of twelve hours a day, and was lucky to manage a week's out-of-season holiday each year. This was not Archie's idea of security. It led but to the grave, via retirement, at sixty-five, on a four-pound-a-week pension.

Archie was not a victim of the post-war neurosis of the unemployed, with an uncertain future. He wanted his fun and frolic now, or next year, or—at the very most—the year after next. So he took the daring step of neglecting to sign on at the labour exchange, spent some of his savings on a second-hand Douglas motor-cycle, and began touring the new housing districts beyond Shirley, in search of a derelict busi-ness that he could buy for fifty pounds or less. Once he had acquired premises, however unpromising, he would think about getting stock on credit.

He was a dogged young man. Sometimes he rode sixty or seventy miles in a day, inspecting new housing sites, asking questions in village pubs, making tiny purchases, usually a box of matches, in any grocery store that had about it an air of defeat, and all the time what he was looking for lay directly under his nose, not a stone's throw from his own front door. It was curious that its discovery was directly

attributable to a disaster that threatened to destroy all hope of
the future he had planned.

2

Archie's girl-friend at this particular time was a well-built
blonde, called Edna Gittens, whose family lived at the far end
of the Avenue, and whose father was a diabetic tram-conductor,
with innumerable children.

Edna worked at a hairdresser's, in the Lower Road. She
was nineteen, matter-of-fact, and incurably lazy. Her disin-
clination to walk more than a few hundred yards from her
home, when Archie called to take her out in the evenings,
had certain advantages prior to the time Archie acquired his
motor-cycle. Limited privacy was available to courting couples
in the Lane, at the foot of the Avenue, and when they were
not at the cinema, where Edna, leaning heavily on Archie,
invariably dropped off to sleep during the first reel of the
big film, they usually sat down on Archie's mackintosh in a
grassy hollow, beneath the dwarf elms of the hedge border-
ing the golf-links.

Here, providing it was reasonably dry, Edna usually
obliged him, and then dropped off to sleep in the long,
sweet-smelling grass. Archie usually took a nap with her,
waking her up when the night chill set in, or he was beginning to feel cramped, and leaving her at his gate (which they
reached first) to yawn her way down the remainder of the
Avenue to Number One-Hundred-and-Four, where she and
her family lived.

It was a very somnolent courtship, and Archie liked it that
way. He had not the remotest intention of letting it develop
beyond its present stage, and it is doubtful whether Edna, on
her part, thought about marriage at all. The same applied to
her father, who had so many daughters that he would not
have recognised Archie as a suitor had he passed him in the
Avenue on the way to or from work.

Archie's motor-cycle was the agency that carried the romance a stage further, that brought it, indeed, to its somewhat complicated climax.

That summer, Archie felt he needed a little holiday, and

suggested that he and Edna should go camping, Archie having acquired, for the sum of thirty shillings, a battered side-car in which the tents and equipment could be stowed.

Edna agreed, as she agreed with practically everything, but she made it a condition that her sister Hilda should accompany them. She did not insist on Hilda's presence as a chaperone, but because Hilda was much more energetic than she was, and at the back of Edna's mind there was a strong suspicion that physical exertion might be associated with camping, that the putting up of tents, the lighting of fires, the cleaning of frying-pans, would demand her attention in an upright position, or at least on her knees. After all, this was supposed to be a holiday, and Hilda was out of work anyway.

Archie raised no objection to Hilda accompanying them on the trip. She was two years older than Edna, and attractive in the same heavy way. Side by side, they looked very much alike. Both had bobbed hair, good complexions, and their father's prominent blue eyes, and both had the heavy pink lower lip that Archie always looked for in women.

The camping holiday was a great success. They took two patrol tents, and the minimum of gear, and set off gaily down the Tonbridge Road, camping the first night on a lightly-wooded slope, immediately above the Penshurst Place.

That first evening, they fried supper over a wood fire that Archie lit and Hilda tended.

When it was quite dark they put out the fire and went to bed, Archie to his tiny tent, the girls to their double patrol tent, pitched a few yards higher up the slope.

Archie's camping experience was limited to reading an article or two on the subject in magazines, and he had chosen an unfortunate spot for his tent. In the night there was a heavy thunderstorm, and streams of water were soon running under the valances, saturating his blankets, and ultimately, despite all his efforts to keep the shelter rigid, dislodging the pegs, and bringing the tent about his ears.

It was still raining hard when he fought his way free of the dripping canvas. The sidecar was full of gear, and too small to accommodate him anyway. There was nothing he could do but crawl into the girls' tent, and this he did without a moment's hesitation, waking Hilda and persuading her to edge over an inch or two.

The tent was small and she made room for him with difficulty. Surprisingly, Edna did not stir, and Hilda and Archie discussed the situation in low tones. They soon made rather more room for themselves by shifting gear on to Edna's feet. Presently, Hilda began to giggle. She had more sense of humour than her younger sister.

"She only brought me to do the chores," she protested, when Archie solicitously endeavoured to give the sleeping Edna even more breathing space.

"There are chores and chores," said Archie, who had now stopped shivering, and was beginning to think there were certain unlooked-for advantages in thunderstorms.

They were both up and about long before Edna climbed out, yawning. Archie's tent was put up, and his blankets were laid out to dry in the morning sun. They breakfasted quietly, Hilda humming to herself, and occasionally winked at Archie over the fire. Edna, who had a lazy woman's healthy appetite, carefully disposed of all the food that was left over. Then Archie had a bright idea.

"Why don't we camp here all the week, and go day trips on the bike?" he suggested. "It'll save pitching somewhere new every night, and give my stuff time to dry."

The girls were agreeable. They re-pitched Archie's tent higher up the slope, and when they returned to the site that evening his blankets were dry.

Edna and Archie wandered off towards the lake, and Hilda remained behind contentedly to cook supper. There were no more thunderstorms, and all three continued to sleep comfortably. Edna's sleep was so much deeper than her sister's.

"It reminds me of that old joke about twin beds," Archie told Hilda, as he wriggled in between them one night, and stretched himself out with a deep, contented sigh.

"Tell me," said Hilda, fitting her head into the hollow of his shoulder.

"Couple put an advert in the paper—twin beds for sale, one almost new!"

"I don't think she'd mind if she knew," Hilda giggled.

"Well, and why should she?" he demanded; "you're keeping me in the family, aren't you?"

3

Archie was not to remain family property for long.

On their return home, Archie realised that the Gittens family were now making impossible demands upon his time. Whereas he could always manage an odd evening or two with one sister, he found it irritating, and altogether too complicated, to plan a courting time-table for three. The result was that his enthusiasm for this concubinal triangle soon cooled, and he was seen less and less in the Avenue and Lane at dusk, but began seeking love-life further afield in Bromley, and sometimes as far away as Brighton. That was the advantage of a motor-cycle; it widened his fields in more spheres than that of commercial reconnaissance.

The girls did not pursue him through the late summer, and Archie had almost forgotten them when, one morning, as he was wheeling his motor-cycle from the alley, preparatory to setting off on another of his long-distance business surveys, he was stopped at the exit by little Mr. Gittens, five-foot four inches in his tram-conductor's uniform, and wheezing rather more agitatedly than usual.

Archie had seen Mr. Gittens pass his door for more than a year, but had never known who he was, and had never connected him with the girls at One-Hundred-and-Four.

"Name o' Carver, *Archie* Carver?" asked Mr. Gittens, apologetically.

He was a very apologetic little man, and spoke with a strong Lancashire accent. This, combined with his stature, and a general air of seeking to please, invested him with a faint aura of the music-hall.

Archie readily admitted his identity, and wondered impatiently what the little man could want. He was very soon enlightened.

"Ah'm Fred Gittens, from a hundred-and-four," said the tram-conductor, very civilly. "You must be t'lad who's put both my girls in t'family way!"

He said it pleasantly, and conversationally, as though this

line of talk was an everyday gambit between neighbours who had met unexpectedly in the street. It was his manner, as much as the information he imparted, that shocked Archie. His stomach contracted, and his jaw dropped. He had difficulty in holding his heavy cycle upright.

Mr. Gittens, however, was not disposed to press charges there and then. He was a very punctual little man, and had merely stopped by on his way to the tram depot. Without waiting for Archie to comment he went on, still very pleasantly.

"Eee, but tha's made a rare to-do in our house, lad, for it's plain enough tha can't marry both! As I said to missus, not an hour since, I said, 'He can marry one, and pay for t'other'; so you'd best coom round tonight, and have it out like! I'm on middle turn, and I get home about five." And with that he touched his peaked cap, and twinkled off down the Avenue towards Shirley Road.

Archie gaped after him, not having uttered one word of denial or affirmation, for Mr. Gittens' lack of rancour had paralysed his tongue. It was almost as though Gittens, himself the father of a huge family, was applauding a casual stranger's virility, but was of the opinion, nevertheless, that certain economic arrangements must be entered into between parties, if only in order to tidy up the situation generally.

Archie stood stock still until Mr. Gittens had rounded the corner of the pillar-box. Then he slowly wheeled his motorcycle back into the shed, and set off on foot for the "Rec". He had to think. He had to sit still and think, and think, and think.

Only one decision emerged from his numbed brain, and as he passed between the brick pillars of the "Rec" and made his way to a bench near the empty tennis-courts, this fact emerged from a sea of panic and stood out like a rock of salvation. It was simply this: whatever he did, or said, in the next few hours would determine the pattern of his life. One false word, one unconsidered step, and he was lost, for all time. There would be no shop, no income, no independence—nothing but years and years of counter-jumping, and prampushing, nothing ahead of him but the prospect of becoming a sort of male Louise, chained to the sink, flanked by rows and rows of nappies, and condemned to potter about a suburban garden, doing without cigarettes and 'bus-rides, in order to make ends meet every Friday.

He gritted his teeth and formed, then and there, an implacable resolve. This wasn't going to happen to him. To anyone else but not to him. Never, never, never, not if every female in the Gittens' family produced triplets, named him the father, and handed him a sheaf of affiliation orders.

He was sweating with the intensity of this resolution when, for the second time that morning, a semi-stranger addressed him in almost the identical terms employed by Mr. Gittens.

"You're Archie Carver, aren't you?"

He looked up, startled, straight into the sad brown eyes of Toni Piretta, the Italian proprietor of the corner shop, that stood at the junction of the Avenue and Shirley Rise.

Mr. Piretta was beaming even more genially than usual. He held out a plump, freckled hand.

CHAPTER VIII

New Worlds For Edith

1

WHEN Ted Hartnell, Edith Clegg's jazz-minded stonemason lodger at Number Four, came home one evening in the autumn of '23, confessed that he had been sacked, and told her shamefacedly that he would have to leave the area in search of a job and cheaper lodgings, Edith Clegg turned very pale, and went straight up to her room for a quiet cry.

Edith was very happy with her lodger and, by this time, looked upon him as a son. The impact of his cheerful personality upon her sister Becky had been wonderful. For years, before Ted came to live with them, Becky had been rather less than half-witted. She seldom said or did a rational thing, and Edith never quite knew when another "spell" was coming. Becky's spells could lead at best to embarrassing complications with neighbours, and at worst to another visit from the doctor, and a renewal of the frightening discussions regarding the advisibility of "sending Becky away".

The absorption of Ted Hartnell, his gramophone, and his banjolele, into the household, had changed all that. Ted and Becky got on famously, and Becky had not had a serious "spell" for years, if one discounted her periodical appeals to the errant Lickapaw from the boundary fence.

Ted had never seemed to realise there was anything seriously the matter with Becky. Lately, he had taken to calling her "Aunt Becky", as he had called Edith "Aunt Edith" ever since he had first carried his gramophone downstairs, and played jazz tunes to them in the kitchen.

Despite Becky's "spells", Number Four had always been a very placid home, but now, with the three of them on such gay and affectionate terms, it was among the happiest in the Avenue. There was never so much as a spurt of irritation to spoil the harmony. Edith put her pianoforte pupils through their pieces whilst Ted was at work, and after they all had their high tea, at 7:30 p.m. they cleared away, and Ted entertained them with his gramophone or, less frequently, with his mouth-organ, and banjolele.

When they played the gramophone, they all sat in the warm kitchen, with Ted tapping out a lively rhythm on the table-top and saucepan lids. When they decided upon an impromptu concert they all went into the front room. Ted provided sheet music, of which he had nearly a trunkful, and Edith accompanied him on the yellow-keyed cottage piano.

Before Ted came to them Edith had never played a dance-tune. She was familiar with the decorous parlour songs of her girlhood, and could accompany any rendering of the sort of number so popular between speeches at public diners, songs like *The Golden Vanity, Glorious Devon,* and *Come in to the Garden, Maud,* but she had never sat down to play the sort of music that Ted introduced into the house. His music had its outside covers decorated with love-lorn young ladies, wearing bandeaux, or couples sitting out under a sickle moon, and palm trees, and his songs all had oddly similar titles about moonlight in Georgia or cabins in Nevada, and lyrics that rhymed "June", "moon", and "soon", or "love" and "above". The scores had familiar crotchets and quavers, but in addition, little gratings, half-filled with dots, that Ted told her were the ukelele accompaniments, and showed him just where to put his fingers when he strummed.

Becky joined in these little soirées with an eagerness that made Edith's heart swell, and sometimes brought a lump into her throat. She even learnt the words of the songs, and bobbed about the front-room, to the utmost peril of the plant-stands, and the carefully-balanced Goss china on the mantelshelf.

At other times she accepted Ted as though he had been living with them since girlhood days, and had been bound up with their life at the Devon Vicarage, long before the coming of Saul, and the cloud that had blotted out all that had happened since.

And now Ted had been sacked, and was talking about finding cheaper lodgings. Suppose he left? What could she tell Becky? How could she begin to explain that Ted would never again sit down to his high tea with them, that there would be no more gramophone recitals, no more songs and junketings round the cottage piano?

Up in his back room, the room he had slept in for more than three years, but had never yet used as a sitting-room, Ted was equally despondent. Edith and Becky meant more to him than anyone in his past, and the billet was certainly the most comfortable he had ever heard of, much less occupied.

The thought of packing his belongings, and moving off into the inhospitable world again, depressed and frightened him. He could not bring himself to begin putting his things into the hold-all that he had dragged from the cistern-loft where it had remained, gathering cobwebs, since he came to Number Four, in the autumn of 1919.

He sat on the edge of his bed, elbows on knees, and cursed himself over and over again for losing his job on account of a piece of downright stupidity, for which he could blame no one but himself.

Ted's abrupt dismissal from the stonemason's yard had a strong element of farce.

It was Ted's habit, when chiselling the pencilled inscrip-

tions on a tombstone, to regulate his taps with the beats of
whatever popular tune that happened to be syncopating in his
mind at the moment.

Hundreds of tombstones that had stood in cemeteries all
over South London had received their inscriptions to the
catchy rhythms of *Alexander's Ragtime Band,* and *Yes, We
Have No Bananas.* Scores of verses from the Scriptures had
been chiselled out of marble to the tap-tap of *The Sheik of
Araby,* or the slow, more painstaking rhythm of *Missouri
City Waltz* and *Bubbles.* When he was at work, Ted never
sang these songs aloud. He hummed them, or crooned them
over and over in his head, as his seamed fingers adjusted their
measure to the letters he was shaping.

Then, unaccountably, a particularly tappy tune had let him
down, and landed him in the Labour Exchange queue.

Beating out the words "Asleep in the arms of Jesus", in
memory of one, Thomas Hitchcock, "who fell asleep on May
23rd, 1922", and who was, it claimed, "secure in the hope of
a glorious resurrection", Ted Hartnell's jazzy jinx selected *The
Red, Red Robin* as an over-all accompaniment.

Ted went right on bob-bob-bobbing long after he should
have laid aside his tools, and shifted his position to begin
another line. He did not even notice his error until he heard
Mr. Foster, his employer, exclaim from his end of the
bench. Then he paused on the words "his own sweet song", to
brush away the dust, and study his handiwork.

He knew at once that there was something odd about the
tablet, but for a moment or two he could not decide what
was amiss.

By then, however, Mr. Foster had sidled round to Ted's
end of the bench, and was gazing at the stone with horror.

"You've run off the line," he kept repeating, "you've gone
and run off the ruddy line!"

Ted had done rather more than run off the ruddy line. He
had concluded the words "Asleep in the arms of Jesus" with,
not one, but a whole crop of inverted commas, setting them
at slowly descending levels, reaching slantwise to the very
edge of the block. The remorseless rhythm of the red, red
robin had bewitched him. He had been hypnotised into the

act of beating away with his mallet, until he had literally syncopated his way off the tablet!

Ted immediately offered to pay for it, but Mr. Foster'was not to be mollified. By habit an ardent churchgoer, and by persuasion a great upholder of memorials to the dead, he was profoundly shocked. The ridiculous association of red, red robins and the late Mr. Thomas Hitchcock's expectations of glory, was more than he was ready to forgive. It savoured too much of blasphemy, and Ted was given notice on the spot. Had he been a good stonemason he might have talked himself out of the scrape, but it had been obvious to Mr. Foster for some time past, that Ted's heart did not repose in memorial tablets. When he considered the matter, in the light of the ruined stone, he concluded that his own work was beginning to deteriorate, under the merciless drip of Ted Hartnell's hummings, jiggings, and bob-bob-bobbings. He was not a vindictive man, and gave Ted a final piece of well-meant advice:

"Get yourself a job in a jazz band, lad. Maybe someone will pay you to bob-bob-bob from morning to night!"

Ted was not disposed to take this advice very seriously. No one was likely to hand him the keys of Paradise on a spoiled headstone.

Hitherto he had striven to keep his life in two separate compartments—those of beating out memorial tablets by day, and pursuing hot-rhythm by night. He was unaware, until the moment he had spoiled Mr. Hitchcock's tablet, how rapidly the one was encroaching on the other, how surely the tide of syncopation was engulfing him, and how little room there was in his mind for anything unconnected with cabins in pines; and moons over Colorado. It had never occurred to him to try and convert his obsession into a means of livelihood. How *did* one make a living from jazz? Who would employ anyone whose soul might be in pawn to the saxophone, but who had never yet handled one, whose musical accomplishments indeed were limited to a few chords on the banjolele, and a certain facility with the mouth-organ?

His sombre musings were cut short by a gentle knock on his door, and "Aunt" Edith came in. Her face was puffy with grief. In her eyes, however, was a glint of resolve.

"I've decided, Teddy; you mustn't leave here. It would be very bad for Becky; besides, wherever you go, they won't let you play your gramophone. I'm going in to talk it over with Mr. Carver! Go down now, and play something for Becky. She's in the kitchen shelling peas."

She did not wait to hear if Ted had any suggestions, but let herself out of the house, and went along the Avenue to Number Twenty.

In the last two or three years she had made a habit of "talking things over" with Mr. Carver. She had respected his judgment in worldly matters ever since the day he had taken her to see the tomb of the Unknown Warrior, in Westminster Abbey, and explained to her the full significance of the phrase: "They buried him among the Kings, because his soul was great." She looked back with quiet pleasure on this, her first visit to the Abbey, and her very first expedition "up West" with a man.

Back in November 1920 it had needed considerable effort on Edith Clegg's part to knock on the door of Number Twenty, and ask Jim Carver to take her to see the Unknown Warrior's Tomb, but he had been very understanding about it, and so kind in getting his daughter Louise to look after Becky while they were gone.

"You see, Mr. Carver," she had said to him that first day they had spoken to one another, "it's almost like going to the funeral of somebody you knew and liked. I *might* have known him. Lots of the boys who came to the Vicarage when I was a girl went to the war, and I expected some of them were killed, poor dears."

Jim Carver had agreed that she might well have known him; and later, when they had shuffled together past the open grave, and glanced at the silent guard of honour, leaning on their reversed arms inside the barrier, he had let his mind range over the possibility that he too might have rubbed shoulders with the man who was buried among the kings. It was not so impossible after all. Perhaps they passed one another on the way up the line with a ration party, or in some crowded estaminet, where men were singing *Keep the Home Fires Burning,* or even as the stretcher parties staggered back from the shambles of some sector like Mametz Wood, carrying the Unknown to a field-dressing station to breathe his last, and be laid in a temporary grave to await immortality.

Jim was touched by this twittery little spinster's eagerness to identify herself with the national symbol, and all that wintry afternoon he had gone out of his way to be gentle, and mildly gallant towards her. He would have been surprised if he had known that this single encounter had elevated him in her mind to the level of a sage.

He now discussed her new problem readily and realistically: "He'll have to get a job, Miss Clegg, and apart from Kidd's there isn't another stonemason's yard round here that I know of."

"But he mustn't *go*," Edith insisted; "it would be so *bad* for Becky. Having him has made such a difference, you'd hardly believe! Besides, he's . . ." she broke off, blushing, ". . . he isn't a gentleman-boarder any more, he's a sort of . . . well . . . *nephew*."

She was going to say "son", but checked herself at the last moment. It crossed her mind that even dear Mr. Carver might misconstrue their true relationship.

"Well," said Jim, flatly, "I don't know your means, Miss Clegg, and I don't know whether you are in a position to feed and board him indefinitely for next to nothing. If he stays on here without a job, he'll only get his dole money. Besides, you'll have to let his room to someone else, won't you?"

"I couldn't do that," replied Edith, firmly, but illogically, "it would always be dear Teddy's room, whoever had it!"

"What else can he do?" asked Jim. He was quite ready to help Miss Clegg with advice, but he had an eye on the clock. He was due at a meeting in fifteen minutes.

"He can sing and play. . . . I . . . I could teach him the piano!" said Edith, desperately.

It had often occurred to her that Ted could be taught to play the piano but, until now, she had never put the thought into words. Jim Carver was scornful. He had the manual worker's contempt for the arts as a means of earning bread.

"There's not much money in that," he said. "Millions of
people can sing and play!" He rose heavily to his feet. "I'll
tell you what I'll do. Let him stay on for a week or so, and
I'll make some enquiries at my depot. Maybe I can find him
some sort of job down there, just something to keep him
going. You'd better ask him to call in and see me tomorrow
evening."

"It's terribly kind of you, Mr. Carver," said Edith. "I knew
you'd think of something immediately."

"I wouldn't count on anything," said Jim, guardedly.
"Whatever it is, it won't be much of a job, I can tell you that
now!"

But in Edith Clegg's mind, as she went blithely back to
Number Four, the matter was as good as settled, and her
drooping spirits were quite restored. She and Becky and Ted
sat down to a mackerel tea as usual, and afterwards they
celebrated the reprieve with a concert.

Coming home after dark that night Jim Carver passed the
cutained window of Number Four, and heard them all at the
piano. They were playing and singing *Horsey, Keep Your
Tail Up.*

Jim did not possess a strong sense of humour, and rarely
smiled, but a bubble of laughter rose to his lips at the vision
of the Misses Clegg and their lodger, greeting the uncertain
future, with a decorous rendering of *Horsey, Keep Your Tail
Up.*

2

In the event it was both Edith and Ted who found jobs.

Jim Carver secured part-time work for Ted as auction-
hand in the sale-room of the firm for which he worked. Ted
donned a green baize apron, and stood round the lots on
Tuesdays, Thursdays, and Saturdays, afterwards assisting in
the deliveries to dealers. He was paid seven-and-six a day, and
Edith accepted twelve-and-six of his earnings for board. Ted
would have gladly given her the whole sum, but she stead-
fastly refused it, pointing out that a young man had to have
something left over for new gramophone records.

Notwithstanding, it was a struggle to keep him on such a

pittance, and when the financial strain became apparent to her she made the most important decision of her life. She took a job as cinema pianist at the Granada, in the Lower Road, and, having taken it, glided into a new and wonderful world.

Now that Ted was home for half the week, she had much more freedom of movement. Becky could be left, and Edith took to going out for her shopping, instead of relying upon tradesmen to call. She found she could shop more economically this way, and also enjoy the occasional change of scene.

It was on one of these shopping expeditions that she' saw the notice on the iron gates of the Granada, a small, ramshackle cinema, that had once been a Methodist Chapel, and was now run by an enterprising gentleman called Billings.

It was a very unpretentious cinema, with a capacity of about 150, one of a small chain run by Mr. Billings, in the outer suburbs, and employing a projectionist, an aged pianist, a cashier, and a single usherette.

Mr. Billings called twice a week to enter up books, bank the takings, and superintend front-of-house publicity. The remainder of the time the premises were nominally in charge of Mr. Billings's nephew, a sleek, hollow-cheeked young man, called Eddie.

On the day Edith happened to be passing, Mr. Billings was featuring a big, forthcoming attraction, Lon Chaney in *The Hunchback of Notre Dame*, and had been interested to discover, among the publicity sent on to him by distributors, a free copy of the theme song, *Song of the Bells*.

Now Mr. Billings was not one of these latter-day motion-picture magnates, whose entry into the profession is brought about by their sound knowledge of accountancy. He was a showman, whose experience dated back to the old bioscope days, and he was, moreover, a serious student of audience reaction. He was also an unashamed sentimentalist, and made a habit of sitting through his own pictures, weeping and guffawing alongside his regular customers. His yardstick, as a professional purveyor of mass entertainment, could be found in the word "mood". He believed that the success of any entertainment lay, not in any qualities it might or might not possess, but in the subtle stimulation of the mood of the audience watching it. Such stimulation he accepted as his own responsibility. He did not, in other words, leave such essentials to Mary Pickford, and Charlie Chaplin. They had their jobs and he had his, and at each of his cinemas, be it ever so lowly, he went out of his way to engage a good pianist, in order to ensure the creation of moods in the correct order.

His pianist at the Granada was an aged musician called Stubbs, known affectionately as "The Professor", who could be relied upon to regulate the emotions of the audience, much as an experienced janitor regulates the steam-heat of a block of flats.

Mr. Billings thought a great deal of Mr. Stubbs, having himself shed many a tear in the privacy of the one-and-threepennies, while witnessing Lilian Gish mount the steps of the guillotine, or sob on the bosom of Ramon Navarro, and the moment Mr. Billings's eye fell on *Song of the Bells* he shouted hoarsely for Eddie, his nephew, and told him to send the mæstro up to the office, which was sited alongside the projection-loft.

"Professor" Stubbs did not appear. Instead Eddie himself looked in, a limp cigarette hanging from his lower lip.

"The old Prof's in hospital," he told the astonished Mr. Billings. "Went there night before last. Ain't comin' back, neither, if you ask me. Looked half-dead when they took him off, smack in the middle of the Custard-Pie!"

This was grave news, and caused Mr. Billings to chew his ragged moustache.

"What you do without him las' night?" he wanted to know.

Eddie shrugged his padded shoulders. "Got a kid in. She played pieces through both houses. Trouble was, she kep' stoppin' to look at the film. Bloody awful it was. Proper shambles!"

"Well," said Mr. Billings finally, "we gotta get someone fer the *Hunchback*, and they gotta be good. No pianer-player, no mood! No mood, no 'ouses! Simple as that, Eddie!"

They found somebody, and they found somebody good, so good indeed that Mr. Billings never again made the mistake of judging an employee's worth on his or her outward appearance.

In later years it made him shudder to think how close he came to denying Miss Edith Clegg the opportunity of proving how well she understood the moods of cinema audiences. He interviewed her because she was the only applicant attracted by the card that he hung on the iron gate, and he decided at a glance that she was too nervous, too dowdy, and obviously quite inexperienced. It was his disparaging glance, however, that put Edith on her mettle. She anticipated his gloomy dismissal, by saying with a pertness that surprised him:

"I can play anything, and play it in the dark. Why don't you try me?"

He was struck by her unexpected forthrightness, and jerked his head towards the dim auditorium. Ahead of her he padded down the central aisle to the tiny railed-off pit, where a cottage piano stood at an angle of forty-five degrees to the screen.

"You don't *'ave* to play in the dark," he told her, "you get a pilot light, see?" and he switched on the light beside the score bracket.

The 15-watt bulb glowed eerily, giving Edith the impression that the cinema was as big as a cathedral. Mr. Billings opened *Song of the Bells,* and placed it reverently on the bracket.

"It's not just a question of *playing,*" he warned her. "It's a question o' *mood.* You gotta foller the story *without* follering it, if you see what I mean. You gotta be ready to switch moods at 'arf-a-sec's notice, to 'ave 'em drippin' into their handkerchiffs one minute, 'oldin' the edge o' their seats the next, and fair bustin' wiv laughter the one after that, see? Now this 'ere *Song o' the Bells* is a noo one on me. They don't usually send along a special like this, but mindjew, it's a good idea. They oughter do more of it. If the toon's good it get under everyone's skin, see? And when they 'um it after, when they come out, what do you think of? Tell me that, now? What do they think of? They think of the picsher—an' that's what we want, ain't it?"

Edith murmured an agreement, but he was not really listening. He was launched on his favourite theme and, because she was his audience, he found himself warming towards her.

"Now the 'Prof', he 'ad routines, see? '*Earts 'n' Flowers* for the sob-stuff, 'Andel's *Water Music* whenever a stream or a river comes on, and *Minuet* and *Yewmer-esk* for costume—always remember that—they got used to it be now, see? *Minuet* and *Yewmer-esk* for wigs and knee-britches, but he flipped about a bit, mindjew, fer the action stuff—*William Tell* fer chases, *'Untin' Song* fer 'untin', and whatnot, but fer straight love, wi' no-niggers-in-woodpiles, and all through the kisses, he plumped fer *Blue Danube*, every time. Got me?"

Edith, who had understood no word of this, except the names of the musical items he had quoted, was grateful for the dark. She felt terribly nervous, but somehow elated, much as she had felt during her last essay into the unknown, the night that Ted had come to them as a lodger.

She sat down, cracked her finger-joints, and sailed into *Song of the Bells*, after which, without waiting for his comment, she played excerpts from all the scores he had mentioned.

Slowly, a wide, satisfied grin settled on Mr. Billings' round face. He knew he had picked a winner. He knew he had no need to tell this skinny little body anything more about the mysteries of audience mood-making, that, despite her old-fashioned appearance, she had got just what he wanted, right at her finger-tips. He would have been aghast had he been informed that this was the first time Edith Clegg had entered a cinema in her whole life.

Thus began a new life for Edith, a warm, exciting life, that had little connection with Becky, or Ted, and all the habits that had fenced her round in the past. She acquired, almost overnight, a new personality. From now on, she lived for the silver screen, and for its priesthood, the stars. She writhed on desert railroad tracks with ill-used ranchers' daughters. She danced minuets with John Barrymore. She trapesed about in the snow with Mary Pickford. She hung from skyscrapers with Harold Lloyd. She was wooed by the saturnine Valentino in tents and Cossack bivouacs, and she could hardly see the keys for tears of laughter, conjured up by Ben Turpin and Buster Keaton. She loved and cherished each and every one of them. They became, as time went on, far more real to her than the people of the Avenue, and she was soon driven to increase her intimacy with them by a close study of their private lives, their marriages, divorces, likes, dislikes, and private swimming-pools, in the film magazines.

Her memory for detail, associated with cinema stars, became phenomenal, and Mr. Billings, who came to regard her as his own personal discovery, often consulted her when he was planning foyer displays and special advertisements.

And with this worship of Edith's went a kind of pride, that grew and grew in her, until she became a sort of moving-picture public relations officer up and down the Avenue. Her enthusiasm overcame her natural shyness with people. She found she could talk glibly to neighbours on the subject of films, whereas, in the past, she had found it difficult to raise her eyes to acknowledge the lift of a neighbour's hat.

The Granada job solved all economic worries at Number Four, for Mr. Billings paid her, at first thirty shillings, and then two pounds a week. He told his wife, in an unguarded moment, that she was worth at least twenty pounds a week to him; but Edith did not assess her value in pounds, shillings, and pence. Had Mr. Billings but known it, she would have gladly played for him for nothing.

CHAPTER IX

Elaine Frith And The Facts Of Life

1

THESE were the halcyon years for Judith Carver, the years when she had Esme Fraser all to herself, years before Elaine Frith, of Number Seventeen, moved between them, and elevated Esme—for a time at any rate—to the verge of Paradise and by so doing consigned poor Judith to the limbo she was to inhabit for most of her 'teens.

Ever since the day they had played *Sleeping Beauty* in Manor Woods, Judy and Esme had been close friends, as close, in some ways, as Bernard and Boxer, and with something of the same relationship to one another.

In their case there were no preliminary consultations, as there were, however nominal they might be, between the twins. In the case of the boy and girl, the boy both proposed and disposed, and the girl merely tagged along, carefully gauging her enthusiasm by an unwavering observation of her lord, devoted to the point of death, unquestioning, unreasoning, enslaved.

As he passed from childhood to boyhood, Esme's dreamworld widened with his reading, from Henty to Scott, from the "B.O.P." and "Chums", to Conan Doyle and Rider Haggard. He was as much in need of an audience as Mr. Billings but, unlike the cinema proprietor, could manage comfortably on an audience of one. Judith was his audience, and paid him in the currency of utter devotion.

Her enslavement was no secret in the Avenue.

"There's Esme Fraser, and the little Carver girl," people would say, as they drifted by, Esme, addressing his dark, Imperial scowl to the paving-stones, Judith a yard or so behind, like an Eastern wife without her burden.

In the early days of their association her family had teased her about him: "Hurry up, Judy; Esme's coming out!", or "Judy won't want any breakfast; Esme's finished his," but Judith, although she blushed a little, did not resent this sort of badinage. Why should she? They could all be forgiven a little teasing. They hadn't got Esme.

Judith's family never found out anything really important about the association—the diary for instance, or the "Esme-Box", that she kept hidden under her hair-ribbons in the lower drawer of the chest she shared with Louise. She never wrote in the diary, or opened the box, unless she was fairly certain that she would not be disturbed.

The entires in the diary were bald statements of fact: *"Thursday: Esme was Lancelot and rescued me. We were late for dinner and Louise didn't mind." "Saturday: Esme was Blackbeard, and set his whiskers alight. He told me about the lady pirate, Mary Read."*

These were summaries of the way in which they spent their hours together, usually in Manor Woods, or in the wide ploughland and copses, along the Kentish border. Sometimes they wandered further afield in search of settings. Esme always had to have the correct settings.

Almost incidentally Judith learned a great deal about books, and the romantic episodes of British history. There was always a role for her in Esme's dreams, Maid Marian, the Lady of Shalott, Queen Dido (this frightened her a little on account of the funeral pyre she had to sit upon), the serving-wench who brought Turpin news of wealthy travellers leaving the inn, women pirates, like Anne Bonney and Mary Read, Llewellyn's wife, who was severely scolded, for leaving the dog to guard the baby, Jack Sheppard's moll, who smuggled files into Newgate, and so on; endlessly she ranged across the centuries, comforting, aiding, bandaging, smuggling, and getting small enough thanks for it from a hero who was very quick to censure an anachronism (as when she sent a pie containing a pistol into Richard the Lionheart's dungeon), the very sparing in praise, even when her loyalty had whisked him from the very shadow of Tyburn Tree.

"Faster! Faster! They've got fresh horses!" "Down! Down! Your heels are showing, and they'll be shot off, like Lord Roberts's were!" So she ran, holding tight to his hand, through briars, and across bogland, or lay, sobbing for breath, in a deep bed of nettles, while Edward the First's cavalry probed for them among the undergrowth.

Desperately she studied and trained to fit herself for these posts of honour. Anxiously she watched for his pale glance of contemptuous anger, when she handed him the wrong key, or gave the wrong pass-word. It was exacting work, all of it, but there were many, many compensations —an odd word of approval, the pressure of his fingers on her shoulders, his blazing fury when he "found" her tied to a tree, awaiting the Minotaur, and the one ecstatic occasion when she sprained her ankle jumping from a high bough, and was carried on his back a whole mile, to the door of Number Twenty.

The "Esme-Box" in her drawer contained carefully collected souvenirs of these occasions: a wild rose she had thrown to him on his instructions, when he was about to tourney in her honour, and which he had subsequently abandoned on the field of honour after being dismounted by his fourth opponent; a few blurred snapshots of him, the result of his one brief incursion into the twentieth century with a box camera, given him by his mother's ever-hopeful suitor; a mother-of-pearl hair-slide he had found, and presented to her, as part of his goodwill when visiting Tartary, on behalf of the West.

These things she showed to nobody, not even Louise, but most days she went quietly upstairs, and took them all out, laying them in a row on her bed, with the open box handy, in case she should hear footsteps on the stairs.

Not once during these days did Esme say or do anything to clarify their true relationship. Never did he touch upon the Paradise which, deep in her heart, she had decided they would ultimately enter; and she on her part was very careful never to broach the subject not even in jest, for her instinct about him was very shrewd, and she knew that, when at last it did come, it must come from him, it must be yet one more game—the final one. One day, one great and glorious day, he would let slip the words. One day he would say, quite casually, as though proposing to dramatise another anecdote from the books: "When we are married", or "After we are married . . ." Then it would be merely a matter of growing up, and of cooking and sewing for him, as Louise cooked and sewed for the boys and the babies. Then she would feel the weight of his arm on her shoulder, not as the sorely-wounded Arthur, being assisted to the barge on the margin of the lake, but as a husband and lover, as the person who would emerge from Shirley Church beside her, to duck laughingly beneath the shower of confetti and hustle her into a beribboned taxi, like those that passed the end of the Avenue so frequently at Easter-time.

Judy too had dreams, but, unlike her lord and master, she saw no occasion to rehearse them, save in her mind's eye.

2

The majority of the people of the Avenue managed to maintain balance between the excessive house-to-house neighbourliness of the small town and village, and the isolation of detached houses in more prosperous districts, such as those of Lucknow and Delhi Roads.

Within these limits they recognised one another in the street, and occasionally chatted over the fences that separated their narrow back-gardens, but they were not the sort of people who were constantly entering one another's kitchens, in order to borrow sugar, or discuss the news they heard over their crystal sets.

Even Mr. Baskerville, the radio enthusiast, who had installed a fabulous four-valve set in the front room of Number Eighty-Four, and thus became a sort of courier to the houses stretching half-a-dozen deep on each side of him, was not an excessively neighbourly person, and had never once crossed the threshold of the Carver or Clegg homes, but confined himself to quickening his step when he saw Jim Carver walking down Shirley Rise towards Woodside Station, and saying: "That chap Lenin's dead! Heard it from a foreign station last night", or to passing on some other item of news that he thought might prove a more interesting beginning to a conversation than the customary comment on the weather.

In spite of this reticence, however, most of the householders knew a little about their neighbours—where they worked, how many children they had, where their children went to school, and so on.

When a bride left one of the houses on her way to the church, or when a coffin was carried out to a hearse stationed in the Avenue, the householders paid the centre of attraction the compliment of stepping out on to their porches and watching the procession move off. Sometimes they sent a wreath, and sometimes, when one of their number was sick, they called without social preliminaries, but on the whole they were neither gregarious nor aloof, but something in between.

The Friths, at Number Seventeen, were the exception.

Number Seventeen stood on the open side of the Avenue, at the corner of the unpaved track that had once been a carriage drive to the Manor itself. It was from this point that urban expansion across the meadow to the woods would begin, for the overgrown track offered natural facilities for the cutting of a new road, and was the sole break in the sweep of the crescent.

The Friths had moved into Number Seventeen long before the war. Nobody knew anything about them, where they came from, or what they were like as people. They were not on speaking terms with the Avenue families, not even with their one next-door neighbour, at Number Fifteen, and the only time they were seen as a family was at 10.15 every Sunday morning, when they emerged from the house · in formation, and set off, two by two, for a Methodist Chapel in a neighbouring suburb, presumably the suburb from which they had come.

Every Sunday morning their exodus was closely observed from several windows. They headed for Shirley Rise at a brisk, even pàce, Mr. and Mrs. Frith in front, the son and daughter a few paces behind, all wearing neat, sober clothes, and with their eyes fixed immediately · ahead. Nobody ever saw them speak to one another. Nobody ever saw them smile, and the frigidity of the little group fascinated people at this end of the Avenue.

As the years went by, and there was no sign of a thaw at Number Seventeen, the Carvers, the Cleggs, the Frasers, and all the other families on the Nursery side of the Avenue that looked across to Number Seventeen, began to be interested in spite of themselves.

No sounds ever came out of the doors and windows of Number Seventeen. The lights went out by nine in winter, by ten in summer. The children never came out into the Avenue to play.

Singly, the Friths were observed more closely. Mr. Frith was over forty, short, balding, and wearing pince-nez spectacles. He reminded Jim Carver vaguely of the late Dr. Crippen, and was seen to catch the Croydon 'bus at 8.45 a.m. every morning.

Mrs. Frith was a rather slender woman who must, at one time, have been attractive, for she still had a good figure, masses of blue-black hair, and a very clear complexion. She was sometimes seen at the shops in the Lower Road. She was several years older than her husband, but no one would have guessed it, indeed, Archie Carver, who often thought about such things, could never decide why a handsome woman like Mrs. Frith had married such an undersized little nonentity as Mr. Frith in the first place, and had decided long since that it must have been on account of money he once had.

The physical contrast between man and wife seemed to have been reproduced in the children. Sydney Frith was a pale, narrow-faced replica of his father. He had about him a strange, furtive air, and seemed to walk on tiptoe, as though terrified of being observed. On the other hand, his sister Elaine, who was some eighteen months his senior, looked everybody she met straight in the eye, with a directness that most people found disconcerting, for there was a challenge in her glance, particularly when she looked at men. Those who met her eyes were always impressed by her striking looks, which did not seem to belong in a London suburb, but were almost Spanish, or South American. She was not pretty, with the delicate, well-formed features of her mother; her face and figure were too plump, even at fifteen, and her complexion, although quite clear, had that waxen quality that sometimes goes with jet-black hair, and blue eyes. Her mouth, however, was very full and red, and she moved with a grace and deliberation unusual in an adolescent, and particularly noticeable alongside the creeping gait of her brother, and the short strides of her father, whom she already topped by several inches.

The Avenue folk might well be intrigued by the Friths, for Number Seventeen was possibly the most unusual household in the crescent. It was certainly the unhappiest, for within it the four occupants lived under great strain, the source of which lay in the cold tyranny of Esther Frith, née Esther Rumbolde, once of Oxted Great Park, Surrey.

3

Esther Frith was the only surviving niece of the Hon. Mrs. Guy Rumbolde, a woman of considerable means, and undoubted eccentricity. She had lived with her aunt ever since she could remember, her parents having died in India when she was a child.

She grew up in a vast, dingy mansion, where her aunt had lived out most of her life as a virtual recluse, her sole interest centring in her cats, of which she maintained over two score.

Esther's grandfather, a near relative of the Surrey Rumboldes, a distinguished Anglo-Indian family, had been a man of considerable wealth. Having made several fortunes in the jute trade he had retired to England in the eighteen-fifties, purchased Oxted Great Park, and crammed it with van-loads of hideous furniture, and massive, ancestral potraits.

The one attractive feature of Oxted Great Park under the Rumbolde regime was its library, which had been bought in with the estate, and it was to this library, a huge room filled with strong-smelling calf-bound books, that Esther Rumbolde owed her marriage, and her social descent to the Avenue.

Shortly before her aunt died, in 1907, the family's solicitors had to make an inventory of the house, and Edgar Frith, who was then employed by a local antique-dealer and bookseller, was sent along to re-edit the library catalogue.

He spent whole weeks perched on the high stools in front of the shelves, and here, driven by her desperate loneliness, Esther found him, hardly daring to raise his eyes from his neat sheets of foolscap, and accepting with pathetic gratitude the mid-morning cup of cocoa she brought him on a tin tray.

As the weeks passed, Esther began to spend more and more of her time assisting him in his work, and they became mildly attached to one another, for no stronger reason than that there were no other living creatures about the place, apart from the crazy old woman, a stone-deaf cook-general, and forty-three cats.

Esther Rumbolde had scarcely ever travelled beyond the village outside the park gates, and her experience of men was limited to a few taciturn gardeners, and visiting tradesmen's boys. She found little to attract her about Edgar Frith, but on the other hand nothing at all to deter her from getting to know him better. He, on his part, was immensely flattered by her obvious desire for his company.

He was a very shy little man, and had entered the big gloomy house with a great deal of awe, hardly lessened by the jocular advice of his employer to "watch his step with the crazy old dame and her perishing menagerie!".

It could hardly be said that the friendship between Esther Rumbolde and Edgar Frith blossomed into love. Even after their marriage, it did not emerge from the bud, but remained static and half-frozen, like a plant nipped to death by an April frost.

There would certainly have been no marriage had it not been for the Hon. Mrs. Rumbolde's sudden death, and her extraordinary will, for she died before Edgar had completed his inventory, leaving everything she possessed to an animals' dispensary.

Esther was so shocked, and so frightened at the prospect of being thrown upon her own resources, that she immediately confided in Edgar. It was the one occasion in his life that he saw her in tears. Summoning up every ounce of courage he possessed, he at once proposed marriage to her. He never quite recovered from the shock of her ready acceptance.

Oxted Great Park and its contents were sold by auction, and the couple were married within three months, Edgar taking a rather better-paid post with a firm of antique dealers off the Cherry Orchard Road, a twopenny 'bus ride from the Avenue. He had been a careful saver, and was later able to buy Number Seventeen outright. There they settled and there the two children, Elaine and Sydney, were born.

The marriage was a dismal failure from the very beginning. It did not take Esther very long to enlarge her experience of the world, and Edgar did not gain in the process. She found him timid, hopelessly indecisive about everything and excessively dull, but these were not the defects that deprived her of all chance of making the best of a bad job, and adjusting herself to married life. The marriage foundered in a single week, on the shoals of their joint inexperience as lovers.

There never were two people less qualified to go on a honeymoon together. Neither had had so much as a nodding acquaintance with romance in the past, both were approaching thirty when they met, and both were modest to the point of prudery, Edgar naturally so, and Esther because of the extreme seclusion of her life up to the time she married Edgar.

What little she knew about sex had been gleaned from the hastily-turned pages of musty books. She knew, of course, that when people married they slept together, but, in the gloomy seclusion of Oxted Park her imagination had carried her no further than that, and Edgar was the last person on earth to make her initiation a natural process.

The result was what might have been expected under the circumstances, frustration and bewilderment on his part, horror and incredulity on hers.

After his first clumsy approaches, during their week's honeymoon at Bournemouth, Esther lay awake night after night, unable to believe that this was the sort of thing to which she was expected to submit for the rest of her life, and longing, bitterly and futilely, for the privacy of her virginal bedroom at Oxted Park, where at least one could rely on the privacy of a bathroom that need not be shared with a hesitant, short-sighted little man, who had thin, hairy legs, and padded about on the ugliest pair of feet she had seen, or had ever expected to see.

Edgar, who was a very well-meaning little man, attributed her lack of response to his own lack of experience, and even went so far as to buy a book he saw in a shop window whilst purchasing his allowance of tobacco for the week. The book was called *The Art of Marriage*, and was said to have been written by an eminent Swedish doctor, with a long string of letters after his name, but when Edgar tried to apply some of the lessons he learned from the book, particularly those found in a disturbingly frank chapter headed "Mutual Stimulation", he found himself unable to frame the solicitous questions set down by the author as a necessary preliminary to the exercise. He tried several times, but the words simply refused to be uttered.

In desperation, he left the book beside Esther, when she

was making up for sleep during an afternoon, but when he returned from a walk along the sea-front the book had disappeared, and he subsequently found it in his trunk, carefully re-tied in its original wrapping. It was quite obvious, as he learnt from his renewed attempts towards the end of the honeymoon, that Esther had put it from her without opening it.

In spite of such an unpropitious beginning, Elaine was born within a year of their marriage, and Sydney eighteen months later. After the birth of the second child Esther Frith made her decision. Never again would she submit to the indignity of Edgar's approaches. By this time she had got the measure of him, and knew that he would never have the strength of character to oppose her successfully, and she was right. When she told him that, henceforth, they would occupy separate rooms—he the back and she the front—he mumbled something inaudible, and then drifted into the garden to syringe his roses, whilst she went upstairs, moved all his clothes into what had been the nursery, and then carried Elaine's cot into the little room over the porch. She kept Sydney's cot alongside the dressing-table in her own room. In a year or so she would have to make other arrangements, but she would think of that when the time came. In the meantime she would never have to look at Edgar's feet again, and there would be an end to his apologetic fumblings after he had switched out the light.

The change of life came early to Esther, and with it a curious intensification of existing traits in her frigid personality. In place of what had been a kind of sullen acquiescence to the marriage, an ice-cold fury took possession of her, not specially directed towards Edgar, whom, for the most part, she ignored, but towards his children, particularly the girl. It was as though she herself had played no willing part in their creation, but regarded them as living evidence of the indignities she had suffered, as witnesses of the silent, stealthy affronts meted out to her by Edgar, during the first three years of their marriage.

Co-existent with this frigid hostility towards the children there glowed in Esther a fiery concern for the welfare of her immortal soul.

She had been brought up a strict Methodist, and perhaps the mad Rumbolde blood in her favoured the growth of something not remote from religious mania. Her unpleasant experiences resolved themselves into sins, not sins of her making, but transgressions that had been thrust upon her, and she became convinced that she was answerable to God for her children's concepts in this particular sphere.

The effect of this obsession on her part was to cut off her family from all normal contact with other children, and it revealed itself in a number of other ways. She set out to regulate their reading matter, their conversation, their very thoughts, in a frantic endeavour to isolate them from the horrid contamination of sex.

In the case of Sydney the task was not difficult. He had inherited his father's timidity, and because he was never quite sure when he would be charged with an unspecified misdemeanour, he was very careful to do and say as little as possible in his mother's presence.

In the case of Elaine, however, the task of supervision was more complicated. Elaine had spirit, and never submitted tamely to the tyranny of her mother. Sometimes, when there was a clash between them, Esther thought she could detect hate rather than fear in the girl's eyes, and in the lines of her ripe, pouting mouth.

When Elaine was nine, and Sydney was approaching eight, Esther bought a cane, and kept it tucked behind a picture in the dining-room. It was seldom used but it was always there, its curved handle projecting above the heavy oak frame of "A Tempting Bait", one of those prints, so popular in the Avenue, portraying the idyllic childhood of manorial children against an early Victorian background.

The children's attitude towards their father was negative. He did not enter into the scheme of things at Number Seventeen. He was either away at work, or pottering about his greenhouse, and sometimes whole hours went by without any of them breaking the silence of the house.

Anything the children brought into the house to read was always submitted to Esther, and either grudgingly approved, and handed back, or confiscated on the spot. This supervision made both children curious to discover what it was in certain books that must never be seen, and by the time Elaine was twelve she had reached a point where the fragmentary knowledge gained at the small private school she attended had to be supplemented by one means or another.

She had a shrewd idea that the books confiscated by her' mother were not destroyed, but were secreted somewhere about the house, and after awaiting a suitable opportunity, she began a thorough search of the premises, beginning in her mother's room, and ending, via the airing cupboard, among her father's few belongings at the back. She found nothing to interest her in either room, and the only place left to search was the small loft above the landing.

One afternoon, when her father was at work, and her mother was shopping, she decided to complete the search by getting the step-ladder, and climbing in through the ceiling-trap.

As this operation could not be carried out in secrecy whilst Sydney was about, and as she was never likely to be left alone in the house, she was obliged to take her brother into her confidence.

There was no bond of sympathy between brother and sister. Esther's principle had always been to divide and rule, and she had encouraged Sydney to act as informer, but Elaine judged correctly when she assumed that Sydney's curiosity was equal to her own, and he readily agreed to partner her in the enterprise. They carried the steps up to the landing and Elaine, mounting, raised the tray and climbed in. With the help of a small electric torch she found a pile of odds and ends alongside the cistern, but the only object that offered any hope was her father's leather trunk, which she at once set about unstrapping.

There was little enough inside but, after rummaging for a moment, she came across a thin book, wrapped in brown paper. She pulled off the wrappings and applied the torch, picking out the title in the thin beam. The book was Edgar's honeymoon purchase, *The Art of Marriage*, long since abandoned and forgotten.

At first glance it did not seem very promising. Sydney called from the landing as she hastily flicked the pages. Then she came across one of the diagrams, and at once knew she was on the right scent, and began reading a passage or two at random.

She did not understand much of what she read but it was at once obvious that she had stumbled on the key to something tremendously important. Life under Esther had taught her to think and act instinctively, in all matters of self-preservation. She knew at once that if she shared this secret with her brother it would be a matter of days at most before it was passed on to her mother, and that would mean, at the very least, the liberal application of the cane. Without another moment's hesitation she thrust the book down the neck of her dress, replaced the paper, closed the trunk, and stepped over the rafters to the aperture.

"There's nothing up here at all," she told Sydney; "just a pile of old junk!"

Sydney's upturned face clouded. "She must burn the stuff as soon as she takes it from us," he grumbled, and slouched away, not even waiting to assist her descent.

Elaine wanted him out of the way. She replaced the trapdoor, climbed down to the landing, and carefully removed all traces of dust and cobwebs from her clothes. She then sought him out, and made a great show of commencing her homework. When his attention was distracted, she ran up to her room, and stuffed the book between the mattress and the springs of her bed. Life with Esther had taught her something else. She had learned how to master impatience, how to control her most pressing desires until a safe and suitable opportunity arose to indulge them in secret.

That night, with the torch snugly hidden under the edge of the bedside rug (Esther sometimes looked under the pillows for various items of contraband) she waited until the house was silent. Then she recovered both book and torch, climbed back into bed, pulled the sheet over her head, and began to apply herself to a careful study of the Swedish doctor's interesting theories.

Many of the longer words drove her to her pocket dictionary, which she kept in her satchel beside the bed, but she was a very determined girl, and made steady progress, despite frequent checks. Having turned the final page, she carefully replaced the book and torch under the mattress, and lay, hands clasped behind her head, thoughtfully digesting the information.

So that was what it was all about! That was the citadel of the forbidden city! That explained all, or nearly all that had been so obscure in her mother's eternal hints, glances, shushings, and sudden, inexplicable punishments. It was all to do with the difference between men and women, with their bodies, with—as she had long suspected—the birth of babies, and what happened before they were born.

She smiled to herself in the darkness, and in her smile there was triumph. She lay there savouring her stupendous victory, a victory over Sydney, over the older, more licensed, giggling children at school, above all, over secrecy, and her mother. She felt like a counter-spy who, after prodigious effort, has at last broken down an enemy's code, and deciphered his plans, not completely, perhaps, but sufficiently to promise a word-perfect interpretation in the near future.

She told herself that there must be other books like this one, books that would not require such frequent reference to a dictionary. Somehow, she would get them, and find a place to hide them, and study them in safety. Then, when she knew it all, when she had grown a little, and was strong enough to wrest the cane from her mother, she would use her knowledge to make people do whatever she wished, to buy her things, to compete for her friendship.

She now had something that none of the other girls at school possessed. She had what Eve in the Bible had been punished for, when she persuaded Adam to eat of the fruit from the tree. Eve had been caught, but she wouldn't be. God had found out about Eve, but nobody would find out about her. Elaine always identified God with her mother, a figure-head to be lied to, and hoodwinked; and if she could hoodwink her mother, as she had in the matter of the book, then she could certainly hoodwink God.

She fell asleep at last, but her brain was too fevered to enable her to rest. In after years she always remembered that this was the night she first dreamed of the water, vast, swirling cataracts of water, that poured over her, beating down, and sweeping away everything that stood between her and the flood.

She woke screaming, to find her father standing beside her in his pyjamas. It was almost dawn, and he looked even smaller and more pitiful than usual, with his sparse hair standing up on end, and his false teeth missing.

"What is it? You were shouting!" he whispered.

Even now, she reflected, he had to whisper, for fear of bringing her mother into the room. Sensing his fear, her own courage flowed back.

"I had a nightmare, I dreamt I was drowning," she told him calmly. "It's all right now. What time is it?"

"Nearly five," he told her. "Go to sleep, Elaine, don't wake your mother—we don't want a scene!"

She turned away from him, comforted less by his presence than by the light that filtered in under the blind. She smiled quietly to herself as she remembered the book. Ah! If they knew . . . if they knew what she knew . . . what a gloriously final scene there would be!

The smile remained on her lips when she slept again.

Softly Edgar padded back to his room, and climbed into bed.

CHAPTER X

Alibi For Archie

1

WHEN Toni Piretta, the wheezing Italian grocer from the corner shop, sat down beside Archie in the "Rec", as that young man was grappling with his insoluble problem of double paternity, Archie's response was terse to the point of rudeness.

"I'm busy thinking," he grunted, ignoring the Italian's freckled, outstretched hand.

Toni was not abashed. He was accustomed to rebuffs on the part of the stolid islanders, among whom he had worked for so long.

"*Si, si,* I know that a'ready, Mister Carver; I see it, when you screw up your face like this—" and Toni puckered his broad, sunburnt face, in comic imitation of Archie's glower, and then suddenly exchanged the grimace for his customary Southern smile.

Blast the old fool, thought Archie; what the hell does he want to come bothering me for? Haven't I enough on my mind at the moment? *Both* of them! Christ. Just think of it! *Both* of them. Edna, who must have been sound asleep when it happened, and that giggling sister of hers, who had it worked out from the beginning! Their fertility infuriated him. It was enough, he reflected, to drive a man into a monastery!

The Italian laid a gentle hand on Archie's knee.

"It's a-time you and me talka da business!" he said, with unexpected seriousness.

Toni had lived in England a long time, but he had never tried to rid himself of his traditional icy-creamo accent. He considered it a valuable business asset. It made people remember him and his wares. It singled him out from British competitors.

Archie's mind groped half-heartedly with the possible reasons Toni Piretta might have for wanting to discuss business with him, almost a stranger. He had a daughter, about Archie's age, but Maria Piretta was very plain, and already running to fat. She had a moist complexion, and prominent, unevenly-spaced front teeth. Archie had never given her more than a distasteful glance when he dropped into the shop now and again for Louise's groceries, or to buy cigarettes. He recalled, however, Toni's solicitous guardianship of his daughter's honour, in the days when they were all children, and Toni had kept a fish-and-chip saloon in Lower Road. The youths who patronised the shop for fish suppers often laughed at father and daughter, and sometimes, after a beer or two, mimicked Toni to his face.

Toni, in those days, was younger and much more excitable. Archie recalled that he had been given to sudden angry outbursts, when the young customers sought cheap entertainment at their host's expense.

"You come in here," Archie had heard him roar, above

the guffaws of youths sitting at the tables, "you come in here, night after night, and whatta you do? Hey? Whatta you *do*? You spenda da sixpence, benda da forks, spilla da vinegar, and play with my little Maria!"

This protest always produced roars of laughter, and at the memory of it a sour smile puckered Archie's sullen face. Mr. Piretta interpreted the smile as a sign of Archie's willingness to talk business.

"They tella me you a grocer-boy, hey?" he pursued cautiously.

"I've worked in provision shops," said Archie, with cold dignity. "What of it? What's that to you, Toni?"

Like most Englishmen of the suburbs, Archie was very proud of his nationality when he conversed with a Latin. Mr. Piretta ignored the snub, and became even more earnest.

"Then I maka da bargain with you!" he said flatly. "You worka for me, and I maka da bargain with you!"

Archie was interested, in spite of himself. Slowly he shook off his mood of self-pity. At the prospect of a commercial deal he found he could forget the Gittens' girls, at least temporarily. It was whispered along the Avenue that Toni Piretta was rich, that he had done extremely well at the corner shop he had opened shortly after Italy joined the ranks of the gallant Allies, and, by so doing, released him from the crippling limitations of an alien in a country at war. What sort of "bargain" could the old boy be contemplating? Some sort of insurance wangle possibly. A fire? Surely not? A claim on damaged goods, that needed some sort of independent verification? Groping with various possibilities, Archie forgot the Gittens' girls altogether.

"What are you getting at, Toni? I can be useful, why don't you speak out?" he asked the Italian.

Toni breathed hard. It seemed to Archie, regarding him closely, that he was very upset about something. He avoided Archie's eyes, and the conviction grew in the younger man that Toni Piretta was in some sort of a jam, and had approached him in a spirit of desperation.

"Well," he prompted, "what's the matter? What have you been up to now, Toni?"

This time Toni met his amused glance steadily.

"I been uppa to nothing. I'm doing a'right down there. It's a good business. I talk to you not about me but abouta my girl, my little Maria."

Archie suppressed a dry chuckle. So it was Maria? Not unnaturally, Archie, today of all days, could think of only one source of anxiety regarding Maria that might account for a father's concern.

"You mean she's in the family way?" he asked incredulously.

The Italian shook his head impatiently. He was not insulted, as an English father might have been.

"I wisha she was," said Toni, deliberately. And then, without reserve, and with his eyes filling slowly with tears, Toni Piretta opened his heart to Archie, as he had opened it to nobody since he left Naples, as a ship's boy, forty years ago.

His had been a hard struggle, he said. There had been but bleak prospects of getting rich, and founding a family, in his own country. Like many of his neighbours he had headed for America, but chance had brought him instead to the East End, where, for a few years, he had fought for work on the wharves in the company of thousands of other aliens. Later he went North, to the shipyard towns, and here he acquired at long last a half-share in an ice-cream cart, progressing thence to full ownership of a hand-propelled snack-wagon, in the Gateshead dock area. He had the strong commercial instincts, and the resilience and physical toughness of all Neapolitan slum-dwellers. Eventually, after Homeric efforts, he had scraped together sufficient money for a shop, the chip shop Archie remembered in the Lower Road, and from this, in 1915, he had moved on to the corner grocery store. Now he considered himself highly successful, and had taken out naturalisation papers.

There was one aspect of his career, however, that left him with a sense of bitter frustration. He had only one child, a daughter, and no prospect of a larger family, for his wife had died during the lean years at Gateshead, and Toni had no inclination to marry again solely for the purpose of begetting a son. Until recently, he had relied upon Maria to provide a grandson, but he was a realist, and was beginning to doubt his chances of perpetuating his line through Maria.

Maria was now twenty-four, and almost middle-aged by his standards. He had to admit it, Maria did not attract men, no matter how persistently he pushed her forward when young men came into the shop for cigarettes and mineral waters. Somehow, her prominent front teeth got in the way of her welcoming smile, and young men simply paid for their purchases and went out again, unimpressed.

Toni had watched them for years, from his ambush behind the till, and, bitterly reluctant as he was to admit it, Maria did not seem at all likely to rope a husband from his side of the counter. When she was still in her teens there had been hope. Youths had cracked jokes with her as she set down the plates of hake and rock salmon on the marble-topped tables. One or two had even pinched her behind, and brought a faint blush to her moist cheeks, but nothing came of these gallant encounters. The young men grew up, and married, but none married Maria. To date, no one had gone so far as to call round and ask her out for a walk.

This, Toni admitted, was a routine problem for the father of a daughter, but the real trouble lay much deeper, in the defeatist attitude of Maria herself; she had grown apathetic and listless, pining, as she undoubtedly was, for a man, almost middle-aged, and not even responsive to his suggestion of getting her over-prominent teeth extracted and replaced.

Back in Naples, Toni had seen what happened to women who passed the age of thirty without getting a man. They turned sour. They grew gaunt, instead of plump and comfortable. They nagged, and became awkardly punctilious about religious observances. They despaired of life, and with very good cause. Toni loved Maria. She was all he had, apart from the shop, and that still carried a small mortgage. He did not want this sort of fate to overtake his child and there was really no reason why it should, for, apart from her teeth, she was not an ill-favoured girl, and her father was on the way to becoming a man of substance.

Archie, who was very quick to follow the drift of the conversation, listened open-mouthed. At first he shied away

from the prospect of getting involved, even as a confidant.
He recalled Maria's lack-lustre eyes, and the droop of her
thickening figure as she reached over the counter, but as
Toni continued to talk, softly, and with a Neapolitan's com-
pelling eloquence, he began to listen more attentively, and it
came into his mind that here, right at his feet, there might
well exist a very practical answer to his problem regarding
business premises.

The question was, how far would the Italian expect him to
go? Would it be possible to get in on Toni's business without
actually marrying Maria? He decided not, almost at once. A
man who would go to these lengths to procure a husband for
his daughter was certain to demand safeguards. The Italian
was at once more shrewd, and more haphazard than tram-
conductor Gittens. Like Archie himself, and unlike Mr. Gittens, he had a business training, and Archie realised that if
the bargain was ever to progress beyond the discussion stage
he would have to be as frank with Piretta as Piretta had been
with him. Sooner or later, he realised, the claims of the
Gittens' sisters would be common knowledge up and down
the Avenue, and Piretta, from his strategic position behind
the counter of the corner shop, would be one of the first to
hear about it. In the absence of frank confession the news
would create too much suspicion in the Italian's mind, and he
might start looking farther afield for a young man. Pondering
this, while Piretta continued to wheedle, Archie decided in
favour of a blunt admission of his own problems. It had one
advantage, presenting as it did incontrovertible proof of the
prospective husband's virility. It made the ultimate appearance of a Piretta grandchild almost a certainty.

One of the more likeable traits of Archie's character was
that he hated to beat about the bush. It wasted time, and
time was currency. He made up his mind on the spot.

"I'll marry Maria, providing you cut me in fifty-fifty on
the business," he told Toni, who was so surprised at the blunt-
ness of this statement that he stopped short in the middle of a
sentence, and sat with his mouth wide open, looking like a
grizzled frog.

"There's one thing, though," Archie went on, before Toni

could utter a word; "I'm already in trouble, big trouble. You know the Gittens' tribe, at a hundred-and-four? They shop in your place. Old Gittens called on me this morning, and he says ..."

Suddenly the Italian recovered his urbanity. He raised his hand, silencing Archie with a decisive gesture.

"Oh, *si*, *si*, I a'ready hear about it! Why else should I follow you in here, and talka da business with you?"

It was now Archie's turn to gape.

"You *heard* about it? But hell, it was only this morning that ..."

Toni spat. He was not addicted to the habit, and reserved it for occasions demanding special emphasis.

"That Gittens' family, they no good to you, son! They breeda like rabbits, yes; but whatta they live on? Whatta they eat? You donna know? Then I tella you! They never cook a good meal, not even Christmas! Tins it is, nothing but tins! *I* tella you this, and I serva them all da time!"

Archie pondered this, and all that it implied. Obviously Mrs. Gittens had been discussing her daughters' condition in public, probably with other housewives, as they waited at Toni's counter to be served. *But Toni didn't mind!* He didn't mind in the least! Archie realised that he had sadly underestimated him. Perhaps it was the very fact that he was the alleged father of two that had decided the Italian to seek him out and put forward this fantastic proposition.

Almost at once Archie began to feel more serene. Things looked like working out, providing he said the right thing, and did nothing at all in too much of a hurry.

"I'm supposed to marry one of 'em and pay for the other," he told Piretta, watching closely in order to note how this tacit admission of responsibility would affect the Italian.

The grocer folded his hands over his broad stomach.

"You don't hava to do that," he said with authority. "I gotta the lawyer, and he's a-good, he's smart. He fix it. You leava this to me, you leava Maria to me, you leava everything to Toni!"

Archie felt himself lifted on a tide of relief. His heart warmed towards Toni. He did not even want to question him as to how he would fix things, how he would cope with the Gittens, how he would begin to explain the situation to Maria. He was convinced that, in all these things, the little Italian was completely sure of himself, that this was no haphazard shot in the dark on his part, but the final, triumphant unfolding of a long, carefully-planned campaign to secure a son-in-law, a lively young partner, and an heir at one stroke. And in this supposition he was quite correct, for Toni Piretta had had an eye cocked in Archie's direction for more than a year, and this encounter in the "Rec" was simply the direct result of a chance remark he had overheard the previous afternoon, whilst serving Mrs. Baines, of Number Eighty-Seven, with half a pound of streaky.

He realised then that he would have to act quickly, and he already knew exactly what instructions he would give to Messrs. Hibson and Corke, the slightly shady solicitors he had employed in the purchase of his shops. He had one supreme advantage, that of knowing Mrs. Gittens, her daughters, and tram-conductor, Gittens. He knew that they too, in their casual, indolent way, were realists, and would assess the value of a lump sum far above that of an affiliation order, or two affiliation orders. He knew all about maintenance and affiliation orders, and how difficult they were to execute on a footloose young fellow like Archie, who could stand up in court and lie or could, in face of the dual claim, find a glib solicitor to plead a family conspiracy on the part of the sisters, or, if pressed too hard, would simply vanish, or emigrate.

Like Archie he made up his mind on the spot. One hundred pounds he would offer. Not a penny more, not a penny less.

And so Archie was never saddled with the fatherhood of the Gittens' babies, and the whole episode came to nothing, at least, in so far as he was concerned.

In the event Toni paid twice as much as he need have done, for Hilda's child was still-born, and Edna soon afterwards married a Danish hairdresser, at her place of employment. The same year the whole family moved to another district, on the far side of the Lower Road, and were seen no more in the Avenue.

2

For Archie, however, the alarm had much more practical results. He went to work for Piretta that very week, and the Italian had no reason to begrudge the dispensation of his hundred pounds, for Archie soon proved his worth, both as a counter-hand and a bringer of colour to the pale cheeks of little Maria, whom he wooed, somewhat off handedly, in the living-room above the shop, and married at the Church of the Sacred Heart at Lewisham that same September.

Maria herself played a very minor role in these occurrences. All her life she had done exactly as her father told her, removing the verdigris from the tea-urns, slicing pounds of potatoes in the crusher, submitting dutifully to having her bottom pinched by regular customers' greasy fingers, parcelling up groceries, and now marrying this broad-chested, florid young man that her father had suddenly introduced into the business, a young man who seemed to be so worried about Mrs. Armstrong's week-end order, even when they were slumped together on the horse-hair sofa, and he was absent-mindedly fondling her breasts.

She said nothing, and did nothing to encourage or discourage him. She accompanied her father to a dentist in Lucknow Road, and had her worst tooth extracted and another, less independent denture, screwed firmly in its place.

Then, as it were, she stood quietly aside, to watch herself being fitted for a wedding gown, to ride to the Church of the Sacred Heart beside her beaming father, sweating in his unaccustomed collar and tie, to listen to toasts proposed by Italian cousins, all the way from Gateshead, to move Toni and Toni's things into the chalet at the botom of the garden, and at length, to climb into bed with a man who despite all this preliminary bustle, was still practically a stranger to her.

In this detached, contemplative mood she watched Archie pour himself a large double whisky before he hung up his new doublebreasted jacket, and folded his trousers carefully over the back of the bedside chair. She knew, of course, that he was not in love with her, in the way she always imagined people who got married were in love, but her previous experience with lovers was negligible, and she soon grew accustomed to his long silences, and put them down to his almost fanatical preoccupation with the business.

He and her father seemed to get along very well and that, after all, was the important thing. In any case, religion taught her that the main purpose of marriage was the procreation of children and, within weeks, she was expecting a child, the first, she supposed, of a number she would produce as the years went by.

Maria Piretta had been born in the shadow of great poverty, and had grown up in a very hard school. One of the lessons she had learnt in that school was that only three things in life really mattered: health, food, and shelter, in that order. Given health one could usually procure food and shelter and from now on she looked like having all three in abundance. To expect anything more was to tempt the Virgin to withhold from her all three.

CHAPTER XI

Harold As Giant-Killer

I

THERE was another wedding in the Avenue that autumn. Harold Godbeer, self-appointed champion of the widowed and the fatherless, finally won his fair lady, and won her, be it said, by a deed of daring, as spectacular, in its modest way, as a chivalric deed in the lists.

Harold, a slight, short-sighted man, concealed within his pigeon-chest the tenacity of many weak and physically insignificant people. He was, without knowing it (for he was modest to a degree), of the breed of clerks and shopkeepers who had recently defied the Prussians in the water-logged fields of Flanders for years on end, and he had never abandoned hope of persuading pretty Eunice Fraser to legalise his

role as provider and protector at Number Twenty-Two. He
held on because, throughout these years, he had never ceased
to tremble when she laid a shapely, white hand on his sleeve,
and murmured:

"You're so *clever*, Harold. . . . You're so *sweet* to me."

But in all this time the romance remained suspended, never
having progressed beyond the sleeve-stroking stage. Never
had Eunice gone on to say, as he always hoped she would:
"If only you were here *all* the time, Harold; if only you were
a *real* father to Esme!", or something along these lines that
would afford him, a professional in the matter of recognising
an opening when he saw one, the chance to spit on his hands,
look to his priming, and storm on to victory.

He was aware, of course, of what held her back, and it had
been some small consolation to him that her reluctance to
marry him had nothing to do with his qualities as a lover.
Left to herself she would have capitulated long ago. Eunice
was over thirty now, and far too delicately bred to let her
mind dwell on his qualifications, or lack of them, as a mate.

What she required, what she had gladly accepted from him
since the day she had drifted into his office in St. Paul's
Churchyard a year or so after she was widowed, was someone
to organise her life, study her rate demands, watch over her
modest investments, launch Esme on the first stages of a
career, bring her a cup of tea in thin china at 8 a.m., teach
her how to live within her income, and when day was done,
read Mrs. Henry Wood to her, beside a rustling, winter fire.

Harold was willing, nay, he was extremely eager to do all
this and more, but Eunice, although by no means an intelligent woman, was a sensitive one. She had little commonsense,
but there was nothing wrong with her instincts, and she was
aware, as Harold knew only too well, that marriage with
Harold would sever her already tenuous link with her difficult thirteen-year-old son.

Ever since Esme had grown from childhood to boyhood
she had been aware of the inadequacy of their relationship. It
was not, she felt, the sort of relationship that should exist
between widowed mother and fatherless boy. Either Esme
should adopt a protective attitude towards her, like Harold's,
or he should submit more readily to her cosseting. As it was,

he regarded her as he might have regarded an older but ad-
mittedly stupid sister, retreating further and further into his
dignified dreams, and showing her even less affection than he
showed that adoring and adorable little girl, who was for ever
following him about.

Watching them, as they crossed the Avenue and took the
path across the meadow to the Manor Woods on Saturdays,
Eunice wished a little forlornly that Esme had been a girl,
who could have come 'up West' with her, and shared her
serene scrutinies of shop-windows. If Esme had been a girl,
she reasoned, the child would have been quick to appreciate
the solid worth of Harold, and the little man's comforting
knack of being in the right place when he was wanted, and
of withdrawing the moment he was not. Even her first husband, from what little she remembered of him, had lacked
Harold's discernment in this last respect, and had been inclined to hang about, making conversation, when she would
have preferred to day-dream.

Esme, alas, was not a girl, but a strange, proud, aloof little
boy, who was growing all too rapidly, into an introspective
young man, with his nose in a book (and such bloodthirsty
books) whenever he was indoors, which was by no means as
often as she could have wished. Contemplating the situation,
balancing the risks that attended a decision one way or the
other, Eunice did what she had done in the face of every
crisis throughout her life, she passed, and left the decision to
somebody else, in this case to Esme himself.

2

Harold Godbeer won his bride, appropriately enough, with
a bag of confetti—or rather, with an entire trayful of confetti,
advertised on a huckster's stall at one penny a bag.

Every Bank Holiday the children of the Avenue trudged
up to the Shirley Hills to the fair, that was held each public
holiday (Christmas and Boxing Day excepted) on the pebble
slopes beyond the last houses.

It wasn't much of a fair, just the usual assortment of
swings, roundabouts, side-shows, and freak-peeps, but it attracted, in addition to a few hundred local children and

young couples, a swarm of hucksters, who paid small sums to the promoters for the privilege of setting up stalls, and selling balloons, mechanical toys, and confetti.

Esme and Judith never missed a fair. They seldom patronised the stalls and amusements, but were content to wander from booth to booth, absorbing the colour and incident of the occasion. Esme enjoyed the brassy tawdriness of it all, it was such a contrast to his neat, ordered home, and Judith liked the strident music, that blared unceasingly from the mechanical organ. Bernard and Boxer could usually be seen, riding the swings, or seated together in one of the tents, in open defiance of the prominently displayed notice: *"Children Under Sixteen Not Admitted"*. Bernard and Boxer regarded such notices as a direct challenge to their manhood, and somehow, by guile, by bluff, or by simply crawling under tent valances, they managed to circumvent the hoarse-voiced men at the entrance-flaps. They had seen everything successive fairs had to offer, having gazed stolidly at so many tattooed ladies, fasting men, and midget honeymoon couples, that they were now recognised playground authorities on these bizarre subjects.

At the Easter Monday fair that year, Esme and Judith had a distressing experience. They started out with threepence to spend but happened to meet Judith's brother Archie at the corner of the Avenue. Archie, learning their destination, jovially presented Judith with half-a-crown.

At the entrance to the fair-ground the children passed a confetti stall, presided over by an aged crone, made up to look like a gypsy. Judith, lagging behind, suddenly made up her mind to buy some confetti. It wasn't to throw at anyone, least of all Esme, who would have resented such an indignity, and it wasn't to throw at anyone else, for no one else within range had the slightest appeal for Judith. Perhaps she wanted it for her Esme-Box, which, in some ways, was her bottom drawer, or perhaps the mere possession of a bag of confetti, shared with Esme, helped her to establish him more materially as her groom of the future. Whatever it was that prompted the purchase, she called out to him to wait, and handed the woman at the stall her half-crown, demanding one bag of confetti.

The old woman took the coin, glanced at it, and slipped it into her leather satchel.

"Thank you, dearie," she said, "help yourself," and at once readdressed herself to the folded newspaper she had been studying.

Esme, impatient, had stopped a few yards away.

Judith held out her hand.

"My change——" she faltered, a horrid suspicion already invading her mind.

The crone looked up, a trifle sharply.

"Change, dearie? That was a penny!"

Judith's stomach cart-wheeled, and Esme, sensing that something was wrong, came back to the stall.

"It was a half-crown," whispered Judith; "you *know* it was a half-crown; you *looked* at it!"

She turned desperately to Esme, beseeching instant corroboration. "I had a half-crown, Archie's half-crown, and she says it was a penny!"

Shame and fear clutched at Esme. Like his mother, he hated a scene, any sort of scene, but his reputation was at stake. There was no evading Judith's appeal.

"She *had* half-a-crown and a threepenny-bit; she didn't have a penny," he said hoarsely.

Judith, immensely relieved, turned back to the woman. "You see, I had two-and-nine altogether. Here's my three-penny-bit," and she began fumbling with the tiny knot in her handkerchief.

The old woman looked at them bleakly, then she turned her head towards a bell tent, pitched immediately behind her stall.

"Fred," she called, "come on out, and get rid o' these bloody little shysters, will yer?"

Fred emerged, ponderously, from the tent. He was a huge, bloated man, about forty years of age, with large red hands, and a curiously mottled complexion, as though he had been peppered with small shot. He tilted his dusty bowler, and then blew his nose with finger and thumb. Even in the stress of the moment Esme thrilled with disgust at the action.

"Whassat?" Fred wanted to know.

The crone explained, without wasting a word.

"Pissorf!" said Fred, fiercely, and turned to re-enter the tent.

Esme began to tremble. From where he stood, at the corner of the stall, Fred looked like a fairy-tale giant, whose enormous hands seemed capable of taking both him and Judith in two spreads, and crushing them to powder, with no more effort than was required to lean across the confetti table and gather them up. Esme began to stutter. He knew that Judith was looking at him, and he knew that to fail her on this occasion was to reduce to pitiable ruins the heroic fabric, he had created for her, piece by piece, since the day they first met, but he could think of no way out of this dreadful trial of strength and his secondary reaction, following closely upon that of sheer terror, was a cold anger that she should have involved him in such an unequal contest.

He looked around helplessly, and his eye rested upon a policeman, who was moving slowly along on the outskirts of the incoming crowd between the stalls. He had the suburban child's implicit faith in the matchless power of the law.

"All right," he said, finally; "I'll tell the policeman!"

He had imagined that this threat would be enough, that at the mere mention of the word "policeman", the old girl would dip her hand into her satchel and produce two-and-fivepence.

Nothing of the kind happened. Fred simply guffawed, and the old woman said flatly: "Go ahead, and tell 'im, sonny!"

For a few seconds Esme stood stock still, his imagination recoiling from the prospect of implementing this terrible threat. Except for the purpose of asking the time, he had never yet spoken to a policeman: but here, surely, was an occasion when the support of the police could not be dispensed with.

Dismally, he turned his back on the stall and crossed the track, quickening his step until he came alongside the constable.

Watching him, Judith saw him tug firmly at the blue sleeve, saw the constable bend and say something, and then turn back towards them, with Esme at his side.

The crone made good use of the diversion. She reached into her bag, found the half-crown, and tossed it to Fred, who slipped it casually in his trouser pocket. He then blew his nose again and awaited the constable with an expression of benign tranquillity. He had had many and protracted dealings with young policemen, and had always found this expression rewarding. Fred had also learned the value of initiative.

"Don't it give yer the sick, orficer," he remarked resignedly, as the constable and Esme presented themselves on the far side of the stall. "All these Sunday Schools 'n wot-not, all this public money spent on ejucashun, an' wot does it end up in? A ruddy little pick-pocket, 'oo talks posh, like 'e's got a bleedin' plum in 'is marth!"

The constable was young, inexperienced, and not too eager to engage. He had gathered from Esme's garbled story that somebody, presumably these hucksters, had cheated somebody else, presumably the children, but Fred's genial and confidential manner disarmed him, as Fred had intended it should.

"What's it all about?" he wanted to know.

"Says she give me 'arf-a-crahn fer a penny. Wants the perishin' confetti *and* two-and-five," growled the old woman; "we'd make a forchune that way, wouldn't we?"

"I *did* give her half-a-crown," protested Judith, and turning anew to Esme, "I *did*, didn't I?"

"Yes," said Esme, wretchedly. He had executed his threat, he had summoned a policeman, but he still felt defeated.

The old woman emptied her satchel on the trestle-board in front of her. A small stream of coppers, and one or two sixpences and threepenny-bits rolled out.

"No arf-crahns there, is there, orficer?" she said.

The constable was not so young or inexperienced that he did not realise at once what had occurred, but he saw, with equal clarity, that he had not the smallest chance of proving it, and therefore took the line of least resistance.

"Run along, kids," he said, not unkindly. "Run along, and don't get into any more trouble."

From the point of view of settling the matter then and there, and returning to his contemplative beat, the constable could not have chosen more unfortunate words.

Esme, in some ways, was oddly adult, and had an uncomplicated appreciation of abstract justice. The blatant injustice of this remark, however kindly it might have been meant, struck him like a whiplash, and supreme indignation lent him courage and oratory.

"*Trouble!*" he squeaked, "*I'm* not in any trouble, it's *them* —they've just pinched our half-a-crown, and you've got to get it from them, or I'll . . . I'll . . ." he struggled for a moment, searching for the correct phrase. Then it came to him, from a school poem about the Cornishmen and Bishop Trelawney:

". . . or I'll know the reason why!"—he concluded with a piping flourish.

Judith gazed with shining eyes at this demi-god, this serious-faced, narrow-shouldered stripling, straight from the pages of an Arthurian saga.

For years she had watched him strut, disposing of imaginary hordes at a blow, fulfilling the most impossible demands made upon him by shadowy commanders-in-chief, vaunting, swash-buckling and gasconading, but although she had genuinely admired his artistry, although her heart was warmed by his facility in changing suburban drabness to a riot of colour, she had never quite believed he was altogether real. Always, shamefully hidden in the back of her mind, ws the faint, nagging suspicion that one day this colourful balloon would burst and she would see him, as a man indeed, and a very desirable one, but an ordinary man nonetheless, and one who lived in one of the new semi-detached on the Wickham Estate, went to work on the 8.20, and pushed a lawnmower across the garden on Saturday afternoons.

Now, in the most dramatic maner, his extravagant boasts were vindicated, and her nagging doubts had been dragged into the open, and seen to be shabby and utterly unworthy. At the recollection of them she had hard work to prevent herself falling at his feet and begging his forgiveness, imploring a second chance to serve him in the humblest capacity, as cook, as drudge, as third shield-bearer removed.

The constable was not so impressed. He looked slightly startled and then irritated, not having the least idea how to proceed from this point onwards. There had been nothing in his textbooks, or in his probationary period talks with the sergeant, to prepare him for this sort of encounter. He could

only bluff one party or the other, and the children had
seemed the easier group to intimidate. Yet he was conscientious. He wanted to be fair and just. It was a great pity he
did not in the least know how to begin.

Sensing his dilemma, Fred emerged from his mood of
injured benevolence.

"You 'eard wot the orficer said," he shouted at Esme; "'op
it, before you gets run in, the pair of yer!"

"It's *you* that'll be run in, unless you come up with two-
and-five!" said Esme, firmly.

He too had sensed the policeman's indecision, and was
determined to make the most of it. He was surprised to note
that his voice was down to its normal key again, and that his
knees had stopped trembling.

This is ridiculous," said the constable at length. "How do
I know you gave him half-a-crown? I wasn't here, was I?"

"Quite right," confirmed Fred, rather more affably.

In a way, Fred was beginning to enjoy himself. He felt
quite safe, and it was always pleasant to embarrass a policeman.

At this juncture, however, Esme had an astonishing stroke
of luck. There was really no satisfactory answer to the
constable's claim. There was the bag, emptied, yet revealing
no half-crown, and it is difficult to see how Esme would have
been able to establish his claim then or later, and even more
difficult to see how, with Judith looking on he could have
abandoned his position with dignity.

But at that precise moment he saw Harold Godbeer,
picking his way carefully through the main stream of people
climbing the shingly hill, and the sight of Harold at this point
in the dispute was like the glimpse of a bobbing lifeboat to a
man floundering in a shark-infested sea. He drew himself
up.

"Very well," he said; "I'll fetch my lawyer!"

Fred exploded with laughter, and even the old crone's lips
cracked in a sour smile.

"Lumme, he's a cool one, he is!" chortled Fred, smiting his
distended stomach. "You oughter take 'im in charge, orficer,
an' no mistake. 'Fetch 'is lawyer!' Lumme, I ain't 'eard
nothin' like that ahtside o' the Ole Bailey!" And he clutched

the edge of the tentflap for support, as Esme sped away down the slope.

The constable turned shamefacedly to Judith.

"You'd better go home, kid," he told her; "this is no place for a little girl. Here . . ." he fumbled in his trouser pocket for conscience money. "I'll buy you a toffee apple!"

"I don't *want* a toffee apple, thank you," said Judith, confidently. "I want to see Esme and Mr. Godbeer get my two-and-fivepence out of him!"

It was not until Judith actually mentioned Mr. Godbeer's name that any of them suspected, for one second, that Esme's lawyer had substance. Within seconds, however, they had irrefutable proof of the fact, for Esme emerged from the crowd piloting Harold towards the stall. As they approached, Esme introduced him, with a certain proprietorial air.

"This is Mr. Godbeer. He's a lawyer. That's the woman, Uncle Harold, and that's the man she must have given it to!"

3

Harold Godbeer's presence at the fair was an accident. Ordinarily, he never attended such functions, but today, Bank Holiday, he had a luncheon appointment with Eunice, and had been sent out with Eunice's dachshund "Scandal" in order to wile away the hour or two it took Eunice to dress for an outing. His steps had led him in the direction of the hills, and his thoughts had been far away when his coat was seized by Esme on the main path.

Esme, sensing triumph, had not made the same mistake as he made when approaching the constable. He told his tale simply and clearly, and Mr. Godbeer's legal mind absorbed the details like a sponge.

In so doing, he saw far beyond the legal aspect. The boy was obviously in trouble, and asking for help. What enormous advantages might accrue for him—Harold—if he emerged as the champion of law and order, as the recoverer of stolen goods, as the superior of a uniformed constable!

Harold did not shrink from an engagement with a pair of hucksters. He had an even more deep-rooted faith in the law than Esme and a good deal more experience in the art of

bluff. He gave Esme "Scandal" to hold, and crunched purposefully over the pebbles towards the booth. He went willingly,
with a song in his heart.

"Now listen here——" began Fred, again seeking the
initiative.

Harold held up his hand, his pale lips forming a thin,
remorseless line. He had seen too many Freds in too many
witness-boxes, to be impressed by their hectoring tone, in or
out of a magistrates' court. He addressed himself to the
constable, now sweating a little under his tight collar.

"This young man is a friend of mine, Constable. My name
is Godbeer, and I happen to be managing clerk of Stillman
and Vickers, Solicitors, St. Paul's Churchyard. It must be
quite obvious to you what has occurred. Hadn't you better
order these people to return the money at once?"

The constable spread his hands. "They've emptied their
bag . . . how can anyone swear to a particular coin? It
doesn't make sense, Mr.—— Mr.——"

"Godbeer," said Harold testily. He disliked uniformed
officials who were unable to make instantaneous mental note
of one's name, but he saw, nevertheless, the grave difficulties
in the constable's path, and his alert brain at once cast about
for a workable alternative.

He found one, almost immediately.

"That's true enough," he admitted; "but then, one knows
the sort of people involved, doesn't one? That being so, one
has to play them at their own game, which is precisely what I
propose to do. Make an apron of your skirt, Judith!"

Instinctively, and without quite knowing why, Judith seized
the hem of her print frock, and held it taut. Into it Harold
began to scoop bag after bag of confetti, ignoring the sputtered protests of Fred, and smartly slapping at the claw-like
hand of the old woman, as she reached out to check him.

Into Esme's eyes came a look of undisguised admiration.
He would never have thought out *that* one, not in a million
years! Now it was his turn to enjoy himself, and the expression on Fred's face, and the fish-like gape of the constable,
were sheer heaven. Gleefully, he began helping Mr. Godbeer
to scoop. Bag after bag, two dozen in all, were swept into
Judith's skirt.

"It's thieving! Lumme, *stop him!*" roared Fred, at last.

"Give the constable particulars, and prosecute," said Harold, coolly, as Judith, with sagging skirt, backed away from the stall. "I, and my . . . er . . . my client, would be happy to contest the case in any court you care to name, sir!"

He turned to the constable. "You may even arrest us all, on the spot, if you wish. We shall offer no resistance. Would you prefer that, or shall we settle it this way, without further trouble and expense?"

With a slight jerk the constable came to himself.

"You'd better leave it at that," he told Fred, and, turning on his heel, crossed rapidly to the path and quickly lost himself in the crowd.

With a pleasant nod towards the astonished vendors, Harold placed a protective hand on the shoulder of each child, and directed their steps towards the main road.

"And now," he said, "we had better dispose of the evidence as rapidly as possible. Half-a-crown, I think you said," and he plunged his hand into his pocket, and presented Esme with a coin of that value.

Esme was overwhelmed.

"Well, thanks . . . thanks . . . Mr. . . . *Uncle* Harold. . . . That was marvellous, just marvellous. . . ."

"Ha, ha," piped Harold, with excusable pride, "you see I know these people, and that man in particular. Now why don't you and Judith play nearer the house? I wouldn't come up here if I were you. Or, better still, why don't we all go for a picnic to Manor Woods? Your mother will be ready now, and we could have fun, the four of us!"

And that was just what they did, the four of them picnicking in Manor Woods, where Judith poured out the story of the confetti battle to a rather startled Eunice, and Harold sat beaming in a glow of triumph that he was quite ready to share with Esme, for presently he said, removing his short briar from his mouth:

"Esme was quite right to stand up to them, and even more sensible to fetch me!"

That night, Esme lay awake thinking a long time and, as a result of his musings, sought out his mother alone the following morning, when she was brushing her long, fair tresses at the dressing-table mirror.

"Mother," he said quietly, "why don't you *marry* Uncle Harold and be done with it?"

Eunice was so surprised that she gave a litltle cry, and let fall the silver-backed hair-brush.

"Esme, you don't *mean* it?" she exclaimed seizing his hands, and pulling him towards her.

Esme held himself stiffly. He resented these spontaneous embraces.

"Well, why not?" he demanded. "He's mad on you, anyone can see that, and I think he's a proper sport, and so does Judith!"

"Oh, Esme, *darling*," was all Eunice could reply for the moment.

4

It was very decorous little wedding at Shirley Church, with Eunice in blue organdie, a white cloche hat, a spray of lilies of the valley, and Judith as a bridesmaid, in a Kate Greenaway gown.

There was no real reception, but later in the day, Eunice having changed into a going-away costume, and reduced the groom to a state of breathless ecstasy by kissing him lightly under the right ear, the couple left for a week's honeymoon at Torquay, taking Esme along with them, because it was holiday time, and they did not care to ask Mrs. Sturge, the daily, to sleep at Number Twenty-Two for the week.

They stayed at a large hotel, and Esme, who had never previously entered a hotel, was impressed by the opulence of the setting, particularly the bemedalled commissionaire, who showed a deferential interest in the boy when he learned the lad's father had been an officer, killed on the Marne.

This piece of information came in useful in the staff-room, where a chambermaid had admitted herself somewhat puzzled by the fact that the little boy in Number Twenty-Seven must be all of thirteen, yet continued to declare, with a leer altogether alarming in one so young, that "his people were having their honeymoon"!

CHAPTER XII

Jim Burns A 'Bus

1

THE Genera₁ Strike of 1926 was a great disappointment to Jim Carver, for the same reason that it disappointed the Kremlin.

Although by no means a violent man, Jim's political education had encouraged him to expect sensational constitutional changes to emerge from an upheaval of this magnitude. When none did, when the Old Gang emerged from it as smug and secure as ever, Jim's general conception of the British political scene underwent a sharp change. From May 1926 onwards, he ceased to regard his political work as an improving hobby, and in the years that led up to the Depression and beyond, his activities in this direction became an obsession. Where householders, opening their doors to receive one of his free pamphlets, had once encountered a social busybody, they now found themselves looking into the eyes of a fanatic.

The General Strike did not seriously involve the people of the Avenue as a community. Few industrial workers lived in the crescent. Some half-dozen, like Mr. Baskerville, of Number Eighty-Four, took a few days' holiday, and marched about the Lower Road, hoping to witness something exciting. They had a feeling that a stoppage of this size should provide some visual evidence of a real revolution. They too went home disappointed. No amount of fiery talk on the part of Jim Carver and his associates could induce the Cleggs, the Friths, the Frasers, or even the Baskervilles, to look upon the event as anything more than a welcome break in the monotony of their everyday lives.

One or two of the Avenue wives, recalling the uninhibited scenes of Armistice Day, went further afield in search of spectacle, but these would-be sensationalists were in a small minority. The Avenue was only twelve miles from London, and almost everyone residing there who had work in the City got to it by one means or another, even if they did little on arrival but gossip, and gaze out of office windows. Some of them used bicycles, a few walked, and the rest gathered in little knots at the junction of Shirley Rise and the Lower Road, to be picked up and transported by volunteer motorists, or "Specials" driving lorries.

There was, among all these people, a curious detachment in their approach to the emergency. Throughout the nine days' wonder they displayed small sense of partisanship, one way or the other. In essence they were pro-Government, but there was no rancour in the suburb towards the strikers. The householders sympathised with the miners, whose case had been given plenty of advance publicity, but whose average wages were recognised as inadequate, having regard to their working conditions. Jim Carver, out stumporating night after night, despaired of persuading them to make common cause with the miners: the nearest coalfields were hundreds of miles from the Avenue, and the injustices of the men, who "talked funny", and worked there, were as remote as those of Chinese coolies, and Tokio rickshaw-runners.

There was, it seemed to Jim, no evidence of true political awareness in the suburb, no true recognition of the class struggle, as set down in his pamphlets and statistical surveys. One could quote facts and figures to these people until one was blue in the face. They listened, occasionally asked in irrelevant question, occasionally made a weak joke at the speaker's expense, but hardly any of them saw beyond their own, pitifully limited, horizons of thought. They were blind to the danger of the Capitalist Conspirators, who were standing by with fetters, waiting for a chance to reshackle them to the Juggernaut of Victorian class-exploitation.

Meantime, those few who did see, those like himself who devoted the whole of their free time to preaching the gospel, were methodically victimised, even as the miners were being victimised.

It was not long before Jim himself felt the weight of this victimisation. Less than a month before the outbreak of the

General Strike he found himself out of a job, and branded as an agitator, without even the chilly consolation of martyrdom.

Jim Carver's political activities, throughout the six years he had worked as vanman for the removal firm of Burtol and Twyfords, were well known to the directors, but had so far resulted in no recrimination on their part. This was mainly because old Hubert Twyford, the dominant figure of the firm, had recognised in Jim a sound, conscientious workman, willing to give a fair day's toil for a limited day's pay, notwithstanding his well-known, radical sympathies.

Hubert Twyford was an old-time Liberal and Free-Trader, whose political thought had been cast in the mould of men like Lloyd George and Sir Edward Grey. Old Man Twyford took a keen interest in his employees. He knew every one of them by name, and although he had long regarded Carver as a mild crank, who sought in Socialism reforms that which could have been achieved by the Liberal Party, he shared Carver's open contempt for the Tories, past and present, and had once gone so far as to tell him as much when he had attended a meeting at which Jim was speaking in support of a Socialist candidate.

Shortly before the strike, however, Hubert Twyford died, and the direction of the firm passed to his only son, Gilbert, who was detested among the yardmen and clerks as a pompous snob, with a hundred half-baked notions of building Burtol and Twyford's—a compact business employing less than fifty men—into a dangerous rival to Carter Paterson's and Pickford's.

Gilbert took over his father's direction in March. By the end of April a dozen of the older men had been sacked, and Jim was one of the first to go.

His dismissal was made known to him at a brief, unpleasant interview.

"I'm making changes," Gilbert Twyford had told him. "From now on, this firm is going to be run on twentieth-century lines. We can forget all about the horse-vans, can't we?"

As Burtol and Twyford's had been using motor-lorries since 1913, this remark struck Jim as particularly fatuous, and when, at the close of his pep talk, young Twyford asked for suggestions, Jim was rash enough, and irritated enough, to make a pointed reference to the rates of subsistence pay issued to teams away from home overnight.

"If we're being brought up-to-date, I suggest we start with a review of journey-money rates for long-distance work," he said. "We get five shillings a night. That might have bought two meals and a bed before the war, but it certainly doesn't now, Mr. Twyford!"

He was as good as out of work before he had finished speaking. Ten minutes later, when they were back in the office, Gilbert Twyford asked his chief clerk for information regarding the man who raised the matter of journey-money. Unlike his father, he had made no pretence of getting to know the men he employed. The chief clerk, who was over fifty, and nervous of his own future, had no hesitation in giving the new proprietor a colourful character-sketch of Jim Carver, stressing his reputation as a Socialist.

"Is that so?" mused Gilbert. "Well, well, we must look into this, mustn't we?"

Look into it he did, with the result that Jim Carver was given his cards within a fortnight of the pep talk. He was under no illusions as to why he was sacked and said so, bluntly, but without heat.

Gilbert Twyford pretended to be shocked.

"You're barking up the wrong tree altogether," he protested. "We don't sack men for political opinions in England, old boy. We leave that sort of thing to Russia. I believe it's quite usual over there. No, no, no; the fact it, we contemplate quite a few changes here, and I'm cutting down on the smaller vehicles, and installing six-wheelers. A six-wheeler is a young man's pigeon—but you'll get something, you'll land something more in keeping with your age, old boy!"

"I've no doubt I will," replied Jim grimly, "but don't talk to me as if I'll find it in a bath-chair!"

Gilbert preferred to take this as a joke, and laughed immoderately, patting Jim's shoulder affectionately. It took all Jim's self-control to check himself from standing clear and planting his fist in Twyford's face. There was, however, the matter of a reference to be thought of, and Carver walked stiffly from the yard and into the seething labour market at the age of forty-seven. He needed no one to tell him that the years ahead would be difficult ones, more difficult perhaps than the period of job-seeking that followed his demobilisation. After all, he was a student of industrial statistics.

2

The month that followed was a very active one for Jim Carver, so active indeed, so studded with open-air meetings, policy-framing committee sessions, and door-to-door canvassing on behalf of local government candidates, that he had no time to reflect on his own future.

During the Strike he was on his feet eighteen hours a day. He spent the greater part of his time on picket work, in the Elephant and Castle area, and this was how he came to be involved in a serious clash between "Specials" and strikers, that resulted in a Tilling 'bus being burned in the Walworth Road.

He did not enjoy the scrimmage, as he thought he might when he joined in it. The 'bus, driven by two university students, each swathed in a colourful scarf, and obviously enjoying themselves, came bowling down from the direction of the river, and was stopped by a small road obstruction, set up by a picket under the leadership of a huge Clydeside docker. What a Clydeside striker was doing so far from home Jim never discovered, but the man's unintelligible directions irritated him, just, as, during the war, he had been irritated by the news that a French General was to command the British Army.

One of the students climbed down from the 'bus to remove the obstruction. The picket closed in, and at that moment a group of three middle-aged "Specials"—office executives by the look of them—ran along the tram-lines to support the driving team.

Jim never understood how the struggle came to involve so many people so quickly. At one moment there were less than a dozen men, shouting at one another, and giving each other provocative little pushes, and the next the whole area round the 'bus was seething with men and women, clawing at one another, punching, shouting, and kicking. Jim heard the Glaswegian shout "Burrrn the bloody thing, burrrn it!" and even in the heat of the moment was vaguely shocked by such a dreadful proposal. He fought his way towards the rear platform of the vehicle, and was surprised to find it jammed with passengers, mostly factory girls.

They looked very frightened indeed, and as Jim approached they began to scream in unison. Before he could mount the platform a uniformed constable struck Jim a glancing blow on the side of the head. The blow did not hurt, it was little more than a tap, but the indignity of the assault caused Jim to lose his temper and he struck back, flooring the policeman with a well-aimed swing to the cheek. The struggling mob on the tram-lines then moved in, and the girl passengers went on screaming above the general uproar. Jim found himself hitting out in all directions. His coat was ripped down from the lapel, and his tie was jerked into a choking knot.

Suddenly there was smoke all round them, and the girls stopped screaming, and began to leap from the platform. It was at that moment that Jim noticed the dog under his feet.

The sight of the animal caused him to forget everything else—the girls, the policemen, the probable results of the picket's action in setting fire to the 'bus. He thought only of the dog, and how to extricate it from this heaving mass. Planting his feet squarely, he bent swiftly and picked it up. It was surprisingly heavy, and its weight anchored him against the stairs. He braced himself, leaped forward, and fell on one knee on the edge of the mêlée. The thickest part of the press was now swirling towards the blazing bonnet, and he was able to stagger upright and run towards the pavement. His size, and the weight of the dog, carried him through. He emerged on to the pavement gasping, and his instinct for cover—returning after a lapse of eight years—directed him to dive into a maze of empty side-streets.

Clear of the main road he stopped to set down the dog and take stock of his injuries. His coat was in ribbons, and his left-hand trouser leg had been cut by the fall. Through the rent he could see that his knee was bleeding.

The dog made no attempt to run away, but stood looking up at him, grinning. It was a mongrel, but a handsome one, two-thirds golden-haired retriever, one-third something else, possibly spaniel, to judge by its over-long ears. It was thin-nish, but unscarred, and its long brown coat seemed to have been cared for. It had no collar.

Jim's first thought, after he had bandaged his knee and made some attempt to pin up the lapel of his jacket, was to take the dog to the nearest police station. Then he reflected that this, together with his appearance, would amount to a tacit admission of his part in the affray.

Looking towards the main road he could see smoke rising from the 'bus, and, judging by the distant uproar, the battle still raged round the half-burned shell. There was nothing to do but take the dog along.

As he bent down to loop a length of pamphlet string round its neck, the dog's long tongue shot out and licked his sweating face. A feeling of comradeship surged through the man and, with it, a curious sense of gratitude towards the mongrel. It had been the means, he felt, of extricating him from an incident that might well have landed him in gaol. Notwithstanding his passionate convictions regarding the jus-tice of the cause, Jim Carver was not a man to look upon a gaol-sentence as a badge of class loyalty. He was too near the era when such a thing branded a man for life, whatever the nature of the offence that brought him behind bars. In addition, deep down, although he brushed it impatiently aside, was a sense of shame that he had taken part in the destruc-tion of public property, and struck out at a uniformed police-man. The dog seemed to have no such misgivings, he went on grinning and lashing his tail, and when Jim headed for London Bridge, he trotted alongside as though he had never known another master.

"Eh, but you got me out of a pickle, pup," Jim said to him. "What'll we call you?"

A name suggested itself very readily as they moved to-gether through the loose stream of sightseers, who were now pouring down the tram-lines towards the 'bus.

"I reckon we'll call you 'Strike'," he said.

The dog executed a half-turn and leapt up at Jim, his pink tongue seeking the big hand that held the string.

It took Jim and Strike nearly three hours to walk home, and both man and dog were tired and thirsty when they turned up Shirley Rise early that afternoon.

Out here things were quiet, quieter even than on a normal day. As Jim approached the corner, a 'bus drew up and a young man, wearing a "Special's" arm-band, jumped off, and began to walk briskly up the rise. Jim recognised the "Special" as Archie.

The arm-band Archie wore was a shock. Of late, father and son had seen very little of one another, and Jim realised that he knew little or nothing of his son's political outlook—if indeed he possessed one, which Jim very much doubted.

The relationship between them had been deteriorating for years. Ever since Jim's return from the war he had sensed the boy's half-concealed contempt for his father's job, his lack of ambition, his entire cast of thought. Archie had never put this contempt into words, but at the dinner-table, when Archie was still living at home, Jim had seen the boy's fleshy lips twitch on hearing his father's comment upon a news item. Jim had never forgotten that passage in his wife's war-time letter ". . . *Archie never seems short of money . . . he helps me sometimes. . . .*" and Jim's quiet contemplation of his son's way of life, as Archie passed from adolescence to manhood, had increased his suspicions regarding Archie's true character. He had heard rumours of the Gittens' children about the time that his son married the grocer's daughter, and the marriage itself had puzzled him, although it seemed to have worked out all right, and to have done something to steady the boy. Once or twice during the past few years Jim had tried, half-heartedly, to improve their relationship, but Archie had shied away from him like a frisky colt, and Jim had not persisted. Somehow, he always felt at a disadvantage with Archie, as though the boy's unspoken contempt undermined his authority as a father, and might even cease to be unspoken if the older man threw down a definite challenge.

But here was something that could not be ignored—his own son, wearing the arm-band of the reactionaries, who were successfully breaking the strike, and putting a padlock on the hatch that had lately been burst open by the dispossessed—the men who, less than a decade ago, had been promised the earth, and everything in it, by a badly frightened oligarchy. Here was his own flesh and blood taking sides against him with people like Gilbert Twyford, and a Government determined to starve the miners into abject submission. He had to do something, and say something. He had to know if the boy realised the enormity of his betrayal of their class, or if he had simply donned the arm-band for a lark, as Jim was convinced was the case with so many of the younger "Specials".

Both men were turning up Shirley Rise towards the Avenue, and they could hardly have avoided walking side by side for a few steps. Jim decided to come straight to the point. He touched Archie's arm-band with his index finger.

"What's that, son?" he asked, striving to sound semijocular.

Archie shrugged, but avoided his father's eye.

"What's it look like, Dad?"

"I'll tell you what it looks like," said Jim, choosing his words very deliberately, "it looks as if somebody's been making a proper monkey out of you!"

Archie stopped. They had reached the corner of Delhi Road, a few yards from Piretta's rear entrance. The younger man pointed to a six-inch rent in Jim's threadbare jacket, and then down to his ruined trousers.

"It looks as if someone's been making a bigger one out of you, Dad!" he replied, civilly.

Jim felt a spurt of irritation in his stomach but he ignored it, in the way he mastered his impatience when a heckler interrupted him at a meeting.

"I've been down the Walworth Road," he told Archie. "They've got a way with scabs down there. The one who did this is probably in hospital, son!"

Archie's eyes widened. "That so?" he said, making no effort to keep the mockery out of his voice. "Then it's a pity they didn't pick you up, and throw you inside. I would have, if I'd been handy!"

Jim knew then that there could never be any sort of

reconciliation between them, that from this moment onwards they would always follow opposite paths—Archie to the right, with the bosses, with Gilbert Twyford, with the arms magnates, and the pipe-sucking Baldwin, he to the left, with the outcasts, the collarless, and the sullen queues outside the exchanges. The inevitability of the cleavage freed him from his duties as a parent. From now on Archie was not a son—just one of the enemy, and could be treated as such, impersonally, if need be, mercilessly.

"Well," he said, with a bitterness that was uncharacteristic of him on public platforms, "I'll tell you one thing, Archie: I'd as lief see you dead as wearing that arm-band. So, from today, don't show up at Number Twenty while I'm there, or I'll make sure you're kicked all the way from the front-gate to the feather-bed you've hooked for yourself with that Eyetie! If you don't think I'm capable of doing it, you're welcome to try me, son, any time you like; and if you've a mind to, right outside the front-windows of your bloody customers!"

Under his father's calm gaze Archie lost the initiative, and fell back on bluster. He had never thought of his father as a political opponent, but simply as a well-meaning failure, whose principles—heard over the kitchen table *ad nauseam* during the first years of Jim's return home—would keep him poor, and shabby, for the rest of his life. Archie was not really interested in the strike, or in politics, generally. Archie's politics were, and always would be, the short-term enrichment of Archie. His enlistment as a "Special", during this present ridiculous business, was an act of simple insurance, agreed upon with Toni, his father-in-law, as a step towards the preservation of law and order, and the rapid return to normal deliveries and business conditions. When he had presented himself at the police station, and volunteered to ride a 'bus platform for an hour or so, he had never even thought of his father, only of the need for business-men to stand together against the *hoipolloi*, whose junketings were beneath notice until they caused a falling off of shop trade. He was shocked, despite his natural arrogance, by his father's edict forbidding him the house.

"There's Louise and the kids," he began, but Jim cut him short.

"As long as they live there they'll do as I say. I can't prevent them calling on you—I wouldn't anyhow—but that doesn't mean they can start a family rumpus by asking you over the threshold, son. I mean that, so don't get to trying anything, Archie!"

He turned away quickly, and walked on up Shirley Rise to the corner of the Avenue. Archie watched him go, noting his loose, shambling stride and slightly stooping shoulders. His surprise and indignation did not prevent him from feeling unhappy at the prospect of being cut off from his family. He had always been fond of Louise, and very generous with her when he made up her weekly order. He valued too the homage of the twins, and of Judith, when he met them in the Avenue, and sometimes tossed one or the other a coin.

Then he shrugged off his regrets. If the Old Man wanted to waste his life rabble-rousing, instead of in the normal pursuit of gathering money, there was nothing that he could do about it. The important thing was to break this idiotic stranglehold on profitmaking, and drive these Bolshies underground where they belonged and where, if he had anything to do with it, they should remain.

He threw up his chin, and crunched up the gravel alley to the back door. His father-in-law was in the spotless kitchen, playing bears with Tony, the baby. He rose excitedly as Archie entered.

"He's a-strong, he's a-forward. Just now he almost walk! Tony, boy, show-a your father, walk-a to grandpa, there's a boy!"

The baby, already ridiculously like Archie about the face and the set of his shoulders, rose uncertainly, and staggered on bandy legs towards the striped humpty on which the Italian sat, beaming, and holding out brown, freckled hands.

Archie grinned at the child, and went into the shop to get the day-book.

CHAPTER XIII

Edith In Mourning

1

EDITH CLEGG never looked back on 1926 as the year of the General Strike. It had, for her, the far greater significance of being "about the time dear Teddy joined a dance-band, and the year poor dear Rudi died, and upset us all so much."

In the summer of that year Ted Hartnell gave up his part-time job in the furniture mart, and moved an appreciable step nearer Elysium He became, to begin with, the only other member of the orchestra at the Granada, in the Lower Road, and his presence in the minute orchestra pit was due less to his ability to twirl drumsticks, and to Edith's pleas on his behalf to Mr. Billings the proprietor, than to the pressing need for noises-off in Mr. Billings' latest attraction, *Ben Hur*.

Mr. Billings had seen a preview of *Ben Hur* at a cinematograph-exhibitors' conference. He immediately recognised the film for what it was, another *Covered Wagon*, with the Bible thrown in, and as such, a possible source of attraction to hitherto cinema-shy audiences, such as Baptists, Congregationalists, perhaps even Plymouth Brethren.

"Point is," he told Edith, when they were packing up after the second house one night, "point is, we gotter put it over proper! It's big, see? Not just another film, not just a *good* film, but a *Birth of a Nation*—a proper '*Unchback* if you see what I mean! Why, lumme, it's even got Jesus in it! You don't *see* 'im, of course—that ain't allowed—but you see 'is arm come out, when 'e gives Ramon Navarro a drink o' water! That's good! That's clever! And we gotter do something about it, something special!"

There was no need to fan Edith's enthusiasm. Jesus or no Jesus she harboured no doubts about liking *Ben Hur*, and she immediately produced one of those intuitive ideas that Mr. Billings had learned to expect from her.

"I always think," she said deliberately, "that it is such a pity we have to *see* things without *hearing* them. What I mean is, I can't do really *convincing* bangs, when buildings fall, and cannons go off. I can only . . . well . . . I can only *suggest* them."

"Go on," urged Mr. Billings, digging away with his splayed tooth-pick. "What you leading up to, Miss Clegg?"

Edith drew a very deep breath. She had been awaiting this opportunity for some considerable time.

"Well," she said finally, "you ought to have an orcehstra for good pictures like this, Mr. Billings . . . no, no . . ." as a haunted look showed in his eyes, "not a *real* orchestra, I know the Granada can't afford *that*, but a one-man orchestra . . . someone who could . . . well, make the bangs with cymbals and drums, and do lots of other things, like blow coach-horns in highwaymen pictures, and tinkle things like sleigh-bells. If only we could have *tinkled* properly, when dear Rudi was driving his sleigh away from those terrible wolves! It would have made *such* a difference, now, wouldn't it?"

Mr. Billings considered. The idea was not exactly new, but somehow he had never given it constructive thought.

"'Ow much would a bloke like that cost?" he demanded.

"Oh, I expect he'd be happy to do it for two pounds ten," said Edith, pressing her stomach, as though the palm could regulate her internal rumblings. "I've got a lodger called Mr. Hartnell, and he can play almost anything by ear. He'd be wonderful, and we could rehearse together at home, if you let me borrow the advance publicity booklets they send you."

Mr. Billings needed little enough persuading. Within twenty-four hours of this conversation Ted Hartnell was installed in the pit, isolated from his delighted sponsor by a second-hand bass drum, a side-drum, a kettle-drum, a pair of cymbals, and a strange-looking instrument of his own invention that came to be known as "The-All-In".

"The-All-In" began life as Edith's clothes-horse. Its struts were covered with green baize, and hung around with tubes of varying length, bottles partly filled with water; and a few coconut shells. Ted could produce almost any combination of sounds with the drums, cymbals, and the "All-In". During that week's showing of *Ben Hur*, he and his instruments were almost as sensational as the film itself. All manner of authentic-sounding noises emerged from the pit, to the huge delight of Mr. Billings, who sat through seven performances in the first half of the week. When the chariots were racing round the arena, Ted beat a most realistic tattoo on the coconut shells; when the Roman heralds raised their clarions to their lips, he leaped to his feet, and blew a series of blasts on his trumpet; when Ben and his fellow galley-slaves toiled at the huge oars, he beat out a drum rhythm with his foot, and repeatedly dropped a long length of harness-chain into an empty bucket.

His real triumph, however, came later, when, within a few weeks of *Ben Hur*, Mr. Billings secured a feature showing of a French Revolution picture called *The Tragic Queen*. There were plenty of routine noises-off in this film, galloping horses, salvoes of cannon, and the clash of arms on the staircase of Versailles; but the scene in which Ted excelled himself was the final act of the tragedy, when Marie Antoinette's tumbril drove through the massed ranks of the terrorists, and the victim attempted to make a scaffold speech above the monotonous roll of drums. Urged on by Edith, who, with shining eyes, was thundering out the *Marseillaise*, Ted flung himself into the business of producing an increasingly rapid tattoo on kettle and side-drums, the rhythm culminating in the final shattering *"kerlunk"* on the bass drum. This signified the fall of the knife, and produced gasp of horror from electrified audiences. Mr. Billings was so excited that he almost tumbled from the front row of the balcony into the one-and-nines.

On the final night of *The Tragic Queen*, Ted had an unexpected visitor.

When the auditorium had cleared, a slim, willowy young man lounged down the centre aisle to the pit, where Ted was packing up for the week-end. Mr. Billings had left early with the takings, and Edith was responsible for locking up.

The young man leaned heavily on the brass rail, introducing himself by a grubby visiting card that read: *"Al Swinger and his Rhythmateers"*, and underneath, in small italics: *"Musical Engagements—Dancing—Occasions—Parties"*. And beneath that again, in even smaller italic: *"Hot and Classy"*.

Al had a waxen complexion, a pigeon chest, a large curved nose, and small, over-bright eyes. Hunched over the rail he looked like an ailing and uncomfortably perched eagle. He used a shiny dress-suit, and a laboriously-acquired Manhattan accent.

"You sure c'n use dem drums, brother," was his opening remark.

Ted flushed. He was a very modest young man.

"I got no room here," he apologised; "you need plenty of space to really beat it up!"

Edith smiled at the visitor. She liked Teddy to be praised.

"I'll have to lock up the front," she told the visitor, "but you can stay, then we can all go out the back way."

After Edith had gone Al slowly extracted a bar of chewing-gum from a packet, and flicked it into his mouth.

"Chew?" he asked Ted, proffering the packet.

Ted shook his head, and began to slip the canvas cover on the big drum. He performed the office lovingly, like a young mother tucking her baby into its cot.

Al Swinger chewed stolidly for a moment. Finally, he said: "How long you been working in this flea-pit?"

"Just a few weeks," Teddy told him.

"Like to play in a real band?"

Ted stopped in the act of loosening the tension of the kettle-drum. He looked hard at the visitor, then at the card on the piano lid. He swallowed once or twice, giving himself time to master his excitement.

"This *your* band?" he asked.

"Ur-huh," said Al. "Nice li'l band. Got a broadcast lined up. Go places. Better all the time. Drummer's left us. Been run in, silly sod. How about a fiver a week? Make more some weeks. Split commission."

Ted Hartnell was unable to speak for a moment. His hands trembled on the drum-braces. Edith came plodding back, the foyer keys jangling in her hand. Al turned to her.

"You the boss?"

Edith said no, the boss had left after first house. Al shook off his lethargy, jumped the rail, and flung open the piano.

"Okay! Let's have *Valencia,* and give it all you got, brother!"

His fingers slipped over the worn keys. It was not the *Valencia* Ted and Edith sometimes played, during their front-room concerts. It was full of what Edith would have called "twiddly-bits", so full indeed that the melody was sometimes difficult to follow, although the rhythm was there, heavy and insistent. Teddy forgot Edith, and forgot where he was; he ripped the cover from the bass drum, and flung himself into an accompaniment. Between him they made the cinema rock with sound:

> Valenciaaaa ! . . .
> Land-of-orange-grove-n-sweet-content
> you-call-me-from-afarrrr . . . di-bom-di-di
> bom-di-bomiddy . . . bom-di-bomiddy . . .

Ted did give it all he had, hurling himself at the drums like a frenzied savage each time Al lifted his fingers from the keys at the end of a phrase. It was a number in which a good drummer could make his presence felt. It left *Red, Red Robin,* and similar numbers a long way behind.

When they had finished and Al slammed down the piano lid, Edith applauded.

"Why, that's splendid, *splendid,* Teddy!"

"We'd do a lot better on a real Joanna," said Al, and Edith notice that the pallor of his cheeks was now relieved by two bright red spots, each the size of sixpence. "You'll pass, brother! We rehearse in the Assembly Rooms off Black Horse Lane. Look in, ten tomorrow. I'll have a contract out."

He climbed out of the pit, and lounged off towards the fire-exit.

Edith moved forward to guide him, but he stopped her with a languid wave. He seemed to be moving in familiar surroundings.

2

Al Swinger was shrewd and business-like. His terse manner of speech, his lounging movements, the impression he gave of trying to be someone or something he had only read about in magazines, or seen in places like the Granada, failed to conceal the fact that he was a dedicated man, dedicated to jazz music in a way that Ted Hartnell would never be. Al carried his obsession a stage further than Ted, into the realm where it ceased to be a pastime, and became a commercial ambition, where it linked up with contracts, white ties, silver-plated saxophones, and dining out in expensive night-clubs. He liked and trusted Ted from the start because he saw in him a devotion to jazz that was objective and unlikely to involve him in competition with the band-leader. Competition for leadership had already caused the dissolution of two of his dance bands, and he had recently turned away some promising material on this account. What he was searching for were bandsmen who loved their work, but lacked personal ambition; in Ted Hartnell he found the ideal drummer.

Al believed in re-investing most of his earning in the orchestra. That was why he paid Ted a starting-wage of five pounds a week, at a time when few of his engagements earned a ten-pound gross. His margin was narrow, but he kept his team at a high pitch of enthusiasm, and the "Rhythmateers" were beginning to be known as far afield as Lewisham and Catford. They had their own transport, a converted lorry, and an excellent array of instruments. They were still small-time, but Al had made up his mind that, providing they kept their heads, they would move into the bigger time in a year or so. Other, less disciplined bands were already there, broadcasting, and touring the seaside resorts in summer and one day, he assured Ted, the name Al Swinger would mean something in the dance-band world.

Edith missed Teddy very much during those first hectic months. He slept late in the mornings, of course, and they were able to take lunch together, but she had the matinée at two o'clock, and he was usually gone by the time she came home to tea. She left coffee in a thermos flask on the kitchen table, and she usually heard him come in, between two and three a.m., but there were no more front-room soirées, no more long, gossipy meals in the kitchen, with Becky, and Lickapaw. It crossed her mind that, now he was on the road to fame and fortune, he might seek more expensive lodgings, but she never let herself seriously entertain the prospect of losing him, any more than she contemplated a future without Becky, or the cat. It was lonely for Becky now, with herself at the cinema from two till five, and from six to eleven, but there were minor consolations. First, the drain on their capital had been stopped and they were even saving a little, then, Lickapaw was getting older, and spent less time away from home on the slates of Delhi Road. Finally, there was her work, and after work, her press-cutting books, and her portrait gallery.

The gallery was very extensive now. All the wall-space of her bedroom had been used up, and glossy pictures of Navarro, Lewis Stone, Adolphe Menjou, and dear Buster, with his large sad eyes, had crept like a tide into the bathroom and even the lavatory. Dotted about the house were nearly a dozen pictures of Rudi, two of them signed. His occult eyes contemplated her from beneath flowing burnous on the landing, and his nostrils flared at her from an unusual angle on the stairway ceiling. Number Four was a shrine to Hollywood, but the ark of its tabernacle was Valentino, Valentino the Sheik, the Son of the Sheik, the Cossack, the Torreador, the Gaucho.

3

Edith saw the poster when she was on her way to work, shortly before two o'clock one afternoon.

It was standing outside the newsagent's, at the corner of Lucknow Road, advertising an early edition of *The Star*. It was scrawled in charcoal capitals and it screamed: *"Valentino Dead."*

Simply that, as if Rudi had been a mere Balkan monarch, or a British Prime Minister. Valentino dead! And nobody even knew that he had been suffering from indigestion, or migraine.

Edith stopped, and gazed fixedly across the width of Shirley Rise. It was as though, after a single, terrifying thunderflash, a yawning chasm had opened up beneath her feet, and the solid structures of the semi-detached houses on her immediate left had begun to bulge, crumble, and slide into rubble beside her.

She stood there for nearly a minute. Unheeding traffic moved up from Lower Road, stirring little eddies of summer dust. An odd pedestrian or two meandered in and out of Piretta's grocery shop, buying Monkey Brand, and Sunlight Soap, and tinned salmon, just as if the sun was still in the sky, and the world was still spinning on its course.

At last she was able to totter across to the shop. She could not ask for a paper, but fumbled in her purse, and put a penny on the counter. Emerging into the bright sunlight again she knew that she could not go on to work. She turned back towards the Lane, found a fallen elm, and sat on it a long time, before she had sufficient resolution to look at the headlines.

To her intense surprise there was nothing in them concerning Rudi. The main headline dealt with the relatively minor event of Germany entering the League of Nations; and lower, down, the excessively trivial one of Spain leaving it. This lack of confirmation afforded her a brief spasm of hope. Perhaps it was all a cruel hoax, or a false rumour?

She began to hunt through the pages, scanning each column. Then she turned the paper over, and saw the stop-press, printed in red. There, at last, was the dreadful confirmation: *"Star's death. Rudolph Valentino, the film star, died after an operation in California today."*

Just that! Just the bald and terrible fact! Not a word about what kind of operation, or the shattering effect such a paragraph would have upon countless millions throughout the world.

She sat on the elm bole a long, long time. She could not remember feeling like this before, not even when Becky ran away, or was found, reclaimed, and brought home to the Vicarage, speechless, bruised, and half an idiot. On that occasion she had been able to act, to argue with her father and the Bishop, to nurse her sister, to throw herself into the desperate search for Becky's lost wits. This was very different. There was nothing whatever she could *do*, not even send a wreath, not even attend the funeral.

At last she got up, and began to walk unsteadily down Shirley Rise towards the cinema. She felt that she had to talk to someone about it, and who better, who handier, than Mr. Billings, who had such a stake in Rudi? She felt light-headed, and faintly bilious.

At the junction of Delhi Road, Archie Carver came out of the shop carrying a tub of apples. He noticed her vacant look and called—as he called to all regular customers:

"Lovely afternoon, Miss Clegg!"

Edith neither heard nor saw him.

4

In a sense, Edith Clegg did attend Valentino's funeral. She bought every edition of every newspaper that came her way. She read every word describing the fantastic scenes at the morticians' parlour (what a funny way to describe an undertaker's shop!) and, unlike the mourners, described in millions of words that poured across the Atlantic, she did not need a slice of onion concealed in a handkerchief. She wept genuine tears all that week, and Becky, who helped her to hang the crêpe over the signed photographs, wept in sympathy, although she had never seen a Valentino film, and regarded the author of all this grief as "a dear boy Edith had liked so much".

When all was over, when Press releases from Hollywood began to filter down to the inside pages, Edith steamed Rudi's pictures from her walls, and put them carefully away in the drawer of her large wardrobe. There were many empty spaces in the gallery and—for the time being—she preferred them empty. Fairbanks was well enough, and Navarro had a good deal of Rudi's charm, but neither of them could take the place of The Sheik.

Nobody ever did.

CHAPTER XIV

Schooldays For Three

THE schooldays of most boys are lit by a single personality. Other men emerge, masters are remembered for an odd trick of speech, an idiosyncrasy of manner, a fad that singles them out as fair game for the Junior School mimic, but these men are seldom more than background figures. There is always one figure that dwarfs them, that remains centre stage, year after year, until his personality is imprinted on a boy's mind for all time.

Such a man, for Esme Fraser, was "Longjohn" Silverton, who reigned as headmaster of Godley Grammar School from the time he limped out of the hospital for plastic surgery cases, in the Spring of 1920, until many of his pupils were old enough to take part in the second round of Armageddon.

In some ways it was a tragedy for Esme that Mr. Silverton made no real impression on him until he had been a pupil at the Grammar School for more than two years. By that time Esme was rising fifteen, and his character was formed. The best that Silverton could do was to give Esme a push or two in a more promising direction, but by then it was nearly too late. The spell of the Carver twins had been laid upon Esme for several years.

Longjohn was not the conventional type of "popular" head-master. His was not the hearty man-to-man approach, the back-slapping, rib-nudging, honour-of-the-school technique. He conjured up no visions of Arnold, or even Mr. Chips. He was lean, ravaged, silent, and terrifyingly down-to-earth in his approach to boys. The staff found him enigmatical, abstracted, and moodily aloof, and to most parents he was blunt to the point of rudeness. Fathers and mothers—particularly mothers—did not take to Mr. Silverton, and many of them were afraid of him. Yet no boy was ever afraid of Silverton, and that was something that staff and parents found hard to understand.

In appearance, Longjohn was spare, frosty, and hard-bitten. The plastic surgeons, whilst repairing most of the exterior damage wrought by a flammenwerfer at Bois des Buttes, had done little to improve his looks. The contours of his cheeks were uneven, and when he was tired, or exasperated, the taut flesh began to twitch. His eyes had miraculously survived the blast of flame. They were deep brown, and extraordinarily mild, but the shrinking of the skin on his forehead, and above the bridge of his nose, had deepened the sockets, and puckered the lids, so that the eyes now appeared sunken and apathetic. He had other injuries, causing a curious, shuffling walk, and an odd posture when he stood on the dais in the main hall, but he made very light of these, so light indeed that he drew no war pension after 1924.

Silverton had that curious sense of peace and balance that was a legacy of front-line survival. Emotionally he was difficult to disturb, but he could pretend to cold, devastating anger if he thought anger served a good purpose. He had a deep love of scholarship, and a strange abiding tolerance with every living creature under the age of eighteen. Beyond that notch, humanity could go hàng, collectively and individually.

Esme moved within range of Longjohn when he was twelve-and-a-half. Eunice, his mother, overrode her second husband, Harold, on the subject of Esme's education. She would not contemplate the prospect of sending him away to school, although she was, perhaps, the one person in the Avenue who could have afforded public-school fees. Harold argued a little but ultimately gave in, as he gave in to Eunice on every issue once Eunice had really made up her mind. Esme was taken away from the private school in Lower Road, and after passing a viva voce examination, was accepted for Godley Grammar School, a fourpenny 'bus-ride north of the Avenue.

Until he attended the Grammar School, Esme had made no real friends among the children of the suburb. Judith was not so much a friend as a shield-bearing acolyte, and throughout his childhood Esme gained no pleasure from the companionship of boys his own age. He found them lamenta-

bly lacking in imagination and on this account dull partners
in his eccentric games of make-believe. Judy was better than
the best of them. At least she never questioned his decisions,
but did what she was told, with the minimum of error.

Esme was not interested in organised games, and his brilliant memory, for anything he cared to remember, might
have resulted in his becoming a teacher's pet. What saved
him from this stigma was his capacity to tell stories, and to
make them sound more credible than those read in adventure
books, together with an incurable romanticism that led him,
more or less cold-bloodedly, into the more extravagant exer-
cises of master-baiting. He soon acquired a reputation among
the boys for solemn buffoonery and, without being exactly a
butt, or a clown, he was able to provoke laughter on a
slightly different level from that usually employed by the
lower-form humorists. His half-girlish appearance assisted
him in this field, for he looked quite innocuous, and it was
some time before the staff penetrated his disguise. The boys
discovered the real Esme almost at once, for, if he fancied
himself humiliated, he could fight back like a tiger and did,
more than once, during his first, turbulent term. The smaller
boys in Lower School learned not to provoke him, and the
bigger boys, like the elephantine Boxer, feared his biting
tongue more than his sudden rages.

Because he was "different", and because he quickly came
to be regarded as something of a crank, his schooldays might
have been very lonely, but he was rescued from isolation by
the twins, with whom he formed a curious alliance, a bond
(it was hardly a friendship) that was to endure most of the
time he was at school. He made no impression at all upon the
rock-like unity of the Carver boys, but they had a marked
effect upon him, not as individuals but as a team, much as
they impressed the adults of the Avenue.

The alliance was forged at the end of Esme's first term,
which happened to coincide with the end of the school year,
and its anvil was the impending, and seemingly unavoidable,
separation of Boxer and Bernard—the one destined for the
"C" forms, the other, Bernard, for the slightly superior grade
of "B."

This would have meant that they occupied different classrooms all the way up the school, and it was a prospect not to be thought of by the Inseparables.

Unlike each other in physical appearance, the twins were also unmatched in mental ability. Bernard was average. He would never be brilliant, but was capable, if he exerted himself, of moving steadily up the school to the Certificate Fifth. It was equally clear that Boxer, without vigorous help, would eddy about in the lower forms until school-leaving age, and by the time he lumbered into 4C would be surrounded by boys two, or even three years his junior.

Boxer excelled at every activity outside the classroom. He was a member of the First Football Eleven by the time he was fourteen, and his successes in athletics ensured his popularity from the moment he ran his first circuit of the playing-field. He could swim, shoot, box, sprint, kick far and straight, throw a ball half as far again as any boy in Middle School, and shin up the gymnasium ropes in two seconds under the bogey set by the games master, Mr. Trevlow. He was a great favourite of Trevlow's, and a considerable asset to the school in all competitive contests. Perhaps it was on account of his usefulness as an athlete that Mr. Silverton tolerated the alliance for so long, but this was something Esme was never able to discover.

The bargain between Esme and the twins was mooted on their way to the main road that last day of term. They took the same way to the 'bus stop in the Cherry Orchard Road. On the way down the Embankment Road, Esme addressed Bernard.

"3-B for you and me next term, Carver Two!"

The twins were always known as "Carver One" and "Carver Two". Nobody was encouraged to use the term of address they invariably employed for one another—Berni and Boxer.

Apparently, Esme's innocent remark had unwittingly touched a hidden spring in Bernard's mind. He stopped short, and turned to Esme. There was desperation in his frown.

"They're going to split us up, young Fraser. Boxer's going to 3-C. I saw the list."

Esme, who had lived next door to the twins for years, was no stranger to their mutual devotion, but even he was mildly surprised by the urgency in Bernard's voice, and the matching gloom in Boxer's genial features. He saw a chance to move in, and took it on the instant. He needed friends, powerful friends like these two, and it occurred to him at once that they would regard any help he gave them now as an immeasurable service, never to be forgotten. He was a shrewd, observant boy, at once more mature and more child-like than the Carver twins.

"If we got together we could *stay* together," he said, very deliberately.

Bernard made a gesture of irritation. "I tell you I've seen the list! I looked in Snowball's register, when he was called out yesterday. Boxer's in 'C', and you and me are in 'B'."

"I dare say," said Esme, with elaborate nonchalance, "but we don't have to *stay* in 'B', do we? Look at Brett-Thomas. He went into 'B' straight off, and they put him down again, soon as he failed the start-of-term test. We don't *have* to pass it, do we? We don't even have to try. There's harder work in 'B', and you can't muck about with 'Sarky'. He sends you to 'Longjohn' for the slightest thing. If you fail the first test they put you down again, like Brett-Thomas."

Bernard's face cleared, but only for a moment.

"We *could* do that once," he objected, "but it'd be the same again next term—we couldn't keep on doing it."

"We wouldn't have to," said Esme, "not if we got into 3-C and sat near Carver One, and that's easy enough, as long as your brother bashes anyone who tries to bag the seats next to the hot-water pipes."

Boxer had taken no part in this conversation. Most of it was too involved for him. He plodded along beside them, idly twirling his satchel at the full extent of its strap. Now he spoke.

"I could do that. You just leave the bashing to me. We could sit one behind the other along the pipes, then you could whisper and pass notes. Old Chesty, him who takes 3-C, is half-blind anyway." He swung his satchel like a flail. "I'd like to *see* anyone who stopped us getting those seats! I'd just like to *see* 'em!"

Bernard could hardly keep the excitement out of his voice.

"We could do that, young Fraser, I reckon we could do that; but there's home-work. You get written subjects in 3-C,

and how are we going to help Boxer do *written* home-
work?"

Esme was now enjoying himself. He always enjoyed a
Machiavellian role.

"We live next door to one another, don't we? I'll do his
home-work, and he can copy it all out."

And so it was arranged, and it amazed all three of them
how smoothly it worked, right from the beginning.

Bernard and Esme remained in 3-B for less than a week.
Their test-papers, turned in that first Saturday morning were
so badly written, and so full of howlers, that Mr. Dodge—
whose classroom irony had earned him the name of "Sarky"
—was thankful to recommend their abrupt transfer to 3-C,
where Boxer, already undisputed king of the Lower School,
had no difficulty at all in persuading the two boys occupying
the desks immediately behind him to abdicate in favour of
Esme and Bernard.

They perfected their system throughout that first term, and
by the end of the year it was very nearly foolproof. It was a
simple but effective technique. Whenever Boxer was stumped
by a question he simply leaned back, and waited for Esme's
cautious prompt from the desk immediately behind. "Chesty",
the form-master, who took them for several subjects, was
indeed short-sighted, and Esme soon acquired the prison
knack of lipless conversation. In a very little while Boxer's
ear became attuned to the pitch of Esme's controlled whisper
and a stream of carefully sifted information moved up from
his rear, like steady reinforcements trickling into a belea-
guered saphead. . . . *Edward the First, Conjunction, The Ten
Commandments, le Cahier, fifty-seven, ten per cent, Joan of
Arc, adjectival Clause* . . . day after day, week after week,
the steady drip went on, until Boxer himself stood in more
danger of moving into the "B" stream than either of his
supporters.

"Chesty", a benign, elderly man, was delighted. Boxer had
been represented to him as a particularly stupid boy. He had
obviously been maligned. He could only conclude that the
boy had never been taught properly. Parker, of Form 2B,
was notoriously impatient with what some teachers called the
"garden-roller type"—the boy who needed a very strong push

to start him off, but who afterwards went rolling forward under his own momentum. "Chesty" even went out of his way to tell Parker as much, during an acrimonious coffee-break discussion in the masters' common-room.

The whispering served equally well for oral and class tests, but the written home-work called for more delicate handling. Esme enjoyed writing essays, and it was no hardship to him to write two compositions a week. The first time he wrote Boxer's essay, however, he was alarmed, and not a little annoyed, to discover that Boxer's work had earned him nine out of ten, while the author had collected a mere seven. Moreover, "Chesty" read Boxer's effort out loud, as an example of how promising an exercise it was, and it galled Esme to be in no position to claim the credit. He went into conference with Bernard on the subject.

"He'll smell a rat if I go on doing that, Carver Two! I'll have to make some spelling mistakes, and keep your brother down to about six or seven."

Bernard agreed, and thereafter Boxer's work dropped off a little, not suddenly, but week by week, until it hovered about the average of six or seven. Esme also made a point of writing his own essay first, when he was fresh.

Outside the classroom Boxer took command. On the sports-field the other two acted as his trainer and second. They could be seen, almost any half-day, patting Boxer's huge calves, lacing his boots, holding his sweater, and giving him little pieces of advice, for all the world as though Boxer was a professional, and they each owned a piece of him.

In the field of mischief, carefully-prepared mischief, the balance of power shifted back to Esme, although the actual commission of a crime was generally assigned to Boxer. Thus it was Boxer who actually lit, and concealed, the cones of pungent-smelling French incense, that Esme purchased from Woolworth's and brought into class, Boxer who actually dropped the stink-bomb into the crevice between the master's dais and the wall, Boxer who gulped down a half-pint of ginger-beer that had been poured by Esme into a well-scoured sulphuric acid bottle on the laboratory shelves. It was this latter incident that caused Mr. Sisley, a young and pitifully earnest chemistry master, to faint on the spot, and later abandon teaching for a snug roost as a manufacturing chemist, at Uxbridge.

Word of these incidents reached Mr. Silverton from time to time, and occasionally he administered justice on the taut trousers of the chief offenders. He hit hard, and accurately, but without malice. On no occasion, when they were sent in to him for punishment, did he comment on the cause of their being there. He caned them absent-mindedly, as though he was filling in a form, or putting coal on the fire, and the twins loved him for his silences. They were broadminded boys, and regarded Longjohn's cane as his legitimate means of defence against them, but they resented lectures and pi-jaw, for such talk embarrassed them.

Esme sometimes wondered at the Head's silences on these occasions. It passed through his mind that there was something sinister about them, and it sometimes seemed to him that Longjohn laid into him with a vigour, and a purposefulness, that were lacking in his address to the twins. It was not until the faintly ridiculous "Miss Reid row", however, that he was fully confirmed in his suspicions, indeed, it was not until that incident had been cleared up that he came to know Longjohn at all.

Up to that time Longjohn had never been a human being, just "The Head"—to whose study one went for a hiding, a lean, scarred man in a neat grey suit, who read prayers at assembly, and was occasionally seen wandering about the corridors.

The "Miss Reid affair" was rather more than a classroom frolic. Miss Reid was the headmistress of the Girls' Grammar School, housed in adjacent buildings, and separated from the boys' school by an eight-foot brick wall, surmounted by embedded glass and three strands of barbed wire.

Miss Reid distrusted men and loathed boys. For years she had carried on a guerilla war against the boys' school, claiming the use of the communal playing-field at short notice, insisting that the boys' time of dismissal should be put back to 4.30, in order to give the girls time to get clear, and discourage association—pinpricks inflicted by a steady stream of memos, recommendations, and suggestions, aimed at segregation, that sometimes caused Mr. Silverton's cheeks to twitch with maddening persistence. The feud between the two staffs was common knowledge among the rank and file of both schools, and the pupils naturally did all they could to exacerbate the situation. One of the boys' counterattacks was their time-honoured method of reclaiming lost balls.

Miss Reid's precise instructions regarding the reclamation of balls that went over the wall were carried out with ironic punctiliousness. Almost every day a boy wearing an expression about half-way between meekness and idiocy would present himself at Miss Reid's study, touch his cap, and ask for permission to reclaim a ball.

There came a day, however, when a football, driven hard and high by the size-nine boot of Boxer Carver, soared over the wall, and bounced on to the roof of the girls' toilets, rolling thence into the gutter, and remaining wedged there.

Impatient for the continuance of the game Boxer waived the customary procedure.

"Aw—give me a hunk up, Berni, and I'll get it without going round."

In the event it was the lighter Bernard who retrieved it, after first climbing on Boxer's shoulders, and then on Esme's. He threw down the ball, and was preparing to scramble back to the wall when Miss Reid herself emerged from the washroom, immediately below. Seeing a boy climbing nimbly over the lavatory roof towards the dividing wall, she squealed with rage.

"Name, boy! Name!" she shouted, spreading her arms in order to prevent girls behind her from emerging into the open.

Bernard, who seldom made a joke, decided to make one now.

"I'm Dan, Dan, the Lavatory Man!" he replied, very pleasantly, and leaping on to the wall, rejoined his brother and Esme in the boys' yard.

He found Boxer, who had overheard the quip, almost hysterical with laughter. Unable to resist an active part in such a gallant demonstration, he ran along to a buttress, clawed his way to the top of the wall, thrust his head between the strands of wire, and shouted: "And I'm his twin-brother, mother!"

Miss Reid came round before afternoon assembly, and the trio owned up before the inevitable identity parade could be organised.

"I demand that the boys be expelled," said Miss Reid, as the Head escorted her into the vestibule; "this is intolerable— quite intolerable!"

"Indeed, it is," was all Mr. Silverton would reply, "and you may rely upon me to deal with it at once, Miss Reid. Thank you for reporting the matter."

Deal with it he did, that same afternoon, and at first Esme had no reason to suppose his method would differ from that employed on previous occasions. He caned the twins first, and dismissed them, breathing hard, and clutching fistfuls of buttock, into the hall, where they were told to remain until supplied with a quire of paper on which to write: *"Ribald remarks seldom fall into the category of humour,"* one thousand times.

"And if I detect the work of sympathisers on any of the pages handed in, you can assure them in advance that they'll write their own lines standing up!" was Longjohn's parting shot.

Esme stood by. He had taken no actual part in the incident, and was already beginning to regret the impulse of quixotic loyalty that had prompted him to join the twins in confession. A dabbing like that! *AND* a thousand lines!

But Longjohn only tossed his cane into a cupboard, and Esme noticed that his cheek was twitching more violently than ever.

"Sit down, Fraser," he said shortly; "it's time you and I had our first intelligent conversation. How old are you now?"

Esme sat, relieved, but uncertain.

"Fifteen, sir," he said, and suddenly realised that he was blushing.

Longjohn took out a pipe and slowly stuffed its bowl.

"Fifteen," he mused, and his face ceased to twitch. *"When* were you fifteen?"

"In February, sir."

Longjohn finished filling his pipe. There was a long silence, during which Esme could hear his heart-beats very distinctly. Presently Longjohn said:

"I've known all about your arrangements with the Carvers for some time past, Fraser. I tell you this straight away so that we can start on open ground. What I *am* anxious to know is how long do you intend to keep it up? Until you leave? Until you've failed School Cert., and thrown away every opportunity you ever had of learning *how* to learn?"

Esme shuffled his feet. He discovered, to his secret chagrin, that he was unable to meet Longjohn's eye. The man's friendliness and reasonableness were agonising. He wished now with all his heart that the Head would reach for his cane and give him the same ration as he had dealt out to the twins. Then he realised that this was all part of Longjohn's treatment. He was deliberately setting out to make him feel small, and mean, and cheap.

"They're my friends," was all he could mumble.

Longjohn lit his pipe, and blew out a cloud of acrid smoke.

"I don't think they are—not really, Fraser," he said. "They have each other, and I don't think you have ever really belonged there, have you?"

Esme felt sick. He saw Longjohn through a haze of smoke, and scalding tears that would not be held back. Then, quite suddenly, the Head was standing beside him, and smiling down at him.

"This had to come, Fraser. You know that, I believe. You see, Fraser, old chap, you have to look at this my way, and Carver One's way: You haven't done him much of a good turn—not really. He would never have learned much, one way or the other, but what you and his brother have done is to take away what little chance he ever had of learning. That's what your sort of cribbing is—a steady knocking-away of footholds from the chap you think you're helping. It's been going on for hundreds of years, and it's always disguised as comradeship. All his life now Carver One will have to rely on somebody else. That isn't your fault, not in the main, and it is difficult to blame his brother either, but it's still a fact, and not a very pleasant one, is it?"

"No, sir," Esme managed, hoarsely; and then, more in an effort to convince himself than any hope of convincing the Head: "They're . . . they're decent chaps, sir."

Longjohn moved away, and stared out of the tall window. The asphalt yard, on which the window looked, was wide and empty. Every boy in the school was in class, all except the twins, slowly massaging their behinds in the hall, and Esme, here in the study, facing the second big crisis in his life.

Longjohn gave the boy a moment or two to collect himself. Then he went on: "It's like this, Fraser, the chaps here fall mainly into two streams, those who are going to have to earn a living with their hands—and I include among those all the fellows who will go out of here into offices, and banks, and shops—and the chaps who are able to *create* something out of themselves, chaps who can do something without big organisations, and lots of apparatus behind them. You're one of that minority. You might not know it yourself yet, but you are, most definitely. In other words, you've got a spark, and all the time you've been here you've been doing your best to stamp it out. Do you follow me?"

"Yes, sir," said Esme, almost inaudibly.

"You've been tagging along with the Carvers because you were scared of being lonely. People like you—and like me, for that matter—will always be lonely, but being lonely is a dam' sight better than playing second-fiddle to people mentally inferior to you, isn't it? You'll find that out in due course. It's part of my job to see that you find it out as soon as possible, soon enough to do something about it. I'm going to put you into 5A. You'll start in there now, this afternoon. But I don't want you to leave here with the impression that I'm doing this solely because I want you to swot, and stuff your head with all the facts and figures you will find in your text-books. That isn't education—the stuffiest intelligence can absorb facts and figures at your age, and still spend a working life cooped up in an artificially-lit concrete box. I want you to do something better than that. I want you to learn *how* to learn, how to select *what* to remember, and what to discard. A mind is much like a body, Fraser. It's got to be trained, and flexed, and kept in condition. You're fond of English and History, aren't you?"

"Yes, sir," said Esme again.

It was all he could think of to say. His mind was in a

ferment, his throat was parched, and in his heart was a strange surge of love and of gratitude for this spare, ravaged man, who spoke to him as if they were equals, as if they had been through the fire together. He knew of the Head's war record and fleetingly Esme thought of his father, and wondered vaguely if their paths had ever crossed in battle.

As if reading his thoughts, Longjohn said:

"Your father was killed in the war, wasn't he?"

"Yes, sir, on the Marne, in 1914. He ... he was an officer, sir."

As he said it Esme felt pride quickening within him. He did not think of his father often nowadays, but it was good to feel that he and Longjohn had once stood up to a common enemy, on common ground.

"Then you never knew him at all?"

"No, sir; my mother married again."

The headmaster remained by the window a moment longer. Then he moved over to the large roll-topped desk that occupied an alcove, and foraged in the centre drawer, taking out a file bulging with clipped, foolscap sheets. Esme instantly recognised them as written examination papers. Longjohn thumbed through them until he found what he sought, a few sheets, covered with Esme's cramped writing.

"You'll be wondering how I know so much about you, Fraser," he said, with one of his swift, schoolboy grins. "Well, here it is, an essay you wrote more than a year ago. Do you remember it?"

Esme remembered it very well. It was a terminal composition exercise, four pages on *"Books I enjoyed"*. He remembered how much he had enjoyed writing that paper, how he had dipped into the memory of the hours and hours of happiness he had extracted from Stevenson, Twain, and Henty. The paper had occupied him ninety minutes that had passed like five.

"I dare say there's hardly one of us who doesn't imagine he can write at your age, Fraser," pursued Longjohn. "Hardly any of us can, of course. We mistake tricks of memory for genuine inspiration. But there's a sentence here ... where is it ... listen ... right at the end:

"The books I liked, I think, are the books that people liked writing. You can tell this somehow. It's like humming a tune, that sticks in your mind. You know that what they are writing about was in their minds a long time before it was written down."

That's the spark I told you about, Esme. Stop treading on it and try blowing on it for a change!"

Esme was dumb with the wonder of it, that a man like Longjohn, until fifteen minutes ago immeasurably remote, should have sat in his holy-of-holies, reading an examination paper written by a boy in 3-C, and then, having read it, filed it away, in a place where he could lay instant hands upon it. It seemed to him, both then and later, the greatest compliment that had ever been paid to him.

He said, "I'd ... I'd ... like to write, sir. I'm not much good at anything else."

Longjohn looked at him steadily, puffing away at his pipe and filling the space between them with smoke so acrid that Esme's eyes smarted.

"You'll write, Fraser," he said; "nothing I could say would ever stop you. You'll write, and write, and write. You'll collect hundreds of rejection slips, but that shouldn't worry you. You'll have had your fun, writing. And I haven't the slightest doubt but that you'll arrive with drums in the end. If you want any blue-pencilling, either now or when you've left here, keep in touch. I'm a professional blue-penciller!"

He stood up, signifying that the strange interview was over.

Esme hesitated near the door.

"You'd better get your things, and bring them back here," said Longjohn; "I'll take you along to Mr. Setchell right away."

Esme still hesitated.

"That thousand lines," he stammered finally, "it's ... it's ... not fair the twins should have that, sir. I ... I was with them, I gave Carver One the bunk up."

"You've got a point there," said Longjohn; "we'll make it fifteen hundred—five hundred apiece. When shall we say? By Monday?"

"Thank you, sir," said Esme, and hurried out into the hall, without closing the door.

Boxer and Bernard were still standing under the clock, and Bernard turned expectantly towards him as he crossed the hall to Middle School corridor.

Esme winked twice and then, without a word, moved on towards the classrooms.

CHAPTER XV

The Ice Cracks At Number Seventeen

1

SOMETIMES more than a decade would pass without anything out of the ordinary occurring inside certain of the houses to break the rhythm of passing years.

Such a house was Number Seventeen, where the four Friths had lived since before the war. It was a very silent house, and its front door, or the back gate that led into the Manor Meadow cart-track that was the sole break in the crescent, were only opened and closed at specified times, when one or other of the family entered or left the house for a specific reason—to go to work, to go shopping, to attend chapel. Even on these occasions their neighbours did not address them and observed, moreover, that members of the family seldom addressed one another.

Then, one October evening in 1928, Number Seventeen erupted. Lights flashed on and off in windows over which the curtains had yet to be drawn for the night. Mr. Frith dived from the front door, ran down to use the telephone kiosk in Shirley Rise, and was back again only minutes ahead of the doctor's car. Later an ambulance called, and after more scurrying about somebody was carried out, but it was too dark to see who was on the stretcher, and who was bobbing about round the porch. The even numbers opposite, and Mrs. Crispin, of Number Fifteen next door, sat up and took notice then, but the ambulance had moved off, and the front door had closed, before somebody plucked up enough courage to make enquiries. Then the Avenue learned that Mrs. Frith had been whisked off to Croydon Hospital with acute appendicitis, and was said to be in a very bad way indeed. From that moment, the veil that had shrouded Number Seventeen for so long was lifted, and although it soon dropped again, there was always a chink in it wide enough for such of the Avenue who were interested to peep through, and guess at what was going on inside.

Very little worth recording had in fact occurred at Number Seventeen since the Friths first came to live there. The house was always dark at 10 p.m., and its inhabitants were only seen as a family when they issued from the front door at 10.30 a.m. each Sunday, and walked, two by two, to the corner of Shirley Rise, and down the hill towards their Chapel.

Edgar Frith, the little man whom Jim Carver thought to look so much like the late Dr. Crippen, always emerged at 8.20 sharp each week-day morning, and boarded the Tilling 'bus for his antique shop, in the Cherry Orchard Road. Occasionally—about once a month—he caught the 8.40 from Woodside for the City.

Esther Frith, his wife, tall, slender, and utterly unbending, emerged to do her shopping in the Lower Road, mid-mornings. She spoke to no one, either en route, or at the counters.

There were, however, one or two small, outward changes over the years.

Elaine Frith, now a shapely girl of sixteen, with masses of dark hair, plaited into decorous "wireless coils", instead of its being shingled, like that of all the other girls in the Avenue, no longer walked to and from school with an attaché case, but went instead to a Commercial College, in East Croydon, five days each week.

Sydney, the boy, was still at school, but he stayed on at an Addiscombe private establishment, and wore a cap with an orange ribbon round it, instead of the dark blue and silver, worn by all the Grammar School boys in the suburb.

Sydney was seen about the most. He had inherited his father's undistinguished looks and, to some degree, his father's poor physique. His front teeth protruded, and his complexion was pale, without the waxy pallor that made his mother's and sister's complexions assets. Sydney's complexion was poor. At fourteen he was much troubled with pimples and, because his front teeth were large, and unevenly spaced, his mouth was usually slightly agape, revealing a moist, lower lip. His legs were thin, and his knees prominent. He still walked with a slight, furtive stoop, and his head, over-big for his body, was never still, but weaved this way and that on a long neck, as though searching out hidden assailants. He was not popular at school, and led a rather solitary life. He was known to weep very easily and, if sufficiently goaded, to flout the sacred canon of every British schoolboy by marching boldly up to the nearest authority and reporting his persecutors by name, delivering his complaint in a flat, non-accusative voice, like a bored bailiff serving a writ.

He had, of course, been bumped, and pelted, ostracised, and even thrashed for this unheard-of breach of juvenile etiquette, but there was within him a tough streak of obstinacy, and he persisted, with the result that authority usually felt obliged to institute half-hearted reprisals.

He was a clever boy, and exceptionally bright in all branches of mathematics, but there was something about the promptness with which he answered questions, and the meticulous neatness of his written work, that disturbed his teachers, and made them cautious in their dealings with him. His quiet arrogance was a bubble that no one was able to prick, and the fact that he was very seldom in trouble with those in authority never quite convinced them that this was due to a law-abiding disposition, but left them with an unhappy conviction that Sydney had yet to be caught out.

In due course, and solely on account of his age, he became head boy at the school, and from then on his complaints, once classified as sneaking, had to be recognised as evidence of zeal in an overseer. As he grew older he began to display more and more confidence in himself, and the somewhat seedy staff at the private school he attended found themselves, without quite knowing why, delegating more and more authority to him, until at length he was in possession of more real power than anyone excepting the Headmaster, who was principal shareholder of the establishment.

Sydney enjoyed himself during his last year at school. His one regret was that he was not allowed to beat smaller boys, and had to remain content with getting them beaten, the more the merrier, and as often as possible. Everybody, including, it must be admitted, the Headmaster, was very relieved when he finally left, to take up a trainee's post in an accountant's office, in Norwood.

At home he had, to a limited extent, picked up the reins of authority abandoned by his father when Sydney was still a child and throughout his teens Esther leaned heavily upon him in matters of business and finance. He completely ignored his father, and was barely civil to Esther. His sister he hectored until one day, in a cold, pitiless fury, she plunged a pair of scissors into his forearm. After that he went out of his way to avoid her, and so helped to increase—if that were possible—the stealthy, almost macabre atmosphere of the house, a house in which meals were often eaten without a word being exchanged, and whole evenings sometimes passed without any remark being offered by anyone, except, maybe, an odd word or two between Sydney and Esther, concerning insurance, or the price of household goods and groceries.

Sydney worked out tables for all this sort of thing, and was able to save Esther a good deal of money over the years, simply by proving that some articles could be bought cheaper at Gudgeon's, in the Lower Road, than at Piretta's, across the way. Esther nursed a secret pride in Sydney's ability to add up columns of figures in his head and translate the latest stock-market prices from the evening paper. There was no real affection between them, but at least there was mutual trust, and their alliance shut out Elaine and Edgar, throwing each of them back upon their own limited resources.

Edgar spent practically all his waking hours at home in his greenhouse at the bottom of the garden. Here he raised a wide variety of indoor plants that must have given him, vicariously, some of the colour and variety so lacking in his everyday life. When it was too dark to work in the green-house there was always his stamp collection, now worth, according to his careful reckoning, at least £500, exclusive of the Mauritius set, worth at least another £100.

Between his stamps and his greenhouse, Edgar was able to efface himself completely from the family circle. He was nearing the fifty mark now, and hungered for nothing, except money to instal a small, central-heating plant in his green-house. This, he felt, he would achieve in time, for he had never told Esther about his last rise in salary, a rise given him by his employer, Mr. Chaffery, when they opened their new branch at Purley.

Edgar's resignation to this mockery of his home-life may well have had something to do with Mr. Chaffery. Chaffery was a huge, amiable extrovert, who had made a great deal of money in post-war property and antique deals. He was a lively and astute business-man, but shop life bored him. He had to be up and about, dodging in and out of sales, sizing up derelict property, ruminating on the possible financial gain to be derived from corner sites, making a pound or two here, a hundred or two there, talking to people, cozening old ladies, and jocularly abusing other dealers; in short, playing a very positive part in life. Nevertheless, he was obliged, by reason of his business, to have a permanent base, and Edgar had proved himself an excellent executive over the last fifteen years. Chaffery recognised him as a good judge of current values, a stonewaller with dealers on the make, and a scrupu-lously honest handler of cash. He therefore treated him well, paid him adequately, and reposed considerable trust in him.

When the new shop was opened at Purley, Edgar's business routine was slightly altered. On the instructions of Chaffery he was now obliged to leave the Cherry Orchard Road shop in charge of the full-time cabinet-maker for three afternoons a week, and take a short 'bus-ride over to Purley, in order to "see how Frances was getting on".

Miss Frances Hopkins, the new assistant, was a shy little woman, of thirty or thereabouts, with pale gold hair, a slightly receding chin, and a self-effacing manner that somehow im-pressed customers with the genuineness of the article she was trying to sell them. Chaffery, a shrewd judge of character, had selected her for this very reason, for she was what he liked to call "genteel" and, as he pointed out to Edgar the first day they installed her, "nothing shifts a doubtful bit like a touch of gentility on our side of the counter!"

"It's like this, old man," he elaborated, for he enjoyed teasing and sometimes shocking the solemn Edgar; "the person who comes in for Queen Anne doesn't want it dished up by someone who looks as though he ought to be flogging a hire-purchase suite! The trouble with our trade is that ninety-per-cent of The Boys (Chaffery invariably referred to his colleagues in the antique trade as "The Boys") overdo the *gen-u-ine* touch, and make a customer suspicious the minute he comes inside. No wonder, either! To hear some of 'em you'd think they were flogging the crown jewels in a scrap-metal yard. Now take Miss Hopkins—she couldn't pull a fast one on a customer if her virginity depended on it! Her family's had money sometime—look at her hands and feet—and she grew up with the stuff all round her. What's more, she loves it, not like you and I do, because our beer money depends on it, but because of its line, and feel. She'll do okay there. All she needs is someone like you to put her wise to The Boys. Look in Thursday to Saturday, no matter where I am, or what I'm up to. Catch on?"

Edgar entered into the new arrangements with misgivings. After all, Esther had been "genteel" and, on this very account appeared to have despised him from the day they were married. Edgar had never had much confidence in himself, but what little he had originally possessed had dissolved under Esther's acid. Accordingly, he approached Miss Hopkins very gingerly, expecting rebuffs, and saying as little as possible. Scarcely a week had elapsed, however, before he began to enjoy her company, finding in it a balm to his self-esteem that was very pleasant; before long, the prospect of spending a few hours with her came to be something to anticipate with mild excitement throughout the first half of the week.

Miss Hopkins' desire to please had, at the outset, very little to do with Edgar. She had, at long last, found a job that interested her, and she looked upon her immediate superior as a man from whom she could learn the trade in the process of earning a living wage. His gentlemanly bearing towards her came as a mild surprise. She would not have been surprised if, in due course, she had not been faced with the choice of being petted in the room behind the shop, or seeking a job elsewhere.

Nothing like this happened. On the contrary, Mr. Frith, her employer's chief assistant, appeared to derive considerable pleasure from teaching her the trade, a duty he took very seriously indeed, and after a time, particularly when, on slack afternoons, they sat before the gas-fire sipping the tea she had made for them, a mellowness stole into their relationshp. Once their mutual shyness had been overcome he reminisced by the hour on china, silver, and the ways of distinguishing the "genuine untouched" from the made-up, or the fake.

Frances Hopkins was a good listener, and on his own subjects—china, English glass, foreign stamps, and indoor plants—Edgar Frith was an interesting talker. As the weeks went by Edgar's personality began to flower under her attentive smile, so that even when they were apart Edgar found himself humming little tunes on his way to and from Purley, and later still indulging in ridiculous little daydreams, in which he rescued Miss Hopkins from the clutches of an amorous dealer, young Mr. Isaacs perhaps, who always looked at young women as though he were mentally undressing them, and he probably was, if Chaffery's stories about Isaacs were only half-true.

For a long time their friendship remained placid, right up to the time when Esther had to go into hospital, in order to have her appendix removed, and Elaine began staying out at night, and Sydney left school, and found himself that job in the City. Then the whole frostiness of Edgar's life began to melt under the sun of Miss Hopkins' shy smile and Edgar discovered that, notwithstanding his middle-age, he did hunger for something more than a central-heating plant for the greenhouse. He was obliged to admit to himself that he was starved of warmth, and friendship, and sympathy, that he needed somebody who thought of him as something more than a silent machine, grinding out money year after year, for rates, housekeeping, and children's education. He wanted the inexpressible joy of *being* wanted, needed, petted and even considered once in a while.

2

The ice cracked half-way through the silent supper at Number Seventeen one October evening.

The four of them were sitting round the table, picking at cold tongue and pickles, when Esther half rose up, pressed her hand to her side, and gave a little scream.

Edgar was so taken aback that he sat stock still, while Sydney ran round to her, and caught her by the shoulders, half-carrying her away from the table, and settling her on the leather couch beside the tiny banked-up fire.

"It's here, *here!*" Esther kept repeating, and when the doctor was fetched, much against her will, he at once diagnosed acute appendicitis, and arranged for Esther to go into hospital that very night.

Ordinarily Esther would have opposed this with every argument at her command, but by the time arrangements were made the pain prevented her from thinking clearly. She only mumbled a few protests when the ambulance arrived, and then closed her eyes, and allowed herself to be carried out on a stretcher, and down the short path to the waiting vehicle.

Edith Clegg and Louise Carver saw her go, and both ran across the road with offers of neighbourly assistance. Edgar received them politely, but told them that he and the children were perfectly capable of looking after themselves, and that once the operation was over, Mrs. Frith was unlikely to be detained more than a fortnight or so.

In the event Esther was in hospital for six weeks, and in that period the dry fabric of the Frith household fell to pieces. For a few days she hovered between life and death, but at length her tough physique pulled her through, and she sat propped up in the ward, saying very little, but effectually silencing the garrulous woman on her right, who was much disposed to go into details about her own complaint, and those of her deceased sisters and husband.

Edgar and Sydney went to see her on visiting days, but Elaine could not be persuaded to take an afternoon off from her commercial course, in order to travel over to the hospital; neither would she take advantage of the week-end visiting periods, or send her mother any message.

Elaine's callousness regarding her mother shocked Sydney. He could not know that there was not, and never would be, the faintest trace of hypocrisy in Elaine's personality, and that she would never, throughout her life, lie to herself on the smallest issue. Neither did he realise that, to Elaine, her mother's removal was like the sudden and unexpected dismissal of an inexorable gaoler, and that having once tested freedom, she resolved to herself that never again, not if she had to fight with her nails and teeth, would she allow herself to be herded back to the cloister on her mother's return.

Esther's absence had a somewhat similar effect upon Edgàr. He was not, like Sydney, shocked by Elaine's unashamed delight at her mother's absence. Dimly he understood Elaine's relief, for—in a sense—he shared it. As long as Esther was about the house he had found it disconcerting to indulge in day-dreams about Miss Hopkins. Such day-dreams seemed to him a kind of infidelity, for despite Esther's treatment of him as a husband, he had never contemplated leaving her. He had nothing but an instinctive affection for his children, and none at all for his wife, but he was a very conscientious little man, ready to accept his responsibilities, however irksome they proved. So far he had never thought far enough ahead to envisage a time when Elaine and Sydney would cease to be his responsibility, and he supposed that Esther would always be there, waiting for the housekeeping money, and attending to his frugal needs in all respects but one. Now that she was no longer there his mind began to range on what he might do if—by some chance—Esther should die, and he was astonished to discover in himself an upsurge of guilty hope that at once related itself to Miss Hopkins.

Miss Hopkins—Frances, he now called her—was single. She had no admirer that he was aware of, and clearly did not regard him with disfavour. She was, moreover, quite alone in the world, her parents having died several years before, leaving her a minute income, quite insufficient to maintain her on more than a subsistence scale.

Suppose Esther should die? Suppose he suddenly found himself free? Would he propose to Miss Hopkins? Would she accept him? And if she did, could they not leave Mr. Chaffery, and drift into Arcady hand-in-hand, somewhere in the country or by the sea, or in one of those little cathedral towns in the West, where there were said to be openings for little antique businesses?

Once launched on this flight his fancy soared upwards like a bird, and presently he found it difficult to fix his mind upon anything else. So abstracted did he become that he let young Isaacs have a Regency commode for less than cost, and incurred Mr. Chaffery's storm of abuse, shamefully administered in front of Miss Hopkins, who gallantly tried to share the blame.

When Chaffery had simmered down and departed, Miss Hopkins at once set about soothing his wounded pride.

"I knew you were worried, Mr. Frith; I knew you were thinking about your wife. He wasn't fair! He was cruel! Let me get you some tea, and some of those nice croissants. Sit down by the fire, and forget all about it! Take two of my aspirins. I think he was horrid! . . . horrid!"

He smiled at her gratefully, and allowed himself to be led to the fireside. As she bent over the hob he noticed, not for the first time, the tiny cluster of curls that strayed, almost playfully, across the nape of her neck. He leaned forward as she poured from the kettle, and suddenly, monstrously, his mind shied away from the turmoil of Esther, and Chaffery, and Isaac's sharp practice, and his hopeless infatuation. He sat quite still, staring and staring at the red-gold tendrils, caught in a shaft of pale sunlight that streamed through the fanlight over the shop door.

She had slipped forward on her knees, and was in the act of laying out the tin tray, when he acted. Hardly knowing what he was doing, but impelled by some force he was powerless to resist, he reached out his right hand, and began to stroke the tendrils with two fingers.

She stopped laying out the tray and remained quite still. Unbelievably she did not recoil from his touch, or exclaim, as he had thought she would when, in his day-dreams, he had half-imagined such a beginning. She seemed, if anything, to draw a little closer to him, and he experienced wonder and incredulity, before a possessive delight surged over him like a giant wave, and he flung his arms round her thin shoulders, and pressed her close against him, showering breathless little kisses on her hair, and ears, and hands.

After the first few moments of ecstasy he released her, and she stood up, but even then she did not move away from the fire. He did not release her hand, and she made no effort to withdraw it. Slowly raising his eyes, he noticed that she was crying, gently and silently, and at the sight of her tears he scrambled to his feet, tenderness almost choking him. He caught her by the waist, pulling her away from the scorching heat of the fire.

"Frances, you mustn't. . . . It isn't like you think. . . . I love you . . . I'll do anything for you . . . anything . . . I love you so much Frances. . . ."

The words came effortlessly, just as they had in his day-dreams, tumbling out half articulately, and no woman could have doubted their utter sincerity.

She said, very softly, "I know, Edgar, I've known a long time now. I love you, too. I'll always love you."

He was speechless with amazement. It was impossible that somebody like her could love him with anything approaching the fervour he felt for her. Respect him, perhaps, enjoy his company even, but not love—not desire to the extent of wanting to be kissed, and held, and caressed. . . . ! He could make no reply. He could only just stand there, gazing at her as if she had been a goddess who had suddenly materialised from among the unsaleable ornaments and half tea-services.

She must have recognised incredulity in his face.

"It's not so difficult," she said, with a wry smile. "Nobody ever treated me as you have; nobody, ever. Not even Philip."

"Philip?" The name meant nothing to him, but even so, he felt a sharp stab of jealousy.

"He was killed in the war," she said. "I thought I'd never get over it; but you do, Edgar, you can get over anything."

She lifted the tea-tray on to the console table, and began to drop sugar into the cups. He marvelled at her steadiness.

How could she bother with a tray of tea at a moment like this? He had never been drunk, but he imagined that it must feel rather like this, uncertain of one's balance, yet filled with a wild desire to run out into the main road and shout the news at the strangers going by, poor luckless devils, with their shopping baskets and tea-time kippers. He wanted to buy armfuls of roses, to write sonnets, to dance, to do things he had never even thought about doing, not as a boy or a youth. This was so different from how he had felt when Esther had accepted his stammered proposal in the ice-cold library of her aunt's ugly mansion. Then, lost for words, and miserably embarrassed as he was, it had seemed no more momentous than the discussion of a sensible arrangement for the pair of them, a wife for him, a provider for her.

The memory of that other declaration helped to steady him. His mind raced among the possibilities that presented themselves, now that she had made the still barely credible admission that she returned his love. A divorce? A secret arrangement? An elopement, with or without sanction of Church and State? What did it matter? What did anything matter? But he had to learn her views. They had to begin making plans at once.

"I'll speak to Esther as soon as she comes out of hospital. I'll tell her she'll have to divorce me!" he babbled.

She smiled, sadly he thought, and handed him his cup.

"You couldn't do that, Edgar—not in the circumstances; you're far too gentle a person."

The note of resignation in her voice alarmed him. The salient factors in their situation buffeted him like a chain of detonations; Esther's ruthlessness, the children, his own sense of duty, and now Frances's generosity, not only towards him, but towards the woman who had made his life so wretched, and for so long. For a moment he felt trapped. Then his yearnings surged over him, a small tide of optimism.

"You don't *know* about Esther," he said, choosing his words deliberately. "She's ... she's never been a wife to me. There were the children, yes ... it still seems impossible, but it wasn't quite as it is now, not at the very beginning. She ... she'd never have much to do with me even then, but we didn't *live* apart, not at the start. It was only after Sydney came that ..."

His voice trailed away. Somehow, urgent as it was that she should understand, he found it impossible to relate the stark facts. It was like explaining something obscene to a child. The words that needed to be said could not be said, yet there were no substitutes, not if she was to understand in the way she must understand. How could he know that she already understood, that his very helplessness in this direction had contributed, in large measure, to her surrender to him?

She took her tea, placed it on the low stool, and settled down beside him, curling her legs under her, and leaning her delicious weight against his knees. The movement soothed him, and for a moment it was quite still in the room, with no sound save the pleasant song of the gas-fire.

"I think I know what your life has been, Edgar. I think I've known a long time," she began, and then, before he could exclaim, "I *knew* as soon as I met you that you were wretched, and lonely, and despairing, and I suppose I knew that because I was the same way for so long, before I got over it, before I won out by *making* myself get over it."

In his amazement he withdrew into the chair.

"That's impossible," he argued; "you've never even been married. . . ."

"I've had a child," she said, simply. "I've got a daughter. She's nearly ten, now ... Pippa ... I want you to meet and like Pippa."

He was not shocked and horrified, as he might have been, had she told him this astounding fact an hour ago. Now, in the warm glow of their love, he felt only tenderness, and kinship, and a strange, anticipatory excitement at the prospect of looking upon a child that had emerged from her body. It brought her, if that was possible, even closer to him. It hardened his joyful determination to protect her, for ever and ever.

"Was it ... Philip?" he asked.

As he spoke the name another sharp spasm of jealousy pricked him, but the pang was momentary. He went on:

"Were you very much in love with him?"

"At the time, very much, Edgar."

He was grateful for so much honesty. "And he with you?"

She shook her head, with one of her fleeting smiles.

"I don't think so, but that wasn't Pip's fault. You see, I imagine he knew he was going to die. It was a bad time to be a young man, Edgar, but perhaps you remember?"

He remembered very clearly, but not from a personal viewpoint. Quite early in the war, seeking escape, he had been rejected by three medical boards, and the war years to him did not mean shells, and gas, and water-logged ditches, but only ration books, and food queues, and patriotic songs. His most poignant memory of the war was the witnessing of a leave-train departure from Victoria on a foggy November night, in 1917. Almost everyone at the barriers had been drunk, weeping and desolate, chivvied by red-capped military policemen who, working in practised pairs, dragged flushed young men from the arms of wailing, tipsy women. It occurred to him that one of those young men might well have been Pip, the father of Frances's child, perhaps the one who had clung so desperately to the sliding metal frames of the platform entrance, cap askew, roaring out:

When this wicked war is overrrrr
Oh, how happy I shall beeeee ...

Quietly, and without embarrassment, she told him about Pip.

Frances's mother had died when she was a child, and Philip had been a distant cousin, who spent odd leaves at her father's bungalow in Caterham. Her father, himself a retired Army officer, had encouraged the boy, particularly after Pip had been commissioned and decorated. Pip was just the sort of young man an ex-major of the Gunners would prefer his only child to marry, and the Major had pictured for himself, and for Frances, the sort of life they would lead after the war, occupying married quarters on hill-stations in India, and sending their boys home to be educated at Clifton, his old and cherished school.

Up to that time, Frances had had little or no opportunity of meeting young men. She was little more than a child when the war began, and all the eligible young men were carried off, as though by plague. Pip was not much older, but he had matured very quickly, as young men did mature on the Somme, in 1916.

There were one or two country walks, and a quiet embrace or two on the downs, during his first leave; then a spate of letters, long and passionate letters from her, laconic and grubby notes from him, for it was difficult to compose love-letters in a roofless barn, shared with eight other mud-spattered men, when one yearned only for the oblivion of sleep from the cold and the dirt, and the lice, and the long-range shelling, that made up one's day-to-day existence.

They were formally engaged, of course, when he came on his final leave, in March, 1918. It was her nineteenth birthday, and he was one year older. There was a little party in the Caterham bungalow, a bottle of war-time champagne, a cake piped with their initialled hearts, and a good deal of reminiscent speech-making on the part of the Major and his cronies.

Then came the telegram, recalling Pip to the Line, where Ludendorff was punching huge holes round St. Quentin. That night, in the small hours, he had crept into her room, and when she started up, alarmed, he was standing there, mutely, already half a ghost, but a greedy one, greedy for that minute part of life that was left to him and demanding it, wordlessly, but with a pitiful urgency.

She was sure then that he would never return, that there would never be an arch of swords at Caterham Parish Church, a hill-station billet, or sons at public schools, but equally sure that these things were remote, and irrelevant when balanced against his need to be comforted, and the inevitability of the troop-train in the morning. He went off, sombrely enough, after breakfast, and they never heard of him again. He just disappeared into the welter of the German army's advance towards the Channel ports.

Pippa was born during the first Christmas of the Peace, and the shock killed her grandfather. He did not subscribe to the new morality, having been born and reared under a Victorian code. It seemed to him, already enfeebled by a war that had destroyed almost everything, yet denied him an opportunity to serve, that every convention had been violated, the sanctity of woman, the canons of hospitality, the very decencies for which, up to that time, he had supposed they were all fighting.

He took to his bed during the 'flu epidemic, and it was clear from the outset that he would neither recover, nor forgive her. There was a tiny income, and she could have that. She would need it, he supposed, for bread, when all decent doors were closed to her.

Pippa was born in the house of an aunt at Sevenoaks, and when Frances realised that she could not keep the child, and also earn a living, she agreed to her aunt's virtual adoption of Pippa. She herself moved closer to London, spending more than she could afford on week-end trips down to Sevenoaks, too tired, after a fifty-hour week in a bookshop, to compete with her aunt's living-in housekeeper for Pippa's affection.

She lived for a long time in a furnished room near her work, but shortly before answering Mr. Chaffery's advertisement she had made a great effort to pull herself together, and chase the drabness from her life. She began by mortgaging her income to buy a tumbledown cottage at Addington, and the cottage—or rather the absorbing work of restoring it—had given her a new interest in life. It was her search for suitable pieces of furniture that had led her into the junk shops, and stimulated her interest in the trade. She was now determined to become a dealer herself, and regarded her job with Chaffery as a form of apprenticeship.

Edgar listened to her story with close attention, but even as she talked his mind raced ahead, for Frances now filled his life, leaving no room for Esther, the children, his potted hyacinths, or his stamp-collection. Esther would have to divorce him, on any terms, and he would then make over to her and the children as much as he could afford. At some time in the future, he and Frances would move right away, and open their business, but in the meantime they would have to continue as employees of Mr. Chaffery, and their relationship, he decided at once, must remain a close secret from Chaffery, and the other dealers. Edgar had heard Chaffery discuss women, and flushed at the prospect of the sniggers and innuendoes he might expect as soon as Frances was out of earshot.

The important thing, he decided, was to do nothing precipitate, to think out each move well in advance, to sound out Esther, perhaps, to begin saving, to work and work towards the fulfilment of a dream that was delicious to contemplate, a dream of going back over the lost years, and starting all over again. At his time of life this might be difficult but with Frances it was not impossible. Nothing was impossible with a woman who cared, who welcomed his capacity to love, and cherish, and protect. This was the one important factor, and, in the ultimate reckoning, the only one that mattered.

"We ought to begin planning, Frances," he began, "we ought to begin now."

She took his hand, and laid it alongside her cheek.

"Don't let's go into all that, Edgar, not now, not yet . . . it isn't important, really. What is important is that we've found one another. I want you to meet Pippa, and I want you to see the cottage. It isn't very far from you. You could walk there, one evening."

His heart began to beat violently. "Any time, this Saturday . . . it's easy now, while . . ."

He was going to say "while Esther is in hospital" but checked himself just in time. She rescued him, with another of her swift smiles.

"You needn't worry about neighbours," she said. "I haven't any, and I'll cook you a supper. What do you like? What do you like especially?"

He abandoned planning in favour of the novel and delightful experience of having his appetite explored. He told her he liked sweetbreads, and kidneys and all manner of savouries, that he preferred potatoes baked in their jackets, and rarebits, and pasties, and apple-and-blackberry tart. For the moment they discussed only the immediate future. It was enough that they would eat supper together—her supper, in her cottage, and that this was no longer a wildly improbable day-dream, but a glorious, established fact, as real and reliable as a railway time-table!

When it was dusk they locked up, and he escorted her to the 'bus stop, standing to watch the receding vehicle until its tail-light winked out in the autumn dusk.

Then he set out to walk home, swinging the neatly-furled

umbrella he carried as a boy swings a stick at thistles in a country lane.

It was not until he was passing the "Rec" gates in Lucknow Road, that his step began to lose its spring, and his mood the boyish ebullience with which he had set out. For here he was passing into the orbit of the Avenue, and Esther, and without being conscious of it his stride began to shorten, until he found himself hardly moving.

Then he remembered that Esther was not there, but still in the ether-smelling ward of the hospital. Illogically, this did not encourage him, and he began to wonder how long it would be before she came home—how long before he must confront her with the demand for a divorce?

And as he thought this a chill struck him, and he admitted to himself that he did not know Esther, that he had never known her, that she might well be capable of anything, of withholding a divorce, of finding some way to destroy both him and his dream.

The rush of fear stopped him dead. Alone, and without the soft pressure of Frances against his knee, it was not so easy to dismiss Esther, even an Esther tucked away in hospital. He felt a desperate need to confide in someone, someone who was neutral, who had experience of these matters, who could explain what to do, what to say, and what not to say.

He had reached the corner of the Avenue, and was loitering in the shadow of the laburnum that dwarfed the front garden of Number One-Hundred-and-Eight, when a man of about his own age passed, moving briskly down the Avenue towards the shorter even numbers. As the passer-by walked into the shadow of the street lamp, Edgar recognised the neat pin-striped trousers, and level-set Homburg of Mr. Harold Godbeer, of Number Twenty-Two. Harold gave him a sidelong glance, and automatically touched his hat. He was one of the very few people in the Avenue who knew Edgar to speak to, for occasionally, when Edgar had business in town, the two had walked down Shirley Rise together, on their way to catch the 8.40. On one occasion they had even travelled up to London Bridge in the same compartment, so that Harold wondered briefly what Mr. Frith could be doing, standing alone, and uncertainly, beneath the laburnum of

Number One-Hundred-and-Eight, on a chill, autumn evening.

He was within a few yards of his own gate, when he heard trotting steps behind him. Mr. Frith caught him up, and laid a nervous hand on his sleeve.

"I beg your pardon, Mr. Godbeer," he said, a little breathlessly, "but ... but I understand you are a practising solicitor!"

Harold regarded the little man with surprise that was not far from alarm.

"Well, I'm ... er ... I'm managing clerk to a *firm* of solicitors," he said, "Messrs.——"

Before he could announce the name of his firm, Frith interrupted, even more breathlessly.

"I have ... I have a matter of some urgency ... I should be extremely grateful if you could advise me," he said.

Ordinarily Harold would have protested that matters of urgency, once brought to the attention of solicitors' clerks, were not discussed in the light of street-lamps, but something in Frith's anxious eyes, and the tremor in his voice, touched his warm heart and he smiled politely.

"Will you come inside, and drink a cup of tea with me?" he asked. "My wife ..." Harold could never manage to keep the pride out of his voice when he referred to Eunice as his wife—"my wife will have it ready now—but perhaps you're expected home?"

"No, no," said Edgar gratefully. "I'm often late, and my wife is away in hospital ... I should be extremely obliged, extremely so, Mr. Godbeer."

Harold pushed open the primrose gate. It was the only primrose gate in the Avenue. All the others were painted chocolate-brown, slate-grey, or at best, a dull, hedgerow-green. Eunice liked unconventional colours. Under her direction Harold had last winter repainted all the interior woodwork of Number Twenty-Two in lilac, cerise, and what she always called "pastel shades of sweet-pea". It was certainly the most original scheme in the crescent, and one of which Harold was just the tiniest bit ashamed.

He selected a key from a ring heavy with keys, yale keys, watch keys, safe-keys, cash-box keys, and padlock keys of deed-boxes.

"Eunice, my dear," he announced from the narrow hall, "we have a visitor!"

He coughed twice, and tried not to notice Edgar's blink of surprise at the rainbow colours of the banister supports.

CHAPTER XVI

Lady In A Tower

1

ELAINE was the first to win liberation.

The bond between her and her father was undeclared, but it had existed for some years, beginning as a wary, defensive alliance, when Sydney began to grow old enough to influence his mother. It was not a very strong alliance, for Elaine was contemptuous of her father, but on his side there was a measure of sympathy for a young girl, whom he saw as someone cut off from all the normal enjoyments of youth, and driven in upon herself to feed, not on dreams, but on a hatred for Esther that she made little attempt to conceal.

As he watched the girl pass from childhood into her teens, Edgar could not help contrasting her with the daughters of other families in the Avenue, girls who now flaunted their post-war emancipation from the pillions of motor-cycles, who, in their shapeless, tube-like clothes, were beginning to look more and more like the youths who hung about their back gates, who came home with their boys in the small hours, and sometimes kept him awake, exchanging interminable and uninhibited good-night embraces, to the accompaniment of giggles, and scuffles, and, on several occasions, the throb of a ukelele.

Like most of his generation, Edgar was genuinely shocked by the new freedom, but it still seemed to him grossly unfair that Elaine should be the only young girl in the neighbourhood to whom it was not extended. He was not unaware of her contempt for him and, although it sometimes saddened him, he did not actively resent it, for he knew that his surrender to Esther had been abject, and that his hasty retreats into the greenhouse, when edicts were issued by his wife, was the act of a craven. He knew that he could have, and should have, asserted himself sometimes, particularly on the occasions when Esther reached for the cane that had hung, for so long, behind "The Tempting Bait", in the living-room; but the fact was that he never had interfered, not once, and he therefore deserved his daughter's opinion of him.

It did not take Elaine very long to realise that something stupendous had happened to her father. At first she attributed the new Edgar to the mere absence of her mother, but when his customary mood towards her changed from mild gentleness to one of clumsy jocularity, when he went so far as to tax her with "not getting out and about enough", and "not meeting more people her own age", she realised that life at Number Seventeen would never be the same again, not even when Esther came home. This realisation determined her to advance her own plans, plans that had now been maturing for more than two years.

Elaine Frith had not the smallest desire to become a flapper. Had she yearned to wear thigh-revealing skirts, to dash about on a pillion, to use make-up, and consort with the wide-trousered youths who flapped here and there as the suburb's corps of beaux, there is little doubt but that she would have long since extended her physical rebellion against Esther to the point of open mutiny, for she was no longer afraid of her mother.

She was taller and stronger than Esther, or Sydney, besides being, in her own smouldering way, a good deal more ruthless than either of them. Faced with defiance, Esther would have been obliged to take refuge in nagging, and choose between giving her daughter the freedom of the suburb, or advertising her impotence to the Avenue every evening. Neither Edgar, nor Esther, nor Sydney really understood the reasons for Elaine's unexpected passivity in this direction. How should they, when they had no inkling of how Elaine passed the time when she was out of the house, or was closeted for all those hours in her little room, over the porch?

Elaine had, in fact, travelled a long way since that far-off day when she had rescued *The Art of Marriage* from the trunk in the cistern loft. It might be said that the study of the little volume had changed her life, for since then she had perfected a complicated network of defensive deceit around her, and the smoke-screen that she added to her defences would have done credit to a depraved bishop, bent on leading a worldly life whilst remaining a spiritual èxample to his flock.

Outwardly, she spent much time studying text-books, relative to her commercial course. Her mother never even bothered to look into these text-books. Had she done so she might have been surprised to discover that every one of them belied its innocuous title. Gregg's *Shortened Course of Double-Entry Book-Keeping*, for instance, camouflaged Miss Elinor Glyn's *This Passion Called Love*. *Shorthand for Beginners* provided covers for Miss Dorothy Dix's advice to the lovelorn, and even Doctor Marie Stopes' *Married Love* had strayed into Elaine's commercial course, and was now carefully rebound between the blue covers of *The Secretarial Questionnaire*.

No fiction was represented, beyond the inevitable one on the outside covers, but under the loose board, beside her washstand, Elaine had accumulated a sizeable fiction library, and in the hours supposedly spent in study she sometimes switched her mind from the technical to the romanticised aspects of love, beginning with Ethel M. Dell's *Way of an Eagle*, and graduating to *Lady Chatterley's Lover*, purchased tenth-hand from a student who had been on Easter Holiday in France. She had all manner of other books down there between the floor-joists, books on female costume throughout the ages, books on etiquette, books on cosmetics. They were all part of the master plan.

She spent a good deal of her time at the public library, but she never took out a book, passing the hours instead in the reference section, where she had long been accepted by the assistants as a fanatical medical student, too poor, it seemed, to attend university. To get here in the daylight she had to falsify her time-table, but this was accomplished easily enough by a bland announcement that she stayed on at

College one hour after other, and less conscientious, students had left, in order to "practise" on one of the establishment's typewriters.

She enjoyed lying to her mother. It gave her a sense of power, and of superiority over Edgar and Sydney. Every successful deceit was a personal triumph, and when she had accomplished something new in this sphere, she always went upstairs to her room, smiling like a cat, to savour her triumph alone.

But Elaine Frith did not spend all her hours of seclusion in reading.

Every night, as soon as the others had retired, she went through her ritual in front of the long mirror of her wardrobe.

The moment her mother's light had flicked out, she scrambled from bed, slipped out of her flannel night-dress, and shed her old personality like a snake sloughing its skin.

She began by re-dressing her hair, looping it in heavy coils over her wide brow, and wetting her fingers to fashion the kiss-curl in the centre. She had got the idea of the kiss-curl from a film poster outside the Granada, advertising *Barbed Wire*, starring Pola Negri. She discovered that kiss-curls suited her, and she bought a small bottle of fixing lotion, so as to be ready for the occasion that she knew would come, sooner or later, when she could emerge from Number Seventeen, and devastate all mankind.

When her hair was arranged to her satisfaction, she would stand before the mirror, carefully examining her body. She looked with satisfaction at her firm breasts, her flat stomach, her long, straight legs, and small feet. She admired the pale shine of her skin, the steep smoothness of the curves above her hips, the firm roundness of her behind, and the way it emphasised her surprisingly small waist.

Standing there, turning this way and that, glancing over her shoulder, posing hand on hip, and studying the reflection of her hundred and one expressions, from the demure to the sultry, from the arch to the downright provocative, she looked like a young, pagan priestess performing some mystic, solitary ceremony. She had the serenity and confidence of a priestess. She did not envy the Avenue flappers their freedom, for she was aware that, in contradiction to the stridency of the decade, men did not really want flat-chested, comradely women, but the kind of woman she would be when her moment arrived. The books had taught her that the art of love was that of sustaining mystery, of promising so much and giving so little, until the time came when one could stupefy with generosity, and enslave the man who would pluck her from the tower, and instal her in a mansion or palace, where she could be done with subterfuge, and spend the livelong day radiating beauty, reigning over a whole troop of lesser men, each of whom would consider it a high privilege to die for her.

This was the traditional destiny of all beautiful women. This was her dream and her plan.

2

It was Edgar's nominal membership of the local branch of the Conservative Association that enabled Elaine to stage-manage her own coming-out.

About a week after his promising talk with Harold Godbeer, when he strode humming about the house, maddening Sydney with unsatisfied curiosity, and leaving them both alone in the house during his unexplained absence at the week-ends, Edgar suddenly presented Elaine with a printed invitation that had been delivered, by hand, to every paid-up Conservative in the Avenue.

It was an elegantly printed invitation from the Honourable Mrs. Stafford-Fyffe, who occupied one of the last of the big manor houses near Chislehurst.

Everybody in Shirley knew Mrs. Stafford-Fyffe, who saw herself as a political hostess, a latter-day Lady Holland; whose husband was not only the prospective Conservative candidate for a Potteries constituency and twenty years her senior, but also fabulously rich. Mr. Stafford-Fyffe still held a controlling interest in a famous jam firm that had become a household word during the war, and in the early 'twenties he took to speculating in real estate on the outskirts of Birmingham, where he was said to have scooped up another fortune.

The Stafford-Fyffes lived in considerable style, and took a very active interest in local politics. Jim Carver, of Number Twenty, knew them as war-profiteers, and the rest of the Avenue knew them by their huge Rolls Royce, that was often to be seen outside the Unionist Headquarters, in the Upper Road.

About the time that Elaine was perfecting her plans, and Esme was on the point of leaving school, Mrs. Stafford-Fyffe launched a vigorous campaign among the youth of the suburb, on behalf of the Junior Imperial League. Being young, gay, and extremely attractive, she had come to terms with post-war youth, and was ready to cover her political pill with large spoonfuls of her husband's jam, or the dividends therefrom. She decided to open her campaign by inviting every young person in the district to a monster party, at "Hillcrest Court", her Chislehurst home. The local association prepared lists, and volunteers delivered the invitations. One for Judy and two for the twins came through the letter-box of Number Twenty, but Jim found them and tore them up with a full-mouthed oath, so that his children did not hear about the party until Esme, who had accepted, mentioned it casually to Judy, over the garden fence. Judy was piqued that she had not been invited, but she knew her father well enough to refrain from raising the subject, and starting a family rumpus.

Judy was not making much progress with Esme these days—indeed, it sometimes seemed to her that she was retrogressing a little, for Esme no longer needed her as a shield-bearer in his games of make-believe, and had taken to spending a good deal of time in his bedroom, now fitted up by Harold and Eunice as a "study". Here, he informed her, he was engaged in writing a book, and Judy sometimes waved to him from the bottom of the garden, when she was on her way out shopping, via the back lane.

Once, he had run down, and read her a page or two of his work, a boys' adventure story about highwaymen, and one Saturday afternoon he had actually asked her to accompany him to Shirley Hills, where they had attended so many bank-holiday fairs together.

That afternoon was one of her happiest memories, and she

longed in vain for endless repetitions of the occasion. Up there, under a cloudless August sky, they had picnicked on the pebble slopes, and he had talked to her as never before, all about his ambitions, and his hopes for the future, how he would soon become a famous novelist, and *write* adventure stories instead of reading them, how he would travel to the uttermost ends of the earth, seeking material for his books, and checking up on his backgrounds. He still failed to use the plural when describing his daydreams, and never once said "*we* shall go", instead of "*I* shall go", but it was nevertheless reassuring to be his confidante again. Clearly he had not mentioned these things to anyone else, not even his mother, or step-father, and after all, he was still at school, and at sixteen Judy could afford to take a slightly more realistic attitude as to their future. No matter what happened, she reasoned, they could not be married for years. According to Esme, it took several to establish oneself as a professional writer of books. However, she could wait. She had waited ten years already, and there was still no sign of any competition in the field. She had made sure of this by a judicious questioning of her brothers, Boxer and Bernard, who had attended the same school as Esme all these years. Boxer had snorted at the bare idea of Esme having a sweetheart.

"What *him? Esme?* Don't be daft, Judy-girl, he never even notices 'em! He's always sucking-up to old Monkhouse, the English master. He passed out with honours in two subjects in matric' this summer, didn't he? He was all right, once, wasn't he, Berni? We had some good fun with Esme when he first went there, didn't we, Berni? But not *now*, not since old Longjohn split us up, and stuck him in with the swots! Girls! Esme?", Boxer grinned his wide-toothed grin; "he wouldn't know what to do with one, not if she fell slap in his lap!"

The twins did not realise how immensely relieved Judith was by Boxer's scornful summary of Esme's qualifications as a philanderer. They themselves, working as a team, of course, had by this time learned what to do with girls—more or less —who fell into their laps. Few had, at this stage, but they had their moments, at Church Institute hops, and on Saturday nights in the Granada.

Longjohn's prophecy regarding the twins' future was proving a shrewd and accurate one. After losing Esme, they had slipped, contentedly enough, to the bottom of every "C" form left to them, and finally they drifted away, without even sitting for School Certificate, to get themselves jobs in a scrap-metal yard at Clockhouse. Somehow, on a pooled salary of four pounds a week, they had acquired an Indian motor-cycle, and now added their quota to the nocturnal undertones of the Avenue. They were in court once or twice for speeding, before they changed their jobs and became mechanics at the Crystal Palace Speedway Track. Here they found a joint niche, standing each night in filthy overalls beside the pits, while the rival teams roared round the cinder-track, sending great spurts of grime over the barrier, and they impatiently awaited the day when they would graduate from pit to track, and earn their own reputation as dirt-track aces.

They appear later on, but briefly. Their big adventure was still more than ten years away, and came at a time when young men in the Avenue could find plenty of full-time employment, with or without school-leaving Certificates.

3

Elaine set out for the Stafford-Fyffe rally in a dance-frock of deep crimson velvet, knee-length, and cut closely to her mature figure. She had never worn such a dress before, and she would not have worn it for very long if the dance had not anticipated Esther's discharge from hospital by two clear days.

Edgar, having accepted the invitation on his daughter's behalf, had given her four pounds to equip herself. He was persuaded that she owned nothing remotely suitable for a party such as this, and Frances had made him curiously reaware of women, and women's problems touching clothes. The gift had, in fact, been prompted by Frances, in whom he had confided, and Elaine went off to a Croydon gown-shop, and chose herself a dress against the carefully-worded advice of the assistant, who deemed her to be at least two years older than she was, likely to become a regular customer, and therefore in dire need of protection against herself.

The reason the assistant tried to persuade Elaine not to buy the dress was that the model she chose was out of fashion, and should never have been seen by a customer. It was much too full in the bust to be currently popular, and the assistant would have preferred to sell the young lady a fringed, low-waisted silk, in tangerine. Elaine, however, was fascinated by the colour of the outmoded frock, and when it was tried on, the assistant had to admit that there was, after all, a good deal still to be said for figure-revealing dance-frocks, sadly dated as they were, and almost as archaic as the crinoline.

Standing before the mirror of the fitting-room, Elaine went through a shortened form of her bedtime ritual, ignoring the hovering fitter, pleased and satisfied with what she saw in the reflection, but not excited and pernickety, like most of the flapper customers.

She then changed, paid the bill, and went out to buy a bag, shoes, and a "choker" necklet. Unknown to Edgar, she had six pounds ten of her own, laid by for just such an occasion.

The Imperial League rally was a huge success. The ball-room of "Hillcrest" could accommodate over a hundred guests, and there was an overflow in the drawing-room, where the sliding doors had been opened to allow games and dancing for the late arrivals.

Two local bands had been engaged, one of them "Al Swinger's Rhythmateers", and by 9 p.m. the Charleston was in full swing, and Ted Hartnell was sweating it out on the dais, leaping from drum to drum, flinging himself at the cymbals, beating out a merciless rhythm with his unemployed left foot, and generally enjoying himself as much as, or more, than anyone on the floor below.

Mrs. Stafford-Fyffe herself led the first Charleston, partnered by a glossy-haired young man, rumoured to be from the Foreign Office, and the two of them were afterwards employed whipping-in the little knots of stragglers that persisted in clustering round the respective cloak-room entrances.

There were few laggards at one of Mrs. Stafford-Fyffe's parties. Every guest was herded briskly on to the floor, including Esme, who, until the moment he was spotted, had been hovering on the outskirts of the throng, looking in vain for some person, male or female, whom he recognised, and wishing with all his heart that his mother had not let him in for what looked like being a dismal and embarrassing evening. He was not a very sociable boy, and had tried very hard to dodge the column.

"It's so silly, dear," Eunice had said, when he protested that he was not likely to know anyone at the ball. "That's the whole *point* of a party, to *get* to know somebody, and to dance, just as I paid for you to learn to dance, at poor Miss Ackroyd's!"

"Poor Miss Ackroyd", late of Number Sixty-Three, had taught several of the Avenue children to dance, just as Edith Clegg had taught others to tinkle the cottage piano. She became poor Miss Ackroyd after she was killed by a skidding 'bus, in the Lower Road.

"I don't think people dance like that nowadays," Esme told his mother; "it's all new stuff—"Black Bottom" and whatnot! I can't get the hang of it at all! It's daft!"

"Whatever it is, it's a lot better than stewing in your study all evening, as you've done all the Christmas holidays so far, now isn't it, Harold, dear?"

"Yes, darling," said Harold dear, from the depths of his leather armchair. Harold replied "Yes, darling" to almost everything Eunice said these days. He hadn't quite realised what a talker she was in the days when they first met, and prattled away in London tea-shops. In those days he was still looking at her long eyelashes, and not really listening to anything she said. He still thought her the prettiest woman in the world, but he was beginning, after four years of marriage, to form an indifferent opinion of her mind. He had once flattered himself that he would set about forming it, as Mr. Murdstone had promised to form Mrs. Copperfield's, but he gave up the attempt within weeks of the Torquay honeymoon, and regarding Eunice's mind there was now a half-humorous understanding between step-father and step-son. Both liked peace, and Eunice—who never lost her temper—

was yet capable of shattering the tranquillity of Number Twenty-Two for days on end, for she never willingly relinquished a topic of conversation, possibly because a search for a new one required a certain amount of preliminary thought.

Standing just outside the door marked "Gentlemen", Esme reflected gloomily that his suspicions had been well-founded. Apparently people did not dance like Miss Ackroyd in the late 'twenties. So far there was no sign at all of a Lancers, or Boston Two-step, or even a good honest polka, there were just walk-around foxtrots, and quick-steps, and Charlestons, and a peculiar hugging-and-bobbing dance, played to the tune of *All By Yourself In The Moonlight*, that was known, he was told, as *The Heebie-Jeebies*. Esme had never learned to Charleston, and it looked a very complicated dance indeed. The Heebie-Jeebies looked a lot easier, but to go out on the floor and practise it would be to fling personal dignity to the winds and despite Mrs. Stafford-Fyffe's chivvyings, he had not the slightest intention of being bullied into trying.

It was in the Paul Jones, close on supper-time, that he first noticed Elaine Frith.

She was circling in the opposite direction, and even before he recognised her as the strange, silent girl of Number Seventeen, he was struck by her grave, unsmiling expression, so unlike the forced smiles of the girls on either side of her.

Then he noticed her dress. It was different somehow, and very striking, not only in colour, but in length. All the other girls' dresses finished well above the knee, but hers ended an inch or so below. She looked so grown-up too, at least eighteen, and for a moment he wondered whether it was indeed the girl he had passed so often in the Avenue, the one who always kept her eyes on the pavement, and appeared oblivious of everything outside her own solemn thoughts.

Then she came round again, and the music stopped, with Esme and Elaine almost but not quite opposite to one another. The girl immediately facing Esme smiled nervously, and stepped forward. Out of the corner of his eye he saw that Elaine had no partner, that the men on each side of him had swung off with other girls. The band began to play *Charmaine*, a tune he had always liked, and he moved towards her at a sharp angle.

"May I, Miss Frith?"

He was a well-mannered boy, with a good deal of his mother's charm.

She nodded gravely, and they moved off, leaving the girl who had been facing Esme to find her own blushing way to a chair.

A waltz was the only dance in which Esme could feel certain of not making a fool of himself, and he found his partner very easy to steer, responding to the slightest pressure of his arm and shoulder. He wondered, as they circled, where she could possibly have learned to dance. He knew enough of the Friths to recall that they were "very chapel", and never let their children out in the evening. Yet no partner at Christmas parties, or at Miss Ackroyd's, had given him so much confidence on the floor. For the first time in his limited experience he was floating, rather than shuffling and suddenly he was glad, very glad indeed, that he had allowed himself to be persuaded to come.

On the completion of their second circuit, he said:

"You're the only person I know here. You live opposite me, don't you?"

"Yes," she said, and he was struck by the low pitch of her voice. It seemed a part of her grownupness, far removed from the high-pitched chatter of the girls all about him, or the voices that came squealing over the wired-in dividing wall, at school.

The music stopped, and couples disengaged to re-form the ring. They stood together a moment, holding hands. She seemed reluctant to leave him.

"You're the only person *I* know," she said, as the marching tune began again; "will you ... will you ask me to dance after this?"

He was elated by the proposal. It restored his confidence, which had been ebbing fast since he had arrived.

"I ... I'd like to, very much," he said, "the next," and was whirled in the grasp of the young man on his right, and could only smile at her when she came round again, finishing up a dozen paces beyond him.

There was no dance immediately following. Mrs. Stafford-Fyffe climbed on to the dais, and invited all guests to take their partners in to supper. Esme spotted the crimson dress, on the far side of the room, and half ran across the polished floor, arriving a little breathlessly at her side.

"Will you ... may I ... take you to supper?"

She smiled and stood up at once. Promptly he offered an arm, for this was one thing poor Miss Ackroyd had insisted upon, and they moved through a laurelled arch into the big hall, where sandwiches, jelly, trifle, and cider-cup were being served from long trestle tables.

He found her a little table, just inside the conservatory, and then went back to queue for sandwiches and drinks.

"I didn't know whether you wanted trifle, or what, Miss Frith," he said, on rejoining her; "there was rather a run on everything decent."

"No," she told him, "I don't want to eat, but please don't keep calling me 'Miss Frith'; it sounds dreadfully stuffy. My name's Elaine, and I know yours, too. It's Esme, isn't it?"

"Yes," he said, marvelling. "How did you find out?"

"I heard the Carver girl ... the younger one, call out to you, oh, years ago. You and she 'go' together, don't you?"

"No," said Esme, slightly taken aback, "not ... not ... in that way. We're just friends, like ... like ... you always are, with people next door."

Abruptly, he moved to safer ground. "I didn't know your name, but I like it. It's—well, it's kind of historical."

He wanted to add that it suited her cool, dark looks, that she reminded him of a picture of Lancelot's Elaine, in his *Myths and Legends of the Middle Ages* on his study shelf, but he was not finding this initial conversation very easy. She was so cool, and composed, while he had always found girls, Judy Carver excepted, difficult to know.

She nibbled a sandwich, and he noticed her long, slender fingers. Everything about her, he decided, was shapely, graceful, and quiet. She differed so sharply from all the other girls, now giggling and screaming over the cider-cup that the young men were ladling into them, but as he glanced sideways at less inhibited couples it struck him that the youths were so much more at ease with their partners than he was, that the thought made him flush. He decided that he must say something that would impress her.

"I . . . I think your frock is a lovely colour," he blurted out, finally. He recalled hearing somewhere that if you couldn't think of anything to say it was always safe to compliment a girl on her appearance. It certainly seemed to work.

"Thank you very much, Esme," she said demurely, and lost a shade of her composure.

It was the first dress compliment she had even been paid, but nobody would have known it, for she knew how to accept a compliment. That was one more thing she had learned from Elinor Glyn.

"I'm not much good at this sort of dancing," he went on, with more confidence, "I went to dancing classes at old Miss Ackroyd's, at Number Sixty-Three, but we didn't learn this sort of dancing, just things like the Lancers, and the Mazurka."

"I don't think you ought to worry," she told him, "you're very 'light' indeed. No other partner I've had is half as light." (What was that in *Eve's World*? "Build up his confidence, make him feel bigger for having met you!" Well, she wasn't doing so badly for a beginner.)

"I say, can *you* Charleston?" he went on, enthusiastically.

"I have, tonight," said Elaine, "and it's a lot easier than it looks."

"But where on earth did you *learn*?"

"In a magazine," she admitted; "then I practised with a chair in the bedroom."

He laughed, and the laugh relaxed him. He saw, in her answering smile, that she had large dimples, and that her eyes were very blue, and prettily flecked, and as he noticed these things, as her lips parted to display her white, evenly-set teeth, a sensation like a mild spasm of cramp stole into his stomach. It caught him by surprise. At first he did not recall ever having experienced such a sensation before, and it occurred to him at once that perhaps this was "it", perhaps this was the thing that all the films were about, the "love-at-first-sight" that seemed to find its way into almost all the books, even straightforward adventure stories, the thing that poets and dance-tune composers wrote so much about, the thing that people said (in jest, he had always imagined) made the world go round. But then he told himself, this wasn't first

sight. He had seen Elaine in the Avenue for years, and had
never given her more than a curious glance, and even those
glances had been prompted more by the monastic reputation
of Number Seventeen than by the girl's appearance or magnetism.

He wondered whether it was anything to do with the way
she looked tonight, or with the soft wail of the saxophone
that still issued from beyond the laurelled arch, or with the
shaded lights that cast a pinkish glow over the crowded conservatory, or with the general background of laughter and
excited voices that surrounded them.

Then it occurred to him that he *had* experienced the
sensation before, or something very like it, on the numerous
occasions when he was standing outside Longjohn's study,
having been sent there with the twins by exasperated form-
masters. It was curious that the two sensations should be so
similar, the one an anticipation of sharp physical pain, the
other a feeling traditionally centred on the heart. The com-
parison appealed to his sense of humour, and he grinned
across at her.

"I'm so glad I came," he admitted, "I nearly didn't—it was
my mother who bullied me into it."

"I think your mother is very pretty," she said. ("Praise his
mother—that's always a good start.") "She doesn't look nearly old enough to have a boy your age." ("Stress her youth if
possible.")

"How old do you think I am?" he asked seriously.

She looked at him steadily. "I *know* how old you are,
Esme. I know much more about you than you know about
me. You're sixteen-and-a-half, aren't you? I know a lot about
most people in the Avenue—our end of it, anyway. I've
watched, you see, and guessed, and then watched again to see
if I was right. I remember when you came, and when the
Carvers came, and when the big boy Carver married the
grocer's daughter, and went into the shop at the corner. A
girl he went with had a baby. Lots of people never knew
that, because the girl moved."

Esme's eyes opened wide, and she acknowledged his surprise with a merry twitch of her mouth.

"He's got a new shop, now, at the bottom of Delhi Road,

and others in Wickham and Addington. And those old maids at Number Four—they don't have parlour concerts any more, because Mr. Hartnell, who lodges there, has joined a jazz band, and plays out every night. He's here now, playing the drums. I could tell you everything about the people in the Avenue, but most of them aren't worth talking about."

He was suitably astonished. She went on:

"I'm never allowed out, you see, and I wouldn't be here now if my mother wasn't in hospital. Daddy's all right, when Mother isn't there; and anyway he's so different lately." She had been skipping away from the etiquette books for some minutes now, and suddenly she went right off the circumscribed path. "I think he's fallen in love with somebody else, and it's made him . . . made him kinder, I suppose."

Esme was obviously shocked. The people in the Avenue weren't the sort of people who conducted themselves in that way. Fathers went to work, and came home at dusk; mothers stayed home in the mornings and cooked, or went shopping, and took the children to and from school; sons and daughters passed in an out of the houses with their satchels and music-cases. There was an unchanging rhythm about each house in particular, and about the Avenue as a whole. Fathers didn't fall in love just like that—not people like her father at any rate, not funny little men with bald patches, and grey, drooping moustaches. She must be what everybody told him *he* was, a romantic, who had had her nose in too many books for too many years.

"You can't possibly *know* that, Elaine," he told her earnestly, "you're just imagining it."

She gave her shoulders an odd little shake, and he interpreted the gesture as impatience on her part to waste precious time talking about dull people in the Avenue.

"The Interval's over now, Esme," she said. "Let's have our dance. It's another waltz."

They had their dance, and all the other dances, for the cider-cup had further enlivened the already boisterous company, and experiments could now be tried out on the floor without fear or shame. In a corner, beneath the dais, a sweating Ted Hartnell beamed down on Elaine and Esme gravely learning to Charleston, and bobbing about in a small orbit to the exhilarating evolutions of the Heebie-Jeebies, and as he watched he noticed that they smiled into one another's eyes, with chaos all round them, and moved to brisk accompaniment of Elaine's commands.

"*Both* hands on my shoulders—that's it—now twist the left foot from the toes, and throw the right out—*that's* it—no, *twist* it . . . hold me a little closer, so that we go up and down on the same beat. . . . *No*, Esme, bob from the waist; your feet don't leave the floor in this one!"

And as the evening progressed, and Mrs. Stafford-Fyffe, expertly squired by the young man from the Foreign Office, glided among the young people with shining eyes, the tide of hilarity began to ebb a little. Bobbed heads were seen to nestle on braided lapels, and moist powder exchange cheek for cheek, trips to the cloak-room became more frequent, in order that swift repairs could be made, and not a moment of such an evening wasted.

Eleven o'clock, midnight, one o'clock. Al Swinger received his instructions to play *Good-night, Sweetheart,* but determined to give generous measure managed to sandwich *I'll See You in my Dreams* and *Ever So Goosey* between the command and the last waltz.

A stuttered vote of thanks to Mrs. Stafford-Fyffe and her diplomatic M.C., *Auld Lang Syne,* with plenty of billowing forward and back, *The King,* and a rush for coats and scarves, for it was snowing outside, or had been, they said. Then it was over, with a tide of eager young voices exclaiming delight, as they poured out on to the snow-covered drive, and piled into the cars and the taxis that moved up to the brightly lit portico.

Shouts, laughter, and more squealing from the girls, most of whom had now tied coloured scarves under their chins, and were letting their coats swing free. The last taxi slipped away, and Mrs. Stafford-Fyffe turned ecstatically to the young diplomat:

"How many new members, Aubrey, darling?"

He told her nearly two hundred, with the promise of more to come when subscribers had small change about them.

"Topping! Oh, *topping!*" she exclaimed, and you were a pet, Aubrey, a *perfect, perfect pet!*"

4

Elaine and Esme had not ordered a taxi, but neither minded the walk home through the soft snow, certainly not Esme, who glowed with delight when Elaine slipped her gloved hand through his arm, and fell into step with him, just as though he had been walking her home through the crisp night for years without end.

It was a perfect night for new lovers. The stage might have been set for them, at least, so thought Esme, dumb with wonder, as they came out from behind the beech clump, and saw the old Shirley Mill silvered in bright moonlight on their left.

The wind had dropped, and the light snowfall made the night very still. Now and then a car glided by, its wheels making no noise beyond a pleasant scrunch, and when they reached the decline, at the crest of Shirley Rise, Elaine's fingers took a firmer grip upon his, lest she should slip in heels that were not made for walking in snow.

They spoke very little, just an odd, occasional remark about the weather, or the dance, and it was not until they had turned into the Avenue that Elaine said:

"I've got to go in the back way. Daddy left the key under a flower-pot in the greenhouse."

The moonlight here was so bright that every house in the Avenue stood out clearly, looking like gabled cottages in a pantomime scene. Not a light showed along the wide sweep of the crescent, and snow had blown into shallow drifts under the dwarf walls of the even numbers.

When they turned the corner by Number Seventeen they were able to look across the meadow, towards the dark mass of Manor Woods, now a blue-black strip between the untrodden snow of the field and the stars. Esme thought he had never seen the woods look so still or so beautiful. Away in the far distance, towards the City, a goods-train rumbled, but there was no other sound as Elaine lifted the latch of the garden door, and beckoned to Esme to follow her inside.

He did so, the cramp in his stomach returning, as she

picked her way down the short path to the tiny greenhouse against the boundary wall.

"It's here," she said, lifting a hyacinth pot from one of the slatted shelves, and slipping the key in her pocket.

He expected her to turn, close the greenhouse door, and walk past him down towards the back door, but she remained standing inside.

"It's always warm in here," she told him, "Daddy must have lit the stove. He's terribly fussy about his old plants. Come inside."

He stepped in, and she pushed the door closed with her foot. The moonlight filtered through the sloping glass roof, and a beam touched her hair, so that it seemed to sparkle like frost rime. There was a heavy, pleasant scent from Edgar's early hyacinths, ranged in dozens of pots along the wall.

"Thank you for being so sweet, Esme," she said, and then, in her low, level voice, and with a little ripple of laughter: "Don't you want to kiss me goodnight?"

He wanted to very much indeed. He was not quite a stranger to kissing. In the last few years he had attended dozens of Christmas parties in the suburb, and there were always plenty of kissing games—winking, and sardines, and murder, and postman's knock. He had often kissed Judy at these parties, but somehow those kisses, and the clumsy embraces that accompanied them, had never seemed worth remembering on the way home. When it came to the actual meeting of lips, neither he, nor the girl he was kissing, seemed able to melt into one another, as the stars did so effortlessly on the Granada screen. It was one of those things that looked easy but wasn't. He knew that party kisses would be little use to him now, just as he knew that Elaine would never kiss the way other girls kissed, stiffly, jerkily, and stifling an embarrassed giggle.

Neither did she.

Her theory was much more sound. He reached out for her, but, as on the dance-floor, it was she who took charge. There was a deliberation about her that was almost frightening. She put one arm round his waist, and the other along his shoulder, with her palm open against the back of his head, and thus drew him towards her gently, but with unquestionable firmness.

She kissed him softly, and then returned his kiss, with lips that were slightly parted. She held him like that for a few seconds, and when he shuddered a little she let her weight incline towards him, not very definitely, but enough to make him conscious of a faint eagerness on her part. Nobody had ever kissed him like that before. When she drew away from him, smiling, he remained quite still, his face burning, his heart hammering as never before. Her lips, he thought, were like petals, and he wanted now to remember and remember their freshness, and texture, and warmth. He seized her hand, and pressed it hard against his mouth.

"Elaine...." Now it was intoxicating to speak her name aloud. "Oh, Elaine ... you're wonderful, wonderful.... I never dreamed ..."

She withdrew her hand, and reached past him for the knob of the flimsy door. She did this with the same gentle decisiveness that she had demonstrated in shutting the door and in the act of kissing him.

"I'll have to go in now, Esme."

("A few moments the first time ... he must walk home remembering one kiss—not one of twenty")

"Yes, of course—but tomorrow ... couldn't we go somewhere? I'd like ... I could come over and——"

"*No!*" She was very emphatic. "You must never call here, Esme. Mother will be home."

"But you said the day after tomorrow!" There was real distress in his voice.

"I shall be busy getting ready for her ... you could write—but not here, to the College."

"I will, I will!"

They were walking swiftly down the garden path towards the back door.

"Goodnight, Elaine——"

"Goodnight, Esme!"

She relented at the very last possible moment, and turning, blew him a kiss. He remained staring at the door for more than a minute, until he saw the reflection of the landing light in the kitchen windows. Then he went slowly out into the

Avenue, and across the road to Number Twenty-Two. He stopped at his gate, and stood regarding his own home for a moment. All these years it had been just a place to live. Now it was the ante-chamber to paradise, within cooing distance of the lady in the tower, who (could it be possible?) lived immediately opposite!

He did not notice the flask of coffee or the plate-shrouded sandwiches that Eunice had left for him on the hall table, but as he was mounting the stairs, a sudden thought made him quicken his step, and slip along the landing into the porch room, now called the "Study". As he flung open the door, a stifled cry of excitement escaped from him. He was right! The porch room was *her* room, and there was a faint shadow, *her* shadow, moving behind the curtains.

It was icily cold in the little room, but he sat there a long time, waiting for the light to go out. Why hadn't he told her he occupied this room, as well as the back bedroom overlooking the nursery? She might then have turned out the light, opened the window, called across to him, or simply looked out into the night, like Juliet.

Presently her light went out, and he dragged himself to his bedroom, where Eunice had instructed Harold to light a small fire. It was burning very low now, but the room was warm to undress in, and pleasant to lie awake in.

Methodically, he began going over the evening from the first moment he had seen her in the Paul Jones, to the final blown kiss from the back door.

He lay awake for an hour or more, listening to the soft rustle of coals in the grate, and wondering if she too was awake, and thinking of him; but not daring to decide whether she was or was not.

He might have spared himself the nag of doubt. Elaine was thinking of him, and while, in his present delirium, he might have found her thoughts mildly flattering, they were hardly the counterpart of his. If she too was ecstatic it was not on account of him but because of her own triumph, and when credit was apportioned most of it went to herself, and to Elinor Glyn, with a few crumbs for the author of *Eve's World*. He was madly in love with her! There was not the slightest doubt about that, and he was good-looking, good company, and gentle, perhaps too gentle. More important still, he was reverent, and reverence was the one thing they all insisted upon, both before and after marriage. Taken all round it was an encouraging start for a totally inexperienced beginner, and the only mistake she could remember making was that of telling him her suspicions regarding her father's philandering. That small error had, however, been more than compensated for by the kiss. She felt quite certain that Elinor Glyn herself could not have improved on that kiss. What was it one of the magazine aunties had published, in reply to a girl who wrote in, asking how she could be certain of recognising "Mr. Right"?

"If the touch of his hand fails to thrill you, if his first kiss does not fill you with unspeakable delight, then, my dear, he is not the man you have been waiting for."

That was it. She remembered it word for word. Well, now, had his kiss and his hand-touch performed these miracles? Hardly, but she was ready to admit that she had found them undeniably pleasing. Perhaps it was difficult to tell after a single encounter? They would meet again, and kiss again, quite soon, for he was writing. . . . She had handled *that* very well, too . . . ! It would be interesting to see what sort of letter he wrote. Would it begin *"Dear Elaine"*, or *"Dearest Elaine"*, or *"Elaine, Dearest"*? All the magazine aunties said that was important, too.

She fell asleep, still pondering.

Across the road, in the porch room she shared with Louise, Judy Carver had been asleep several hours, but before she undressed she had taken out her Esme Box, and written a few words in her diary, using the only few minutes she would have alone, before Louise came up.

She wrote:

"Today it snowed. Esme went to the big party at Mrs. Stafford-Fyffe's. I wish I could have gone. I have a feeling something would have happened there, and anyway, we should have walked home together."

It seemed futile to write more.

She put the diary back in the box, and the box in the drawer, covering it with clean underclothes. She was a long time getting off to sleep, and when she did she slept fitfully, starting up in the middle of the night, and hurrying to the window when she heard a car stop in Shirley Rise, and someone turn into the Avenue, whistling.

It wasn't Esme, however, but Ted Hartnell, Miss Clegg's lodger.

Ted walked slowly up the Avenue to the gate of Number Four, eight doors down. He had been crooning jazz tunes for five hours, with a twenty-minute supper break, but he still had enough breath left for a few bars of *The Broadway Melody*.

CHAPTER XVII

Carver Roundabout. I

1

THE Spring of 1930 proved a memorable one for the Carvers, of Number Twenty. The majority of the people in the Avenue slid into the new decade almost without noticing it. They had little reason to suppose that the 'thirties would differ from the 'twenties. The upheaval and the anxieties of the war were now a long way behind them—so far, in most of the houses, that children were now growing up in the Avenue who thought of Kaiser Bill, and Earl Haig, as Jim Carver might have thought of Bismarck, and Buller. Too many sensations had interposed between the mafficking of Armistice Day and the enthronement of Amy Johnson. Small-powered cars were now commonplace in the Avenue, and it was a waste of time to send children out with bucket and shovel to collect manure for the rosebeds. Few tradesmen used horse-vans nowadays, but overhead aircraft droned and spluttered into Croydon Aerodrome all day long, and their passage failed to distract young Tony Carver, and his pot-bellied grandfather from their daily game of hopscotch or bears in Piretta's storeyard.

The first Spring of the decade was memorable for the Carvers because it heralded a general reshuffle at Number Twenty.

To begin with the twins left home, renting a furnished room near their Speedway, at Anerley. Jim, Louise, and Judy were sorry to see them go, for they were good company, but they were very glad of their living-space. Since Archie had married there had been an end to the 10 p.m. bedtime-drill downstairs, but for some years now the accommodation at Number Twenty had been limited, particularly in bedrooms. Louise and Judy had squeezed into the porch room, Jim and the boys shared the front room, and the babies, "Fetch" and "Carry", slept in the rear room, overlooking the nursery. Now Jim changed with the elder girls, and Louise and Judy at last had space to make their beds properly.

The house seemed very empty without Boxer's lumbering bulk and Berni's tuneless whistle, but Jim was grateful for a privacy he had not been able to enjoy since joining the army, in 1914. He found that a room to himself enabled him to think more clearly, and to keep his quick temper in check. In addition, there was now room to unpack, and even display his small library, and file away his vast stocks of pamphlets.

Jim spent a good deal of his time in preparing speeches and compiling current cost-of-living indexes. Often enough there was little else for him to do, for his jobs, since leaving the furniture firm, had been of a temporary nature, and had recently begun to be spaced out by longer intervals, as the wind of depression whipped the seedy queues outside the Labour Exchange.

Jim could see little future for himself, or his country, in the way things were going just now, notwithstanding the Socialist victory at the polls the previous summer. Much as the realisation galled him he was obliged to admit that the Labour Party might as well be out of office as dependent on the Liberal rump for its slender majority in Westminister. He was beginning to wonder, in fact, whether the victory of MacDonald was a triumph at all, for they said it had been

welcomed at Tory Headquarters, as a heaven-sent opportunity
to pass the buck. In additiòn, Jim found it difficult to display
more than lukewarm enthusiasm for his Premier, with his
slightly unctuous "My Friennnnnds . . .", and his disconcerting habit of hobnobbing with duchesses. Somehow, reputation
notwithstanding, Ramsay MacDonald did not fit into Jim's
preconceived idea of a Socialist prime minister. His speeches
lacked the positive drive of a legally-elected rabble-rouser,
and there was a disconcerting aura of patronage about a man
who had been raised to eminence by the jobless, and collarless, yet was said to be impatient of advice from colleagues
who did not receive invitations to Devonshire House.

There was something else, too. Although it was illogical to
distrust a man who had been a pacifist in a capitalist war,
Jim found himself distrusting his leader on this very account.
He tried, desperately hard, to rid himself of these unworthy
doubts but he did not wholly succeed, for his political faith
was deeply rooted in the comradeship of slimey shellholes,
where he had awaited the commands of young officers,
almost all of them from Tory homes, to get up and come to
grips with the Hun. It saddened him to reflect that some of
the officer survivors of those years were now his beloved
party's bitterest enemies.

He was pondering over these heresies on his way home
from a party rally in Hyde Park one gusty March evening,
when something happened to change the course of his life,
and to return to him, on a plate as it were, the limited
security he had forefeited in the 1926 strike.

Jim had stayed behind after the rally to distribute literature and pack up chairs. He was that sort of convert, a man
who performed the routine jobs, leaving others to climb on to
soap-boxes, or continue the arguments long after they had
descended from them, and the crowds had gone home.

It was dark by the time Jim turned for the Avenue,
intending to catch a tube from Marble Arch to Charing
Cross, there to take the 9.30 p.m. for Addiscombe Road.

Because it was dry and keen he decided to walk as far as
the Circus, and he was about half-way along Oxford Street
when he heard, but was hardly conscious of, a crash of glass
from the direction of New Bond Street.

A moment later, when he was level with the crossing, a large touring car shot from the turning, and tried to veer north, but the turn was made at too high a speed, and the car mounted the pavement, missed him by inches, and struck the base of a lampstandard, where it ricochetted and stopped dead.

Jim, darting back, had a good view into the car's interior. A bare-headed young man was at the wheel, feverishingly trying to reverse, and beside him was an older, bulkier man, who was looking nervously over his shoulder in the direction from which the car had come.

As the vehicle shot back Jim's brain linked the crash of glass with the presence of the car, and his eye took in the pile of furs in the rear seat, and the panic of the young driver.

Three years on and off the dole had not slowed his reflexes. Before his eye had taken in the pursuing car, or the scattering group of pedestrians on the pavement, he had jumped on to the running-board, grabbed the driver by his upturned collar, and driven his fist hard into the boy's ear, pitching him across the older man, who was in the act of opening the car door to escape.

The blow was powerful and well-judged. The boy was stunned and fell across the empty seat, just as the nearside door flew open, and his companion landed in the street on all fours.

At that moment another car roared past, braked powerfully, and came to a shuddering halt at an acute angle, boxing the tourer between lamp-standard and corner shop. A police-sergeant jumped from the running-board and pounced on the man in the road. Another policeman scrambled out, and dived headlong into the car.

"You don't want to worry about him, officer," said Jim, a little shakily, "he's out cold, I reckon. What the hell's going on?"

The policeman grinned without answering, and called across to the sergeant.

"Pedestrian got him, Sarge! How about your baby?"

The sergeant's prisoner was already handcuffed, and the policeman slipped a pair on to the boy's wrists as he sat up, vomiting. Two other constables suddenly appeared on the scene, one reversing the police car from the pavement, the other shepherding the curious crowd away from the corner.

"Move along, please, move along!" he said, prodding Jim in the small of the back.

"Hi, hold on," said the constable who had dived into the car; "he's the chap who slugged the driver!"

In the respectful gleam of the policeman's eyes Jim read publicity, and shrank from it. Mumbling something inaudible he tried to edge round the constable and lose himself in the gathering crowd, but the sergeant saw the movement.

"You mustn't go, sir," he said; "we shall need you as a witness. You'd better come along to the station with us now."

They went, in two cars, Jim and the sergeant in one, and the two bandits and three constables in the damaged tourer.

It was long after midnight when the police car deposited him outside Number Twenty, and Louise, who had been peering anxiously up and down the Avenue, let out a yelp of dismay when the lamplight fell on the sergeant's helmet. The policeman was in high good humour.

"There you are, Mr. Carver—now you can tell the missis all about it!"

"I haven't got a missis," said Jim, with a reluctant grin, "but I dare say the kids will be interested."

The dog Strike ran growling on to the pavement, and at the sight of the dog Jim chuckled inwardly. He wondered what the police sergeant would say if he was told in what circumstances Strike had been acquired, nearly four years before.

2

Jim did not enjoy being a hero, even for the one day following, when his action was splashed all over the evening papers, and a number of photographers called at the house, or during the two-day period of the trial, when he shared the publicity with the police.

Before the trial ended he found himself feeling slightly ashamed of his part in arresting the boy, who turned out to be only eighteen, and a graduate of Borstal, where he seemed to have spent most of his adolescence after emerging from a State orphanage.

Jim thought the sentence severe—seven years—the same as that meted out to the older man, who had a long record of crimes of violence. When the judge pronounced sentence the boy looked stunned, and turned mutely towards the witness bench, his eyes meeting Jim's in a kind of appeal. Jim found himself unable to meet the boy's eye. Instantly, and, as he tried to console himself, quite illogically, his mind went back to the dead boy on the bank, outside Mons, and suddenly he felt sick and defeated. Was this all that Society could do for the product of an orphanage, who had probably turned to crime because he could find companionship only among criminals? Had anyone gone an inch out of their way to help this kid to find himself, when he was thrown on to the crowded labour market? God knows, it was difficult enough to get a job without a record. What must it be like with no training or background beyond Borstal? In any case, Borstal or Council School, how much would anyone pay a kid like this, even if they found him a job washing dishes in some airless basement, or heaving luggage about a railway station, or up and down the backstairs of a provincial hotel? He saw the boy as a symptom of the whole rotten system, a system of exploitation, and dividends, and gold standards, and endless hair-splitting over conference tables. What did it matter to a boy like this whether they built big ships, or little ships, or no ships at all? How did it improve his chances of survival if statesmen's signatures were scrawled over a dozen Kellogg Pacts? A boy like this would always be at war, if not with the Germans, then with the social conditions into which he had been born; all his life he would be involved in the hopeless fight of the under-privileged against the snug, and the well-breeched.

Jim got up, found his way to the street, and was about to board a 'bus when somebody plucked his sleeve. He turned to look into the coarse, wrinkled face of Jacob Sokolski, the owner of the furs that had been stolen.

During the trial Sokolski had struck him as being a gentle old man, somewhat distressed by the case, and certainly not on show, like most of the other witnesses. He had given his evidence in mangled English, and Jim guessed that he originated from Eastern Europe.

"Vait, mister," he invited, "you'n me take tea, eh? You'n me get the taste of bloddy polis from our troats, eh?"

Jim regarded him with surprise. In spite of the man's benevolent appearance it struck him as odd that a successful businessman, whose goods had been yanked from the shopwindow by professional criminals, should now refer to those who had arrested the raiders as "bloddy polis". He let the 'bus go.

"I'd like some tea, yes, Mr. Sokolski," he said civilly, "but you might as well know that it didn't give me any satisfaction to see that kid sent up for seven years. Two would have been ample. Either that, or the chap that organised it should have got fourteen. As it is, it doesn't make sense."

"You an' me, we tink the zame," said Mr. Sokolski, grasping his arm, and leading him purposefully towards an A.B.C. "These polis here, they no so dam bad. No guns and no knouts, but still they are polis, eh? Vunce a polis, alvays a bloddy polis. They hit the peoples. Like that—dum-dum!"

And Mr. Sokolski withdrew his arm, and smote his open palm very hard, signifying police oppression the world over.

They took a fancy to one another from the beginning. Jim, who had read a good deal about Tsarist oppression, was genuinely interested in Sokolski's first-hand information on the subject.

As a child, the furrier had been hounded from home by Cossacks, and had starved in a Lithuanian hovel. He had seen his father flogged, and his brothers marched into exile. He himself had escaped, at the age of eleven, into the relative haven of a cabin-boy's berth on a Baltic trader, where the life would have killed most children in a month, but Sokolski took a great deal of killing, and had survived to jump ship in Philadelphia, and make his way, speaking no English, and almost penniless, across a wide continent to the fruit-farms of California. A chance meeting with another Russian had brought about his entry into the fur trade, and because he had natural shrewdness, and could save ninety-five dollars out of every hundred he earned, he soon prospered, and later moved to London. His terrible childhood, and the grind ing poverty of his early manhood, had not soured him, or made him arrogant in success, for, throughout his pilgrimage, he had hung on to his two major characteristics, a strong sense of humour, and a bitter distrust of all men in uniform.

"Even my commissionaire, Carver.... I say to him, 'No bloddy uniform ... no bloddy medals'! With the uniform it is alvays the same for the peoples—dum-dum!", and this time he smote his fist to signify the world-wide tyranny of the military.

Jim went to work for Sokolski the following week. He began as shopman, cleaning windows, stoking boilers, and carrying out all the menial tasks that presented themselves. Within the first year, however, Sokolski made him a van driver, and not long afterwards, when the furrier bought a controlling interest in a group of ready-made clothing shops in the north-west suburbs, he promoted him to the post of transport overseer, with a salary of six pounds a week, more money than Jim had ever drawn in the past.

He knew all about Jim's socialism, and tolerated it with a mixture of scorn and amusement.

"Ach," he would say, as he stood about the transport yard watching stock-loading, "you bloddy socialists set the vorld to rights, eh? No, no, my frien' ... nobody set the vorld right! Not socialist, not Bolshevik, not priest! I dell you somding, Carver. You make effryvun rich, and comforts see, like me, but you not set the vorld right, not for ten minute! Because vy? Because half the peoples go to sleep right off, and the odders run avay vith vot the sleeping vons leave lying around!"

This quaintly-phrased philosophy did not irritate Jim, for he recognised the Russian as possessing something that had been overlooked in all the pamphlets he had read, and the speeches he had heard. Perhaps it was common-sense, or perhaps the gospel of a battered human heart that had never quite forgotten how to laugh.

3

Archie Carver remembered the Spring of 1930 because it was the season in which he began his expansion.

Archie's dream had changed with the years. When he had first joined the Pirettas, in the days when he was roving the countryside looking for empty premises, the acquisition of a business had not been an end in itself, but merely a means to furnish the quick capital, and freedom of movement, necessary to provide him with A Good Time.

His outlook had undergone some important changes since then. Somehow, his adolescent conception of A Good Time had crept into a till, and never found its way out again. He came across it now and again, when he opened the drawer for loose change, but he no longer recognised it. A Good Time, as he had understood it when he was twenty-one, had nothing whatever to do with his latter-day dreams of commerce.

It_was not that he denied himself very much. He smoked as much as ever, drank a good deal, and even seduced the odd female customer whenever the opportunity presented itself, but these diversions were no longer important to him. What was important, what occupied most of his waking thoughts and even invaded his dreams, was The Chain.

It was stupid, he reasoned, to spend one's time and one's entire creative energy on operating a single business. Piretta's shop paid off well enough. In the five years he had been the Italian's son-in-law and partner the turnover had trebled itself. There was, however, a definite limit to the yield of a small grocery business in an outlying suburb. What was needed was a *chain* of such businesses—all small, all staffed by not more than two people, and all overseen and regulated by himself.

His experiences at multiple stores had shown him the weak spot in such enterprises. The weak spot was the local manager, who had to possess enterprise and initiative, a limited amount perhaps, but still of a type superior to the ordinary counter-hand. Yet this man, the key man, was denied a stake in the business, and because of this he was, given time, certain to go sour, to become dishonest, or disillusioned and slack. Archie understood this very well. He had worked with shop assistants long enough to know that the one thing they shied away from was responsibility. They would work, sometimes until they dropped, at any kind of manual task, but to ask them to think for themselves, to make decisions involving cash, to back their judgments about goods, and customers, was to ask more than they were able to give. Loaded with responsibility against their will, they became sullen, or sick, or so nervous that they were liable to fly off the handle at awkward moments. They had to have someone at their elbow, someone on whom they could unload their worries. Provide them with someone like this and they were usually prepared to give him their unstinted labour and—what was even more essential—their personal loyalty.

Archie considered this aspect very carefully when he thought about his Chain. When he began forging it, he told himself he would have no managers as master links. A branch would consist of one or two assistants, carefully picked for lack of initiative and robust physique, and of premises that were sited in a back street near a housing estate, or among fields that would soon become a housing estate. It was a mistake, he thought, to choose premises on main roads. Motor traffic was getting heavier all the time, and it would not be long before parking problems began to affect turnover. South London was constantly expanding, and roads that were now main thoroughfares might not remain so for much longer; nor would they remain within easy shopping distance of the suburban population. What was wanted— what could be made to pay off handsomely if a man had foresight and patience—was a series of tiny shops in villages that would soon cease to be villages. Land and real estate was still cheap in these areas, and premises in village side-streets could be acquired for trifling sums, particularly when old folk died off, and their modest estates were sold up by impatient families.

In his mind Archie called these dream-shops "Pop-Ins". Before he was thirty-five, he told himself, he would have at least a dozen Pop-Ins, all within a five-mile radius of his present business. He would pay each of them two visits a day, one to check stock and watch service, the other to check books, and satisfy himself that his employees still lacked his sort of initiative.

He made his first move in February 1930. He had never lost touch with Piretta's slightly shady solicitor, and it occurred to him that here was a man who might put him in touch with the sort of property-owners he was looking for. His hunch was correct. The solicitor put him on to two families, each with a small property to sell.

Archie donned his best suit, called, and made offers that were at once indignantly refused by both beneficiaries. He retired unruffled. He was an expert in sizing-up people and premises. Within ten days he had both the properties in his possession, and the chain of Pop-Ins was a two-link reality.

He did not consult Piretta about this, but he did have the foresight to buy both shops in his wife's name. Maria was called in to sign papers, and two small banking accounts were opened, also in her name.

By this time Maria had three children, two boys and a girl. She seldom appeared at the counter, where Piretta had once hoped she might find a husband among the Woodbine regulars,

She was occupied all day long, cooking and washing for the children, her father, and her husband. She said very little, except when she was alone with the little girl, Juanita. She talked to Juanita a great deal, but no one ever heard what she said to her. The baby, an attractive child, with her grandfather's mild brown eyes, watched her intently as she fussed about the cot and the play-pen. Juanita must have been puzzled why her mother was so silent in company and yet so talkative when they were alone.

Maria took little interest in the two boys, who were always playing with their grandfather, but she remained very dutiful in the performance of wifely obligations towards Archie. Archie accepted her ministrations in the same spirit as he accepted the services of a 'bus conductor, or bar-tender. He was never actively unkind to her, and never criticised her. He simply ate what she put before him, dressed in the clothes she laid out for him, and paid swift and silent court to her whenever he had been too preoccupied with business to call upon one of his mistresses.

It did not occur to him that both Maria and her father knew all about these mistresses; and if he had known he would not have shown the faintest concern, or troubled to make an excuse. He himself did not take them very seriously and was very careful to keep each relationship on an unemotional plane. He remembered Rita Ramage; having once learnt a lesson, he never forgot it.

Thus, Archie geared himself for the new decade, and was soon to be seen in his bull-nosed Morris Cowley, flitting between Addington, Wickham, and Shirley, a slightly thickening figure, with rapidly receding hair, and a confident way of carrying himself that was just short of a swagger. A businessman, a husband, a father, and a future Czar of South London Pop-Ins.

4

Louise remembered the Spring of 1930 because it was her first mating season.

At the age of thirty Louise was thin, flat-chested, and slightly stooping. Nearly two-and-a-half decades over sink and stove showed in Louise's figure, but not in her character, which was as sweet and pliant and motherly as it had always been.

Nobody had ever heard Louise complain about anything, and nobody ever caught her with her pursey little mouth puckered into a frown, or her prominent, grey eyes unsmiling. All her life she had been the steady provider of clean towels, and beautifully-ironed underwear for any Carver who needed towels or underwear, at any time of the day or night, and all her life she had performed a thrice-daily miracle of serving up hot, nourishing meals from the limited housekeeping money given her by Jim. It was on this account that all the Carvers had good teeth and excellent digestions, and each of them, in their own way, loved Louise for her gentleness and her monumental unselfishness. Perhaps this was why they welcomed Jack Strawbridge, notwithstanding the alarming possibilities his courtship presented at Number Twenty.

Jack Strawbridge was a jobbing gardener in the employ of whoever happened to be renting Stannard's nurseries, behind the Avenue. In the winter of 1929 he was sent to clear ground that had been left fallow for thirteen years, and the task of freeing the nursery from its acres of bramble, and bindweed and dandelion, seemed likely to occupy him for some considerable time.

He was a big, shambling man, with a brick-red face, and a large head on which was balanced a cloth cap at least two sizes too small for him. The cap always looked as if it would fall off at the first sweep of Jack's long-handled bill-hook, but it never did, and Judy formed the opinion that it was fixed there by some means unknown to her—a strip of adhesive tape perhaps, that linked the lining to Jack's shining pate.

He had the stolid nature and soft burr of a Kentish countryman. Nobody ever discovered what had brought him to the suburb in the first place. He would have looked much more at home behind a plough or a lowing herd of cows. His movements were slow, deliberate, and immensely powerful. He could crack a Brazil nut between finger and thumb, and whenever he did so, or performed any similar feat of strength, he would show his delight by a short, rasping chuckle, that sounded rather like a St. Bernard's warning bark. His eyes were a vivid blue, and there was always a short, gingery stubble on his chin. He was as comfortable and as engaging as an old cart-horse, and when he made his ponderous way from the nursery into the Carvers' garden, via a gap in the rotting fence, he looked like one, recently relieved of its harness.

He and Louise might never have met had that gap in the fence been opposite any other back gate. He came blundering through the gap about eleven o'clock one morning, holding a forearm in a huge fist, and grunting somewhat with the pain of a four-inch gash, caused by the bill-hook.

He was losing blood rapidly when he reached the Carvers' kitchen door, and Louise, who happened to be hanging up washing, saw that there was no time to send for a doctor, and rendered first-aid on the spot.

They did not so much as speak until a tourniquet was fixed, the bandaging was done, and Jack was sipping hot, sweet tea at the kitchen table. Then she made use of an expression that was familiar to everyone who knew her, and fitted almost every situation in which she had found herself since babyhood. She said:

"There, now! What a pity it is!"

Practically everything was a pity to Louise—a stray cat's appetite, the dog Strike's suspicious barks at tradesmen, minor mishaps such as Jack's cut, or a train disaster involving the deaths of hundreds of passengers. The expression covered the entire range of humanity's ills, from earthquakes, plagues, and famines, to spilt milk, mosquito bites, and ingrown toenails.

Jack Strawbridge, sipping his tea, looked at her with interest. He did not see the sagging flatness of her figure, or the startling prominence of the eyes, only an immense compassion, that seemed to emanate from her like a lighthouse beam, and was now directed exclusively on him. For a few seconds he basked in its warmth, then he made up his mind.

"I'm a widower," he said, simply and without ambiguity.

It seems hard to believe that their courtship was launched by that single remark, but such was the case. No man had ever made an approach to Louise, direct or indirect, and possibly this had something to do with the complete success of Jack Strawbridge's assault. Or it may have been that Louise, having so much to do about the house, found no time or opportunity to be coy, even at that first meeting. At all events, they made up their minds on the spot, and from that day on Jack ate all his mid-day meals in the kitchen of Number Twenty, and returned there, washed and changed, but not shaved, at precisely seven each evening, in order to take Louise for a stroll as far as the mill.

They never went further than the mill, and once they were out they never turned back before reaching it. If it was raining they sat in the kitchen and read the evening paper together. Occasionally they went down to the Granada and watched a film through twice from the nine-pennies. It was a placid undemanding courtship on both sides, and it was hard to see how it could ever progress towards marriage, for Jack supported an invalid mother on his two pounds fifteen a week, and Louise never once contemplated leaving her father and sisters to fend for themselves.

The strange thing about this static element in their association was that it did not appear to worry either of them, and in time Jim, Judy, both sets of twins, and Jack's mother (who never appeared on the scene at all) accepted it with the same equanimity as that of the two people most concerned. The Carvers liked Jack, and Jack liked the Carvers. That was all there was to it, and all, presumably, there ever would be to it. Whether or not his daughter embraced her suitor in the shadow of the old mill when they went for their walk, Jim never knew, and whether they would ever get married he did not know either. His elder daughter's admirer ate a good many meals in the kitchen, but his appetite was no strain on the household budget, because he more than made up for what he consumed by a steady supply of fresh vegetables, taken from the now cultivated nursery over the fence. After a time, when the south end of the plot was cleared and planted, Louise stopped buying vegetables altogether. This distressed her a little, for she hated disappointing the tradesmen who called for orders.

"I've got so much fruit, I don't know what to do with it," she told the disgruntled greengrocer's van-man, throwing open the pantry door, and displaying apples, and plums, and gooseberries, and red currants, stacked neatly along the shelves in rows of boxes and punnets.

"Lumme, you 'ave, 'aven't you?" said the van-man.

"Yes," said Louise apologetically, "it's such a pity!"

5

It did not take Judy Carver very long to discover that she had lost Esme for ever.

Her suspicions were aroused within hours of Esme's first kiss in the greenhouse, but a period of some weeks elapsed between the first nagging doubts, and the shattering realisation that her dream would always remain a dream, and that nothing short of a miracle would ever transform it into reality.

But by that time Judy had ceased to believe in miracles, ancient or modern, for she had ceased to believe in divine mercy and justice. She longed desperately to die, and be done with it all.

People of the Avenue saw their dreams recede and fade every day, and most of them rode out the shock wave within hours. But their cases were different. For them there were always new dreams.

Judy's dream was a good deal more insistent than the dreams of the other people of the Avenue. Some might even have called it an obsession. All along the crescent people had dreams but, for the most part, they were recognised as such, and kept handy for odd moments, when nothing much was doing. They were aspirins, not opium pipes, stage dressing, not the stage itself.

Judy's dream had never been tailored to fit a plan, like Archie's, or Elaine Frith's, whose dreams were always being adapted to meet expanding opportunities. Their dreams confined themselves to the present and the future, but Judy's went back into the past, back to the hot summer morning, ten years ago, when she and Esme had played Sleeping Beauty in the gazebo beside the Manor Lake. Fundamentally, it had not changed in all that time, it was still centred on marriage to Esme. Only the scenery had been changed a little as Judy passed from childhood to adolescence.

In the beginning they were to marry in a Cathedral, later, more modestly at Shirley Church, and later still, after Esme had expressed certain doubts concerning his spiritual beliefs, the wedding moved to the Register Office, in East Croydon. In the same way, the threshold that he was to carry her over had been modified, to keep it in line with practicalities. Once, they were going to share a Manor, like the old mansion in the woods, later a country cottage, with diamond-latticed panes, lupins, and an undulating thatched roof where swallows nested, but by the time Esme had left school the cottage had become one of the new semi-detached villas that they were beginning to build in the new roads half-way between Wickham and Shirley Church Road. In the end, had circumstances demanded it, it might have become a caravan, or a hut on one of the allotments. It was Esme that mattered, Esme and the child—the "cherub", as Judy called her, for the child was a girl, who could wear pretty little poke bonnets, and suck her thumb gravely as she bounced along in her shiny new pram, pushed by Judy, an unusually silent child, who saved all her gurgles for Esme's evening homecomings.

All these years Judy had been waiting for a sign. Sooner or

later, she reasoned, her dream must communicate itself to Esme. At the magic of the password or countersign it would then unfold, like the miraculous dragonfly in *Water Babies*, and their future would merge, as it was fated to merge from the very beginning, from the first touch of his lips in the gazebo. God had promised her, and God did not lead the devout and the prayerful up garden paths. Judy still said her prayers out of bed, even in the depths of winter, and Esme's name had never been dropped from those prayers, not once, since the day they had met.

Sometimes it had seemed as though God were giving Esme a gentle nudge. There was the day when she sprained her ankle, and he carried her for a mile home through the woods. There were the occasions when they both attended the same Avenue parties, and he called her out in "Postman's Knock", or blinked solemnly at her in "Winking". There was the recent and more mature moment, when he had talked to her of his ambitions during their picnic on Shirley Hills. These were the modest peaks of Judy's love-graph and, while the field was still open, she asked for no more than the limited reassurance they brought her. It was the day following the Stafford-Fyffe dance that the graph took its first plunge; after that it went on plunging until it shot off the page.

Judy had half-hoped that Esme would come in and tell her about the dance before she went off to work that morning. When he did not, when her lunch hour went by, and she had seen nothing of him, she made up her mind to call after tea, and hear his account first-hand.

Since leaving school the previous year, Judy had been working as a counter-hand at Boots, at the corner of Cawnpore Road. She liked it well enough. The shop had a certain aura of luxury, absent at other chemists. Most of the girls who worked there came on from the Grammar School, and Judy, who had remained at Lucknow Road Council School until she was fifteen, was agreeably surprised by their friendliness and lack of snobbery. She worked in the toilet department, selling soap, toothbrushes, and hot-water bottles, and there was a chance of graduating to cosmetics in time. It was what her father had described as a "clean job", with some sort

of prospects, providing "she didn't get uppity, as so many of
the flappers did nowadays."

About six o'clock that evening Judy slipped next door via
the fence. As the former bridesmaid she was on excellent
terms with Eunice and Harold, and Eunice invariably made
her very welcome, for the years with Esme had made Judy a
good listener, and Harold usually spent the two hours following supper with *The Times*, which he read page by page,
resenting interruptions.

Esme, Judy learned, was in his study, and had asked not to
be disturbed.

"How did he enjoy last night?" she asked.

Eunice sighed and pouted. "I haven't been able to get a
word out of him, have I, Harold dear?"

Harold grunted, and Eunice ran on: "Come to think of it,
Judith, he's been very odd all day; he was moody at breakfast—well, not exactly moody—preoccupied would describe
it better perhaps, preoccupied and . . . and *distrait*, you
know?"

Not knowing the precise meaning of "distrait", Judy said
loyally: "I suppose he was tired. Mr. Hartnell, the bandsman,
didn't get home until very late. I heard him come in."

"Well, dear," said Eunice, "after all the fuss and bother I
had to get him to go, I *was* looking forward to hearing all
about it. If you can't go to dances yourself"—she looked
reproachfully at Harold's paper—"you can at least hear
about them! Perhaps *you* can get it out of him. He'll tell *you*
what he wouldn't tell me! Now why don't you slip up and ask
him? Then you could tell me, couldn't you?"

Harold looked up from his paper. "Esme said he was
writing, and didn't want to be disturbed."

"Yes, I know he did, dear," said Eunice placidly, "but you
men always say that when you've got something worth talking about, it just saves you bother. Sometimes, Judy, you'd
hardly believe me, but *sometimes* a whole evening goes by,
and neither of them says a word!"

She got up. "I know—I'll make the coffee, and you shall
take it up, just to surprise him!"

Had Judy been less curious to hear about the dance she
would have declined this invitation, but the announcement

that Esme was writing reassured her. She knew of Esme's need for an audience and imagined that he would be glad to read aloud what he had written.

She took the tray, containing her own coffee and his, mounted the stairs, and knocked softly on the porch-room door.

There was no answer, and so she went straight in. He was sitting crouched over his desk, and her entry surprised him— so much so that he seemed to her to start up, and bite back an angry exclamation. At the same time his hand shot protectively across the page he was writing, but not quickly enough to mask the size of the note-paper. She had time to see that it was a small sheet, and obviously a letter, for Judy remembered that he always wrote his stories on foolscap.

His nervousness communicated itself to her. She set down the tray, trembling a little.

"It's just your coffee, Esme, your mother thought——"

He flung himself round on her. He had never looked at her, or spoken to her like this before. His face was clouded, almost sulky, his tone tetchy, and complaining.

"Hang it, it's impossible to get any privacy in this blasted house!" he shouted, and then, seeing sudden misery in her face, "—it's not you, Judy, it's . . . Mother. She . . . she will *poke* into everything! It's enough to drive a man mad!"

Judy remained uncertainly by the door. She was always at a loss when Esme flared up, but he had never been quite like this. Her eye returned to the edge of the half-written letter under his hand. Hastily he tucked it inside a blotter. His action made her heart leap.

"It was just that we . . . we wanted to hear about the dance, Esme," she faltered. "Was there anyone you knew?"

He was clearly feeling very uncomfortable about something, for he found it difficult to meet her eye, and turned sharply away, drifting over to the window.

"Yes, there was someone," he said in a low voice. "It was Elaine."

"Elaine?"

"Elaine Frith, the girl opposite. I didn't like the show at first, but later on it warmed up." He turned back to her, but still failed to look her in the face. "It was a pretty marvellous

'do,' Judy . . . must have cost them a small fortune. Look—
would you mind, I . . . I've got to work now? Would you tell
Mum I meant what I said about not being disturbed?"

"Yes, of course."

She took her cup and went swiftly downstairs. She was
confused rather than alarmed by his information and irritabil-
ity. He obviously resented being questioned about the dance.
He was writing a letter that he wanted no one to see. Could
he have got into some sort of trouble last night? Was he
writing an apology to Mrs. Stafford-Fyffe, or the someone to
whom he had been rude? Elaine Frith, the girl opposite?
That was incredible, surely? She was never allowed out for a
walk, much less to a dance, scheduled to end at 1 a.m. Her
mother was in hospital. *That* might account for Elaine being
at the dance, but why should Esme be writing to her, when
she only lived at Number Seventeen, immediately opposite?

She could make nothing of it and after gulping her coffee,
excused herself and went home.

She tried to read, but it was useless. The memory of
Esme's manner, and the way his hand had shot over his letter
the moment she entered the study, kept returning to her. The
more she thought about it, the more convinced she was that
Esme had been involved in some sort of scene at Mrs.
Stafford-Fyffe's, and was bitterly ashamed of his part in it,
and at pains to conceal the facts if that were possible. If he
was in trouble it was her privilege to help him, but how,
when he spun round like a disturbed thief the moment she
spoke to him?

She went to bed early, and lay awake long after Louise
had come up. The memory of Esme's clouded face invaded
her dreams.

Judy got her answer about a week later, when the shop
was crowded with Christmas shoppers, and she was struggling
to get some bath-salts out of the window for a particularly
trying customer.

Kneeling there, trying to avoid bringing a loaded stand
crashing down, she saw Esme turn into the shop. In her
eagerness to climb out she knocked over a stand behind her,
and Mr. Myrtle, the Manager, heard the crash, and came
bustling over from the cash-desk. He was a nervous little man

and was finding it very difficult to keep his head in the rush
of business.

"What's happened? What are you doing in the window,
Miss Carver?"

Judy explained that a customer had insisted on a particular
box of bath salts from the front of the window.

"All right, all right," he said, "straighten it up, and I'll
serve her . . . just hand it out to me—quickly . . . quickly!"

Judy gave him the bath salts and set about rebuilding the
window. It occupied her at least ten minutes, and when at
last she climbed out, Esme had made his purchase and gone.

She waited impatiently until lunch-hour, and then began
questioning the girls. She fancied that Miss Symes must have
served him, and described Esme, feature by feature. Miss
Symes was amused.

"Boy friend of yours? Yes, I think I remember him. He
bought an enamel powder-compact, and wanted it initialled. I
told him that was hopeless if it was a Christmas present, so
he gave up the idea, and wrote a note to send with it."

"A note? You mean *we're* sending the compact?"

"It's in the post hamper . . . hi, what's the idea? If it's your
present you shouldn't spoil the surprise. . . ."

But Judy was already burrowing in the hamper, searching
desperately for a box that might contain a powder-compact.
The parcels were not yet made up for post, and she found
the flat box almost at once. Inside was a sealed envelope, in
Esme's familiar handwriting, addressed to *"Miss Elaine Frith,
c/o Sutler's Commercial College, Lowel Road, East Croydon."*

For a few moments she was stunned. Mercifully, Miss
Symes was due back on duty, and left her. She sat back on
her heels beside the hamper, holding the compact, and staring at the neat angular characters of the address on the
envelope. It was incredible—Esme sending *her* a powder-
compact for Christmas, and doing it from her shop, just as
though Elaine Frith had been an aunt, or a cousin! Suppose
she hadn't been in the window when he bought it? She might
then have had the humiliation of helping him to choose it!
And what did this mean, quite apart from the fact that Esme
was "going with" Elaine? Clearly it meant that he did not even

take her into account, that he did not in the least mind her knowing about it! And this could only mean that either he wanted to hurt her—which, even now, she refused to believe —or what was far worse, that he had never so much as thought of her as his sweetheart.

For a moment she thought she was going to faint. She got up unsteadily, and went into the toilet, a tiny partitioned-off room, with a single wash-basin. She looked at herself in the spotted mirror, seeing a small, pointed face, desperate with anxiety, and pale with shock.

Suddenly she realised that she could not remain at work, devoting the entire afternoon and early evening to indecisive women and bored or bewildered men. She had to get out in the open, to think, and think, and think. She had to reason things out, fight her panic, and come to some sort of terms with herself. She made a decision instantly, hurried into the shop, and sought out Mr. Myrtle.

"I'm sorry, Mr. Myrtle, I've got to go home . . . I . . . I . . . I'm not well . . . I feel terribly sick."

Mr. Myrtle began to protest.

"You can't go home, Miss Carver; it's Christmas . . . we can't cope. . . ."

"I'm sorry—I've got to, I've got to!", and Judy ran back into the lobby, peeled off her overall, snatched her coat, and was gone before he had time to argue.

She did not go home. Home—with Louise, and the twins, would be worse than staying at work. There would be explanations, cossetings, cups of tea, and sedatives. She did not want tea, sympathy, and sedatives. What she knew she must have was *time*, and a few hours' solitude in which to collect herself, catch her breath, and screw up enough courage to face this appalling crisis.

She hurried up Shirley Rise towards the mill, taking the path that ran beside Oaks Road, towards the Old Roman Well. When she reached the clearing she sat down on a half-rotted seat. It was very quiet here, and she was quite alone. Last week's snow had turned to slush, and the countryside looked cheerless and desolate. All the way up the hill she had been fighting to keep back the tears, but up here there was no one to see her, and tears began to flow, bringing some sort of relief from the choking sensation that had caught at her throat ever since she had seen the envelope.

Commonsense told her to make no effort to check the tears, and soon she began to feel a little calmer. Her rage against God began to abate, and with it came the first feeble glimmerings of objectivity, a promise, no more as yet, of being able to extricate herself emotionally, and look at the situation from outside.

It was then that she realised for the first time that perhaps she was being unfair to Esme, that she alone was able to assess the depths of her devotion, and that in all these years she had never once confessed her love, not even to Louise, or to one of her few school friends—certainly not to Esme himself. It was suddenly quite clear to her that he had never thought about her as a girl—had even perhaps found her vassalage a nuisance at times.

The thought made the tears flow again, but this time she resisted them. It was too late for tears, and too late, it seemed, for a new approach to Esme, one that might conceivably make him aware of her as something more than a mere hanger-on. She made a great effort to think progressively, and bit by bit she was able to come to grips with the main issues. What were the issues? She tried to tick them off, one by one. She was in love with Esme. Esme was not in love with her. Esme was now in love with somebody else, and that somebody else was an elegant and attractive girl, with the added attraction of mystery surrounding her.

What could she do about it? Could she go to him and explain how she felt? That was unthinkable. To acquaint him now with her true state of mind would be to court his contempt or pity, and it was common knowledge that men ran away from women who stalked or plagued them. Perhaps this had been her wrong turning from the beginning, although she had always been dimly aware of this danger, and had tried hard to guard against it. In the main she had set out to make herself indispensable to him, and when they were still children, she had, she was sure, succeeded in doing so. Then this wasn't the wrong turning, and the fact that he was unaware of her love was proof that it wasn't. It was more likely that her trust in God was at fault. She had always felt quite certain that, sooner or later, Esme would do something, or say something, that would point them directly towards the altar or, failing this, that something dramatic would happen to reveal her to him—something like the blindness of Amyas, that had steered the hero into the waiting arms of Ayacanora, in the final, touching pages of *Westward Ho!*

Then again, she had always been told that men did not grow up as quickly as women, and had believed it for, until this moment, Esme had not shown the slightest interest in girls, not even in the way her brothers Archie, Berni, and Boxer regarded them, and she had imagined, poor fool, that this was proof of the fact that he considered himself spoken for!

She went at her problem relentlessly, plucking and plucking at the tangle to find a loose end that she could follow, and her mind was still trying to gauge the strength of his infatuation for Elaine, when she heard a sharp crackling from the bushes on her right. She looked up, and was astonished to see a big, chestnut horse step sedately into the clearing, and lower its head over a few blades of grass that sprouted beside the seat.

She was so startled that for a moment or two she completely forgot her misery. The horse was saddled, and its reins trailed in front of it, hampering its movements.

Judy looked round in all directions but there was no sign of the rider. The horse appeared to be lost, and straying.

She went over to it and picked up the reins, finding a little solace in its presence. She was standing here, not knowing what to do next, when she heard a harsh rattle of gravel on the path beyond the clearing, and a woman cantered into the clearing, riding an equally big grey, lathered with sweat.

Judy glanced at the horsewoman apprehensively, and at once thought her the most formidable-looking woman she had ever seen. She was thick-set, heavy-limbed, and coarse-featured, with little button eyes that blinked above a monstrously hooked nose. Judy thought she looked rather like a powerfully-built witch, and instinctively let go of the bridle she was holding. The horse-woman braced herself in the saddle as the grey reared and flung its head about, straining at her control.

"Don't let her go, girl!" she shouted in a harsh, rasping voice.

Judy grabbed the bridle again, just as the chestnut was turning to run. The jerk made her stagger, but she hung on, and was surprised to see the woman backing the grey towards the path.

"Lead her over there—over there by the Well!" shouted the woman, now hunched into a concentration of bulging muscle, as she wrestled with the nervous grey. "Wait a minute. . . . I'll come to you. . . . *Stand*, Pipeclay! *Stand*, damn you!", and she raised her crop, and slashed viciously at the animal's hindquarters, at the same time straining back on the double bit.

Judy watched her manœuvers with interest, expecting to see the grey rear again, or turn and bolt up the steep path behind it. It did nothing like this. Under the liberal application of the crop it suddenly became cowed, and began sidling away, quietening under the woman's gently hissed commands—"*Quiet*, Pipeclay. . . . *Quiet*, now. . . . *Stand!* . . . there's a boy! *Stand*, Pipeclay!"

When the horse was quite still, the woman flung herself from the saddle, and deftly knotted the reins to a silver birch. Then she came squelching across the clearing, with long, lumbering strides.

"I'm obliged to you, whoever you are. They hate one another. . . . Don't worry about Miriam, she wouldn't harm a fly, so long as Pipeclay keeps his distance. . . ."

She turned to the quivering chestnut. "There, now . . . easy, now, easy! What the hell have you done with Mr. Goodchild, Miriam?"

She went on soothing the chestnut, taking a knob of sugar from her pocket, and slipping it into its mouth.

"Do you ride, girl?" she suddenly flung at Judy.

"No, I'm afraid I don't—but did you say they hated one another—the horses?"

"I certainly did! Happens sometimes! Nobody knows why, but it happens! I want my head examining, taking them out together. Always had some crazy notion they'd grow out of it, but they won't. Asking for trouble, I was, especially with that fool of a Goodchild. He's a mile back I wouldn't wonder—two, maybe. But serve him dam'well right. He *will* sit forward, no matter what I tell him."

"Do you mean Miriam has thrown him off?" asked Judy.

The woman gave a short laugh. "Thrown him?" She slipped the stirrup-irons up the leathers. "I'll say she threw him . . . never saw such a thing in my life. Shot him out like a catapult, flat on his face in the gorse—over there, by the Mill."

"But—but oughtn't we to find out if he's hurt?" asked Judy.

"No!" said the woman, "let the silly ape look after himself! I've got my hands full, haven't I? Look here, gel, I can't get Miriam back to the stables on the leading rein, there's a stretch of main road, and I tell you they hate the sight of one another! Can't you ride *at all?*"

"No," said Judy, very promptly indeed, "I've never yet sat on a horse!"

The riding-mistress sucked her big teeth.

"You could walk her—she's like a lamb with young gels. Don't ask me why, but she is—look at her now."

As though to confirm the statement the horse stood perfectly still. Judy reached out, took the reins, and walked a few paces across the clearing. The horse followed her, placidly.

"You see?" said the woman. "Look here, I'll go ahead, and you follow me." Then, as an afterthought, "You're not doing anything special, are you?"

"No," said Judy ruefully, "nothing really special."

They moved off down Oaks Road towards the Mill, the woman riding ahead at a prancing walk. They turned off above the mill, and crossed a muddy path of common and several by-roads. After nearly an hour's walk they topped a rise, and Judy saw what appeared to be a small farm in a shallow valley, with a line of one-storey outbuildings adjoining it. She had never been this far afield, and fancied she must be somewhere near Keston.

At the head of a winding cart-track stood a weather-beaten board. It read:

FIRHILL RIDING STABLES—Prop. Maud Somerton
LESSONS GIVEN—LIVERIES RECEIVED

Judy wondered vaguely what a livery was, and how Miss Somerton, who, she gathered, was the woman riding ahead, would receive one if it was offered.

She was soon to find out. Miss Somerton gave both the horses to a man in a sweat-soiled yellow shirt, and on learning that Mr. Goodchild had phoned, and gone home by taxi, she jerked off her bowler, threw down her crop, and clanked into the house, beckoning Judy to follow.

The room they entered was an old farm kitchen, partially converted into a living-room. It had a spartan look. All the furniture was black oak, and the stone floor was covered, here and there, with worn strips of coconut matting. There were no pictures, and no curtains, but a huge root smouldered in the vast fire-place. The place had a warm, cosy smell, suggesting baking bread and chicken mash.

The woman took a purse from behind the mantelshelf clock.

"What shall we say—five shillings?"

"I don't want paying," said Judy, surprised. "I—I liked leading her, it was fun."

The woman looked at her for a long moment.

"You'd better have tea, at any rate," she barked. "Dam' decent of you, to tramp all out here. Kettle's boiling. Won't be a minute."

Judy watched her make tea from a huge, black kettle, suspended over the smoke on an iron bar. Cups and scones were fetched from a cupboard beside the fireplace, and the woman flung them about carelessly, her spurs ringing on the slabs as she stamped to and fro.

"You say you've *never* ridden?" she asked presently.

"Never," said Judy, still faintly intimidated by her brusque manner and staccato sentences.

"Lord," grunted Miss Somerton, half to herself, "you might as well be dead! What do you do?"

"I work in a chemist's," Judy told here, "at least, I *did.* I shall probably be sacked when I go back there."

"Why?"

"I walked out—sort of."

"Huh!" snapped Miss Somerton, stabbing a spoon into the

tea, and stirring it with such vigour that tea spurted on to her lapel.

"I—I suppose I was upset," added Judy.

"Upset?" snapped Miss Somerton. "What about, money?"

Then an unaccountable impulse stirred in Judy. For years she had nursed her feelings about Esme to herself. Not once had she risen to the tiresome teasing of the family, or the exploratory questions of girls at school, and at work, as to whether or not she had ever been out with a boy. Now, without a moment's hesitation, she found herself pouring out the entire story to this big, horsey, buck-toothed woman, who was a complete stranger, and had never set eyes on Esme.

She told her how they had first met in Manor Woods, of her long apprenticeship as Esme's "squire", of the interminable wait for Esme to pronounce upon her future, and finally of his sudden infatuation for a girl opposite who, to Judy's certain knowledge, he had never spoken to, a week before.

She told it all rather breathlessly, and it was not until she had finished that the enormity of her confession brought the blood rushing to her cheeks. She got up and snatched at her coat.

Miss Somerton made a gesture with her big hand, the sort of gesture she might have made to a restive horse, and it had the same effect.

"Sit down, gel! Have another cup of tea! Eat a scone! Only thing I can make! Here——" and she pushed the plate across the table.

"That place you work . . . this chemist's . . . what do you sell, besides powder-compacts?"

It seemed a very irrelevant question, but Judy told her.

"Well . . . soap, and hot-water bottles, and . . . aspirins, and things."

"*Hot-water bottles!*" Miss Somerton made it sound as if a hot-water bottle was lethal. "What sort of life is *that* for a gel? *Hot-water bottles!* And you can't even ride! Never so much as sat a horse!"

She leaned across the table, and held Judy with black, boot-button eyes.

"Know your trouble? You're one-track! I can spot it! I'm

one-track, too. Only thing to do when you're one-track, and you find out it's a cul-de-sac, is turn back, and try the next turning! Change your life! Start now! Make the break! Mooning won't help! Stand up! Walk about!"

Judy stood up. Her acute embarrassment, that had succeeded confession, gave way to bewildered uncertainty. She was beginning to wonder if this odd woman was quite sane. Obediently, but without taking her eyes off Miss Somerton, she walked a few steps towards the fireplace, and then back.

"There! Knew it! You've got the figure! You've got hands, too! I'm never wrong about these things! Would you like to learn to ride, gel?"

"To ride?" Judy regarded her with astonishment. "You mean *pay* to learn . . . on Wednesday afternoons off?"

"No, no, *no*! Who ever learned to ride a horse walk—trot—canter routine on a leading rein? *That* isn't riding, it's being carried about the countryside! I mean *work* here, with me— and there wouldn't be so much riding yet awhile, either! It'll be mucking out, cleaning tack, answering the phone, making out bills—I can never get around to making out bills, and some of 'em run on for years. You see for yourself what comes of that!"

She waved her hand, indicating the peeling walls and comfortless furniture, then returned abruptly to the business on hand: "Well? Wouldn't that be better than selling hot-water bottles?"

Judy felt she could answer the question quite safely. "Yes, Miss Somerton," she whispered, "I rather think it would!"

That night she borrowed Miss Somerton's aged bicycle and cycled home, returning the following morning on Boxer's bike, piloting Miss Somerton's cycle with her left hand.

When Jim heard that a riding-mistress was offering Judy thirty shillings, for a seven-day week, he protested, but finally gave his approval. He was always prejudiced in favour of open-air jobs, and there was not a great deal to choose from these days.

Thus it was that Judy never returned to Boots, in the main road; she sold (much to Miss Somerton's relief) no more hot-water bottles. Moreover, Miss Somerton's prophecy was speedily fulfilled, for Judy emerged from her cul-de-sac, found her alternative track, and enjoyed the process of exploring it. It was not only working in the open, and getting to know the horses that appealed to her, but Miss Somerton herself, whose gruffness concealed an intelligent kindness, and whose patience with pupils who were not frightened of occasional tumbles was infinite.

Many happy hours were spent at "Firhill" that Spring, hours of polishing and furbishing, in the musty old tackroom, where Miss Somerton sat alongside her, soaping saddles, and talking of "cracking days", and gymkhanas long ago; of her early triumphs as a professional show-jumper, and her hard-riding father, the mere mention of whom brought a wistful look into her boot-button eyes.

Then there were strenuous hours on the cinder-track, in the field behind the farm; mounting, dismounting, walking, trotting, jumping a pole on the ground, jumping a hurdle six inches high, walking over a low brushwood fence and, at long last, clearing the regulation hurdle at the gallop.

It was all new and exhilarating, and Judy loved every moment of it, even the long, rather harassing rides with the six-year-olds, who prattled and prattled as she urged them to grip with their fat little knees, and "keep-the-pony's-head-up-head-up-and-don't-let-him-nibble!"

It was not that she forgot Esme. She thought of him often and, for a long time, not without pain, but there was always so much else to think about now, and so much to do during the day; and when she had cycled four miles home, she was far too tired to do more than eat and sleep, in readiness for the 6 a.m. ride to the stables the next morning.

As for Miss Somerton, she kept her at it the whole of that first year, until the memory of Esme began to recede, and take its place in among other childhood memories. Then, at last, Judy began to see Esme as he really was, a rather self-conscious young man, with freshly slicked hair, and a dreamy expression, who pottered about the Avenue, waiting and waiting, in the hope of catching a momentary glimpse of Elaine coming or going about Number Seventeen, and looking, Judy thought, faintly ridiculous into the bargain.

Sometimes, when she watched him objectively from her bedroom window, she was even a little sorry for him. The important thing was, that she was no longer sorry for herself.

CHAPTER XVIII

Changes At Number Four

1

SOME of the colours had faded for Edith Clegg, of Number Four.

She no longer worked as pianist, at the Granada in the Lower Road. The spell was broken at last, for with the coming of the talkies, Edith not only lost her job, but was made redundant. The new decade found her left behind in the march of events, cut off from her Temple, and forbidden to worship, for the new cult obliged her to regard all her gods and goddesses as quaint and dated, like the nursery scraps she had once pasted on the screen in Becky's bedroom.

Mr. Billings had partly replaced her by an ex-sergeant-major commissionaire, whose principal duty was the handling of queues that now thronged the pavement outside the foyer. Harsh, metallic songs had replaced Edith's *Hearts and Flowers* and *Water Music* and heroines now wept to the accompaniment of orchestral recordings of *Blue Danube* and *Minuet*. There were no bangs and thumps needed from one end of the piano, and no trills and grace-notes from the other end. The piano itself had been moved out, and sold for a song, for pianos were at a discount everywhere, and this one had taken a terrible beating since Edith had first used it to play the *Song of the Bells*, for Lon Chaney's *Hunchback*, and *Yes, We Have No Bananas*, for the antics of Ben Turpin and Charlie Chaplin.

It had all happened with dramatic suddenness, like the fall of an Empire, whose entire forces had been brought to battle and annihilated in a single encounter. In the summer of 1928 Edith was still sitting in the little pit, her head at an acute angle as she followed the stalking of Alice Terry by the suave and sinister Lewis Stone, in a reissue of *Scaramouche*. Less than a year later the stalls were snuffling at Al Jolson's domestic troubles and on their way out through the foyer humming:

> When dare are grey skies,
> Ah doan mind de grey skies . . .

Sonny Boy had proved the swang-song of an era. Stars that had once seemed as permanent as St. Paul's Cathedral disappeared overnight, and it astonished Edith how soon the public forgot them, how eager they were to sweep them into the lumber-room. New faces, new voices took their place, like people moving up a 'bus queue, and suddenly, for Edith, all the magic ebbed from the silver screen.

To do him justice Mr. Billings did not welcome the change-over. For him it meant trouble and expense, besides losing Edith, whom he had come to admire and respect. He resisted the tide for as long as he could, with business dropping off at an alarming rate as soon as the big Croydon cinemas installed their machines. He even scoffed at talkies during the transition period.

"Stunt! That's all it is, Miss Clegg, nothin' but a stunt! You won't catch me investing no money in it!"

But as time went on he did invest money in it, more money than he had, or expected to earn in two years, and in the end, as much as he could possibly borrow, and although his new apparatus broke down twenty-seven times during the first showing of *The Singing Fool*, he survived to see *Sold Out* notices in the foyer for twelve weeks in succession. In the excitement of the boom he almost forgot Edith, who stayed on a few weeks as cashier, but ultimately gave in her notice and sadly abdicated.

She was not sacked. Mr. Billings was genuinely fond of her, and would have preferred her to have stayed on as house-manager, at a pianist's salary.

An executive post at a cinema, however, was not for Edith.

It meant sitting in the cash-desk after the first house had gone in, and later, when the second house had come out, taking the cash into the office, and coping with all the paper work.

The long columns of figures worried her, and the atmosphere of bustle and stress overwhelmed her. In these circumstances she could never watch a picture through; indeed, she hardly ever managed to see more than a scene or two of any one feature. Moreover, she disliked the type of patron that the talkies seemed to attract. They clamoured for music, and more music, at the price of romance and enchantment. They booed and whistled, and made many other rude noises when the action was interrupted by a temporary break in the projectionist's loft. They jeered openly at the tearjerkers, so that Edith made up her mind to leave before her happiest memories were debased. She stayed on just long enough to develop a mild affection for Charles Farrell and Janet Gaynor— but they, and all the other newcomers, could never compete in her heart with John Gilbert, Gloria Swanson, the Gishes, John Barrymore, and Mary Pickford. They were not *big* enough. They were too much like people in 'buses, and trams, and shops. They danced their steps, strummed their ukes, and sang little songs like *I'm in the Market for You-hoo,* from a ledge less than half-way up the slopes of Olympus. It wasn't their fault. It wasn't Mr. Billings' fault. It was just progress.

The night Edith left the Granada she called on Jim Carver, at Number Twenty. She had got into the habit of consulting Jim whenever a crisis interrupted the rhythm of her life, and she found him, as always, courteous, patient, and wonderfully understanding.

"I suppose you know best, Miss Clegg," he told her, when she explained why she had been obliged to leave the cinema, "but it isn't going to be easy to get another job at your age. Things are getting worse all the time. There's a big slump just around the corner, and we'll have three million unemployed before we know where we are. When we do—when the figure reaches breaking-point, then look out for squalls! I think the best thing you can do is take another lodger. How

about your porch-room? Couldn't you let that, and board someone at twenty-five shillings a week?"

Miss Clegg thought not, it was too pokey, but she approved
the idea in principle. If another boarder did come to Number
Four, then she and Becky would have to re-deploy themselves, and let their own bedroom to the newcomer. In spite
of her insistence on happy endings she behaved realistically
outside the cinema, and she supposed it was either that or find
alternative employment.

In the end she took Jim's advice, put Becky in the porch-
room, and made up a bed for herself in the parlour, a section
of which she curtained off. They hardly ever went in the
parlour these days. It was warmer and cosier in the kitchen,
and Teddy—poor dear—had little leisure for soirées round
the cottage piano. She still took in music pupils, though it
had been difficult to fit them in whilst working at the cinema,
but there had been a slump in this sphere as well, for more
and more families in the Avenue were installing wireless-sets,
and fathers and brothers were not often disposed to forgo the
Savoy Orpheans to order to listen to little Milly's experimental
jabs at *The Merry Peasant Returning from Work*, or *Down
on the Farm*.

Edith's new lodger was a nineteen-year-old Scots girl,
called Jean McInroy. She came in response to an advertisement in the *Croydon Advertiser*, and moved in, one summer
evening, in 1930, bringing with her, in addition to a large
cardboard suitcase, a shapeless bundle of impedimenta, that
looked like the sort of equipment Edith had sometimes seen
scattered around absorbed landscape artists, at work on Shirley Hills.

Edith welcomed her at the gate, and was at once struck by
the pleasing contrast of her elfin prettiness and sturdy figure.
Jean had thick, very fair hair, cut short, and bundled under a
coloured scarf. Her clear blue eyes and fresh complexion
gave Edith the impression that she was but lately come to
town. She had a small and ripe mouth, with very red lips,
and big dimples. Edith's first thought was that poor Teddy
must fall head over heels in love with her at first-sight—she
was certain that *she* would, if she was a young man—but the
girl's strange reluctance to speak, and her painfully hesitant

manner defeated her for a moment, for she felt this could not wholly be accounted for by shyness, the sort of shyness Teddy had shown when he arrived on the doorstep of Number Four long ago.

Edith greeted her, and asked her upstairs to inspect the room. The girl seemed satisfied, but in response to Edith's chatter she said nothing at all, and Edith could make no sense of her little gasps and murmurs. It was only when she asked her flatly if the room would do that the girl coloured, and blurted out her approval in three or four words that were only just intelligible.

Then Edith realised at once that the poor thing had a terrible impediment—so bad indeed that most of the words she tried to utter emerged from her pretty mouth mangled beyond recognition.

Edith knew it was very wrong of her but she instantly felt relieved. Perhaps her relief was the expression of her deep maternal instinct, fostered by Becky's helplessness, and Teddy's need to be mothered all these years, or perhaps it was simply relief that Teddy would not, after all, be likely to fall in love with the new lodger and marry her, and go away to live somewhere else, for this was something she always feared now that he was so much better off, and getting so well known in the suburb.

The girl Jean seemed to sense the rush of sympathy that succeeded Edith's relief. She smiled, and took off her headscarf, folding it neatly, and putting it on the chair beside the bed. Edith thought she had never seen a sweeter smile. It made her want to reach out and pat the girl, who now began to unpack her equipment. Edith looked curiously at the easel, and the rectangular slabs of cardboard that were laced to it with clean, white tape.

"Are you a painter, dear?"

She spoke in such a way as to imply that there was no need for a spoken reply.

Jean pulled the bow of the tape and the slabs fell apart. Between them were large sheets of drawing paper, covered with neat charcoal drawings, and scores of smaller pencil sketches. The sketches were beautifully drawn but they did not look like any of the landscapes Edith had seen the artists paint on Shirley Hills. Every one of them reminded her of an advertisement of something—something one used about the house, like a broom, or a carpet sweeper, or a gas-cooker.

"Well, fancy!" Edith was delighted. "You do sketches for advertisements? Well I never!" She pressed her hands together and beamed.

Now, under one roof, she had a musician and an artist. Becky would be terribly excited.

The girl spread the drawings on the bed. Edith looked through them, smiling, and watched Jean set up her easel at right angles to the window. All the time the girl did not speak, and Edith felt it was almost like conducting an interview with a foreigner, or a dumb person, although by the girl's signs, and air of bustle, Edith quickly realised that she was trying to stave off the necessity of speaking. Pity glowed in her like a brazier, and their relationship began to build from this pantomime, Edith articulating the girl's meaning, and slipping into the habit of answering her own questions.

"For *magazines*? Why that's *splendid*! I think they're lovely! One doesn't realise that all those things in papers have to be actually *drawn* by somebody. Becky, my sister downstairs —she used to draw, but I don't, I *play*. And we've got a young man here, who plays in a dance band, and doesn't come in until very late. He'll be *most* interested. Now you get unpacked, dear, and I'll get you some supper, shall I? No, dear, *not* in here, downstairs . . . but you . . . you needn't worry, dear, we'll understand."

She gently backed from the room, and hurried downstairs to describe Jean to Becky, who was cutting up fish for Lickapaw, the cat having just returned from a two-day jaunt in the Nursery.

"You'll have to be most tactful with her, Becky dear," said Edith. "You see . . . she . . . she can't talk very well—no, dear, she's not a foreigner, more like Mr. Butterworth, the grave-digger—you remember? I think she must have something very wrong with her, like this . . ." and Edith made an unsuccessful attempt to say "ninety-nine" without moving her tongue. "Poor girl," she sighed. "We oughtn't to grumble, did we? And so pretty too, as pretty as a picture. Now take

Lickapaw off the table, dear; I'm sure Miss McInroy would
think that was most unhygienic!"

2

With the settling of Jean McInroy into Number Four a
new dream came to the Avenue. This time it was the dream
of a perfect man. Notwithstanding her impediment, Jean
McInroy was much more articulate than most of the Avenue
dreamers and had been trying to put her dream on cartridge
paper for two years now, the period she had been employed
as an artist for Dyke and Dobson's, the advertising agency, in
Long Acre, W.C.2.

Dyke and Dobson's were an enterprising firm, employing a
score of artist and copywriters on the premises, and twice as
many free-lance artists, all engaged on a piece-work basis.

Jean had begun to send them sketches and rhyming copy
from Glasgow, when she was hardly sixteen, and her father,
a ship's riveter, was still alive. She had earned a few odd
pounds this way, and when her father died, and her mother
married again, she left home, and came south, living for a
time in a Y.W.C.A. Hostel.

Her disability regulated her life, setting her apart from
other young people. She could have come to terms with it,
perhaps, had she been less personable. As it was, her freshness and charm attracted both men and women everywhere
she went, but her friendships always failed to develop. The
men slid away the moment they found out about her, and the
women adopted an air of patronage that made her life in
mixed company a torment not to be borne.

She found consolation in her work, which was held in high
esteem at Dyke and Dobson's, where Mr. Keith, the staff
manager, was always hoping to coax her on to the permanent
staff. He had a conviction that she could not but be grateful
to him, and might be inclined to repay his patronage in a
form of association that could be conducted with a minimum
of conversation. Jean, however, did not respond, not only
because she had left her Scots home in terrifying innocence
of the Mr. Keiths she might encounter, but simply because he
did not conform to her conception of the ideal man.

This man was already beginning to be a feature of Jean's copy. He was seen, from time to time, in all the women's magazines, pipe in mouth, brown hand on blonde wife's shoulder, the two of them speculating on the possibility of redecorating the lounge, or buying a carpet, or pruning the roses. She even had a name for him—"Philip", never shortened to "Phil"—and she knew, down to the last detail, how he looked when he smiled, or frowned, or came home with a surprise parcel tucked under his raincoat. She also knew what he looked like when he was shaving, or laying a stair-carpet, how strong and lithe he looked in a swim-suit, how handsome in plus-fours, emerging from a smart blue coupé. She had learned to love the strong lines of his jaw, and the way his hair grew thickly at the back, both with and without the application of "Sunset" brilliantine. She knew what he liked to eat, and how gaily and expertly he could romp with the children at Christmas, and on summer holidays. She got up with him every morning, and cooked his favourite breakfast— ham, eggs, and cereals. She lay down with him every night, on a "Luxuro" mattress, and snuggled into his strong, rapturous embrace, her hand sometimes reaching up to stroke the firm flesh of his throat, so smooth and cool, after countless applications of "Snow Cream" shaving soap.

She drew Philip, sometimes half-a-dozen times a day, and when she received a magazine serial assignment from Dyke and Dobson's, she sometimes coaxed him out of the semi-detached villa, where he spent most of his time, and dressed him in hunting-rig for a gallop with the Pytchley, or put him into tennis flannels with a knife-edged crease, and set him to woo under the chestnuts of a stately home.

On these occasions sub-editors usually added a caption under her pictures, and gave her something more to think about when the proof was sent to her. She was then able to extend the dream, by identifying herself with the girl of the story, and she heard him say: *"This thing is bigger than us, Jean, we must stop fighting it!"* or *"I knew you would come to me Jean, if only I waited long enough!"*

She preferred, however, the more impersonal, more enigmatic captions, such as—*"Philip knew that her heart was his, but there was Sybil to think of! What could a man do in a dilemma like this?"* or *"Trevor could offer her everything; what had Philip to offer, beyond lifelong devotion?"*

She kept a sharp look-out for Philip in trains, and tubes, and 'bus queues, but she never found him. There were hundreds of men of about thirty, who smoked pipes, and had lean, brown faces, and Empire-building eyes, but when they caught her looking hard at them they usually looked back in a way that Philip would have considered ungentlemanly, or worse.

She settled into Number Four with relief. It had been difficult to work properly at the hostel, and here, at last, she had a room of her own, where she could set up her easel, lay out her pens and brushes, and make a sort of shrine to Philip. The old maids downstairs seemed to be quiet, gentle people, and the sane one went out of her way to mother her, yet without seeking to engage her in conversations. She did not set eyes on their Mr. Hartnell, the jazz-band drummer, until she had been living in the house for some weeks. He came in so late, and was always in bed when she was moving about the house.

For the rest, she made her own bed, took nearly all her meals in her room, and went for long walks in Manor Woods during the afternoons. She was happier than most people in the Avenue, for not only could she put her dreams on paper, but was paid for dreaming them.

3

Ted Hartnell did not fall in love with Jean McInroy, as Edith had feared when she first set eyes on her new lodger. There was, indeed, something about Ted that Edith did not know, and about which he had, as yet, breathed no word, although he had long regarded her as a comfortable cross between a mother and a favourite aunt.

The fact of the matter was, Ted was already in love, and his love was reciprocated wholeheartedly. Everything had happened with the neatness of a well-turned dance-lyric. From the opening bar of the introduction "moon" had rhymed with "June", "love" with "above", "miss" with "kiss", and "eyes", with "skies".

He had first seen her at the record counter of Woolworth's, in the Old Orchard Road, having gone there to buy a cheap recording of a current hit, written in honour of Amy Johnson, the famous flier.

He saw, and heard her, over the heads of a hundred dawdling shoppers, standing on her little dais, beside the gramophone and plugging *Tiptoe Through the Tulips*.

She was small, dark, and vivacious, with brown eyes that roved expertly here and there among women buying toilet-rolls, and cheap note-paper, as though seeking someone—preferably a man, at whom she could aim the lyric. She saw Ted, moving down past the tool counter, and their eyes met, steadily on her part, bashfully, but gratefully, on his.

> . . . knee-deep, in flowers we'll stray
> And chase the shadows away . . .

she sang, and Ted was accounted for, just like that, proving for all time the potency of cheap music that Mr. Coward was making such a point about just then, in his *Private Lives*.

He waited until she stepped down, and then crossed over and promptly bought the record, together with *Wonderful Amy*, and several others that he had not intended to buy.

Because he was a customer, she was at liberty to dally with him, and for the next fifteen minutes they talked dance-tunes, before he led off by asking the name of her favourite.

"It's *Margy*," she told him. "You see, I'm *called* Margy."

"Sing it, will you?"

She smiled, climbed back on to the dais, and sang it through for him, in a husky little voice that was tuned in to dance hits. "It's nice, isn't it?" she said, stepping down again.

"Wonderful," he told her, "the way you sing it."

He did not add that it was last year's, and already a back number. Instead, he told her his name, and how he earned his living.

She was excited and made no pretence of concealing her pleasure.

"Drummer! For *Al Swinger*! Then you must have broadcast!"

He told her, modestly, that he had broadcast on several

occasions, and added that in his opinion Al was "going
places".

"You were at the football club dance on Wednesday,
weren't you? But this is marvellous . . . do you mind if I fetch
Mr. Cooper? He's our manager, and I know he'd like to hear
you've been buying," and, as he hesitated, not wanting to
terminate their tête-à-tête, ". . . it'll do me no end of good
. . . 'specially if you . . . you . . . told him I put them over
well!"

At this he could not refuse, and Mr. Cooper was fetched,
introduced, and duly impressed. He patted his saleswoman
with a proprietary air. "And what do you think o' my little
plugger, Mr. Harper?" he wanted to know.

"I think she puts them over marvellously," said Ted,
watching the colour rush to Margy's cheeks. "She doesn't
overdo it, like so many of them. . . . She lets the number
unwind itself!"

Mr. Cooper thumped him enthusiastically between the
shoulders, and launched himself into a disjointed conversation.

"That's exactly it!" he endorsed. "I couldn't have put it
better myself . . . just-a-minute-Miss-Gregson-I'm-busy-can't-
you-see. . . . Now look here, Mr. Hartwell, you could do me
an' Miss Shearing here a real turn if you put that in writing!
You know—uns'licited testimonial—keep-your-eye-on-that-
one-with-the-red-shopping-bag-Miss-Gregson-I-don't-like-the-
look-of-her—coming from you, in the business. It'd be something for the area-manager to chew over. Between you'n me,
I had a big job getting establishment for a plugger in this
branch, and this about clinches it. What do you say, Mr. Harper?"

"I'll do it with pleasure," said Ted, and was instantly
rewarded by Margy's dazzling smile.

He wrote the letter and it gave him the freedom of the
shop.

He began getting up earlier, and going down to the Old
Orchard Road at 11 a.m. every morning. Sometimes he took
up his position under the dais, but more often he stood well
back, over against the confectionery counter, and heard Margy sing her way to the lunch-break.

He bought, on an average, two records a day, but he was a shy young man, with very little experience in courting, and it was difficult to know how he would have progressed had not Margy herself made the next move.

One morning, between plugs, she said: "I'd just love to do a cabaret number with your band, Ted."

Her brown eyes made him reckless.

"Why not?" he argued. "I'll fix it with Al, he'd jump at it!"

"Would he? Oh, *would* he?"

"Sure! Why not, Margy?"

But it wasn't as easy as all that. Al Swinger was moving up in the world, and when Ted had finished singing Margy's praises to him, he remained doubtful.

"Woolworth's, you say? I dunno. . . . If we do have a vocalist she ought to have class. What's she doing, song-plugging at Woolworth's?"

"She's great, Al, great . . . she's . . . she's *got* something . . . it's the way she puts them over!"

"Okay," said Al, finally, "but as a favour to you, Ted, and if she doesn't come classy, she's out—understand?"

"She's classy," said Ted, breathlessly, "she's the classiest plugger I ever heard. Dammit, Al, even the best of 'em have got to start somewhere!"

"Yeah," said Al, cryptically, "but it doesn't have to be Woolworth's."

Margy, however, while she did not produce the same devastating effect upon Al as she had on Ted, satisfied the band-leader that she possessed—or might come to possess, sufficient "class" to appear as solo vocalist at one or two of Al's minor engagements.

Her first engagement was a Rotary Club Dance, in the Lewisham area. She had the sort of voice that is ideal for dance lyrics, throaty and eager, with a trick of hanging on to the words at the end of each couplet, and, as Al put it, "making them drip!"

She was too slightly built to make a very impressive figure at the microphone, but she looked trim, and appealingly wistful, in a yellow silk frock, with her dark hair freshly waved, and her hard-working eyes roving among the couples as she crooned *Moonlight on the River Colorado* and *If I Had a Talking Picture of You.*

If Ted Hartnell had needed a pushover he would have received it that first night, watching her from behind the drums, and tapping out the rhythm with his unemployed left foot. Her two numbers earned generous applause, and from then on she became a feature of the band, working part-time through the summer, and giving up her daytime job when the season got under way in October.

Al paid her generously, more than twice as much as she had received song-plugging, but she never forgot that she owed her opportunity to Ted Hartnell, and because of this they seemed to drift together, without any of the customary preliminaries.

She liked his modesty and his sunny temperament, but not his lack of ambition, and his willingness to let Al make all the decisions, or his tendency to underrate himself as a professional.

In the Spring of 1931 Ted was introduced to her family. They lived in one of the terraced streets, off the Millwood Lower Road, and the house seemed to be full of brothers and sisters, all tumbling round the four-valve wireless set, and humming snatches of popular hits. It was the sort of house in which Ted could not fail to feel at home, and it wasn't long before they became engaged, Al Swinger himself making an interval announcement of the news at the Licensed Victuallers' Ball, in Croydon.

It seemed to Ted then, as he took her by the hand, and announced her solo number above the clatter of glasses and ice-cream saucers, that he had everything a man could possibly desire, a well-paid job with a dance-band, a comfortable lodge, and Margy—Margy, who kissed him gently when the taxi dropped them off at her gate round about 2 a.m. that morning, and said:

"I love you, Ted, and you've always been sweet to me. Now I'm going to start being sweet to you. I'm going to see that you get somewhere. Like you deserve."

He was mildly surprised that the prospect of marriage should set her thinking along these lines.

"Aw, I'm happy enough with Al, Margy," he told her.

She pressed her cheek against his. "Oh, Al's all right for a start, Ted, but some day, soon, you're going to have a band of your own, you'll see."

A band of his own! He had never yet let his imagination carry him that far, and he put it down to her exuberance of the moment.

He held her for a moment and then, laughing for sheer joy, lifted her and swung her over the low railing of her front garden.

"I don't want a band of my own, Margy. I want things to go on as they are, for ever and ever. That's all I want, Margy."

She said nothing to this, but leaned over the railing, kissed him once more, and quietly let herself in.

He went off towards the Avenue, hands in pockets, shoulders hunched against the wind.

Lying awake, Edith heard him turn in from Shirley Rise, whistling *Happy Days are Here Again*.

Dear Teddy, she thought to herself; how long has he been here . . . twelve years? Good heavens, he must be over thirty, and he still looks such a boy! I wonder if he'll ever get married, and go away? I hope not . . . oh, I hope not!

CHAPTER XIX

Esme

1

ESME FRASER also heard Ted Hartnell come whistling home on the night of his engagement.

He was sitting in the porch-room, where, sleepless, he had drifted to look out across the Avenue at Number Seventeen, the house where his beloved had lived for so long, but lived no longer. The crisis had come and gone at Number Seventeen, and Elaine had departed, in the wake of her father.

Esme had been sleeping very badly during the last few

weeks. He would try and tire himself, physically, by long solitary walks, and then go to bed well before midnight, but usually he was awake again by 2 o'clock, and at this hour, when there was nothing to distract him, his brain was helpless against the memories and regrets it had accumulated since Elaine had decided to anticipate his rescue, and effect her solitary escape from the tower.

For this was how he had always seen her—a captive princess in a tower, waiting to be snatched from dragons below, and carried away on his saddle-bow as a bride, hard won, and suitably grateful. This was how he had regarded her since the early, idyllic days of their courtship; it was his private tragedy that she had always seen him, and herself, in a somewhat more prosaic light.

Lying awake, on a bed that had become lumpy, between sheets that had rucked and wrinkled, or ultimately getting up and mooching into the study, he slipped into the profitless habit of going back over every detail of their association, from the first moment he saw her in the "Paul Jones" at the Stafford-Fyffes' Dance, to the dismal night when she suddenly informed him of her decision to go north and join her father.

He recalled, a little bitterly, just how she had told him, lightly and gaily, as if she was setting out on a high adventure, and he had been obliged to admit at last that they had been moving on different planes from the very beginning, that while he had seen her as a goddess, she had seen their association as a kind of experiment, an experiment in love.

There could seldom have been a more complicated romance, or one more fraught with lies and deceits, with fictitious friends she was supposed to meet at fictitious rendezvous, with stolen moments, subterfuges, and alibis—but all this, according to her, had been imperative on account of her mother, whose discovery of the affair, she declared, would have put an end to it altogether.

Deep down, and far from willingly, Esme had never altogether believed this. He sometimes had an uncomfortable suspicion that Elaine was using her mother as a bogey, in order to subject his devotion to a series of excruciating tests, and this, in fact, was a fairly accurate assessment of the position. He could hardly be blamed for failing to guess that her motives were even more complicated and that she had now come to regard every stolen moment with Esme as a secret blow at Esther, a penny, so to speak, off the account of all her years of seclusion and prohibition, of rule by cane and edict in a court of no appeal.

Elaine had been gone three months or more now.

Sitting on the window-seat of the porch-room in the small hours, Esme thought back over the past year, and wondered if his own account balanced, if the joy and fulfilment of those first weeks had been worth the misery and the frustration of the weeks that followed. He was inclined to think not; if this was love, he reasoned, then they could have it for all he cared.

There had been good times, of course, like the day they spent at the Crystal Palace, when he had told her about the prehistoric monsters, and basked in her appraisal of his vast store of general knowledge. There had been the lovely afternoon they had gone up West, and seen a matinée of *Autumn Crocus*, and afterwards had tea in Lyons, and a compartment to themselves all the way from Charing Cross to Woodside. There had been the dozen or so stolen walks on warm summer evenings, when Elaine had slipped out of the side gate, and they had met by appointment at the bend of the lane, crossing the field to the copse behind Wickham. There had been plenty of kisses, depending more on her mood of the moment than the intervals of privacy they could expect on these occasions, for Elaine, if she felt like kissing, was never deterred by a passer-by.

In fact it was her moods that governed the tempo of each occasion. He had never dreamed that a woman could have so many moods or, possessing them, could employ them with such devilish skill, for the sole purpose, it would appear, of producing matching moods in her companion. They had so little time together that Esme felt they should have wasted no single second in bickering over trivial issues, but Elaine did not see it this way, and he could never really admit to himself that the bickering was all part of the experiment, like her sudden impulses to run up and down the scale of his emotions, or enfold him in an embrace so fierce and uninhibited that it frightened him.

Sometimes he parted from her feeling like a cork that had been swept along in a tide-race. Sometimes he felt humiliated, and defeated by it all, but sometimes he was uplifted and half-demented with gratitude, with no adequate way of expressing it. Usually it was her talk that shocked him, but he dared not show as much, lest she should think him naïve. Yet, for all this, he thought of little but her when they were apart, and as time went on, his long ride on an emotional switchback did a good deal to mature him.

The day she shocked him most deeply was the day she told him of the latest developments at Number Seventeen.

It happened one Saturday afternoon, when they had met by appointment in the "Rec".

Saturday was their best day for meetings, Elaine having given her mother the impression that she left her work at one o'clock, whereas she was often able to get home by mid-day. This was one of her smaller deceits, without which, she assured him, they could never have met at all.

She came down the main avenue of the "Rec", smiling, and sat down beside him on the seat furthest from the tennis-courts.

"Daddy's gone," she said flatly.

"Gone? Gone where?"

"Why, gone off with his mistress, the one at the shop!"

She enjoyed the startled expression she produced on his face.

"Mother's not going to give him a divorce," she went on, in a voice that conveyed the blandest satisfaction; "she says she's not going to make it easy for him to fornicate!" Here she threw back her head and laughed. "Mother gets those words out of the Bible, and I've always thought she likes saying them. It's funny . . ."—she now seemed to be talking more to herself than to him—". . . but I think she's always been a bit sexy, but not with Father, if you see what I mean! I think it went sour on her, soon after they were married, and she turned to religion as a sort of second-best. People do do that sometimes, Esme. I've read about it."

Esme, hating this conversation, and dreading where it might lead, tried to steer her back to the main facts.

"You mean your father's left home altogether?" he demanded.

"Yes, of course—they've gone off somewhere, Daddy and his woman, Frances she's called. She's about thirty."

"But where?" asked Esme, very much out of his depth. "Where could they have gone?"

"Oh, to Wales, I think," she told him airily. "He said he'd write me at the office. It's no good him writing home. Mother would never let me have the letters. She says he's an adulterer now, and that Sydney and I are to have nothing more to do with him."

"And will you?"

She laughed again. "Why, of course! I think he's marvellous! I never dreamed he had it in him!"

Her calmness astounded him. He tried to think how it would feel if a blow like this had descended on Number Twenty-Two; if Harold, for instance, had suddenly taken it into his head to walk out, and set up with a mistress "about thirty", in Wales—but his imagination boggled at the idea, and it occurred to him again, this time with a little tremor of fear, that if she could talk like this about the betrayal of her mother by her father, she must be incapable of feeling anything.

"But . . . but what *happened*, Elaine?" he stuttered, "how did it all come about?"

"*You* ought to know," she said, "considering it was your step-father who fixed it all."

"My step-father! Old Harold?"

"Of course, he was Daddy's solicitor, and he 'acted for him'——"

He remembered then that Edgar Frith had had meetings with Harold, and that Edgar had come to the house on two occasions. But Harold would never commit such a breach of etiquette as to discuss his clients' affairs round the dinner-table, and Esme told her this.

She was not impressed.

"Oh, there must be lots and lots of juicy sides to a solicitor's life," she said, "but I heard most of it myself, lying on the floor upstairs, with my ear to loose boards in front of the fireplace. I've found out lots of things that way, but it's a pity I can always hear Daddy so much better than Mother. I did this time. He was talking and talking about 'connubial rights'. Do you know anything about connubial rights, Esme?"

"Not much," he told her gruffly, and seeing that she was predisposed to tell him, added: "Let's walk as far as the allotments, and round home that way."

"No!" she said firmly, "I don't want to walk. I want you to hear about what happened. Don't you *want* to hear?"

"No——" he said, "not really," and then: "It's all so . . . so awful for you. I can't bear to think of you going on living in a house like that, with your mother, and that little squirt Sydney. I want to take you away from it, for always!"

She squeezed his hand encouragingly. "Don't be silly, Esme, how could you? Besides, I'm not even sure I want to be married, not yet, anyway. But I've told you that before, haven't I?"

"Yes," he said, his eyes on the concrete base of the seat, "but now I think I know why—it's because you think marriage is being like your father and mother, and it isn't, Elaine. Ours wouldn't be. Your father and mother could never have been in love, not from the start."

She considered this a moment. "I don't know about that," she said at length; "they got me, didn't they? And later on they got Sydney. It was only after that they stopped sleeping together."

"That isn't love," he said contemptuously, "not the sort of love I feel for you."

She gave a little chirrup of laughter, and hugged his arm.

"Isn't it? Oh, isn't it, Mr. Launcelot? Then why do you like kissing me?"

He shook his arm free, and stood up.

She smiled at him without moving, for she had no fear that he would sulk himself out of her company, and she enjoyed teasing him.

"Sometimes," she said deliberately, "*sometimes*, Esme, you're most terribly stuffy!"

He flung himself round on her, his face drawn and tense.

"I'm *not* stuffy," he shouted, "I'm just . . . just . . . *different* about that sort of thing, and you ought to be, too, Elaine. All the fellows at school used to talk that way. They were always telling each other stories . . . about honeymoon couples and . . . and sex. I could never see anything funny in them, and some of the chaps used to think I was a sissy, because of it. They all found out if I was, sooner or later! Kissing's different, and you know it's different! You're just trying to make me mad!"

She had never provoked him this far and she recognised the danger-signal. The laughter went out of her eyes, and her mood changed abruptly.

"Sit down, Esme dear," she said softly. "I'm sorry I teased you, and I know you love me. I'm proud of it—much prouder than you'll ever know, so there! Now sit down, and don't let's waste time quarrelling. I've only got another quarter of an hour."

He sat down, and his temper went out like a snuffed candle.

"All right. I hate quarrelling with you, but I've got to know what difference this is going to make to our seeing one another, Elaine? You won't move from here, will you?"

"No, we won't move. Daddy's given Mother the house, and he'll have to go on sending her money."

"How much?"

"As much as he can afford. He doesn't have to pay for us now, because we're both over sixteen, but he's got to go on keeping Mother, whether she divorces him or not."

"But don't you feel upset by it at all, Elaine? I mean, honestly, without joking about it?"

She considered. "No. No, I don't. I think he's done the right thing. I've always hated Mother, and the funny thing is I don't think he ever has, in spite of everything. I suppose he's a bit like you, really, or perhaps most men are—you know—always putting women on pedestals, and refusing to take them off, no matter what. I think he would have gone on just the same all his life if he hadn't met this woman, Frances, at the shop. He had to do something then, because he fell in love with her. I suppose she was kind to him, and he felt he hadn't much time left. I've seen her, you know, and I think she looks rather nice."

"Where did you see her?"

"Directly I heard about it I followed him to work. They both run a furniture shop in Purley, and I saw him go to her, and start telling her what had happened at home. I could see them quite well through the shop window. They talked for a minute, and then Daddy started crying. It was funny seeing him cry like that, I've never seen him cry before."

"Well?"

"Well, then they went into the back room, and shut the door, and I couldn't see any more. But I'm glad I saw her. The funny thing is, Esme, she isn't bad looking, and I can't imagine what she could possibly see in a man like Daddy. I mean, he's old, and going bald, and he's such a little man. I wouldn't ever let a little man touch me, or an old man, either, but perhaps some women are different, perhaps you're right, Esme, and love isn't the same for everyone, though it always seems to add up to the same in books, and plays, and everything, no matter how much they dress it up. It always comes down to sex in the end, doesn't it? I mean, if you didn't find me nice to look at, and to kiss, and touch, you wouldn't want to marry me, would you? You wouldn't want me just to talk to, and to look after the house?"

"No, I wouldn't," admitted Esme, "and of course I think you're terribly pretty, and exciting to be with, but the way people go on they'd have you believe that getting married was all sex and nothing else. I think I thought so, too, before I met you—but it's different now. I ... I ... don't only think of making love to you, I don't think of that at all when I'm away from you."

"What do you think of?" she wanted to know.

"I don't know ... just of writing things for you, and ... and ... doing things for you, and going places with you—of you just *being* there, and sometimes not even talking, but just ... well, just sharing everything, the way people do when they're married. It's awfully hard to put into words, Elaine, but I think I could write it, in a letter to you." His face lit up with the prospect. "Would you like that? Would you like me to write you a letter?"

She was not much impressed by the offer.

"Yes, Esme, I'd love it, but we'll have to go now. You'd

better kiss me before somebody comes. Then we can go
home round the allotments, and I'll try and slip out for a
little while tonight, about eight."

They kissed, but lightly, for there were people down on the
cricket pitch, and then they went home, hand in hand, via the
allotments in Brooklyn Road.

They parted before turning into the Avenue.

2

He did not see her that night. He did not see her again
until more than a week later. He wrote to her office, and
when he received no answer, he called there, and learned
that she had given notice that very day, and was understood
to be taking another job.

Frantically he hung about the unmade road, that flanked
her side gate, and waited for her to appear at her bedroom
window, but for days Number Seventeen might have been
unoccupied. Its curtains were drawn, upstairs and down.

At last, on the Saturday following their meeting in the
"Rec", there was a scribbled note for him, pushed—he knew
not how, or when—under the back door of Number Twenty-
Two. It told him to be in the greenhouse of Number Seventeen, at midnight, on Sunday. The hour she proposed for the
tryst did not surprise him overmuch. On three or four occasions she had been able to slip out to the greenhouse for a
few moments, when everyone at Number Seventeen was
asleep, and it was a simple matter for him to leave Number
Twenty-Two by the back door, without disturbing Harold or
his mother, because he occupied the back bedroom and had
no occasion to cross the landing and pass their door.

He was in the greenhouse long before midnight. Edgar's
carefully tended plants were dying for want of water. No one
had touched them, it seemed, since Edgar had gone away,
and Esme, feeling sorry for them, occupied the time watering
the pots with a tin cup. There was no necessity to run the
tap, for Edgar had installed an open tank, and it was full.

She came out about fifteen minutes after midnight, and he
saw her step into the bright patch of moonlight, that lit up
Edgar's little array of outhouses, adjoining the back door,

and pause there for a moment, listening and silhouetted against the kitchen window.

He thought he had never seen her look so beautiful, standing there motionless, like an alerted nymph on a classical frieze. Then he saw that her mass of hair was unbound, and swinging free to her waist, and as she turned towards the path, it glowed in the pale light, and his wild longing for her rose in his throat in a surge of pain.

He remained quite still, watching her move noiselessly down the path to the greenhouse door. It opened very quietly, for they had oiled the hinges. The greenhouse was built against the boundary wall, and the moonlight penetrated but one corner of it, the section nearest the road.

She called softly: "Are you there, Esme?"

"Yes, Elaine, yes!"

"Wait a minute, I'll shut the door again."

She did so, and he moved out of the deep shadow. He saw that she was wearing a kind of housecoat, or kimono, tight-fitting, and reaching to her ankles. She was holding its folds in one hand. He noticed, too, that she was wearing bedroom slippers, with large feather pom-poms. He touched the fingers of her free hand, finding them cool and firm.

"Have you been to bed?" he whispered.

"I had to. *She* came in. I think she suspects something."

"About me being here?" His heart was beating violently, and the scent of her hair engulfed him like a wave.

"No, no, Esme"——her voice, as always, was calm and steady——"but she saw me writing that note to you. Don't worry, she's sound asleep now, and so is Sydney. I listened at both their doors."

"Why couldn't you get out this week?"

"There was a lot to do. I didn't have a chance. I've got something important to tell you, Esme."

"What?"

"It can wait."

For the first time he seemed to detect excitement in her voice. She came closer to him, moving out of the light.

"Darling Esme! How long have you been here?"

"About half an hour, but it doesn't matter. I watered the plants. They were all dying."

She laughed. "Silly boy!"

He put his arms round her, and found her mouth.

"Oh, Elaine, darling, *darling*! I'm so terribly in love with you. You're beautiful. . . . I've never seen you with your hair loose before, and it's like I dreamed—like a girl in a wonderful painting."

With his left hand he reached behind her and gathered a handful, pressing it to his lips. Quite suddenly she began to shiver.

"You're cold! You must be——"

"No, no . . . kiss me, Esme . . . it's too dark here . . . over by the door . . . I want to *see* you!"

She seized both his hands, and pulled him violently out of the shadow, throwing both arms round his neck, and pressing herself to him so strongly that he reeled against the slatted shelves. She began kissing him—not as she had returned his kisses before, but greedily, with her lips parted, and as she kissed she held his face tight between her palms, pressed against his cheeks.

For Esme the universe seemed to disintegrate. His heart seemed to burst with the intoxicating nearness of her, and his hands, freed by the intensity of her embrace, roved over her neck and shoulders, and plunged again and again into her hair.

For a long minute they stood thus; then she suddenly went limp, and her hands left his face, and forced themselves between their straining bodies. He interpreted her movement as a rebuke, and loosened his hold slightly. She broke away, and turned back towards the shadow.

"Wait, Esme! Wait a minute" she said breathlessly.

She began fumbling with the top buttons of her long housecoat. They were tiny buttons, about the size of peas, and her fingers bungled twice before she got two of them undone. Then she lost her patience and tore at the fastenings. Two or three buttons flew off and her coat came open as far as her waist. She turned full into the moonlight, twisting the coat so that it slipped from one shoulder, revealing a full, white breast.

He stared at her, petrified with wonder, the desire of a moment ago ebbing from him; then, with a little sob, he bent his head, and kissed her breast—not as he had kissed her mouth in their first embrace, but softly, and very reverently.

She stood quite still, her head flung back, her hands loose beside her, as though his kiss was an act of homage, respectfully given, indifferently received. It was only when he reached out, and drew the folds of her housecoat back on to her shoulder, that she suddenly drew away from him, her back pressed to the frame of the little cistern.

"What's the matter? Don't you want me?"

His mouth puckered like a child's. He was appalled at the hardness of her tone.

"Not want you? I'm terribly in love with you, Elaine . . . surely you must . . ."

She braced herself away from the frame.

"But you *don't* want me—not like this—not as a *woman!*"

"Elaine . . . darling . . ."

He could barely speak as the terms of her challenge penetrated to him.

"Can't you *begin* to understand . . ."

"No, I *can't!*" She was almost shouting now. "No woman could! I don't want to be loved like that . . . like a . . . like a statue or something! I want to be wanted for myself—like any woman!"

Her fingers were wrestling furiously with the tiny buttons, and her voice was hard and grating.

"But not *here*, Elaine—not like *this* . . . not yet, Elaine——"

She finished her rebuttoning.

"Then it's never, Esme! *Never!* Do you understand?" She drew a long breath. "I'm going away! Tomorrow! So it's never!"

For the second time in a few minutes Esme's universe exploded. Her voice seemed to reach him from an incredible distance.

"Going away . . . tomorrow. . . . Where? . . . Why?"

"I made up my mind. I'm sick of all this, sick of being watched, and spied on, and having nothing to look forward to in this awful house! I'm going to my father. He's got a job for me, a job where I can meet people! I mightn't have gone, if you'd been different—but you never *will* be different, not about me! I don't *want* to be worshipped! Can't you understand a simple thing like that? I want to be wanted, every minute of every day. . . . I want you to look at me all the time, and want me, and want me! *Now* do you see?"

He did not see, not till much later.

At the moment, at seventeen, her needs were far beyond the range of his experience' and comprehension. This was little to be wondered at, for he had known only one woman, his mother, and she, so like himself, saw life in terms of knights, and steeds, and princesses in towers. He had tried to explain this to her so many times and had failed. Tonight his failure had been so spectacular that he saw quite clearly that he had sacrificed all chances of convincing her in the future. Even the crushing weight of misery in his heart could not extinguish that spark of truth. He said very quietly:

"When? When are you going, Elaine?"

"I told you—tomorrow!"

"Doesn't your mother know?"

She chuckled, and seemed to recover her humour in an instant.

"Of course she doesn't! I shall go to work as usual only I won't really go, I'll go to the station instead. I've got a letter ready to post, in case she asks the police to start looking for me when I don't come home after tea. This time tomorrow I shall be in Llandudno, and I'm going to be an hotel receptionist. What do you think of that?"

He thought nothing of it, being incapable of coherent thought.

"Then I won't see you again?"

She considered, pursing her lips, and a little of his misery touched her.

"I don't know—it depends—perhaps."

"I could write . . . can't I write to you?"

"Yes, of course, if you want to. I'd like to have someone to tell about everything."

Suddenly he saw a tiny glimmer of hope. "I could get a job there . . . there must be jobs going in a place like that . . . especially in summer. . . ."

"No! Esme." She was very definite. "This time I want to

do something myself. Don't you see, I've never done anything for myself before."

"Then you can't love me at all, and you couldn't have done from the start."

She regarded him steadily, and without pity.

"I don't know how you can say that, not after just now. You could have had all of me, and I'd have loved you for wanting to, for not being able to stop yourself. It's just that we're different, Esme—you don't want a girl like me, really. I even frighten you, don't I? There must be heaps of girls who'd suit you better than I do. That Carver girl, for instance, the one that was always following you around when you were young. . . . Why don't you fall in love with her?"

He made a little gesture of hopelessness.

"Elaine . . . you . . . you . . . just don't fall in love like that. . . . That just proves you could never have been in love. If you had, you couldn't believe that. I'll never love anyone but you—never."

She was not disposed to argue with him. The draught from the door was blowing on her, and her feet were getting cold.

"I must go now," she told him, "I've more packing to do."

At once he became desperate. "I'll come to the station with you—you'll have luggage, I'll see you off. . . ."

"No! Esme." Again she was adamant. "I've sent most of my stuff on in parcels, and I'd rather you didn't come to the station. I told you—I want to do this on my own."

She took his hand and squeezed it.

"I'd still sooner we parted friends, Esme, and I'd like you to wish me good luck. You'll do that, won't you?"

"I'll write, like I said," he told her, withdrawing his hand. "You'd better go now; you'll get cold, and it's late." He opened the door for her, and held it.

She moved one step, and smiled.

"Won't you even kiss me goodbye?"

He hesitated for a brief moment and it occurred to him that even now it might not be too late. If he shut the door, took her in his arms, made love to her in the way she demanded to be loved, then she might change her mind, and stay on in the Avenue after all, just to be near him.

She read his thoughts with the facility she had read them so many times before.

"It's too late for that now, Esme. It wasn't quite true what I said just now—about me not going if you'd been different— I made up my mind to go weeks ago, and I'll go anyway. Besides, I don't feel that way any longer, and you can't really blame me, can you? No woman would, not after being refused."

There was no kind of answer to this. They went out and down the path, and he watched her let herself in. She turned on the threshold, and blew a kiss to him. Even in the agony of the moment he noticed how gracefully she made the gesture, sweeping her arm in an arc, like a ballet-dancer.

He had turned away, when she called: "Esme!"

He hesitated, trying to force himself to go.

"When you get in, creep across the landing, and sit in the porch-room for a moment. Will you promise? In about ten minutes?"

He nodded dumbly. He did not notice the bubble of laughter in her voice.

He crept back across the moonlit Avenue, and into the deep shadow of the alley, between his own house and Number Twenty-Four.

As he crept through the kitchen, and up the stairs, he raised his hand to his face, and brushed away the first tears he had shed since he was a child.

But he had not finished with her, not even then. Not quite.

He sat glumly on his bed for a few moments, and had begun to take off his clothes when he recalled her last words to him—"Sit in the porch-room for a moment." He jumped up, his heart leaping with hope. Why had she said that? What might it imply? Perhaps after all, she had no real intention of going, perhaps—oh God make it so—the whole thing was an elaborate tease!

He tiptoed quickly across the landing, grateful for Eunice's fitted carpet, and into the "study", standing close to the window, and peering out across the moonlit Avenue to the porch-room window that was hers. The light was on. He could see that, although the heavy curtains were tightly drawn. He imagined her moving about, smiling to herself as she stuffed things into her attaché case, putting the finishing touches on the letter she was to send her mother.

Then, when he least expected it, the left-hand curtain was suddenly whipped back, and he saw her stand, for a few fleeting seconds, within inches of the pane. He could see her very clearly.

She stood quite still, facing directly across at him, her weight poised lightly on hands that rested on the narrow window-ledge, her head held slightly forward, with a dark mass of hair tumbling across her shoulders. She was stark naked.

Before he could gasp she had slipped back into the room, and the light went out. He saw a white arm flash, and the curtain was re-drawn.

Suddenly he was seized with a fit of violent shivering. He felt defiled, as though she had screamed something obscene across the Avenue, as though she had shouted *"Here I am! This is me! This is what you spurned! Take a good last look at me, silly little man!"*

She had said her farewell, and its ruthless mockery made him cry out in despair.

There was a swift movement immediately behind him, and his light flicked on.

Esme choked back a cry, and swung round to see Harold standing there, tousled, and blinking short-sightedly without his essential spectacles.

"What is it, old chap? What's happened?" he said sleepily. Then, seeing Esme's expression, he stepped swiftly over the threshold, and touched his shoulder.

"You're not ill, old chap?"

"No—Harold," Esme managed to croak, "I'm not ill."

Harold stood blinking at him. The utter wretchedness of the boy's face alarmed him and he shook off his drowsiness.

"If there's any way I can help, I'd like to," he said. "Suppose we go downstairs, and make some tea? Your mother's sound asleep. She won't butt in, old chap."

Esme said nothing, but nodded. Harold hesitated a moment longer, then winked solemnly, strictly as one man to another.

CHAPTER XX

Jim Hears Rumblings

1

BECAUSE Jim Carver was dedicated to suffering humanity he seldom devoted much thought to that section of it that constituted his own family. Whenever he did he derived little satisfaction from his reflections.

They were not, as he was obliged to admit to himself, a bad set of kids as a whole, but neither were they much to write home about. Individually, they seemed to him to possess average intelligence. Collectively, they were a little disappointing, and better left to their own devices.

It would have shocked him very much to discover that they interpreted this attitude on his part not as tolerance, but as lack of interest. Not one of them would have considered coming to him for advice, in the way that Miss Clegg, of Number Four, sought him out whenever she was faced with a problem. He had always gone his way, and they had gone theirs. Apart from his single brush with Archie, he had never tried to mould the political outlook of any one of them and, if he had thought about it at all, he would have concluded that they had no views at all, beyond a bland acceptance of life as something to be lived day by day.

He had broken with Archie, presumably the most original of them, on the third day of the General Strike, and the rupture had never healed, although they had decided, independently of one another, that it would be childish to pass one another as strangers in the street. Accordingly they nodded, and perhaps exchanged a vague handwave on the rare occasions that they did meet in Shirley Rise, or in the Lower Road.

Jim never went into the corner shop, although Archie was hardly ever there these days, and Archie never came to the house when Jim was likely to be about. Jim heard a little of his son's business expansion through the girls, chattering over their meals at Number Twenty, but he made no attempt to expand the odd scraps of news that he picked up from this source. He had never cared for Archie since receiving those letters from his wife, when he was still in the trenches, and the boy's thinly veiled contempt for him had put Jim on the defensive long before Archie married, and set up in business with the Pirettas.

He had much more respect for Louise but, like everyone else at Number Twenty, had long since taken her for granted, and this attitude now extended to Louise's suitor, Jack, who still hung about the house of an evening. Louise was a good, kind, hard-working girl, but not the sort of daughter a man needed to think about, unless, of course, clean pants were not to be found in the airing-cupboard, or there was no soap in the bathroom basin.

The twins, Berni and Boxer, Jim had written off as typical products of a speed-crazy age. Their scholastic career had been punctuated with minor irritations for him, beginning with that crazy attack on the Headmaster, at Havelock Park, and ending with the Grammar School Headmaster's laconic comment on their final school report. Longjohn had simply written: "They are lazy, but fundamentally decent boys. They will never be persuaded to act independently of each other."

Since they had left school, and gone out to work, Jim had seen even less of them than he saw of Archie.

Judy, his second daughter, had always been his favourite, ever since she had burst into tears on the day he came home from Germany to find his wife lying dead, and he had been able to coax a smile out of her with a newly-minted sixpence, but even Judy seemed to have moved off into a world of her own since she had grown-up, and stopped following that Fraser boy about. He saw a good deal more of her than he saw of the boys, for she still lived at home, but she was always out of the house before he had finished shaving in the morning, and if he missed her at his evening meal she was in bed before he came home from the Unemployed Workers'

Club, or from political meetings at Lewisham, or Clockhouse.

He thought her rather pretty, and trim, in her well-worn jodhpurs, and roll-neck sweater (he never saw her wear anything else these days), and he sometimes wondered why she never seemed to bother with boys, but spent all her waking hours up at that stable. It never occurred to him to link this fact with the abrupt ending of her friendship with Esme, next door. He was, in fact, like all men with strong political convictions, concerned with the mass, rather than the individuals who make up the mass. He would have shown immediate concern if any of his children had seemed obviously unhappy, but nobody at Number Twenty ever appeared to be anything more than moderately content, and each was quite capable of looking out for himself, even as Archie had done from earliest childhood.

Finally there were the girl twins, "Fetch" and "Carrie" as everybody called them, and they had made less impression upon Jim than any of his children.

As babies they had lain silently in their cots, while Louise fed and changed them. As toddlers, they had sat side by side on the tiny veranda, facing the nursery fence, munching slice after slice of bread and dripping spread thickly with "jelly", that Louise stored for them in a pudding-basin. As children they had gone to and from school without incident or accident, and the only 'teenage characteristic Jim could recall about them was their persistent humming of an endless succession of jazz tunes. They were not like Bernard and Boxer, who, although operating as a team, always displayed widely differing personalities. Fetch and Carry had no diverse characteristics at all. They sat together, slept together, ate their meals side by side, and even spoke in unison, or very nearly so, for each would begin to echo her twin's remark before the other had finished speaking, so that they usually finished every sentence with the late starter a short head behind. To listen to them engaged in a discussion with a third party was like listening to an echo. They were, withal, so much alike that Louise was the only person in the Avenue who could tell one from the other.

Jim was reminded of his responsibilities as a father one

morning when he was invited by a police-constable neighbour to attend a local Police Court the following morning, when Bernard and Boxer were due to appear on charges connected with a motoring offence.

It turned out to be nothing very serious. They had ridden their motor-cycles at full speed through a pool in the road, caused by a broken water-main, and the direct result of this act of derring-do was a miniature tidal wave of flood-water, that swept into shops on each side of the highway, causing considerable annoyance to customers and staff. They were charged, on this account, with driving without due care and attention, and because they were speedway riders the case attracted a certain amount of local attention.

Jim asked his employer, Jacob Sokolski, for the morning off, in order that he might attend Court, and it irritated him to have to do this and explain his reasons. Nevertheless, he felt it his duty to attend.

He was even more irritated when he arrived at the Court, and discovered that the prosecution was regarded as a huge joke by the fans of the local Speedway Track, many of whom were in Court, and earned a sharp rebuke from the Chairman of the Bench during the proceedings for laughing uproariously at the evidence given by Boxer on his own behalf.

Boxer was not impressed by the majesty of the Court. He stood in the box, wrapped in a huge leather jerkin, and nothing could wipe the clownish grin from his face. When asked by the police superintendent to estimate the speed of his machine he looked at Bernard for the usual inspiration.

"Whatdysay, Berni?" he asked amiably.

"I'm asking *you*!" snapped the Inspector.

"Okay," rejoined Boxer equably, "then about ten miles an hour, sir!"

This frivolous understatement delighted his supporters in the body of the Court.

"Lumme, 'ear that, gov'nor?" chuckled a small, hard-bitten man, swathed in a violet choker, who was bobbing about beside Jim. "That ''Urricane Carver' that is, an' if you ast me 'e never did less'n a steady thirty in 'is bleedin' push-cart, did 'e, 'Orace?"

'Orace, a fat, jovial man on Jim's left, gave a long, rasping chuckle.

"Not 'im, not 'im, Charlie!" he corroborated, "he's got the lap record, ain't he?" And seeing the man in the choker shake his head, added: "He '*as*, you know, I sore him get it, against Harringay lars Toosday week!"

"It ain't 'im, it's 'is bruvver," muttered the little man authoritatively; "it's the little 'un, ain't it, Bert?" and he turned to a third fan, whose supplementary information was cut short by a Court usher's bellow for silence.

Thereafter the specators confined themselves to indistinct mutterings, and Jim settled down to form his own judgment of the case.

The hearing did not improve his temper. From what he could learn, when the witnesses' answers were not lost in the subdued buzz arising from the fans, the shopkeepers had been perfectly justified in their complaint, and the boys' act seemed to Jim oafish and inconsiderate, quite apart from the element of danger involved. He was therefore relieved to hear the magistrate find them guilty, and fine them five pounds apiece, plus Court costs, but he was somewhat taken aback when both pulled wads of notes from their hip-pockets, and paid over the money on the spot. Seeking more information on the matter, he turned to the man beside him.

"What sort of money do these Speedway chaps make?" he asked.

"Ah, they do all right, gov-nor, take it from me, they do all right, don't they, 'Orace?"

'Orace said they did very well indeed.

"It ain't the pay so much," he added sagely, "it's the perks they git from garridges, and manyfacturers!"

Awaiting his sons outside the Court Jim reflected, a little ruefully, that his family seemed to be far more successful at money-making than he had ever been.

The twins greeted him cheerfully, hardly bothering to refer to the case. Boxer, especially, seemed delighted to see his father in Court.

"Not bad, was it? I figured on a tenner. Even brought the money with me," he said. And then, slapping Bernard on the shoulder, "What do you say to some grub, before taking Pop over to see the track? Whad'ysay, Berni?"

Berni gave his approval, and they at once adjourned to a large and cheerful public-house, where Jim was left in no doubt as to the local popularity of the boys. The moment it was known that he was their father everyone in the bar wanted to stand him a pint, and they were still drinking, and wolfing slabs of bread and cheese, when the barman called time, at 2 p.m.

Jim had remained behind after Court with the earnest intention of lecturing the boys on their social responsibility, or lack of it, but somehow, what with the rivers of beer, and the noisy company, and all those people congratulating him on possessing two such stalwarts for sons, he had no opportunity to begin a serious conversation. It was, he reflected, through a haze of beer fumes and tobacco smoke, a sad comment on the age that an incident like this should increase, rather than diminish, the popularity of the culprits. Any ill-feeling that did show itself in the pub conversation was directed against the unsportsmanlike attitude of the shopkeepers, for daring to resent the intrusion of a wall of flood-water into their premises, when it had been directed thence by two such daring track-riders.

Soon, however, the initial cause of the get-together was forgotten in a babel of speculation on next Saturday's inter-track contest, and Jim found himself jostled down to the Speedway to inspect the new machines the boys were to ride on the occasion. He had never visited a Speedway track before, and was mildly intrigued by all he saw and heard.

"Isn't it a bit dangerous?" he asked Bernard, as the boy pointed out the most hazardous corner of the circuit.

"Not half as dangerous as it looks, Pop," Bernard told him. "Boxer and me, we tackle it together, see, and I usually block the opposition, and let Boxer through. It works okay, Pop!"

And that's about it, thought Jim, as they walked him cheerfully to the 'bus stop, Bernard as the buffer, and Boxer the one who gathers the laurels.

So he never delivered his lecture on social behaviour after all. When they had put him on the 'bus for Addiscombe, and were standing by the kerb waiting for it to start, Boxer looked up at him with a wide grin, and said:

"Well, so long, Pop! Decent of you to look us up! Keep clear of the cops, won't you, now!"

It was ironic and exasperating that this was precisely what Jim failed to do, for in less than a month it was his turn to stand in a dock, on a somewhat more serious charge than that of swooshing flood-water into shop doorways.

2

If most of the Avenue folk were able to watch the General Strike from the kerbside, a number of them found themselves taking a far less detached view of the Depression of five years later.

Nobody bothered to make a statistical review of the Avenue's unemployed during the autumn and winter of 1931–2, but had they done so they might have found more residents on the dole than at any period since the crescent had been built.

The previous slumps had hit the artisans, and labourers, men like Carver, who, for the most part, earned their bread with their hands, but the latest depression was something quite new in slumps. Small firms, with limited reserves, began to close all over the city, and the tide of unemployment soon lapped into the outer suburbs, where the clerks, insurance agents, and the small non-salaried commercial travellers lived and dreamed.

The collapse of the Socialist Government, in the early autumn of 1931, put an end to a number of Avenue dreams. Some Avenue dwellers stopped dreaming for fourteen years, and did not begin again until the whole world had been turned upside-down, and there were things to dream about that did not exist in 1931.

Jim Carver was not unduly cast down by the Labour landslide in October that year, and the virtual collapse of the party that was to have ushered in the Millennium. He was a dedicated Socialist, but very far from being a pedant, and he had to admit that, minority notwithstanding, the Second Labour Government had made a pretty poor showing, and misused its golden opportunities. Unlike many of his colleagues, who were inclined to think that Labour was finished for all time, Jim remained optimistic. There were sound reasons for his optimism. From far off he could hear rumblings, and he reasoned that if an earthquake was to follow the landslide, then it was far better that Tories should be sitting in Westminster, where eruptions were usually centralised.

He anticipated a phrase that was to become fatuous a few years later, and told his dispirited colleagues, at a gloomy Labour Committee Meeting, that "time was on their side", if only because no one party, least of all a Tory Party, could hope to solve the unemployment problem. A figure of three million unemployed, he argued, meant big trouble for someone, and they had already seen how damaging failure to tackle the problem could be for the Government in power!

In the event the explosion was heard a good deal sooner than he anticipated, and Jim found himself rather more closely involved in it than he could have wished. With him, even deeper in trouble, was his genial employer, Jacob Sokolski, who had never yet cast a vote for Socialism, or any other Ism, having a deep-rooted conviction, dating from earliest childhood, that "bloody bolitick iss a bloddy nuisance for efferyun".

It all began when Jim turned up to work one morning in his best suit, a serviceable blue serge, and looked in on Mr. Sokolski to ask for another day off.

"Vot's der matter now? Iss your boys in drouble again?" Sokolski wanted to know.

Jim told him no, this was a private matter, concerning an unemployment rally.

The Russian grunted. "Ach! Der bloddy bolitick again," he said.

"Bloody politics it is, Mr. Sokolski," admitted Jim, with a grin. "I've promised to receive the hunger-marchers, when they get in for the big Rally. The last time I attended a rally up West I saved your furs, remember?"

"Hunger-marchers!" snorted the furrier; "you make me laugh, you Pritisch! *Hunger*, you say! God'lmighty, you doan know vot hunger iss, not none of you!"

"I don't know about that, sir," said Jim cheerfully, for no

one could take Sokolski very seriously, "I reckon an empty belly feels the same in Manchester as it does in Moscow. These chaps come from Jarrow, on the Tyne, and from the Rhondda mines. They've been rotting out there for years. You must have read about it, Mr. Sokolski."

"Sure I read about it," said Sokolski, "but vot dam' good dey do coming here? Dere's no zense in marching on empty bellies, iss there? Dey do more good sitting still on their arses, right vere dey live! Vot you say to that, my Zocialist frien'?"

"I'll tell you what I say to that, Mr. Sokolski," said Jim deliberately. "I'd say that these chaps are about desperate, and that they've got to do something that'll draw attention to what's happening to them! There were those chaps in the paper the other day, maybe you read about them, too. They'd been out of work for so long that they didn't care any more. They'd lost their grip, so what did they do, Mr. Sokolski? They clubbed together, four of them, and bought an old car with their last few pounds. Then they sat in it, and drove it slap over a cliff! Can you cap that, where you come from?"

Sokolski's thick eyebrows came sharply together, and he whistled, softly.

"So? They did that?" he said admiringly. "But that's pig! That's Russian!"

"But it didn't happen in Russia, Mr. Sokolski, it happened in Bristol, only the other day!"

The old man sat thinking for a moment, his hands clasped together over his huge, round belly. Suddenly he got up.

"It is enough," he said, "I do more dan give you the time off, my friend, I come wid you! Let us go, hey?"

Jim was taken by surprise. "You'll come . . . but you don't believe in us, you've always said . . ."

"I begin to believe in der Zocialists ven dey spit so hard," said Sokolski. "Besides, it vill be interesting to watch how you Pritisch make der Revolutions!"

Jim grinned. "You're going to be disappointed. We don't believe in revolutions, over here. Even those chaps in the car didn't, Mr. Sokolski," He was touched, nevertheless, and added: "Are you *sure* you want to come?"

"I'm sure, my frien'. We go now."

He pounded the desk bell, and the wizened little caretaker trotted in. Sokolski used him as a kind of valet, and the man helped him on with his long black overcoat, and handed him his wide-brimmed felt hat, his woollen mittens, and his bone-handled umbrella. They passed out into the street, and turned towards the park.

"A hundred years ago," Jim told him, as they walked briskly down Oxford Street, "the chap who wrote *The French Revolution* came into the West End one Sunday to watch the Chartists revolt."

"So," puffed Sokolski, "shorten your stride, my frien', I haf der pig veight to carry—and how many did they kill that day?"

"They didn't kill anyone," said Jim, "it came on to rain, so they all went home!"

It was raining now, a thin, depressing drizzle, but there was some evidence of the demonstration at Hyde Park Corner, where caped police stood about in knots of three and four. The crowd, sensing tension, were loitering about the speakers' pitch, where orators were already at work, and their home-made placards had been planted. The lettering was already beginning to run in the rain. One placard said: *"Jarrow! What is to become of Us?"* Another: *"Ashton-Under-Lyne. We Claim The Right to Work, even for Next to Nothing!"*

Sokolski spelled out the placards slowly, shaking his ponderous head as he did so, and hissing through his teeth.

"Dis is a strange vay of making the revolutions," he said. "Vould it not be better to pull da policeman from his horse, and kick his face ten times?"

"It isn't a revolution, Mr. Sokolski," insisted Jim, "simply mass protest, and that's quite different! God knows, bloodshed won't help any; it's the one thing we all want to avoid!"

The crowd was increasing every moment, and scraps of stump oratory, flung into the wind, reached them from the speakers' rostrums: ". . . the Socialist government were blocked by a capitalist conspiracy . . ." ". . . the cartels need a permanent pool of unemployed labour . . ." "MacDonald and Snowden were bought by the bosses. . . ."

The number of walking police began to multiply along the pavements of Park Lane, and immediately behind Jim and his employer, where they stood on the fringe of the trees, a group of mounted policemen began to edge their horses on to the grass, gently shepherding the crowds away from the more open ground.

"I'm supposed to report to my reception committee at mid-day," said Jim, turning up his collar against the drizzle. "Suppose we have a coffee to warm us? There's a little place I know off Cumberland Place, if we can get there."

They were unable to get to the café, for crowds were now lining Oxford Street ten deep, and a phalanx of police held the kerbsiders in a solid wedge along the edge of both pavements. Slowly the two of them worked their way to the kerb and stood there, blocked by the broad back of a Metropolitan policeman.

"Vot's diss?" Sokolski wanted to know. "Vy we stuck here by bloddy polis?"

Jim glanced at him curiously, noting the change in the Jew's demeanour. He had set out almost in protest, but later on, after they had stood in the Park for a few moments, he began to catch a little of the general excitement, and had looked around on all sides with considerable interest. Now there was a hard look in his eye, and a very determined set to his jaw. Jim noticed, with some apprehension, that the old man was beginning to look almost belligerent. He said cautiously:

"We'd better stay here for a bit, Mr. Sokolski. I've just heard that the Merthyr Tydvil contingent is coming in from Earl's Court. This is their finishing point, and that'll be them, now."

From over on their left, in the general direction of Bayswater, came a confused murmur from the crowd, and above it the faint sound of men's voices, singing in harmony. Jim edged back a few inches, and hoisted himself up on the base of a lamp-standard. As he was over six feet his additional height enabled him to see two or three hundred yards down the Bayswater Road, to a point where a procession was moving slowly in their direction. He could just pick out the cluster of banners, advancing through the murk.

Here and there, good-natured chaff was being exchanged between police and sightseers.

"Move your great blue behind, copper, and let's see something worth seeing!" piped one Cockney.

"What are all the Flatfeet here for? Do they think we're going to blow up bloody Parliament?" asked another, within hearing of a knot of policemen.

Two or three mounted policemen clattered by, riding briskly towards the procession. Their batons were drawn, and Jim was struck by the tenseness of their expressions.

Shortly afterwards, marching to the slow rhythm of *Cwm Rhondda*, the procession moved into general view, its leading ranks swinging slowly round to the right as its standard-bearer made for the area fronting the speakers' platforms. Jim and Sokolski now had a good view of the pinched, exultant faces in the front ranks, small men, most of them, inadequately clothed against the wind and the driving rain.

Then, as though by pre-arranged signal, two flanking bodies of police moved forward, one from each side of Park Lane, and the procession halted in some confusion. The song ceased as the men behind lost the rhythm. A mounted police-inspector, not ten yards from the spot where Jim and his employer were standing, trotted over to the now halted leading files, leaned forward over his crupper, and said something, pointing with his baton towards Oxford Street.

"Not this way," he shouted; "down there—keep moving down there!"

"They're heading them off," exclaimed Jim incredulously. "The bloody fools, they'll have a riot on their hands if they head them off!"

The solid wedges of spectators immediately behind suddenly surged forward, presumably in the hope of getting a better view of what was going on, and Jim had barely time to grab Sokolski's coat sleeve before the pair of them were projected into the road. Simultaneously the police cordon broke.

At the same moment, the halted ranks behind the Welsh banners broke formation, and pushed forward in a solid wedge, shouting and cat-calling. Police from the shattered cordon began to rally to the mounted group, fumbling for their batons as they ran.

As the first of them reached him, the mounted inspector stretched out and grabbed at the banner of the man he had first addressed, but the standard-bearer, a short, stocky, white-faced man, refused to surrender it, and clung to the pole with both hands as the horse swung round, jerking him off his feet. For a second or two he hung there, while another policeman pounced on him from behind, and a third doubled round the hind-quarters of the horse and began belabouring the standard-bearer's shoulders with his baton.

It was difficult to discover how Sokolski became involved. One moment he was beside Jim, a few yards from the scuffle, and the next he was clear of Jim and lashing out at the third constable with his umbrella.

Jim, horrified, darted forward with the intention of catching and somehow extricating the old man from the mêlée, but by this time the main body of miners had surged to the rescue, and the scuffle had become general, men going down on all sides, with fists and batons flailing.

A burly miner beside Jim darted forward and seized the leg of the struggling inspector, tearing him from his saddle. The banner-pole snapped off short, and the little man who was holding it began using it as a club. Police helmets began to tumble off, and Jim caught a last glimpse of Sokolski, about three yards away, wielding his umbrella by its end, and screaming something at the group of police who had converged on the prostrate inspector. Then a salvo of silver-starred rockets exploded in Jim's face, and he fell beside the riderless horse.

3

When he opened his eyes the first thing he noticed was an enclosed electric bulb, wired into the ceiling. He blinked at it, conscious only of the brightness of the bulb, and of an agonising throbbing at the right side of his head. He put up his hand to rub it, and touched congealed blood. His hair was matted with blood, and he felt violently sick.

He lay still for a moment until the nausea passed. Then he noticed that he was lying on a hard floor, and that round about him was a great deal of confused noise, and several pairs of legs. Gradually the noise resolved itself into the rise and fall of men's voices, using an unfamiliar accent, and it was the accent that gave him the clue, and caused him to remember the scuffle, the flailing batons, and the blinding flash that had brought the curtain down on the fight.

He sat up unsteadily, and discovered that he was sharing a plain, white-washed room with about a dozen other men. They were all so crowded together that they found difficulty in moving without treading on him. He looked slowly round, recognising no one. Then his jaw dropped, for sitting on the closet lid, not a yard away from him, was Jacob Sokolski, hatless, his overcoat lapel ripped and hanging, his shirt torn open, and a large patch of dried mud adhering to his seamed cheek.

Jim struggled to his knees and called to Jacob.

"What happened, Mr. Sokolski? What are we doing here? How did *you* get here?"

The old man's face lit up. He climbed slowly off the closet seat, and shouldered his way to Jim. He appeared to be in excellent spirits.

"Ha, ha, my zocialist frien', you see vat you do for me? Dere *iss* no revolution, you say! Yet, here ve are, locked in a dungeon for fighting the bloddy polis!"

One of the miners, the big man whom Jim now recalled as the one who had unhorsed the Inspector, slapped the Jew on the back.

"And it's a bloody marvel you were, Granpa, with that brolly of yours!" He turned to the others, with a wide grin, that reminded Jim of Boxer. "Man, but it was worth the tramp, it wass! All the way from the Valley we come now, to see a gentleman take our part, and lambast the bloody bobbies, isn't it?"

Jim momentarily forgot his throbbing temple.

"What the hell happened down there?" he asked, and then by way of introducing himself: "I'm from the Croydon Unemployed Workers' Union. I was supposed to welcome you chaps at the Park!"

"Aye, you wass that, Bach," said the miner, "but they tried to turn the procession into the West End. They wouldn't let us stop, you see? Christ, you come all this way, and they won't even let you say your piece when you get here!"

"You'll get your chance to say your piece, Dai, from the ruddy dock!" grinned another man. "My word, but this'll be something for the Press, won't it? How many of us would you say were in here?"

"They scooped up about twenty of us before the reinforcements broke it up," somebody told him; "there were hundreds of the bleeders, bashing right and left and centre!"

"There'll be questions, there will, in Parliament," said another, but Sokolski broke in, violently, suddenly catching the attention of everyone in the cell.

"Parliament!" he snorted. "Ach, you Pritisch do so much talking, and so little spitting! Vy you not pull bloddy Parliament down, and throw it in de bloddy river, brick by brick."

"Not a bad idea, Granpa," grinned the big man, but Jim noticed vague suspicion in the eyes of some of the other men.

"Who the hell is he?" whispered a miner to Jim, "and how did he come to get mixed up in it?"

"He's a furrier, from Bond Street," Jim told him, "and he's my boss. It's my fault, I reckon, I shouldn't have brought him here. He's a decent old stick, and those blasted bobbies might have killed him."

Indignantly, he turned back to Sokolski.

"I'm sorry I got you mixed up in this, Mr. Sokolski, but you were as much to blame as me, going for them with that umbrella the way you did! When we get up in Court don't say anything, you leave all the talking to me, understand?"

But Sokolski had now resumed his seat upon the closet, and was folding his hands over his stomach with the air of a man relaxing after a trying day.

"You make no excuses for me, my Zocialist frien'," he said quietly. "Me? I learn someding good today. And vat is it I learn? I learn your bloddy polis remind me of my Cossacks, and that's good! For why? I tell you."

He addressed the cell at large, and they listened with interest.

"Today I hit three Cossacks, bom, bom, bom! And I learn someding else that time." He winked at the admiring giant among the miners. "I learn I not forget how to dodge, for how many times dey hit me back? Not vonce!"

"Christ!" said one of the Welshmen, "so the old chap's a Bolshie, is he?"

Jim slowly massaged his head. "No, he isn't," he said irritably, "he left Russia years before Bolshies were heard of, but I reckon he must have forgotten where he was, and that's what I'd better tell them when he's hauled up. Is there any water in this stinking place? My head's giving me hell!"

There was no water, and getting no response to their shouts the men began to sing *Cwm Rhondda* again. Jim stood it for three verses. Then he was sick, and Jacob held him over the toilet.

4

They were brought before the magistrate that same afternoon, nineteen of them in all, charged with assaulting the police and resisting arrest.

Jim, who considered that he had a clean conscience in the matter, was highly indignant, but the Welshmen were exhilarated by the prospect of further newspaper publicity. Jacob Sokolski remained strangely silent, both throughout the initial hearing, and after their release on bail, pending appearances in Court the following Monday.

There had been several clashes that day, and Jim made headlines again. It was noticeable that Authority showed some reluctance to press home the prosecutions, and Jim's guess that the charges would soon be reduced to those of obstruction proved correct. They discussed the matter with Jacob's solicitor, a bullet-headed little Pole, called Kossovitch, to whom they repaired after the hearing.

Kossovitch, to whom Jacob had brought a good deal of business in the past, held out prospects of the case against Jim being dismissed. He had been able to locate two of the Reception Committee who were not involved in the fight, and these men were willing to swear that they had seen Jim Carver pushed into the road, and struck from behind, after Sokolski had broken away from him.

It was difficult, however, to enter a similar plea on behalf of the furrier, for a press photographer had recorded his attack on the policeman with his umbrella, and the photograph appeared in a left-wing periodical that week-end. Contemplating the picture, captioned: *"Indignant bystander is moved to support provoked miners!"* Jacob at last broke the brooding silence that he had maintained ever since their release.

"My mudder," he said, "I tink she would hab been more proud of dis dan all the money I make since leaving her."

Jim regarded the old man with affectionate amusement.

"What made you do it, Mr. Sokolski? Was it just the excitement of the moment?"

The Jew shook his head. "I tink you could not understan', my Zocialist frien'," he said, with a slow smile, that sent the wrinkles gliding over his face like a shoal of tiny fish, "but my mudder—she would understan', and maybe my fadder, too."

He settled low in his swivel chair, linking his hands over his stomach, and he seemed to be looking beyond Jim, out over miles of brick and stone and across the North Sea, to the squalid Lithuanian village where he was born. He was seeing, perhaps, a snow-covered landscape, churned into slush by the Cossacks' horses, as yet another pogrom swept down on the half-starved community, and men were dragged screaming from their timber dwellings in the light of pine torches and burning barns. He saw his father staggering this way and that, under the knouts of the Little Father's horsemen, his mother standing in the open doorway, screeching defiance, and himself and his brothers running swiftly across the snow towards the birch forests.

"I ran den . . ." he said quietly, ". . . but dis time I did not run. Instead, I felt the bone of my umbrella strike against de skull of de red-faced one, and before he could catch it, and break it, I had knocked de *pikelhaube* from de head of yet anudder one! I felt good doing dis! I tell you dis, my Zocialist friend, because I am proud to have done dis for my fadder and my mudder. It was in me to do dis thing, but I did not know it, not until de one on de horse broke de stick of de banner."

Jim found this story interesting but unhelpful.

"It isn't the slightest good telling that yarn in Court," he said. "It's very picturesque, but it won't help you in the slightest."

The Jew shrugged. "I pay vot I have to pay and go home," he said. "Stepan, my frien'," he turned to the lawyer, "I leave you to say vot you tink best, and me—I keep my mouth tight shut. I remember dis ting because it is good, but I do not want to speak of it, only to you. Do you understan'?"

The Pole nodded. He understood a good deal better than Jim, for to him "pogrom" was more than a word in a social tract.

On the day of the trial he contented himself with advancing a plea of the extreme provocation of a bystander, who was jostled by combatants, and had regrettably lost his temper, and struck out at those nearest him.

The case against Jim was dismissed on the evidence of the Committee men. Jacob was fined ten pounds, ordered to pay Court costs, and bound over to keep the peace for one year. The miners were fined five pounds apiece, with the option of one month's imprisonment. A left-wing periodical came forward with the fines later that same day, but, by that time, the men were already on their way home to the Rhondda. Jacob Sokolski, a Russian Jew who had sneered at political agitation all his life, had paid out more than a hundred pounds on their behalf and in addition to paying the fines he had given each man the money for his railway fare to Wales. This was a gesture that Jim never forgot.

Jim Carver was possibly the only defendant who felt humiliated by his appearance in Court, and this was not simply because his presence there ran contrary to his innate respect for law and order but because, in the course of the hearing, he looked into the public gallery and caught a glimpse of Boxer's grin. Later he was obliged to suffer that young man's genial congratulations, when they met in the corridor after the case was over.

"Well, Pop, so you beat the rap?" chuckled Boxer. "Berni's here somewhere—we both came over, soon as we heard. Berni!—hi—Berni! We got to go out an' celebrate like we did last time. Whatdysay, Berni, whatdysay?"

But Bernard, having more discernment than his big twin,

shook his blond head, and laid a gentle hand on his brother's leather-encased shoulder.

"It's not the same, Boxer. I don't reckon Pop's getting a kick out of it like we did."

Jim shot the smaller twin a grateful glance. It seemed to him then that he had underestimated Bernard.

"That's about right, son," he said, "this sort of thing doesn't do anyone any good, and that's a fact. It's something the whole lot of us ought to be dam' well ashamed of, especially at a time like this."

A time like this.

Jim Carver's reading, and his habit of reflecting on what he read, was taking him further and further from the parish pump these days. He listened, with some impatience, when his colleagues in committee argued interminably over wage minimums, and pit-head baths, and workers' compensation charters, for he realised that the real fight was moving away from these traditional cock-pits, that something was happening across the Channel that made the wranglings between the cartels and the unions ridiculous, as fatuous as the arguments of wayfarers lost in a wood, disputing the ownership of a broken compass. The French Socialists were aware of it, and were striving to form a popular front against the strident bullies on the far side of their Maginot Line, but the French were old and wise, and knew that these same bullies would stop at nothing, not even firing their own Chancellory to win the support of reaction all over the world. Jim knew this too and recognised, in the strutting Jew-baiters of Berlin, the men who had the insufferable arrogance to assure *him* that they had been unbeaten in the autumn of 1918—*unbeaten*, when Jim, and his gaunt trench veterans, had herded them back over the Rhine, and had kept their children alive for months with sly gifts of chocolate, and tinned milk.

That was where the real trouble was going to come from if the League, and the bemused politicians over here, were content to see Germany flout the treaty, and build up an army, in the vain hope that their legions would turn east, and leave the west to vegetate until the time came to make a new treaty of their own devising.

To Jim Carver, whose political work brought him into
touch with refugee groups from Central Europe, "Pogrom"
was ceasing to be a word in a tract. Delegates he had met at
conferences in the 'twenties were already inside the concentration camps, camps with names that were soon to ring
across the world, marking a new low-water mark of Teuton
bestiality.

These, he felt, were the issues that should be debated in
committee rooms, and this was the enemy against whom all
democrats, blue, red, or yellow, should make common cause.
Sometimes he expressed himself in these terms, but scarcely
anyone listened to him, for he was never anything but a
halting speaker, who lost his audience's attention the moment
his mind began to grope for a quotation, or a set of figures.
"Sit down and stick to the agenda, Jim, old man," they would
tell him, or "Let's put our own pig-sty in order, before we
start sweeping up somebody else's muck!"

So Jim went back to Jacob Sokolski, and discussed these
things with the old Jew, for their personal relationship had
been cemented by the skirmish at Hyde Park Corner. Sokolski was more disposed to listen to him than his Socialist
colleagues, but he held out even less hope of a political truce
between capital and labour, in the face of militant Fascism in
Germany and Italy.

"Ach, my dreaming frien'," he said, "in dis ting dere are
no nations, no flags, only dose dat hab, and dose dat hab not,
and would take it from dem. It is no different in Red Russia,
my frien', believe me. I hab it from dose who come here,
since de Revolution. De trouble is *here*, my frien'," and he
plunged his hand into his pocket, and pulled out a fistful of
silver, throwing it across his blotter. "It is here, and *here*"—
and he lifted his hand from the coins, and solemnly tapped his
heart.

Jim quoted the boy on the bank, at Mons.

"Not with everyone, Mr. Sokolski, not with the youngsters.
That kid wasn't interested in money."

"Dat is so," said Sokolski, "but only because boys like dat
hab no time to discover de truth. My people are born wid dis
knowledge, for you Christians hab seen to dat, wid your
pogroms and spittle, but in dis country you have not suffered

enough. Dat is someding dat can be put right, eh? Dat is
someding de flying machines vill teach you ven der moment
it come!"

CHAPTER XXI

Abdication And Usurpation

I

SOMEONE else living in the Avenue heard rumblings in the
early 'thirties, but although they originated from the same
source, they fell upon his ear somewhat more melodiously
than upon Jim's.

In the Spring of 1934, Sydney Frith, of Number Seventeen, joined the British Union of Fascists and, for a brief
moment in history, constituted the Avenue's extreme right
wing, just as Oliver Rawlings, of Number Eighty-Eight (who
was soon to leave his bones on the glacis of the Alcazar),
might be said to have carried the red banner of the Avenue's
extreme left wing.

Sydney's abrupt and uncharacteristic incursion into the
realm of militant politics was the direct result of his friendship with the splendid Boyd-Thompson, nephew and heir of
Horace Boyd, of Boyd's, Chartered Accountants, Queen
Victoria Street, where Sydney had worked since leaving
school.

Vincent Boyd-Thompson, or "Boydie" as he preferred to be
known in the private bars of the City's more select hostelries,
was a bizarre character, of the type that later found its extreme expression in a small band of stalwarts who did the
washing-up for Propaganda Minister Goebbels, and lived on to
regret their bedevilment.

Not that Boydie went the whole way with these gentlemen;
indeed, he was ultimately to recant absolutely, and leave his
right leg in a field dressing-station, near Benghazi. In 1934,
however, this was unforeseen, for Hitler appealed to a cer-

tain section of British youth, as the sole means left to them of keeping The Rabble in its pre-ordained place.

The Rabble, to Boydie and his cronies, was made up of everyone who had not had the advantages of a private education, who sought their leisure on street-corners instead of on a golf course, who bathed once a week instead of once a day, who had a tendency to drop their aitches, and who sometimes referred to their female companions as "pushers".

The Rabble, as Boydie saw it, had been getting badly out of hand since the General Strike and the Depression of 1931. The Rabble was now demanding work with menaces, and if something wasn't done pretty soon, to bring it back into line, it was conceivable that it might cause heads to roll in Trafalgar Square or, what was much worse, it might use democratic machinery (to which, through some surprising oversight, it appeared to have access) to vote in yet another Labour Government and slap on a capital levy.

Sir Oswald Mosley's appeal for patriotic Britons to unite, and forestall such disasters, was in Boydie's view very timely; he had been one of the first to go out and buy himself some natty riding breeches, a black shirt, and a pair of shining jackboots, in order that he might be suitably attired for lectures at B.U.F. Headquarters, and for the hawking of copies of *Action* outside suburban railway stations.

Sydney had been under Boydie's spell for two years or more. He saw him as the prototype of young English manhood, the sort of fellow that Sydney himself had always longed to be, a man with a public-school background, who owned a nippy, blue sports car, and drove it down to Virginia Water every Saturday, to drink "snifters" in the clubhouse, after playing a round with other young executives. To Sydney these young men were the élite, for they were people who knew London waiters at famous restaurants by their Christion names, who would one day marry glacial-looking girls seen in *The Tatler*, and breed sons who would be entered at Harrow the day they were born, and daughters who, in their turn, would also be photographed for *The Tatler*, with their ears projecting from the bowler hats they wore at gymkhanas in the Home Counties.

All the time Sydney had been at Boyd's Ltd. he had

carefully modelled himself on Boydie. He studied his ties, his plus-fours, his gestures, and his tricks of speech, that somehow managed to convey to people that he was bored by their conversation but far too well-bred to show it.

He began by using the same slang words and phrases as Boydie—"old fruit", "sick'nin'", and "a bit much, don't you think". He watched his "a"s, and tried hard to turn them into "e"s, so that *match* became *metch*, and *back* became *beck*. He paid a dozen visits to the toilet during working hours, in order to make quite sure that his finger-nails retained no scrap of London grime after handling telephone directories and ledger-pages. He volunteered readily for the firm's sporting activities, and gave money that he could ill afford to the office appeals, launched in conjunction with patriotic Lord Mayor's Funds. He even learned to carry his gloves, and his evening paper, the way Boydie carried them, gloves nonchalantly bunched in one hand, the paper tucked under the right arm, at an angle of forty-five degrees. In short he *was* Boydie, a Boydie of the outer suburbs, and before long Boydie himself could not help becoming aware of Sydney's worship. He began to pay Sydney the compliment of addressing him by name, notwithstanding the fact that Sydney was only one among thirty clerks studying for their articles in the main office.

By the time Boydie had enlisted in the B.U.F. Sydney had become Boydie's man, body and soul, so that it was only natural that Sydney should now go out and buy himself an identical outfit, that set him back three weeks' wages, even though he got the boots second-hand, and they pinched him like mediæval instruments of torture.

Then began, for Sydney, a year of unadulterated bliss.

Every week-end, and at least four nights during the week, he accompanied Boydie to rallies, demonstrations, and lecture tours all over the London area. Sometimes, on Sundays, they travelled as far afield as Brighton, or Chelmsford, and on these occasions Sydney had little to do but stand up very straight in front of Boydie's rostrum, with his feet planted *so*, his arms folded *so*, his narrow jaw clamped into a Mussolini scowl, and his large, myopic eyes fixed unblinkingly on curious passers-by, who loitered to hear Boydie's colourful denunciations of red plots in Moscow, yellow perils in Pekin, and black omissions in Westminster.

Nobody ever argued with Boydie when he was stumporating. Sometimes, Sydney wished that somebody would, so that he could hear Boydie humiliate them with a well-judged thrust, or a feathered shaft of wit. Sometimes there was a little half-hearted heckling from louts, standing well back across the road, but these interruptions failed to grow to the proportions that would justify the ordering of *Number One Routine*, which had been prepared for just such an occasion.

For on the command *Number One Routine* Boydie's bodyguard were supposed to close up, and move in a compact body towards the hecklers, to seize them, and to frog-march them into the direction of the nearest horse-trough, pond, or puddle, there to teach them that the B.U.F. had a programme, and was not a new kind of circus.

Unfortunately, Sydney did not possess the sort of physique that went with riding breeches and jackboots but, overlooked from the Rostrum by Boydie, he was confident that, if necessary, he would be quite capable of ducking a dozen town roughs singlehanded.

He did not, however, welcome hecklers, for street scuffles were beneath his dignity. He much preferred to remain glowering and statuesque, quelling possible opponents by hypnotic glare, rather than by strong-arm techniques, and this he continued to do, until the dreadful night of the Aldgate Massacre, when an incident occurred that not only led to his summary resignation from the Union, but a change of job, and loss of Boydie as boss and gauleiter.

The group had gone down to Aldgate Pump one Saturday night to hold a street-corner meeting, choosing this time, and venue, in order to coincide their meeting with the advertised march of local Communists, who were said to be parading through the East End in honour of May Day.

The Blackshirts took up a strategic position at the junction of two main roads, and there was some altercation between Boydie and a friendly police-sergeant, as to whether or not the phalanx constituted a traffic obstruction. A compromise was agreed upon, and the bodyguard moved on, to re-form a few hundred yards further east, where some old buildings had been levelled, and there was a half-acre of broken ground.

Scarcely had Boydie begun to speak, however, when The Rabble converged on the meeting from several different directions. Police squads arrived, and kept up a moving patrol in the immediate area of the rostrum but, in spite of this, the crowd continued to press in, until its front ranks were within easy throwing distance of the storm-troopers. There were choruses of jeers and cat-calls at the end of every sentence Boydie uttered, and occasionally a cabbage-stalk or a sodden ball of newspaper would sail through the air in the general direction of the bodyguard.

Finally, Boydie was unable to make himself heard, but still the crowd pressed in, their behaviour and epithets growing more and more menacing, despite several stern warnings by the police sergeant.

Suddenly a powerfully-built man of about thirty-five stepped forward, and stood looking up from immediately below the platform.

"Will ye no', shut up and get to hell out o' here, sonny?" he demanded, in a thick, Glasgow accent.

The crowd laughed, and the man next to Sydney moved over and laid a restraining hand on the Scotsman's arm.

"I say, look here . . ." began the henchman.

The Scotsman shook him off, much as an absorbed newspaper reader rids himself of a hovering wasp, and again addressed Boydie directly:

"Did ye no' hear me, ye bloody little jackanapes? Will ye no' pack up, an' get to hell out o' here, before we help ye to it?"

Boydie at length deigned to stop explaining how Fascist Germany was able to plan a magnificent Reichautobahn, while the effete British motorist was still content to crawl through innumerable bottlenecks on the Great North Road. He broke off, and looked the Glaswegian blandly in the face.

"*Number One Routine!*" he barked suddenly.

In three seconds the tableau had dissolved. The Blackshirts on Sydney's right and left closed in on the Scotsman, but before they had taken hold of him the front ranks of The

Rabble bulged, and the rostrum was up-ended in a sharp frontal attack, Boydie falling into the arms of the troopers immediately behind him. These were quickly seized and over-thrown by men who ran round each side of the platform, and by the time the police had moved in, the wasteland was a battlefield.

Sydney hardly had time to unfold his arms and raise them to shield his face. A spotty youth, of about his own age, flung his arms round his neck, and twisting his head under his arm, held it there in a pitiless grip, whilst he punched and punched with his free fist.

The pain was agonising. No one blow was powerful enough to daze Sydney, but each was distinctly and separate-ly felt, as bony knuckles smashed into nose, mouth, and eyes. Sydney screamed, and kicked out with his boot, but his feet were grabbed by somebody else, and his body became in-volved in a tug-of-war between two parties, each of whom seemed bent on carrying away some piece of him as a trophy.

Finally, the methodically punching youth surrendered his claims, and Sydney was dragged, feet foremost, across the uneven ground, his nose streaming blood, his bruised mouth still wide-open in an uninterrupted scream. He remembered the side of his face striking a sharp object, a tin can or piece of iron, and then came the dreadful shock of sudden immer-sion in filthy water, and the merciful oblivion that he thought of as death.

Miraculously he was not dead, not even severely injured. Within seconds the police had fished him out of a few inches of muddy water in the adjoining claypit, and after first-aid treatment had bundled him into the ambulance, together with three or four other Blackshirts.

He came to himself while the vehicle was still on its way to hospital, and immediately began screaming again. He went right on screaming until they rushed him into the out-patients' ward, and an exasperated probationer nurse washed his face and began bandaging a cut on his cheek.

After that, they gave him something to make him sleep, and put him to bed for twelve hours.

When he awoke in the morning the first person he saw was Boydie, who was standing looking down at him with a pair of black eyes that seemed to Sydney—stiff, sore, and only half-awake—to belong to someone in one of the comic picture-postcards he had often seen hanging outside a stationer's in the Lower Road.

Boydie grinned, and patted Sydney's shoulder.

"Well done, Frith old fruit! Well done!" he commended; "they were twenty to one, but we gave a rattlin' good account of ourselves, what?"

Sydney made no reply. His nose felt as if it had been clogged with cotton wool, his cheek throbbed, there was a sour taste in his mouth, and his body, which he now gently probed, seemed to have been thrashed with an iron club, not one square inch having been overlooked.

"I'm popping along to see Forde and Semphill. They are in here, too, Semphill with a suspected rib fracture. All the others were patched up and sent home. Dirty swine—they attacked us from behind, you know! Cheery-pip, Old Fruit! It's a good war!"

And Boydie was gone—out of the ward, and out of Sydney's life. The injured Blackshirt remained in hospital all that day, until Esther, his mother, came to fetch him in a taxi.

During that long day, Sydney had ample time to reflect, and the one clear decision to emerge from his reflection was that he would never, not even for Boydie, not for the British Empire, with Sir Oswald Mosley at its head, expose himself to such terrible risks and indignities in the future.

He did not return to Boyd's, but found himself another post in Lewisham. He burned his black shirt, but he wrapped his breeches and boots in brown paper, and put them away in the drawer of his sister's empty wardrobe. After all, he reflected, he might need them for Rotten Row in the future, for there must be other ways of getting into high society and *The Tatler* than via an East End claypit and a casualty ward.

Sydney had listened carefully to the Continental rumblings, but from now on he decided to ignore them, even if they brought the house down about his ears.

2

Esther Frith was relieved to discover that her son had severed his connections with the B.U.F. Not until she had helped him out of the hospital, and into the taxi that took them back to Number Seventeen, did she realise the frightful risks he had been inviting by clumping about the streets in those absurd jackboots, and that common-looking shirt, in which he was likely to catch his death of cold, notwithstanding the woolly vest she insisted on his wearing underneath.

It had been a very trying year for Esther. Although she continued to present a frozen face to the world, Edgar's betrayal had been a terrible shock to her, outraging her pride and her entire outlook on life. She had been so shocked, in fact, that the full impact of his desertion had not been absorbed by her until he had been gone from the house for several weeks, and then, just as she was readjusting herself, Elaine had run away, and she was obliged to face the fact that the girl preferred a sinful father to a blameless mother.

For Esther thought of herself as blameless. She could never bring herself to believe that her consistent refusal to sleep with Edgar, over a period of fifteen years, justified him in so much as handing another woman out of a 'bus, much less abandoning home and family on that account. She thought of Frances—the woman with whom he had become involved—in terms of sex, and sex only. It never occurred to her that, in making such a decision, Edgar was in search of anything beyond the gratification of animal lust. The fact that lust alone was sufficiently powerful to shatter the pattern of their lives after all these years, astonished more than angered her; so much so that, when Edgar was half-way through his initial confession, it even crossed her mind to offer to share bedrooms with him again.

Mercifully, this last humiliation was spared her, for Edgar, whilst appearing subdued, and a little sorrowful, left no doubt in her mind but that he had made up his mind to abandon her. Indeed, he had already visited a solicitor, and had investigated the possibilities of his divorce on the grounds of desertion. It was only when she told him bluntly that nothing would induce her to connive at such a plan, that, by so doing, she would be tacitly approving his bestiality, that he came out with a fantastic notion of divorcing *her*, on the grounds of her refusal to sleep with him!

He even had the legal jargon for this new approach, calling it "restitution of conjugal rights", or some such nonsense, and he had assured her, with evident sincerity, that provision was actually made for such cases in the Courts of Law. She did not believe him at the time, but when the solicitor to whom she turned assured her that such was indeed the case, her entire faith in the English legal system suffered a setback from which it never recovered. It was only when she had time to reflect that laws were made by men, all of whom, it would appear, considered access to a woman's body an inalienable right, that she could bring herself to believe her solicitor, and only then did she consent, and with the utmost reluctance, to a divorce going forwards on grounds of desertion. She comforted herself that this at least would mean that Edgar could not marry his harlot for years, even though he might live with her, and pass her off as his wife in the meantime.

She did not commit the indignity of asking Edgar to reconsider his decision. She felt no pangs on parting with him, as a person with whom she had shared a house for nearly twenty years, but she claimed the maximum allowances, and the future care of the children, and in these respects he made no difficulties at all, committing himself to send her, month by month, two-thirds of his income, and agreeing to take no steps at all to prevent either Elaine or Sydney from continuing to reside with her at Number Seventeen. He also made over to her the house and furniture, and was obviously anxious to depart as quickly and as quietly as possible.

With the flight of Elaine the leadership at Number Seventeen slipped from Esther's hands. For years she had dominated all three of them, but now, alone with Sydney, she began to show indecision, and he was very quick to notice it, and take advantage. She did not actively resent his usurping her position as head of the household, but when he was out of an evening, or away for the week-end, her loneliness began to trouble her as it had never troubled her in the past, either before or since marriage.

She turned more and more to her Chapel for solace, and joined the mid-week sewing circle. Even here, however, she found it impossible to escape from her gloomy thoughts, for after so many years of disciplined silence sewing-circle chatter did not come easily to her, and she made no friends. She found herself worrying more and more about Sydney during his absences, with the result that, when he did come in, she irritated him with her questions. He stood it in silence for a long time, but one night, soon after his resignation from B.U.F., he turned on her almost savagely.

"What is it to you where I've been? I'm not a kid now, and I can stop out all night if I want to. If you must know, I've been out with a girl, and I'm going out with her whenever I like. Who's going to stop me?"

She was almost as shocked by this admission as she had been by Edgar's. It seemed incredible that Sydney should want to go out with a girl.

He noted her astonishment and it piqued him.

"What's so strange about that? All the chaps at the office have got girls. What's different about me? You didn't do anything about Elaine, when she was here?"

"Elaine?"

"Of course! What do you imagine she was doing, when she went for her walks? Studying the scenery?"

"You mean she . . . she *went* with men?"

"Not men!" He laughed, shortly. "You really are incredible, mother—she had a pash on the boy over the road, Esme Fraser, and she imagined I didn't know, but I did, almost at once. I saw them in the "Rec", and sometimes she used to meet him in the Lane. She even used to see him in the greenhouse at night."

"Why didn't you tell me?"

"Why should I tell you? We've never been allowed to do anything, but it's different now, and you've got to see that it's different. This girl I'm going with"—swiftly he tried to gauge the measure of his ascendancy in her bewildered face—"I'm going to bring her home, on Sunday!"

For days he had been nerving himself to say, "I should like

to bring her home," but he changed his mind at the last moment.

Esther compressed her lips. She too had some gauging to do, and for a moment there was a silent struggle between them, each realising that this was the crisis, that whoever emerged winner of this contest would henceforth rule Number Seventeen.

It was Sydney who won.

Esther had lost the power of making snap decisions, and betrayed as much by her inability to meet his eye.

"Very well, Sydney," she said meekly, "bring her on Sunday, and you needn't fear that I won't be nice to her. It's better like that—I'd sooner you brought her home, and that I got to know her."

She retreated into the kitchen to mask her defeat, and he heard her filling the kettle.

Smiling, he lowered himself into her chair (Edgar had always occupied a hard chair, furthest from the fire) and defied a fifteen-year-old edict by placing his feet on the polished fender. Then he set the final seal on his triumph. Groping into his pocket, he brought out pipe and tobacco pouch. He had been smoking, in secrecy, since before he left school, but never before had he dared to display the pipe in the house.

He filled the bowl, applied a match, and deliberately blew a thick cloud of smoke towards the open door.

3

Esther was correct in her guess that Edgar and Frances were already living together as man and wife, and thanks to Frances they had not had to wait long for their dream shop. It was not situated in a West-country Cathedral town, but in a narrow street off the sea-front of the Welsh holiday resort of Llandudno, and to get it, and stock it, Frances had sold her cottage and furniture, and mortgaged all that remained of her father's small legacy.

She had, in effect, staked everything on Edgar, and her impulsive generosity had paid off more quickly than most gambles, for Edgar, released at last into a sphere where he

could employ his natural abilities, and determined above all
to prove to Frances that he possessed such abilities, began to
develop a new personality within a week of his abdication
from Number Seventeen.

The change was astonishing, even to Frances, who had
seen how near he had come to foundering during the transition period. He lost his timidity and reserve, and w'th it the
slight stutter that he had exhibited when dealing with the
tougher type of customer. He gained, with this confidence, an
excess of physical energy, that swept him into sale-rooms,
and house-auctions, to stand hour after hour, while the auc-
tioneers barked their way through the lots. When his moments
arrived, when the lots that he had ticked off on his catalogue
came under the hammer, he sang out his bids in a loud, clear
voice, and went on bidding, right up to his limit, his steadiness
giving other dealers the impression that he was a man not to
be trifled with, one quite prepared to pay "over the odds" for
anything he had set his heart upon. He even started local
fashions among amateur collectors, popularising paper-
weights, Toby jugs, and china cottages, so that, within a year
of their settling in Llandudno, there were no paper-weights,
or Toby jugs, or china cottages to be found for miles around.

People, often professional people, began to canvass his
opinions about pictures and china at the sales and views.
"Would you go for that, Mr. Frith?" "Is it really Doctor
Wall, or is it much later, Mr. Frith?", and under this modest
flattery he began to expand, like a wispy little plant in strong
sunshine. And Frances, noting as much, was proud and glad.

Frances he treated like a young wife in the first flush of
married courtship. He brought her flowers—freesia, cream
roses, and huge, golden iris. He held back little pieces of
antique jewellery that he came across at the sales, brooches,
cameos, and earrings, and presented them to her not as
anniversary gifts, but small, unexpected tokens of his love,
offering them with reverence, like a pagan worshipper expressing gratitude for a rich harvest, or a male firstborn.

When his ardour showed no signs of cooling, when she was
sure that his devotion had little to do with physical gratification, but was simply the outward manifestation of a great
humility, she was able to see him as she had never previously

seen him, a small man, with an infinite capacity to create happiness in people around him, a little man with vast reserves of patience, and a rare, male gentleness, that made him seem so much bigger than most of the men she had known. When she saw him like this she sometimes wondered about Esther, his wife, and, because she was herself both generous and gentle, the realisation of all that Esther had missed, and all that Edgar must have suffered during the sterile years of his marriage, made her a little sad.

When the business was fully established, and when Elaine (whose catlike smile frightened Frances somewhat) had left their little flat over the shop, and gone her way as a living-in receptionist at The Falconer, over at Colwyn Bay, Frances sent down into Kent for Pippa, her twelve-year-old daughter. Pippa arrived, wide-eyed and wondering, with just enough coltish curiosity to ask embarrassingly direct questions about "Uncle Edgar". This questioning phase did not last very long, for Pippa loved the Middle Ages and learning this Edgar took time off from his sales to conduct her on personal tours of the local castles. He need not have bothered to revisit Conway and Beaumaris, for he won Pippa's confidence and affection on the first of these expeditions to Caernarvon, introducing her, as it were, to an Edward the First who obligingly stepped out of the history text-books in order to explain to her just why he came to Wales and why he built the castles.

After that there were no more questions and no more lifted eyebrows on her part when Edgar jumped up to anticipate the slightest wish of her mother, or display old-world courtesy in piloting Frances to a chair near the fire, lifting her feet to place them on the humpty.

Pippa was a good-tempered child, grateful for the smaller mercies of life. She had not been very happy in her aunt's spotless bungalow, at Sevenoaks, and had been very bored there during the week-ends, when Aunt Phoebe spent so much of her time at church. Aunt Phoebe, she reflected, seemed to know very little history, only a few facts about the Protestant Martyrs, while "Uncle Edgar", who made such a fuss of mother, seemed to know almost everything, and never answered a question with "Because it *is* so!", not even when it was close to bedtime.

Whenever he was explaining anything to her, Pippa noticed that her mother listened and smiled, her feet on the humpty, her book lowered to her lap, and the child came to the conclusion that she smiled because Edgar's patience with questions was one more proof that he was hopelessly in love with her. She did not fully understand how this state of affairs could exist. Aunt Phoebe had told her that the man mummy had "gone into partnership with" was married, and lived in London, and these facts were difficult to reconcile with the knowledge that he obviously lived there, with her mother, and had nothing whatever to do with a wife in London or anywhere else.

The mystery, however, intrigued her more than it worried her, and after a time she came to take Uncle Edgar for granted, supposing that certain business partnerships demand-ed a closer collaboration than others, and that some partners even had to share a bedroom in order that business projects might be discussed far into the night.

Perhaps life with Aunt Phoebe, who was a spinster, and Chairman of the St. Andrews' Church Guild, had left Pippa more naïve than most twelve-year-olds. Perhaps both Edgar and Frances encouraged her in her views on the partnership, or perhaps they were all three too happy to bother, one way or the other.

4

Elaine Frith stayed on as receptionist at The Falconer for nearly two years after she had left the flat over the antique shop at Llandudno, in order to make way for Pippa.

She was a good receptionist, popular with guests and management, and she might have stayed at the hotel much longer than two years, had it not been for the arrival, in the Spring of 1934, of the Great Eugene, illusionist and spell-binder, who stayed at the best hotels whenever he was playing, whether he could afford it or not.

The Great Eugene swept into the foyer of The Falconer with a swish of his crimson-lined cloak, and an imperious tapping of his gold-headed cane upon Elaine's glass-topped reception desk. He tapped because Elaine, at that moment, was working the telephone switchboard, and had kept him waiting a moment or two. When she looked up and saw him she abandoned the switchboard, and turned upon him that demure, yet oddly provocative look that had once caused the middle-aged males of the Avenue to glance over their shoulders at her slowly receding figure as she passed to and from Number Seventeen.

The Great Eugene was not specially privileged in this respect. Every unaccompanied male who showed up at Elaine's reception desk was the target, for a few fleeting seconds, of this curiously disturbing look, a glance that hovered somewhere between extreme feminine modesty, sweet feminine submissiveness, and the merest hint of something a little more up-to-date.

The Great Eugene, a specialist in illusion of every kind was not fooled by it for an instant, but he nevertheless stopped tapping, stood back, and bowed from the waist, recognising at once that Elaine was not the kind of receptionist one tapped for.

He then reciprocated her look by turning upon her his full battery of charm, a charm that had coaxed shy young ladies out of their seats and into his stage sentry-box all the way from Fort William to Sheerness, simply in order that they might disappear and reappear at the staccato clap of his hands. This clap usually prefaced heartier clapping from the auditorium, for the Great Eugene, at his best, had been a very popular turn, and his guillotine trick had been said to conjure screams of horror from strong men and once, on the Northern Circuit, cause a retired Major-General to faint into the arms of a programme-seller.

All this, however, had happened some time ago, before the talkies and the radio had tapped his audiences. He was past his best now, still impressive, still unrivalled in the field of ironic patter, and still almost handsome in white tie, tails, and crimson-lined cloak, but perhaps a little too heavily veined about the nose and cheeks, and a little too obviously breathless if second-house patter was demanded too soon after the interval.

Elaine looked at him with lively interest. She had seen him
billed about the town during the previous week, and there
was no mistaking his spare, impressive figure, his Mephisto-
phelian eyebrows, and trim, French Imperial.

"Have you a booking, Mr. Eugene?"

She knew, none better, that he had no booking, but she
wanted to show him that he was recognised. She had met a
number of people in show business since coming to work at
The Falconer, and soon learned that this was the best method
of impressing them.

His hooded eyes held her in a warm smile.

"You know me? But this is flattering, this is balm, dear
lady!"

He always addressed young women in this way. It was a
kind of double bluff, a means of informing them that he was
quite prepared to pretend that he was modest, but that they
must never let themselves be persuaded that he actually was.

"But of course I know you, Mr. Eugene! You were at
Llandudno last week, and Rhyl the week before. *Everybody*
knows you!"

She did not tell him that she made a point of reading the
show column in the local weekly, but let it be assumed,
without exactly saying as much, that she followed his career
breathlessly, week after week. Perhaps because he was getting old and tired, he began to glow, and took her plump
hand in his, raising it to his lips with an air of restrained
bravado.

"You are kind, most kind," he said, "and there is not so
much kindness abroad but that it should go unrewarded! Tell
me, dear lady, what do you say to us making an exchange of
bookings? You will book me, in your best single with bath,
and I will book you, in the best stall unsold?"

"I think that's a lovely idea, Mr. Eugene." She smiled into
his eyes, and made a pretence of looking at the sheet in front
of her, moving her forefinger up and down the columns
before adding: "Number Twelve! That's our best single. It's
on the side, but it has a wonderful view of the woods."

She rang the bell for the page, and unhooked a key. While
her back was turned he took a ticket from his pocket, and

scrawled *"Complimentary—Eugene"* across it, in handwriting that matched his cloak.

"This is for tonight," he said, with another little bow. "Perhaps, if you are amused, you may wish to come a second time. Is tonight convenient?"

It was quite convenient. Elaine had a choice of three nights a week off during the early part of the season, and seven-thirty found her settled in the front row of the stalls, waiting impatiently through a juggling act, the turn of a Lancashire comedian, and a tenor who sang *Boots* and then *The Road to Mandalay* as an encore, until at last the Great Eugene swept on from the wings. He struck a conventional attitude while the stagehands wrestled with his gilded paraphernalia, and the orchestra obliged with excerpts moderately suggestive of snake-charmers, caravans, nautch-girls, bazaars, dromedaries, and the Battle of Tel-el-Kebir.

Elaine was surprised to find herself liking the act. There was, it was true, nothing very original about his performance as a whole. A young woman wearing tights and a glacial smile appeared and disappeared with bewildering rapidity, coloured handkerchiefs were produced by the dozen from transparent jars, strings of razor blades dripped steadily from Eugene's mouth, and a duck, protesting bitterly, was whisked from beneath the brown trilby hat of a volunteer, who might or might not have been a stand-in.

It was all very polished and effective, but Elaine had a feeling that either she had seen it all before, or, she had once heard someone describe it, movement by movement.

It was his guillotine act that made the audience sit up and gasp. From where she was sitting Elaine was able to make the maximum allowance for the part played in the performance of this trick by Eugene's swirling cloak, which interposed between audience and pinioned girl at inconvenient moments. Nevertheless, she cried out with the rest when the knife went *"clonk"*, and a head—*somebody's* head—bumped into the gilded basket, at the very moment the victim sat up and shouted *"Hoi!"*, without so much as disturbing her exact smile.

It was in the performance of this particular trick that Eugene's showmanship revealed itself. Although alone on the stage, except for his strapped victim, he seemed to be in every corner at once, declaiming his patter in French, in English, and in a mixture of both languages. But although he impressed Elaine, she could not help comparing this splendidly confident figure with the slightly pathetic man who had handed her the complimentary ticket that morning. Up here, in front of his audience, Eugene was great indeed, twirling, pattering, skipping, and clapping his hands. He was the kind of man, she thought, whom any girl might be happy to accompany to a smart London restaurant, or even a Paris boulevard, and he was not far short of the man of her dream, the one who would eventually carry her off, and install her in a mansion, with a terrace for the swains to swoon upon. It was a pity that she had met him in mufti, when the tiny network of nasal veins were visible from the far side of the reception desk, and the steaks of grey showed in the magnificent eyebrows. Still, for all that, he might be worth encouraging—just a little, just enough to launch her one more step in the direction she had made up her mind to go when she became a receptionist two years ago.

It was just possible, she decided, that the Great Eugene, carefully handled, might compensate her for two almost wasted years behind the reception desk, years that had promised much but given, as yet, very little.

5

In the meantime Eugene had been making plans of his own, and Elaine might have been disturbed to learn how important a part she was playing in them.

The Great Eugene was not like other vaudeville artists, his vanity having little to do with his art as an entertainer. It had never had, not since the earliest days, when he had been climbing to the top of the bill of the Number Two circuit. He was vain only in respect of his conquests, and as middle-age and insecurity overtook him it became more and more important to him that he should make new conquests, and make them among younger women. For Eugene saw himself not as Houdini, or a Maskelyne, but as a Juan or a Cellini, a man whose finesse in the lists of love no woman could resist, so bold, yet so calculated, was his initial approach, so novel, yet so practised, his ultimate technique.

In the years leading up to the Great War, when he was in his early 'thirties, and at the peak of his earning powers, he had enjoyed a very considerable success with women, particularly among women of the theatre. They were amused by his macaw-like flamboyance, and often agreeably surprised by his virility. Over the years Eugene had kept a diary, and in that diary were the names of fifty-seven women with whom he had shared a bed for seven or more consecutive nights. He did not bother to enter up casual encounters, being of opinion that mere promiscuity deserved no laurels. He had no particular preferences for one type or another. He had, in his time, consorted with Poles, Hungarians, Creoles, Finns, and even Chinese. He had been married, for a time, to an Italian trapeze artist, and had exchanged her, in Macclesfield, for a French seal-trainer. He himself had never been to France, or anywhere abroad, not even to Dieppe or Boulogne, but he had masqueraded as a Frenchman for so long now that he almost believed himself to be a native of Nantes, whose father and grandfather had been magicians before him, and whose secrets were derived from Cagliostro.

He spoke with a slight French accent, even when asking the time, and he thought of himself as a French lover, a man to whom the current affaire was the most important thing in the cosmos. In his more successful days he had loved outside the profession, but now that this free range was denied him for economic reasons he practised a somewhat limiting combination of business and pleasure. In short, his mistress had to be his assistant as well, and be guillotined twice nightly in exchange for the privilege of sharing his bed, board, and patronage.

His arrival in Colwyn Bay coincided with his parting from Maggie, the girl with the glacial smile, for when the curtain descended on the second house at Llandudno the previous Saturday, Maggie had given him notice. She was marrying, she told him, her childhood sweetheart, now a master-baker in Doncaster, and had received from him a firm proposal earlier that week.

They parted without rancour. In some ways he sympathised with Maggie's need for security, and could well understand why she sought it in a baker's shop in Doncaster. There had been times, particularly of late, when a few slices of bread, with or without the butter, would have been a welcome addition to his own menu whilst he was "resting" between engagements.

Maggie was a generous girl, and promised to see him through the opening night at Colwyn Bay. She had even persuaded a stagehand to stand-in for her until a new girl assistant could be engaged for the act. Like most of her predecessors of late she felt rather sorry for him. He tried so hard, and it was not his fault that he was half way through his fifties.

"You'll soon find somebody, Eugene," she comforted him, in the tiny dressing-room they shared that night.

Eugene could not bear to be pitied.

"I already have, my dear," he snapped, and wondered vaguely how much a week The Falconer paid its receptionist, and whether she was likely to be sufficiently stagestruck to be interested in a certain proposition he had in mind. He continued to ponder along these lines during his walk home, and was still abstracted when he passed in at the revolving doors of the hotel.

There was nobody to warn him that, notwithstanding the fifty-seven names in his diary, which included a Finn, he had yet to encounter anyone as cold-blooded as Elaine Frith, who was even now placing a large double whisky and a chicken sandwich in his room, with a note thanking him for "a wonderful wonderful evening at the theatre".

It was all very much easier to manage than he had supposed. A few light-hearted conversations over the reception desk, and a pleasant tête-à-tête in a café on the Pier during her afternoon break, and she had consented to replace Maggie's stagehand at the Wednesday matinée. He told her that it was all perfectly simple, and indeed it was, for all she had to do was march up from the audience, and do everything he said the moment he said it. She was unable to satisfy her curiosity regarding the mechanics of some of his tricks on this occasion, for most of the time she was either shut up in his sentry-box, or lying, face downward, on his guillotine. But the audience gave her a very sporting hand when Eugene gushed his thanks, and the experience as a whole proved enormously stimulating. She went again the following evening, and again to the Saturday matinée, Eugene readily providing the tickets, but not calling upon her to assist him for fear that it should get abroad that his appeals for volunteers from the audience were bogus.

In the meantime she saw a good deal of him offstage. They lunched together at another hotel, and shared a bottle of champagne in his dressing-room on Thursday night. He was due to move on to Chester on Sunday, and throughout Saturday evening, when she was on late shift, and he was at the theatre, she wondered what further approaches he would make in the short time left to them.

She looked back on the week with pleasure. It was some time since she had been able to purr at the hunger in a man's eyes. She did not count Esme, who had always made her feel like a marble statue in a museum, but there had been two or three promising flirtations with married men at the office, and three brief associations with hotel guests during the previous season. None of these flirtations had amounted to much. The men at the office had proved too timid when it came to the touch, and the manager of the hotel actively discouraged staff associations with visitors. She had not wanted to lose the job, and had been discreet, but since meeting Eugene, and since hearing the burst of applause when he took her hand as she wriggled from the guillotine, the reception desk at The Falconer had lost much of its original attraction. She suddenly realised how terribly bored she was with keys and bills and idiotic requests for hot-water bottles on summer nights. In fact, the job that had once promised so much looked like becoming a dead end, whereas the stage was surely the traditional springboard for beautiful young women, anxious to beguile men out of their senses. Suppose Eugene was to offer her a position as his assistant? Surely it would not be long before she was noticed by somebody bigger, wealthier, and more personable? She had discerned, in his conversations, a hint or two in the right direction, but the fact that he had not enlarged upon the possibility, yet was due to catch the train for Chester next morning, began to depress her. It would have been nice, she reflected, to decline his offer, or temporise, even if common-sense did tell her the whole idea of going on the stage was preposterous.

She was aware that she interested him physically for she had never had any difficulty in recognising the patterns of speculative thought that began to be woven in the minds of most men she encountered. As far back as the Avenue days she had always been able to sort out the mildly intrigued from the frankly sensual. There was a scale in her mind for measuring this kind of speculation, and Eugene's thoughts regarding her could be read in clear print. His courtly approach was something left over from his act, and she was never in the least doubt as to what he was after, from the very first moment she looked up at him from her telephone switchboard. What did puzzle her was that he seemed to have snarled up on something, as though he had sensed in her response, or lack of it, a physical distaste for him that she did not feel, as though he imagined that the moment he ceased to flirt in the Edwardian sense of the word and said or did something slightly more definite, he would get his face slapped, and there would be an end to it. On the other hand, he was not the sort of man a girl could encourage with impunity, for he wore his considerable experience with women like his cloak. Again, as with this spectacular mantle, he used his experience to throw dust into the eyes of his audience, never quite relinquishing his hold upon courtesy, and striving hard to create an impression that he was really a man of honour as far as the ladies were concerned.

Altogether she found him a difficult nut to crack, and one so far quite outside her experience. She spent the last hour before midnight rehearsing her farewell speech to him, but she went upstairs to her room in a sulky mood when she had no opportunity to deliver it. For although she waited until 12.30, pretending to busy herself with bills, he did not come strutting through the revolving doors, so that she finally decided to wait no longer, and punish him with pertness in the morning.

For once Elaine was caught off guard. When she opened her door, and turned on the light, he was sitting in her little armchair, in front of the dressing-table. It took her at least thirty seconds to recover her poise and shut the door.

He sprang up and bowed the moment he saw her. His cloak and opera hat were lying on the bed and he had beside him a bottle of champagne and two tumblers, thick and chipped, that he had obviously borrowed from the theatre. She saw at once that she had misread his diffidence, that he could read her as well, or better, than she could read him. This called for an entire reassessment of the situation at a moment when she was tired and he had a distinct advantage over her.

"Forgive me, my dear, there was no other alternative," he said crisply. "You were on duty until midnight, and I must leave on the ten-five tomorrow. This week has been a very delightful one for me, and I did not want it to fade out, as it looked like doing. Is it presumptuous of me to imagine that you sympathise with that viewpoint?"

He was giving her an opening and she took it, gracefully.

"It's been a very happy time for me, Eugene," she said. (It was the first time she had ever addressed him as "Eugene" and not "Mr. Eugene".) "All the same, you shouldn't be here. You must know that."

He laughed softly, and she decided that he looked much younger when he laughed. His teeth were good, and his eyebrows were eyebrows consistent with laughter.

"I feel sure, my dear, that both you and I will always be the sort of people who get the most fun out of being where we shouldn't be *when* we shouldn't. I brought champagne, but you must forgive the glasses. Perhaps you would prefer your tooth-glass?"

No, she told him, the tumbler would do, and he opened the bottle with the air of a man who has opened an infinite number of bottles, and with another bow from the waist handed her the least chipped tumbler.

The champagne relaxed her. For a moment or two they talked about the show that night. Then she kicked off her shoes, and curled her legs under her on the bed. It passed through her mind then to ask him outright about the possibilities of entering show business, but her instinct told her to wait, that it must come from him. So all she said was: "How did you find my room?"

He looked at her steadily. "I found it the first night I was here. I watched you go in, and tonight I came here an hour ago, through the side entrance, and up the service stairs. Nobody saw me, you can be quite sure of that. After all, I'm a professional at disappearing acts."

"You'll have to go now," she said firmly, "and I hope you'll be just as clever at getting out."

"I must know something first," he said, and she was suddenly aware that he was flushing, and it needed an effort to keep his voice steady.

"Well?"

"Are you happy in this job? Do you think you're getting anywhere?"

She bit her lip, reflecting that it was irritating to be as transparent as all that, but she answered honestly enough:

"No, I'm not getting anywhere, Eugene, but I'd reconciled myself to that before I met you!"

His hesitancy left him. He got up from the chair, re-seated himself on the edge of the bed, and took one of her hands in both of his, regarding her earnestly, but affectionately.

"My dear, you're such a waste, stuck in that little glass box downstairs. You should have adventure while you're young! The world's waiting to play in! Have you ever thought of that?"

She had expected him to be much more original. This speech, she thought, might have been lifted from one of the first batch of paper-backed reprints that she had once hidden under the floor of her bedroom, at Number Seventeen. He did not even look like a lover, pleading his cause, but more like a family doctor, prescribing a convalescent holiday.

She left her hand limply in his. "Where could I go, and what could I do?" she wanted to know.

"You could come with me. You could join me next week, before I move on to Shrewsbury. I need somebody like you in the act; the fact is, I'd get much better bookings with a girl like you."

She was surprised to hear him say this. She had imagined, until that moment, that he used his act as a bait for mistresses, that an invitation to join him in show business was merely his' shop window, of a kind employed by all men of the theatre with designs upon women much younger than themselves. It was so in the books, and all she had to go upon as yet were the books.

"But what would I have to *do*?" she demanded with a directness that he, in turn, found irritating.

"The same as you did at the matinée, but we should improve on it of course. With you I could work up new business"—he used the word "business" in the entertainer's, not the tradesman's sense—"and an act like mine is always enhanced by the presence of a pretty woman, whether she takes an active part, or simply stands around, handing me the things I need."

As he spoke he saw her in the kind of costume he would provide for her out of an agent's advance, an ice-rink costume, perhaps, of tight satin, trimmed with fur, or better still an extravagent, feminine parody of an early nineteenth-century military costume, with rakishly-tilted shako, and skin-tight breeches, and half-length Russian boots. Benny Boy, his agent, would like that, he might even pay for a set of photographs to display in the foyer. He would tell her just how to stand and just how to turn upstage with a slight flounce. Her next question cut harshly into his speculations.

"How much would I get?"

He shrugged. "What do they pay you here?"

She told him, thirty-five shillings and full board. It was the truth. Usually she only lied to her mother.

"I could do better than that, even on Number Two circuits," he told her.

"But it wouldn't be steady, not like this job."

"No, that's true, but at least you'd be free to go where you liked, and do what you liked on seven mornings and five afternoons a week," he reminded her.

There certainly was that about it. She had already timed his act—twenty minutes, twice nightly, and an extra forty minutes for matinées. In all only three- and-a-half hours a week!

He watched her working out the sum, and suddenly decided that he had sadly underestimated her intelligence. He was sure now that she would accept his offer as an assistant on stage, but beyond that he was sure of nothing. How long might he have to support her in separate hotel rooms? How likely was she to make a fool of him by forming a romantic association with another and younger artiste, so that he would be faced with the prospect of paying for somebody else's fun? He began to panic a little. Perhaps he had been too hasty, perhaps she would be wildly indignant when she discovered that he was already supporting a wife and child, neither of whom he had seen for years, and was, in addition, contributing irregular sums towards the maintenance of another child, not many years younger than herself? After all, she had no theatrical background, and probably did not understand these things. Her accent told him that she had been brought up in a London suburb; even suppose he did, after a tedious spell of wooing, manage to get her to bed, wasn't she the type who would expect him to marry her on that account? He had neither time nor money to waste on wooing. He was getting on, and good bookings weren't too easy to find.

He made up his mind to put everything to the touch. It might end in a scene, but he was accustomed to scenes, and an expert in escaping from them. It was better than this uncertainty, and far safer than the terrifying risk of saddling himself with a dud, who might easily develop into a dismal obligation.

He got up, and took her other hand, raising them slowly to his lips, and looking down on her.

"This is a very big decision to make, my dear. Perhaps you should sleep on it. I am not sure how much you understand of these things?"

She understood far more than he had imagined, as her next action proved beyond doubt. Firmly she withdrew her hands and swung her legs round to the floor. For a moment he thought that she was going to walk out on him, and his mind, trained in such reflexes, grappled with the physical problems of getting clear before she could call the manager. He even began to rehearse high-toned rebuttals of the hysterical accusations she might make, should he fail to escape.

But it was her turn to surprise him. She crossed the little

room, turned the key in the door, and came straight back to him. He looked so astonished that she laughed, outright.

"I'm *not* a child, Eugene, " she said, "and even when I was I always understood 'these things', as you put it!"

She picked up his hat and cloak, and tossed them on the armchair. Methodically, and without the slightest sign of haste or embarrassment, she began to unbutton her high-necked blouse.

CHAPTER XXII

Progress For Two

ABOUT the time that Elaine was being fitted for her hussar costume, and Sydney was introducing his typist girl-friend to his mother, a beribboned taxi drew up outside Number Four, and the Misses Clegg, both dressed in green costumes, smelling strongly of camphor and lavender, issued sedately from the gate and rode off in chirrupy high spirits to attend dear Teddy's wedding, at the Outram Crescent Primitive Methodist Chapel.

There were, indeed, active stirrings in several of the houses at that end of the Avenue, as the big lilac at Number One Hundred and Fourteen began to bloom, and tiny, white flowers appeared on the privets behind the looped chains that linked the gateposts of the crescent.

It was the Spring during which Esme Fraser set out on his three-year Odyssey and the month that Jim Carver took to ruminating in Manor Woods, which he had seldom had time to visit throughout these committee-studded years; it was the season that his younger daughter, Judith, moved away from the Avenue, and went down into Devonshire, with that hatchet-faced employer of hers, in order to start a new riding-school on the edge of the moors, overlooking the Channel. It was also the season that Louise decided she could regulate her cooking time-table by inviting her silent fiancé to take up permanent residence in Number Twenty, instead of having him come in from the Nursery at mid-day, and cause her to begin cooking all over again at six p.m. when Jim returned for his evening meal.

These events might appear to be unrelated to one another. They were, after all, the outcome of unrelated dreams, on the part of the individuals who ordered them, but in another sense they were related. It was the bustle of Teddy's wedding, to which she and her father had been invited, that had stirred the placid Louise into considering her own prospects of marriage, and it was Louise's decision that decided Judy to accept Maud Somerton's invitation to accompany her to Devonshire.

Similarly, it was Edgar Frith's letter to Sydney, telling him that Elaine had thrown up her hotel job and gone on the stage, that finally decided Esme to accept his former Headmaster's advice, and set out on his writer's apprenticeship journey around Britain. Sydney knew all about Esme's hopeless infatuation for his sister, and was unable to resist passing on the astonishing news of her second flight, if only for the pleasure of watching Esme's expression when he realised that Elaine had now passed out of his life for ever. Sydney often went out of his way to pass bad news on to acquaintances. He had never quite found a substitute for the little spurts of pleasure he had once derived from reporting delinquents to the Headmaster, when he was head boy of the private school in the Lower Road.

So Esme and Judith disappeared from the Avenue for a period, and Jim Carver took time off from his party rallies and open-air meetings in order to marshal his thoughts regarding the state of the world as he walked the cool aisles of the Old Manor beeches. But Ted Hartnell, to Edith's unspeakable delight, did not disappear from the Avenue. He took Harold Godbeer's advice, and made a down-payment on Number Forty-Five, not two minutes' walk down the Avenue; here he brought Margy, his bride, when they returned from their honeymoon in Blackpool, to set up a dance orchestra with a style, and a *sound* of its own, more ambi-

tious, and more original than Al Swingers' "Rhythmateers".
For so Margy had decided, and Margy was now sole custodi-
an of Ted's future.

Neither the bride nor the groom were Primitive Method-
ists. Margy had never been inside a church since she was
christened, and Ted spent his Sundays rehearsing, or playing
gramophone records. Margy's "comfortable" aunt, however,
was an active Primitive Methodist. As it was she who
provided the wedding breakfast, and gave them a walnut
bedroom suite for a wedding present, they felt they owed it
to her to be married in the church for which she had also
provided hassocks and hymn-books, and where the Reverend
Owen B. Hughes, resident minister, regarded her as more
essential than all his worshippers lumped together.

It is to be wondered, perhaps, what the Reverend Owen B.
Hughes thought of the arch of band instruments under which
the happy couple walked when they emerged from the Chapel, with his nuptial advice ringing in their ears. Jazz bands
were not encouraged among the congregation of the Outram
Crescent Chapel. True, jazzy orchestras of sackbuts, dulci-
mers, and timbrels cropped up in the Old Testament from
time to time, but these were almost invariably played upon
by unbelievers, or at times during the active persecution of
the elect, as on the occasion when Shadrach, Meshach, and
Abednego were thrust into a fiery furnace. However, the
bride's aunt was a very generous friend of the Chapel, and
even had she not been, Al Swinger and his boys had served
no formal notice on Mr. Hughes that they intended to regard
the wedding of their drummer as an occasion to make merry
and advertise the band.

Accordingly, the minister was obliged to stand aside with a
tolerant smile while flash-bulbs sparked off on his church
steps, and Ted and Margy paused for photographs under an
arch of saxophones and drumsticks. Then they went rushing
into the taxi, and shot off down Outram Crescent with a "Just
Married" notice on the luggage grid, and the remains of an
old kettledrum trailing on ten yards of string.

Edith Clegg wept during the ceremony. She had, by now,
both met and approved Teddy's wife, a pleasant, animated
little thing, she thought, nothing like as pretty as her new

lodger, Jean McIntyre, but just the kind of wife dear Teddy needed—someone to *plan* for him, and to make sure that he *got* somewhere, someone to offset his willingness to be *used*, as that horrid, pasty-faced Al Swinger had used him so shamelessly all these years.

Edith made up her mind about Margy the first day that Teddy brought her into Number Four for supper. From that day forth she never ceased to encourage Teddy to marry, and settle down. Margy, having no mother-in-law to cope with, did not underestimate Edith's influence on him, and had taken swift advantage of Teddy's brief absence after supper. With the wide-eyed Becky looking on she had said:

"He won't push for himself, Miss Clegg, he just lets people use him, and bully him, and he's great, Miss Clegg, he's got something hardly any of us have got . . . a sort of . . . *reverence* for rhythm, that's so different from the attitude of the run-of-the-mill drummers. He's got an ear too, a wonderful ear . . . he can play any instrument he tries, the trumpet, the sax, the piano even. . . . I've heard him, when we've been rehearsing, and he's got a *beat*, the sort of beat that can take him right to the top, if only he's carefully handled!"

She looked full into Edith's radiant face. "I'm going to *see* that he gets there, Miss Clegg, you just watch! He doesn't know it yet, but I'm going to *see* that he gets there!"

He soon did know it, for she told him on the final day of their honeymoon, when they had settled themselves in the main-line train at Crewe, on the last lap of their journey back to London.

They had had a wonderful time, thirteen recklessly extravagant days of eating, and dancing, and Big Dipper riding, and thirteen wonderful nights, such as are given to few honeymooners. Although very much in love, they were an unexacting couple, and made love almost absentmindedly, their thoughts continuing to range on other subjects, even as they lay silently together in the impressively appointed hotel suite, listening to the scamper of hurrying feet on the pavements outside, and the goodnight lullabies of the Tower Ballroom Orchestra, playing *Roll Along Kentucky Moon,* and *Stormy Weather.*

Sometimes they would even discuss these numbers as Margy nestled lower on his shoulder.

"They're going back a bit with that one, aren't they, Ted ...? They don't seem to use the latest ones much up here. Never hear *A Night in Napoli* or *A Street in Old Seville*."

And he would reply: "Aw—that vocalist they've got this week isn't all she's cracked up to be, Margy! She doesn't *give* the way you do, she's too stiff somehow. That interval number tonight, what was it, again?"

"Let's Put Out the Light and Go to Bed?"

"That was it! Well, it's a relaxed number, and you've got to swing *with* it, not against it. You could put it over, Margy! You could put it over swell!"

It was an odd conversation for honeymooners, comfortably in bed, and enfolded in one another's arms, but Ted and Margy had settled for one another long ago, and stood in small need of fresh adjustments.

She purposely avoided mentioning her plan until the honeymoon was practically over. Then she launched it at him, sure of herself, and sure of his reaction to it. As the train moved out of Crewe she said:

"We're not going back to Al, Ted."

He stared at her, overwhelmed by the announcement.

"Not going to Al . . . you mean we've left Al . . . ? Margy love, you're dreaming!"

She opened her new handbag, and took out a folded sheet of newsprint. It was a page torn from the trade periodical, and one of the "Wanted" advertisements was ringed. It read:

> *Wanted for auditions. Instrumentalists specialising in dance-music. New Orchestra. Good prospects. Write c/o Mrs. E. Hartnell, c/o 71a Cawnpore Road, Addiscombe, Surrey.*

He read it slowly, and then waited, while she handed the collector their tickets to punch.

"This is crazy, Margy! You need capital for a thing like this, and we've spent practically everything we've got on the furniture and the honeymoon."

"We haven't, Ted; at least, *I* haven't. Look!"

She dived into her bag again, and gave him a post-office savings book. It was totted up in pencil and he saw that there was a credit balance of £260.

"Where did you get two hundred and sixty pounds?" he asked faintly.

She squeezed his hand. "Aunt Dolly gave me one hundred pounds that I didn't tell you about She said it would be a nest-egg for a baby, but we just can't have babies—not yet, Ted. Dad gave me another ten pounds, and the rest is what I've saved. It's enough to start with. We need down payments on instruments, and an advertising campaign. We'll make out, you see if we don't!"

He contemplated her with awe and admiration.

"Margy, you're wonderful, but suppose we don't get any engagements, how will we pay the people we engage?"

"Well, that's a silly way to start a business!" she exclaimed. "You just make up your mind that you'll get engagements. Al always got them, didn't he? And we're going to be a lot better than Al. We're going to *have* class, not just *tell* people we've got it."

She patted him, like a mother reassuring a small boy on his way to begin first term at Boarding School. "Don't worry, Ted, leave everything to me."

He did worry, all the way to East Croydon Station, but he need not have done, for on arrival at her home they found, in addition to scores of requests for auditions, an invitation, sponsored by Margy's father, to quote for a string of socials organised by the area branches of the British Legion. They quoted low, even before the orchestra was selected, and then paid a month's rent in advance on a local rehearsal room. The day their tender was accepted by the Legion Ted took the final plunge, and fixed the day for auditions.

One of the first musicians to appear was Al. He was seeking not an audition but an explanation. Margy had sent in their notices from Blackpool, but Al knew Ted, and was confident that he could talk him round.

"You can't go through with this, pal," he told him. "I gave you your first chance, didn't I?"

Ted was wretchedly embarrassed, but Margy was at hand

to do the talking for him. She stood squarely in front of
Al.

"Everyone's got to get a first chance from somewhere,"
she snapped, "and Ted would have been a drummer no
matter what! Your finding him was just your good luck, not
his!"

"Oh, I dunno, Margy . . ." protested Ted miserably. "Al
and me . . ."

"Shut up, Ted," said Margy, very firmly.

Al tried a flank attack.

"I never could stick seeing a man run by his missus," he
said, an unlit cigarette wobbling slackly on his lower lip, "and
I must say you seem to have handed over your trousers even
quicker than most honeymooners, pal!"

It was the last exchange of conversation that was to pass
between them, and it was terminated by a slap from Margy
that brought a vivid flush to Al's pale cheeks, and sent him
staggering back against the piano.

Margy then followed him up, ignoring Ted's yelp of protest.

"Don't, Margy . . . don't do that to Al!"

"You talk cheap and you *are* cheap," she shouted at the
band leader. "I've always thought so, right from the first day
I sang for you, and now Ted's going to have a real band, not
a half-baked imitation of a Yank set-up like yours! You get
out of here! We've paid for our rehearsal rooms and that's
something you never did until you were County Courted!"

Al regarded her steadily for a moment, then slowly withdrew his hand from his injured cheek and hitched his narrow
shoulders.

"Ted, old boy," he drawled, "I'm real sorry for you,
brother! You seemed to have hitched yourself to a first-class
bitch!"

He turned, intending to drift out through the wide door,
and for a couple of yards he moved at his accustomed pace,
half-roll, half-slouch. But as he crossed the threshold his exit
was suddenly accelerated, not by Margy, but by Ted, who
suddenly shot past the piano, and planted his toe squarely,
and with terrible force, into the seat of Al's dirty flannels.

It was the first time either of them had seen Al move fast.

He seemed to fly horizontally out through the door, and half-way along the entrance passage, slithering to a stop, face down, at the feet of a spare, bespectacled young man, who was on the way in, a violin case tucked under his arm. He was on his feet again in a flash, and before Ted could lay hands on him he was gone, with the violinist still poised on the doorstep, his eyebrows raised in an expression of quizzical interest.

"Was he *that* bad?" he asked Ted, and then, hearing Margy's peal of laughter, "I do hope I make a rather better impression!"

From that moment nothing seemed to go wrong.

It was as though the final brush with Al had released in Ted some secret store of energy, converting him, in a matter of seconds, from a shambling, good-natured, patient drudge, into an alert, cool-headed executive, a fit mate for the dynamic Margy, who hereafter made all the decisions. She simply passed them in private to Ted, so that the Hartnell Eight, as they came to be known, were never quite sure from whom the real power originated, and learned to obey man or wife with equal promptness.

There was nothing jazzy about the Hartnell Eight. They never appeared in fancy uniforms, like other dance orchestras, but wore sober, well-pressed dinner-jackets, and addressed one another in quiet, sober tones between the numbers. They soon acquired a local reputation for sobriety and deportment, but there was no stuffiness about their work on the platform. Their time and their harmony were faultless, and they obviously put in plenty of hard work at rehearsals.

Margy accompanied them to all their engagements, though she was not officially included in their number. Sometimes she sang an interval number, and sometimes she played the sax solo. Sometimes, when Ted was back with the drums, she made announcements, and judged competitions.

Wherever she went she always seemed to bring them luck, and to make friends that led to other engagements, but most of the time they were playing she stood quietly beside the piano, looking across at Ted. Arthur, the violinist who had witnessed Al's expulsion, often saw a glance pass between them, initiated by Margy. Arthur was a very observant young man, and it seemed to him, at times like these, that Margy was simply saying:

"I told you! We're on our way up, Ted, so don't worry about it. Leave everything to me."

CHAPTER XXIII

Carver Roundabout. II

1

LICKAPAW, the prodigal cat of Number Four, died suddenly in the mid-thirties.

He was, according to Becky Clegg's reckoning, fifteen years old, and all things considered he had worn very well, for although, in the years of his decline, he spent much more time at home, and left the roofs of Delhi and Cawnpore Roads comparatively free for younger bloods, he enjoyed a brief Indian summer of romance, and in his extreme old age set out on a last hegira for the purpose of discovering new wives.

Whether he actually found any or not it is impossible to say, for after a few days' absence he was discovered dying in the Nursery by Louise's fiancé, Jack Strawbridge, who carried him into Number Twenty, for Jim to take home to Becky.

He died in the kitchen of Number Four, surrounded, like some feline Charles II, by respectful courtiers, and Becky, the chief mourner, dug a grave over against the highboard fence that divided their garden from the Nursery.

Jim Carver, who was very fond of Becky, made her a little cross with *Lickapaw*, 1919–35 scored on it with a red-hot poker.

The dog Strike did not die. Strike seemed to have lapped the elixir of permanent puppyhood, for he never quieted down, and took to wheezing in his basket like other old dogs, but continued to prance madly about the kitchen the moment Jim returned from work. Jim had half-trained him to fetch slippers and carry newspapers, but he was never very good at this sort of thing. He gambolled and wriggled too much, and seemed unable to forget the lively circumstances in which they had met at the Elephant and Castle.

Strike was getting plenty of exercise these days, for Jim Carver was wrestling with his conscience, and when Jim did this he felt compelled to march. Whenever he had a problem on his mind Jim did not walk, but marched, as he had once marched to and fro along the greasy *pavé* in France.

Jim's conscience was giving him a great deal of trouble nowadays, so much in fact that it was upsetting his entire conception of Brotherly Love and International Socialism. For seventeen years now Jim had been a passionately convinced pacifist, a very militant pacifist it is true, but still a pacifist, that is, one who had pledged himself never again to fight for King, Country, and Empire and one who was opposed, to the point of bloody revolution, to rearmament and the traffic in weapons of war. His feelings regarding these matters had once been the burning convictions of a convert, not in any way subject to the fluctuations of the international scene. He had seen the boy on the bank at Mons and had therefore seen the light. War was a capitalists' racket. War was a profiteers' ruse. War was fought by the masses, who were the inevitable losers thereby. Therefore war was wrong. All wars were wrong.

But were they? What happened in cases like those of Manchuria and Abyssinia? What must a democrat do when Democracy itself was challenged, when the machinery for the outlawing of war was seen to be outmoded and useless? What did a man do when faced by the kind of challenge already looming up from Germany, where thousands of pacifists, as earnest as himself, were being torn from their beds, thrust into camps, and left to rot and starve, or to die under the bullets of uniformed thugs? What happened in one's own Avenue, when a young fool like Sydney Frith, the boy opposite, donned a black shirt and topboots, and promised to start the same sort of thing over here? In other words, where did one draw the line between doctrinaire pacifism and downright cowardice?

To find answers to these questions Jim began taking long evening walks in Manor Woods, and in the winding paths that converged on the derelict manor he found, ultimately, some sort of compromise. It was quiet in here, especially down by the broken terrace in front of the lake, where the weed had multiplied with the years, and water-lilies still floated about round the rotting pagoda.

All these years Jim had leaned heavily upon the League, and while the League remained pacifism seemed practical. More than fifty nations had signed their willingness to accept Jim's ideas about war, and surely it was not possible to flout more than fifty nations, with their sanctions, and shrill threats of diplomatic ostracism? Unfortunately Mussolini, and before him the Japanese War-lords, had shown that such a thing was indeed possible. Japan had carried full-scale war into Manchuria four years ago, and Mussolini was obviously not going to allow the League's frowns to frighten him out of Abyssinia. Meantime, Hitler, the noisiest lunatic of them all, was behaving as though the League of Nations was an elderly spinster aunt, who disapproved of rough games but need on no account be taken very seriously.

The point was, where would this defiance end and did it mean that, in order to preserve world authority, Geneva would have to become an arsenal? Would loyal signatories be obliged to go to war to stop a war, to kill Italians in order to save Abyssinians?

For several weeks Jim put his faith in sanctions, but when Mussolini swept gleefully into Addis Ababa, and the sad-eyed Negus began wandering cheerlessly about Britain, Jim's vision of the boy on the bank began to fade; he became very strident, even for a pacifist, in demanding instant action against the people who were playing ducks and drakes with his conscience.

Unfortunately for him he was a very just and reasonable man. For sixteen years he had been howling for disarmament and, unlike most pacifists, he could follow the arguments of the Tory politicians when they said that wars could not be fought with rolled-up Order Papers. The election of the autumn of 1935 was the most wretched Jim had ever entered upon, for here was Baldwin, pledging support for the League, yet asking for a mandate to rearm, while here was Jim's candidate, trotting out all the familiar clichés about capitalist arms barons, but coupling them with a noisy demand to sit on Mussolini! Small wonder that Jim took to the woods, and when tired of marching sat moodily on the terrace, throwing sticks for Strike.

Meanwhile the beeches behind him turned bronze, and russet, and crimson, and yet more plaster trickled from the façade of the old, blind-eyed Manor, that seemed to Jim to stand waiting, ringed in woods, for the Armageddon that had moved up in the queue, and taken the place of the Social Millennium.

Things were worse instead of better by the time the beech leaves turned green again.

With the outbreak of the Spanish Civil War, and the idiotic farce of Non-Intervention, the vision of the boy on the bank faded completely, and Jim began to have the gravest doubts about pacifism, the League, the Kellogg Pact, and every other topic of so many street-corner orators.

Here was an entire people struggling against a feudalism that had held them in thrall for centuries, and here were madmen like Hitler and Mussolini pouring in men and material to beat them to their knees. Standing aside, like two elderly parsons who were the unwilling spectators of a murder, were his own country and Republican France, both terrified of becoming involved, and doing nothing except to direct a few pious, and none too emphatic protests at the criminals. Eden and Duff Cooper resigned in disgust, and Jim never forgot their courageous action. For a brief moment hope had flared up in Jim, when public opinion failed to swallow the cynical Hoare-Laval plan to partition Abyssinia, but the flame soon died down again. In sullen rage Jim wrote to the headquarters of Canon Dick Sheppard's Peace Pledge Union, demanding the return of his card, the card on which he had pledged himself never again to fight for King or Country.

When it arrived, with the Union's regrets, he tore it up and threw the pieces into Manor Lake. The dog Strike cocked an ear, puzzled by the flimsiness of the object he was expected to retrieve. Jim noted his expression and his face cleared a little.

"Don't go in after that, Strike," he told him; "that's no use to anyone any more. Try this boy—after it!"

And he threw a length of stick, perhaps the very piece Esme Fraser had stuck in his belt for a pistol all those years ago, at a time in history when everyone was agreed that another war was unthinkable, and children thought of weapons in terms of pistols, rather than poison-gas, and high-explosives dropped from aeroplanes.

He got up and called briefly to the dog. As he turned back towards the briar-strewn path he saw a young man mooching along ahead of him, hands deep in trouser pockets and shoulders hunched. He recognised him from the back as young Esme Fraser, of Number Twenty-Two, and his mind drifted away from international problems for a moment, to ponder on the boy next door, the one his girl Judith had once cared for so deeply. What did the boy do for a living? Why did he spend so much time up in that little room of his above the porch? Why had Judy suddenly cooled towards him, and flung herself so whole-heartedly into this horse-riding business?

He did not pursue these questions for they did not really interest him. His mind was still preoccupied with the mass rather than the individual, but before he forgot about Esme he reflected that the boy was of the age group most liable to be killed in the next war, as indeed were his own younger boys, Boxer and Berni.

He wondered, for a mere second or so, what Boxer and Berni were up to now. He had heard they had left the Speedway, and found themselves some sort of work in an Amusement Park. Then he smelled burning weeds, from a bonfire on the allotments beyond the woods, and the smell reminded him again of the pitiless war in Spain. They were forming an International Brigade he had heard, to fight for the People, whom some called Nationalists, and others called the Rebels. That was the trouble nowadays. Nothing had a proper label. Nothing was clear-cut, like the black-and-white issues of the 'twenties.

2

Jim might have spared a longer moment to reflect on the twins had he been aware of the exact nature of the "odd job" they had found themselves in an Amusement Park.

They were now stunt-riders, who travelled about with a Nine Days' Wonder known as "The Wall of Death".

Five times nightly, and several times during afternoon shows, they climbed into a deep, metal well, lashed out at their kick-starts. and began to weave frantic patterns round and round the sides of the pit, crossing and recrossing at breathtaking speeds, to the horror and amazement of patrons who paid sixpence a time to peer at them over the fenced-in rim of the well.

They had quit Speedway racing as soon as it began to bore them, and they now earned better money for doing what looked so dangerous but was, to them, as safe as circling a track.

As time went on they improved on their performances, inventing little thrills for the benefit of the more *blasé* spectators, pretending to fight their way out of speed-wobbles, or folding their arms over their leather-encased chests as they roared up, down, and around the enclosed space. For a time, a very little time, the sport satisfied their craving for noise, movement, and public adulation.

They moved about the country with the promoter, who regarded them as his most valuable asset. They were billed as "The Suicide Twins" and between shows they had their pick of the local girls, who came to see them ride, and were flattered to be seen with them in seafront cafés and cinemas.

None of these mild flirtations developed into a romance, for the twins could never find their counterpart among the young women of the towns they visited. Sometimes Boxer found himself a girl whose company seemed worth cultivating, and sometimes Berni hovered for a moment or two on the point of falling in love, but they were never able to find the pair who could make up a cosy foursome, and it never seemed to occur to them to separate, and go separate ways, not even when the moon was up.

This sometimes proved embarrassing to the girls they invited out. Boxer would turn up with an adoring blonde, "with hair like Veronica Lake", and propose an expedition to the cinema, but the young lady was invariably disconcerted by the permanent presence of Berni, who tagged along on the other side of her, holding long, technical conversations, about over-drives and expansion chambers with his twin.

It was just the same when Berni found a girl. He would make an appointment to take her out to supper, but when she appeared, dolled up for the occasion, she found two swains instead of one, and spent an evening trying to impress both of them, with the not unnatural result that she scored a low average with each, and was left on her doorstep without a subsequent date being arranged.

What would have proved ideal for the twins, who were just as susceptible to pretty faces and slim legs as any normal young men, would have been a pair of identical twins, like their sisters Fetch and Carry. These might have been interchangeable during the early stages of courtship, and perhaps, in due course, Bernard and Boxer might have come to prefer one to the other, but they never had the good fortune to meet such a pair. Largely on this account their spectacular career as the Suicide Twins came to an abrupt and somewhat muddled end, after Boxer had proposed to Jackie Gulliver during the Carnival Ball at Folkestone.

Jackie Gulliver was a pretty, impulsive, determined young woman, reputedly an extremely good match, for she was the youngest child of Sam Gulliver, of Gulliver's Accessories, a well-known motor-cycle manufacturing firm, in the Midlands.

The twins were using Gulliver's machines at that time, and their dare-devil likenesses, reproduced upside down on streamlined 750-c.c. motor-cycles, appeared in all the trade literature issued by the firm, and in some of Gulliver's advertisements in the popular press.

Sam Gulliver was a genial, self-made man, and when Jackie confessed to him that she had fallen hopelessly in love with Boxer, and had every intention of marrying him, he surprised her by raising no objection whatever. Sam, in fact, was fond of the twins himself, and he reasoned that a son-in-

law like Boxer would be more likely to prove a business asset
than some of the spotty young men Jackie had already
introduced into the house, gawky and spoiled youths, for the
most part, who stood around calling him "sir", and haw-
hawing to Brenda, his wife, about drivelling novels, paintings,
and similar nonsense.

Sam and Jackie had driven down to Folkestone for the
summer carnival that year, and the Wall of Death was
carrying a big spread of Gulliver advertising. Sam had even
chartered an aeroplane to write *"Gulliver's For Speed"* in the
sky above the Leas, and the promoter of the Wall of Death
had laid on a special benefit show on behalf of the charities
expecting to profit from the carnival.

At the carnival dance on Saturday night Boxer drank more
than he could carry, which was quite a lot, and Berni, who
made a habit of being two or three pints in arrears, would
have persuaded him into the open and sobered him up had he
been given the chance. Instead, Jackie Gulliver intervened,
and accepted responsibility for him, getting her father's
chauffeur to pilot the wavering Boxer to the back of her own
Bentley sports-car, which was parked near the Pavilion.

Here Bernard was obliged to leave him, in order to 'phone
Sam Gulliver, and inform him that his daughter was returning to London that night. Bernard was glad to convey such a
message, for Jackie's possessive ministrations were beginning
to irritate him. He and only he knew how to handle Boxer
when he was drunk, and he resented assistance, however
well-meant.

He made the 'phone call, but when he returned to the
Pavilion parking-ground the Bentley was gone. He did not
see or hear from Boxer again for the better part of a
week.

Both he and the Wall of Death promoter made exhaustive
enquiries. They even went to the police, and it was through
them that they finally learned where Boxer had gone. It
seemed that Jackie Gulliver had not gone home to London at
all, but had spirited Boxer down to the Gulliver's week-end
chalet, near Pevensey, there to make doubly sure that Papa
succeeded in talking the less accommodating Mamma into
accepting Boxer as a son-in-law.

Bernard was both furious and alarmed. To begin with he felt half-crippled without Boxer around. In all these years they had never been separated for more than a few hours at a time, and it occurred to Bernard that unless he did something to end this romance the present separation might prove but a foretaste of lonely years ahead.

As it happened, Boxer escaped from his idyll without any help, and turned up at their lodgings in Folkestone, looking more than a little sheepish. He found Bernard on the boarding-house steps, booted and spurred for a kidnapping trip to Pevensey.

"Wotcher, Berni?" he said, with a brave attempt at his wide, clownish grin; "I gave her the slip. I got out of the larder window early this morning, and hitch-hiked over here before she twigged I was gone!"

Bernard looked him over, anxious possibilities crowding his mind.

"You're a saphead, Boxer!" he grunted. "How far did you go with her?"

"Oh *that*," said Boxer carelessly; "all the way, I reckon—there was no holding her—but so what? I wasn't born yesterday, and neither was she, so you don't have to worry, Berni boy."

The 'phone interrupted this clinical discussion, and Bernard clumped into the corridor to answer it. He came back looking grave.

"It's her," he said, "and she's coming right after you."

"Jese!" said Boxer emphatically, "maybe we'd better move on. Whad'ysay Berni? Whad'ysay?"

Bernard weighed the chances, just as he had weighed them when Boxer had proposed to vary the tedium of "Knocking Down Ginger" with a game of "String and Parcel".

"That's not going to work, Boxer," he said slowly. "She says you promised to marry her next Saturday. She's 'phoned through and told her old man."

"Jese!" said Boxer unhelpfully.

"Well, did you?"

Bernard kept his eye on his twin as he spoke and Boxer, unable to meet the accusation in it, dropped his glance to the rubber mat on the boarding-house porch.

"I . . . I dunno, Berni, honest I don't. *She* says so, she kept on saying so. I might have, but then again, I might not, and if I did, like she says, it was the night I passed out. I never promised anything after that, honest!"

He looked so much as if he was going to burst into tears that the familiar spasm of pity gripped Bernard's heart. He reached out, and laid a soothing hand on Boxer's massive, hairy wrist.

"Don't you worry, Boxer, I'll take care o' this. You . . . you clear off back home, and tell Dad we're taking a holiday. You let me fix it. Whad'ysay, Boxer?"

What could Boxer say? He had not made an independent decision in twenty years, not since the day he had decided to test the ice on the pond in the lane. He winked gratefully at his twin and then, without a word, lumbered off down the steps towards the railway station. Bernard called after him.

"Hi! You got money for the fare?"

Boxer hadn't, so Bernard ran after him, and gave him three pound notes. Then he went slowly back into the frowsty sitting-room, to wait the arrival of Jackie Gulliver.

She roared up about an hour later, and ran lightly up the steps of the boarding-house calling:

"Boxer, darling! Are you there, Boxer-pet?"

She threw open the door of the guest-room and saw Bernard, sitting stiffly on a horsehair sofa, and regarding her with cold hostility.

"He's gone," said Bernard, and somehow made it sound as though Boxer was now senseless and shackled in the hold of a West Indian banana boat.

"Gone where?" demanded Jackie, her lips quivering.

"Just gone," said Bernard, without taking his hard, blue eyes from her.

Jackie flew into one of her tantrums, but nevertheless she continued to observe Bernard very closely. She believed sincerely in Napoleon's maxim of never letting rage mount higher than the chin. She had discovered, as a small child, that a tantrum paid a dividend if you did this.

"You're hiding him! You don't *want* him to marry me! But he's going to, he promised to .. he's ... he's *got* to now; Daddy'll see to that! So just you tell me where he is, or I'll get you the sack! I'll get straight on the 'phone to Daddy, and get you the sack!"

Sam Gulliver was not the twins' direct employer, but the threat was not an idle one. A word from Gulliver to the Wall of Death promoter would have certainly sent them packing, but Bernard remained unmoved. He sat there, hands on knees, watching her stamp about the room, with tears of rage coursing down her powdered cheeks. If anything was needed to strengthen him in his resolve to get Boxer out of this situation Jackie Gulliver was providing it, here and now, for Boxer, he decided, would be better off at the bottom of the frozen pond than married to this spoiled, hysterical vixen.

"You won't get him," he said at last and with great deliberation, "you won't ever get Boxer, not while I'm alive!"

His tone, and the odd way he was looking at her, made her artificial temper seem ridiculous. She stopped moving about, and came closer to him.

"You don't understand," she said, in a slightly more reasonable tone; "he loves me, and he's promised to marry me."

"He doesn't love anyone, and he only promised when he was blotto," said Bernard. "I don't reckon that counts. I don't reckon it would count anywhere!"

At once she snapped back into a blazing temper.

"You'll have to prove that," she screamed. "I'll sue him for breach ... it'll be in all the papers, and if I have a baby he'll have to marry me, d'you hear? *He'll have to!*"

Bernard rose slowly to his feet. She noticed that he was pale, and was curiously rigid, as though he was himself fighting hysteria, real hysteria. Suddenly she was very much afraid of him. He looked so squat, menacing, and implacable.

"You won't have a baby," he said, "and if you did it wouldn't be Boxer's. You just remember that, Jackie Gulliver ... *it wouldn't be Boxer's*. If you said it was you'd be sorry, and wish to God you never run across Boxer, or me either!"

She gave a little gasp and then, as he moved forward, stepped quickly aside to let him reach the door. Rage ebbed out of her, and her knees began to tremble. By the time she had some sort of control of herself he was gone, and she heard him run down the steps, and stab at his kick-start. A moment later his powerful engine began to roar, and when she ran to the window he was already zooming into the distance.

She rang the visitors' bell, and presently an aged Boots shuffled in.

"Do you think you could get me a little brandy?" she asked shakily.

"I'll see, Miss," said the Boots, and shuffled out again.

Jackie Gulliver sat down on the sofa, opened her handbag, and began to repair the ravages caused by her tears. She might be spoiled, and highly-strung, but she was no fool. She had already decided to forget Boxer, and make that cruise to the Med. with "Jumbo" Coombes-Bister, and his sister Joyce, the children of the Marmalade King, whom she had met at Le Touquet the previous April.

3

Louise and Jack Strawbridge were married at East Croydon Registrar's office that same autumn.

With Judith gone, and the twins Fetch and Carry out at work all day, there was no point in waiting any longer. She was thirty-five, and Jack was a year older. If they didn't marry now, she reasoned, what small chance they had of having children would be gone. The prospect of a childless marriage saddened Louise, for she had been attending to children from first light until nightfall for as long as she could remember.

Her father tried to persuade her to get married at Shirley Church, but she said she was too old for that sort of wedding, and anyway it would cost too much. All she wanted was for Jack to move into Number Twenty, and eat his breakfast with them, before he went out to work in the Nursery. He had been eating his mid-day meals and his suppers at the house for years now, and they could share the bed she had shared with Judy for so long. In her eyes it was not really marriage at all, simply a domestic adjustment.

Judith came up from Devonshire to be her bridesmaid. They all thought she looked radiantly healthy. Her skin was tanned and clear, her thick, brown hair was waved for the occasion, her little figure trim and taut, after so many hours in the saddle. She brought them a canteen of cutlery as a wedding gift, and Louise was glad of it, for her table-ware had not been renewed since before the war, and the knife-handles were shrinking away from the thin blades.

Archie called round the night before the wedding. For the first time in ten years he and Jim sat in the kitchen together, while Louise made them both tea, and fussed about, putting finishing touches to the cake she had baked herself.

Father and son looked a little uncomfortable facing one another over the table, but honoured an unspoken agreement to bury the hatchet, at least for the time being, for Louise's sake.

Jack Strawbridge came round to show Louise his new, navy blue suit, bought for the occasion. He looked very odd in it, for none of them had ever seen him in anything but corduroys, an open-necked shirt, and a converted army tunic. His neck looked redder than ever wnere it strained over his stiff, white collar, and Louise, straightening his tie, said that if he took a really deep breath, fragments of serge and cotton would fly all over the kitchen. He sat down very carefully, and drank tea with the spoon still in the cup. He seemed horribly nervous, and Archie tried to reassure him.

"There's absolutely nothing to it, Jack. It only takes about a hundred seconds. They pass the couples through on a sort of conveyer-belt!"

He was not far wrong. The ceremony occupied just over three minutes, from the moment they were beckoned into the inner office by the clerk, to the moment they emerged into the autumn sunshine, and Bernard and Boxer scattered hand-fuls of confetti over them, while Judith stood back smiling, and Jim opened the taxi door.

"Aren't you and Judy riding home with us?" asked the bride, as he closed it again.

"Not today, Lou; we wouldn't be seen dead with you, would we, Pop?" said Archie, grinning.

"We'll follow on," Jim told her. "Miss Clegg will have everything ready."

Edith opened the door to them when she heard the taxi. She was wearing the same tight, green costume that she had worn at Teddy's wedding, and it still smelled of camphor and lavender. Edith loved a wedding and had been delighted when Jim asked her to act as hostess. They all crowded round the table in the front room, and all their jovial protests could not prevent Louise getting up to help Edith serve the cold chicken and trifle.

After Archie had proposed a toast Jack was given permission to take off his collar, and only then could he be persuaded to get up and make a speech. It was the first and last of his life.

"Well, everyone," he said, "I dunno what to say, except thanks for bein' zo good to us. I reckon we're too long in the tooth, the both of us, for this sort o' lark, but it's nice havin' it just the same, and something to remember. Me an' Lou, we been kind of meaning to get married a long time now, but somehow we never got around to it. Well, now we have, as you c'n zee, and I reckon we oughter make a go of it. Anyone could with Lou here, or he'd be dam' hard to please, that he would!"

He sat down, amid laughter, applause, and a discreetly wiped tear from the smiling Edith.

Later in the afternoon they all surged on to the pavement to speed the couple away on their honeymoon to Clacton, and in addition to the wedding party a sprinkling of Avenue folk drifted out to their front gates to watch the send-off. Archie's wife and family waited on the corner to wave, while Harold and Eunice came out from next door to shake hands, and join in the laughter as the inevitable old boot bumped out from under the rear axle. Esther Frith and Sydney did not emerge from Number Seventeen, but they watched the scene from their front-room window, and as the taxi moved off, to a chorus of shouting and laughter, Sydney said:

"I've always thought those Carvers were rather common!"

Esther said nothing, but went back to her needlework. Perhaps she was remembering another wedding, away in the

remote past, long before the war, when she had driven for
the last time down the ill-tended drive of her aunt's gaunt
house, to meet Edgar, in his frock coat and topper, at the
little chapel in the village. A thought may have crossed her
mind that perhaps this was what had been wrong about her
own marriage, it hadn't been common enough.

4

Old Piretta died that autumn. His chest had been giving
him trouble for a long time, but now the doctor said it was
his heart, and he must rest, and cease to play bears with his
younger grandchildren, James and Juanita. Tony, the elder
boy, was beyond the bear stage, but the old man still tired
himself out making catapults, and bows and arrows for the
boy.

The old Italian did not take his doctor's advice very
seriously. In any case he did not consider 'that a few more
years on a sofa, or in an armchair, were worth the sacrifice
of his games with the youngsters.

They all loved him far more than they loved their father
or mother, and he on his part, worshipped all three to
distraction, and often cocked a speculative eye at Maria's
ageing figure, to see if there was any likelihood of a fourth
grandchild coming along. Juanita, the youngest, he reflected,
was five now, and it was time somebody got busy.

From Piretta's standpoint the marriage had been a great
success. Archie had expanded the business beyond the old
man's wildest dreams. He now had nine shops, all within
twenty minutes' drive of each other, and all but the one at
Ketley (where the manager had embezzled six crates of
stock) were showing steady profit.

There was little or no affection between his daughter and
her big husband, but Piretta did not set much store on
affection between man and wife. The purpose of marriage, as
he saw it, was to get extra help in the shop, and to beget
children, and in these spheres everything had gone according
to plan. It was true that Maria never seemed very pleased
with her life. She hardly ever spoke, and moved about the
house so quietly, as though someone was lying dead in one of

the bedrooms, but then she had always been a vague, unde-monstrative girl—that was how he came to have so much trouble finding a husband for her. She certainly loved her daughter Juanita, and turned her out for her little parties looking like a fairy on top of a Christmas Tree, all pink frills and blue bows, and with every black curl in its proper place.

Toni Piretta spent nearly all his time playing with the children these days. His daughter managed the corner shop and Archie, in addition to doing the books, superintended the chain of satellites.

One sunny morning in November the old man took little Juanita across to the meadow that separated the odd num-bers of the Avenue from the woods. It was one of their favourite playgrounds and whenever they went there Juanita insisted that they should play "Buried Treasure".

This was a game of Toni's invention. It had, he felt, the twin advantages of amusing the child and stimulating her acquisitive instincts. He would pretend to go away and search out a likely spot for treasure-seeking, and then, the moment her back was turned, he would ram half-a-dozen threepenny bits and pennies into the soft ground, and mark the spot with a heel clip.

He would then call her over and begin to scrabble in the ground close by, having first indicated to Juanita exactly where she should dig.

Her excitement, when she turned up the first penny, never failed to delight him, and he would caper about shouting his congratulations, and urging her to dig deeper, and "finda da throopnies" that "musta be there". In the meantime, he would dig, with many exclamations of disgust, in his own barren claim, and when he failed to find anything would slap his face in despair, and shout "Poor Toni, poor Toni, he nevva havva da luck!"

On this occasion he buried three sixpences, and when Juanita had uncovered the last of them he tore her wooden spade from her, and flung himself into a frenzy of digging a yard or so away. Juanita, rubbing her sixpences with the corner of her handkerchief, watched him gleefully. She knew that he would never be lucky. He never was.

Suddenly he stopped digging, and tried to stand upright. The spade fell from his hand, and she saw that his face was purpling. She gave a little squeal of terror and ran to him, but he made a stiff gesture with his arm, warding her off. Then, as he fell forward on his knees, he pointed towards the houses.

Juanita was an alert little girl. She understood at once, and fled across the meadow towards the Avenue, bursting into the shop, where Maria was handing Louise Strawbridge her week-end groceries, and screaming: "Come quick, come quick! Grandpa's going blue!"

When they reached him he was unconscious. They got help, and carried him home, but although he recovered consciousness he never spoke again. They propped him up in the biggest bedroom, overlooking Shirley Rise and the big clump of elms that screened the entrance to the Lane. The doctor came, then Archie, then a nurse, but he gave no signs of recognising anybody.

That evening they brought the children in to see him. His eyes smiled but he made no other sign. The children bent over the bed, and kissed his bluish cheeks, but beyond the smile in his eyes he gave no indication of pleasure.

The truth was that he had recognised them but in the last few hours seemed to have moved a vast distance away from them and away from everything in the present, as though he was looking at them all through reversed binoculars. He was not seriously interested in them, for his mind was now occupied with the past, and the phases of his life drifted by like galleons in convoy.

He saw the fruit market at Naples, a riot of colour and cries, under brilliant Italian sunshine. He saw the gleaming galley of the cargo-boat on which he had worked his passage to England, and smelled again the rank, oily smell of the Tower wharves, where he had once fought for work for a few pence an hour. He saw his dead wife, her face infinitely strained, as she helped him to haul their first ice-cream barrow up the steep, grimy terraces of Newcastle, and he sniffed the cloying smell of fat that issued from her clothes as she stood beside him, peeling potatoes in the little scullery behind their first fish-shop. He saw Maria, sidling past guffawing youths in the Lower Road shop, and then, at the very tail of the procession, he saw Archie's clouded profile, as he had sat beside him on the bench in the "Rec" on the day he had made the proposal that had changed their lives, and brought joy into his heart.

As he recognised Archie he slowly puffed out his breath, so that the wisps of his heavy moustache stirred, and settled again. They had forgotten to pull the curtains and he could see the full moon riding behind the elms, and even make out the black blobs that were last year's rookery. Then a shredded bank of cloud closed over its face, and he shut his eyes, and slept.

The nurse came up after supper and felt his pulse. She stood looking at her watch for a moment, and then slipped her hand inside his pyjama jacket, noting, with detached interest, a faded tattoo sketch of a simpering woman, with an exaggerated hour-glass waist, that covered half his broad chest. Finally she laid both his hands on Maria's beautifully starched sheets, and went to the top of the stairs, calling:

"Mrs. Carver! Are you there, Mrs. Carver? Please come at once!"

There were hurrying feet on the stairs as she turned back to the bed. Toni opened his eyes again but he did not see them crowd into the room, or hear Maria's sobs, and Archie's questions. Instead he heard the voices of boys singing a ditty of long ago, half a jeer and half a greeting, as he pushed his painted cart up the Newcastle terraces, and the urchins sang, in their thick, Geordie brogue:

Oh, oh Antonio,
You left me on my own-y-o!

The moon over the Lane elms sailed out behind the cloud-banks, and in silent wonder he watched it ride. Then the grey hairs of his moustache stirred once again and were still.

CHAPTER XXIV

Edith And The House Of Windsor

MANY of the Avenue folk trailed up to the West End in May 1935 and spent an amusing, uncomfortable night on the pavements, awaiting the Jubilee procession.

On the whole they were mildly impressed by the spectacle, and more so by the warm domesticity of the occasion, but the older ones among them went home a little disappointed, declaring that, as a spectacle, it was not to be compared with Victoria's Diamond Jubilee.

Neither was it, thought Jim, reflecting that in June, 1897, when the Avenue was not even built, the Cockneys who lined the streets to see the little old lady pass had never heard of Depressions and Strikes, or Mons and the Somme. They had thought of the German Emperor as a huge joke, much funnier (yet somehow built on a much grander scale) than his successor, even now screaming away at the Berlin Chancellery, and looking more like Charlie Chaplin than someone out of a Wagnerian opera, and wearing a clipped moustache, instead of that ridiculous, eagle-crested helmet the Kaiser had worn.

Everything, indeed, had been on a greatly reduced scale: the street decorations, good as they were, the uniforms of the troops, and even the monarch himself. Yet the Avenue would not have had him any different, for they felt that a personal relationship existed between this King and themselves. Victoria had always seemed to them an exalted, aloof Lady-of-the-Manor, whereas this kind and earnest man spoke to them all so naturally over the radio each Christmas Day, and went to

Bognor, just as they did, when he needed a convalescent holiday.

Most of the Avenue were there, and cheered lustily, particularly when the Prince of Wales came past their pitch, and no one gave him a louder cheer than Edith Clegg, who was responsible for the outing, having persuaded Jim Carver to organise a party from their end of the Avenue, and travel up the night before, in order to be sure of an uninterrupted view.

Edith had always loved young Edward, whom they had usually called 'Bertie' in her younger days. In her affections he ran a close second to poor, dear Rudi, and, in some ways, of course, one must even put him in front of Rudi, for had he not travelled all over the world on their behalf, and given the generals, it was said, so much worry during the war, by insisting upon going within range of German shells, which was something kings and princes (not to say generals) never did these days?

So when the Prince rode by, soon after the little Princesses in their pretty pink bonnets had passed, and smiled at her from under his enormous bearskin (it must be ter.ibly hot for him on a day like this, thought Edith), she stood on tiptoe, and asked Jim to steady her, so that she could continue to wave her Union Jack until he was cut off from her view by the Lancers and Hussars, who followed him.

Then the roar of the crowd, thought Edith, sounded like the winter breakers under the cliffs at Hartland so long ago, and Jim told her laughingly that she must reserve a little energy for the King and Queen, who had certainly earned a cheer after all these years of stress and strain.

The day after the Jubilee Edith and Becky set out on their first holiday in more than twenty years. Ted and Margy Hartnell made this possible by inviting them to ride in the back seats of their new Morris, for a short orchestral tour of the West.

Edith accepted gladly, not only because she would have gone anywhere with dear Teddy and his busy little wife, but because she was curious to discover what effect a visit to the West country would have upon her after so many years in the suburb.

It was a very sentimental journey for Edith and Becky. The "Hartnell Eight" established their headquarters at Exeter, playing at a string of seaside resorts close by each night, but on most afternoons Edith and Becky took charabanc trips to all the places they remembered as children. They even visited their father's little parish, now not so little, and rather spoiled, Edith thought, by rows and rows of red-roofed bungalows, a huddle of caravans, and hordes of tall, sunburned girls, with long, bare legs, who walked shamelessly up and down the village street, and powdered their noses at the lych gate of the old, grey church.

They laid some flowers on their parents' grave, and Becky dabbed her eyes a little while they were doing it, but Edith was content to click her tongue, and say "There, there, Daddy!" It was all so long ago, and so much had happened since, and she was quite sure that dear Daddy was far happier where he was now that half-naked girls were powdering their noses on the threshold of his church.

They were back in the Avenue again long before the King began to ail, and they heard the radio announcer say that his life was drawing peacefully to a close, as they sat over the little portable set that Margy had given them for Christmas that year.

Edith would have liked to have gone to Westminster, to see the King lying-in-state, but the weather was so bad, and Jim persuaded her not to go, and perhaps it was just as well, for poor, paralysed Miss Baker, of Number One opposite, caught influenza that winter, and nearly died after the day-nurse had left, so that Edith was at hand to look after her throughout January. By Springtime Miss Baker was about again, and could be seen from her downstairs window, looking out through lace curtains on the Shirley end of the Avenue, and thereby restoring a sense of permanence to this end of the crescent.

There was no real permanence, however, for soon that awful business of the Abdication ravaged the odd and even numbers, setting one house against another with a venom that Edith found distressing, for she herself was rabidly pro-Edward, and was always becoming involved with people who seemed to forget everything the poor boy had done for the Empire, ever since he was a child.

The "Domestic Crisis", as the papers called it, might have passed off in a few indeterminate tiffs and growls, had it not been for Mrs. Rolfe, a cross-grained woman, who had recently moved into Number Eight. She now set herself up as a kind of censor of royal morals, thereby causing Edith, who had always thought twice about swatting a fly in the kitchen, to commit the single physical assault of a blameless lifetime.

It happened in the twopenny library, at the corner of Cawnpore Road, on the morning after Edward VIII had made his farewell speech over the wireless.

Edith, feeling unusually depressed, had gone to the Lower Road, hoping to find a novel that would take her mind off the dismal news, and here she heard Mrs. Rolfe holding forth on the Abdication, to an unwilling audience of Mr. Carter, the proprietor, and his two girl assistants.

"All I can say," said Mrs. Rolfe, "is Good Riddance! It's the best thing he could have done, and it'll make everyone happy!"

Edith heard herself addressing Mrs. Rolfe in a cold, edgy voice.

"It doesn't make *me* happy," she protested, "not one little bit, and I'd go so far as to say it shouldn't make *anyone* happy, losing a fine man like that, and making all this stupid, wicked fuss over the poor woman he wanted to marry!"

Mr. Carter, sensing a strained atmosphere between two regular customers, chipped in with a "Now, now, ladies . . .", and the girl assistants began to giggle, but Mrs. Rolfe was the kind of woman who very much enjoyed a friendly argument, particularly with such a poor opponent as the little spinster from Number Four, and she swung round on Edith with:

"So you agree with it, eh? You agree with it? Well, I must say that's a fine thing, coming from someone *I* always thought of as *respectable*, not to say a bit behind the times, if you don't mind me being so frank, Miss Clegg!"

Edith began to tremble, as she invariably did when she was drawn into a quarrel, however mild, but she was by no means ready to back down and abandon her championship in front of three uncommitted witnesses.

"All I say is that everyone's been *most* ungrateful," she said, her voice shooting up a key under the stress of emotion. "Last week nobody would hear a word against him, and this week everybody's running him down! That's not fair ... it's ... it's ..." she struggled for the right word, and found it, "it's downright *sanctimonious*! That's what it is, sanctimonious! And you're not the one to talk either, Mrs. Rolfe, seeing as you've been divorced yourself, so there!"

It was a very reckless speech to make in public, and for a moment Mrs. Rolfe was too surprised, and too outraged, to reply. Edith took advantage of her momentary triumph, to try and effect a rapid exit, but Mrs. Rolfe, who was built on generous lines grabbed her by the arm as she made for the door, and screamed:

"How *dare* you! How *dare* you! What's my being divorced got to do with it? And me the innercent party! Don't you run off, Miss Clegg! I've got more to say to you! Don't you run off!"

Mr. Carter tried, half-heartedly, to intervene, but Mrs. Rolfe shouldered him aside, with a "You stay out o' this, it's nothing to do with you!"

"Kindly let go of my arm," said Edith, still shaking a little, but with ice-cold rage rather than fear. "If you don't let go of my arm, Mrs. Rolfe, I shall hit you!"

Mrs. Rolfe guffawed. She was, in the opinion of the Avenue, a little too raucous for the neighbourhood, and she had no friends among her neighbours.

"Haw! You will, eh? You and who else? Mrs. Simpson maybe?"

The gibe finished what was left of Edith's self-control. Half-turning, she swung her shopping bag with her free hand, and brought it down with all her force on Mrs. Rolfe's head, sending the pro-Abdicationist staggering back against a revolving display frame of picture-postcards and this, in turn, overthrew a balanced pyramid of books built upon Carter's counter. Frame, cards, books, and Mrs. Rolfe crashed through the open counter-flap on to the floor.

Edith waited no longer. Appalled by what she had done

she fled into the Lower Road, but Mrs. Rolfe's cries pursued her—"I'll sue you! Mark me words, I'll sue you!", and then something about "witnesses".

Edith arrived home in a state of collapse, and Jean McInroy at once sent for Jim Carver, who happened to be home. Between sniffs of smelling-salts and sips of strong tea Edith recounted what had happened, and as a result of her recital Jim visited both Mr. Carter's and Mrs. Rolfe that same day.

What information he obtained from the library, or what emerged from his lengthy interview with Mrs. Rolfe, Edith never discovered, nor did it ever become known along the Avenue. But whatever he said, or threatened, he succeeded in preventing any retaliative action by the aggrieved party. Within weeks of the incident Mrs. Rolfe packed up and moved out, much to the relief of Mrs. Hooper, of Number Six, and of Mrs. Burridge, of Number Ten, although their relief was nothing to that of Edith, who had been picturing herself, despite Jim's constant reassurances, as an inmate of Holloway, without the glory that attached itself to those poor dears of more than twenty years ago, whose incarceration, she recalled, always seemed to begin by their having chained themselves to railings.

So, with this relatively small ripple, the two kings went their ways, and the Avenue soon got used to the new King reigning in their stead. He soon proved that he would follow in his father's footsteps, for he was pictured, in the newspapers, as enjoying a game of *Underneath the Spreading Chestnut Tree*, together with his family, and a group of Boy Scouts.

As the months passed Edith was able to forget poor Edward, even as she had almost fogotten poor dear Rudi, and after all, it *was* rather exciting to reflect that if she outlived this monarch, as she had already outlived his father, grandfather, and great-grandmother, she would be a privileged subject of Elizabeth the Second, and share, perhaps, in the glories of a new and splendid age.

CHAPTER XXV

Esme's Odyssey

1

THE long, "heart-to-heart" talk that Esme had with Harold, his stepfather, after Elaine had told him that she was leaving the Avenue, cemented the warm relationship between them that had its origins as far back as Harold's adroit handling of the woman at the fair. From the moment the gypsy woman had been vanquished Esme had respected Harold, and Harold, for his part, had delighted in Esme's confidences. Now he listened to him gravely over a conspiratorial pot of tea in the snug, gaily-painted kitchen and Esme talked freely about Elaine.

Harold did not make the middle-aged error of dismissing the boy's obsession as an infatuation, that "he would soon forget in another girl, or a new interest". He did not even use the words "calf-love", for he had suffered enough, during his long courtship of Eunice, to recognise true misery in the boy's face. For all that, he was brisk and realistic in his approach to the matter.

"You have to face the fact that, however encouraging she might have been when the mood took her, old chap, she quite obviously isn't the sort of person capable of deep feelings about anyone," he said gently. "Confound it, old man, you can judge that from her attitude towards what's happened inside her own family! Most girls, I imagine, would be extremely upset by that sort of hash, yet you say she regards the break-up of her parents' marriage as a joke?"

"More or less," said Esme glumly. "Sometimes I think there's a . . . well a sort of *devil* in her. She seems to like hurting people."

Harold nodded, as though he was all too familiar with devil-ridden women.

"I wouldn't tell your mother anything about this if I were you," he advised, "but I'm glad you've told me. It's always good to have someone to talk to, even if you don't take much notice of anything they might have to say on the subject. Talking about it helps to clarify one's own ideas, and I suppose that's more than half the reason why people have lawyers."

"Do you think she'll stay away always?" asked Esme.

Harold began to approach the matter as a solicitor.

"I think that depends entirely how she makes out earning her own living," he said. "You know, Esme, deep down, if you can look at it objectively enough, you've got to admire the girl. It takes a great deal of courage to strike out on your own at her age. She's not as lucky as you, you know."

Esme sensed gentle criticism in this. He was uncomfortably aware that, although Harold's attitude to his determination to write for a living had been a tolerant one, his stepfather did not altogether approve of a young man leaving school and remaining at home all day. He might well have opposed the idea had it not been for the knowledge that, at twenty-one, Esme would come into half his father's and grandmother's estates. There would be no lump sum to squander, and no sufficiency calculated to throw a young man off his balance, for the money had been invested in sound, unimaginative concerns long ago, and would feed a trust-account. For all that Esme would start his adult life with immense advantages over most young men. Harold estimated that his unearned income, less tax, would soon amount to rather more than three hundred a year, and this would certainly be doubled in the event of his mother's death.

"The point is," went on Harold, sensing a slight advantage, "you'll do yourself no good at all sitting here moping. As a matter of fact, before this happened I was going to suggest that you came in with me, and read law, but your Headmaster was very frank about you the last time I talked to him. He told me flatly that you'd never make a solicitor, and that you ought to be encouraged to train for an artistic profession of one sort or another."

"How *does* one train to be a writer?" asked Esme suddenly.

It was something he had been asking himself, ruefully enough, for the past six months. Sitting up there in his room, scratching away with a pen hour after hour, reading and re-reading pages he had covered with his neat but childish handwriting, he had become uncomfortably aware of the fact that it is far easier to dream romantic stories than to concoct them.

There was a curious flatness about his writing. It began well enough, but fell away steeply after the first few pages, and finally expired under the increasingly desperate pressure he applied to it. He had already commenced three books, a long school-story, a saga of a dragoon in the Peninsular War, and an Elizabethan seayarn, but neither book had progressed beyond half the requisite number of words.

Harold was a wide reader. He had read a large number of biographies of writers, and was glad to take advantage of Esme's change of subject, edge away from the uncharted realm of women possessed of devils, and tread the firmer ground of English literature.

"Nearly all writers begin by being something else, Esme, and write their early stuff in their spare time. There was Dickens, for instance, he was a Parliamentary journalist, and in our own times Ian Hay, a schoolmaster, and Edgar Wallace, another journalist. There's Cronin, he's still a doctor, I believe, and Conrad and Masefield, both seamen. One could go on indefinitely. The only person I can recall who actually began as a poet was Browning, and after all, he was a bit of a genius, wasn't he?"

The obvious commonsense in Harold's line of talk did not make his avuncular approach more palatable to Esme. Now that he had laid bare his soul, and freely admitted to uncertainty regarding his future as a writer, he felt angry and ashamed, but his genuine liking for Harold, and the man's obvious desire to be helpful, compelled him to prolong the conversation.

"What you mean is, didn't I ought to get something to write *about* and *then* write . . . go to sea, for instance, or join the army?"

Harold winced a little. It occurred to him that Esme's announcement that he was going to sea, or joining the Army, on his stepfather's direct recommendation, would involve him, Harold, in a situation with Eunice that might deny him the undisturbed perusal of *The Times* for a hundred nights in a row.

"Well ... er ... no, not exactly, old chap!" he protested. "There's no need to go to extremes. Look here, why don't you trot around in the morning and have a chat with that Head of yours? Quite frankly, he struck me as a rather arty type of chap, but I got the distinct impression that he was very fond of you, and had high hopes of you in one direction or another."

Esme considered. It was strange, he thought, that such an idea had not occurred to him before. He had not seen Longjohn since he had left school, and had not even written to him.

Having neatly passed the buck Harold yawned, and got up, piling the tea-cups on a tray, and carrying them out into the scullery.

"We'd better wash these up, son," he told Esme, "or your mother will begin asking awkward questions in the morning."

They washed up and went softly upstairs. On the carpeted landing Harold said, without any hint of patronage:

"Feel any better, old chap?"

Esme did feel better, if only because he had more than Elaine to think about now.

"Yes, I do, Harold, and thanks, thanks a lot."

Harold glowed inwardly. He loved helping people, any person, and it was immaterial to him whether he was paid for it or not.

"Any time, old man, any time. Hang it, that's what I'm here for, isn't it? Goodnight, Esme."

"Goodnight, Harold."

They crept into their rooms, Harold to slip noiselessly out of his dressing-gown, and inch himself cautiously into bed beside his sleeping wife, and Esme to take down his school satchel, and commence filling it with the manuscripts of his three half-finished stories. When he had done this he took down his copy of Browning, got into bed, and forced himself to begin reading *Sordello*. He had used *Sordello* as a soporific ever since he and Eunice had seen *The Barretts of Wimpole Street*, and had never yet got beyond the third page. He progressed well beyond it that night, for the memory of Elaine's brief, mocking appearance at her window was too clear to be banished by the verse of perhaps the only man in English letters who actually began his working life as a poet.

2

Esme left the manuscripts at the school with a note, apologising for them in advance, and asking if Longjohn would see him when he had had an opportunity to read the work. He received a summons within forty-eight hours, and was soon seated once more in the famous leather armchair, in the room where he had so often stood, with shrinking stomach, during his first years at school.

Longjohn, shrouded as usual in blue and pungent tobacco smoke, took the manuscripts from his desk drawer.

"Well, Fraser, I've read them without skipping a page," he said, "and I'll tell you what's good about them first. You can write readable English, but I knew that a long time ago, and you do seem to have avoided the routine pitfall of most beginners, the purple passages!"

"But they're kind of flat, aren't they, sir?"

"No, not exactly flat, imitative perhaps, but that isn't nearly so depressing. Every writer of your age is bound to be imitative. It's a good deal easier to draw on a retentive memory than a store of experience, particularly when you haven't any! I came across paraphrased Stevenson, paraphrased Dumas, and even bowdlerised Henty, but that shouldn't worry you; at least your subconscious had enough sense to mix 'em up a bit! What I *am* interested to know is why you didn't finish any one of them? They might, just possibly, have interested a minor agent, and got you started."

Esme considered, then answered the question truthfully.

"Because I was bored with them, sir."

Longjohn chuckled. "Well, that's a hopeful answer anyway," he said, with a twinkle. "If you'd ploughed on regardless you might have had me worried." He settled forward on his creaky, swivel chair. "Now this is how I see it, Fraser. Every man-jack who puts pen to paper in obedience to a creative impulse has a Niagara of dirty water to get off his chest. You started getting yours off pretty smartly, partly because you began young, but mostly because you're naturally impatient. Have you ever considered what that misnomer 'inspiration' really is?"

"I suppose a sudden idea that must be got on with," suggested Esme.

"But how does the idea originate?" asked Longjohn.

Esme considered: "Well, sir, I imagine it just hits you, like something flying by, and then sticks."

"That's a very popular misconception," said Longjohn. "The fact is the impulse that starts you writing, or painting, or shaping something with your hands is only the spark igniting the bonfire of ideas, usually ideas that have been piling up in your mind ever since you could toddle."

"Er . . . what sort of ideas?" asked Esme.

"How should I know? Sounds, smells, colours, snatches of conversation you weren't meant to overhear, street-scenes, the exasperated look a mother gives her child when he throws a cake out of the pram, the steam rising from the wet clothes of a 'bus queue, the patterns of frost-rime on hedgerows—this is the raw material of a writer's bonfire, and the 'thing-flying by', as you put it, merely sets it off. You can't really start writing until the bonfire's showing red. Do I make sense?"

"Yes, sir, a great deal. It rather ties up with my step-father's suggestion. He said I ought to take an ordinary job and sort of graduate. The point is, sir, what sort of job, and would it have to be one that left me time for writing?"

Longjohn puffed out three clouds of smoke before answering. Esme had forgotten how strongly everything about Longjohn stank of his coarse tobacco, and it occurred to him that some of the parents who called on him must find the atmosphere of the study insupportable.

"That's what most writers do I admit," he said at last, "but I don't think it suits your book, not yet at all events. What you need is a travelling apprenticeship. I think that would show a richer dividend than a steady job, whatever the job happened to be."

"You mean travel abroad, sir?" said Esme, hopefully.

"No, I don't," said Longjohn emphatically. "I mean travel *here*, among your own people! Damn it, man, London's stiff with half-baked 'moderns', who have spent a few, jaded months on the Left Bank, and come back here, where publishers pay them money to sneer at us! I don't mean that at all. Even supposing you could afford to travel, and possibly live abroad for a time, what would we get from you? A few second-hand opinions from shifty boulevardiers, embedded in a mash of sex. For God's sake give us more honest writing! Tell us what the Industrial Revolution has made of the people whose grandfathers drifted into the Northern and Midland towns from the farms and cottage looms. Distil for us some of the traditional humour of the Cockney, and the Lancashire people. Find us a latter-day Weller, or Micawber, *That's* the sort of shot in the arm that English fiction needs today, and I think you're a person who could do it! Go on a journey, an *English* journey! Don't stick at one job too long, irrespective of whether it pays off or doesn't. Drift about, and keep a notebook rather than a soul-searching diary. Don't scrabble for stuff, let it come to *you*, and soak into you, as the stink of my foul tobacco sinks into everything in this room! That's my advice, Fraser, for what it's worth, but you'll have to square it with your family. They might have other ideas, and you're off my hook now. Well?"

Esme thought for a moment. Then he said:

"My father left me some money, sir, but I don't get it until I'm twenty-one. Should I wait until then?"

"Not if you can help it, boy. With even a little money in your pocket you won't see half as much as you will if you're broke! Besides, you're more absorbent now than you'll ever be. If you're going, go right away, and if you feel like writing to me write, but don't spend yourself in letters. No one's going to pay you for writing letters, and remember Johnson's dictum—no one but a born fool writes for anything other than money!"

That was the gist of Longjohn's interview, and it was the springboard from which Esme began his two-year Odyssey.

It threw Eunice, his mother, into a dither that fulfilled Harold's gloomiest prophecies regarding his leisure to absorb the leading articles of *The Times*, but, to his credit, he ultimately ranged himself behind Esme, and even insisted on mailing him thirty shillings a week, wherever he might be.

Eunice wept and Eunice argued, but Harold was no longer fighting a lone battle, as he had when he lost the fight to send Esme away to school. Esme himself took slow fire at Longjohn's suggestion, and the early summer of that year saw him fitting himself out with strong brogues, a good mackintosh, a capacious knapsack with innumerable pockets, and a supply of maps and notebooks.

It was early May when he left the Avenue and set out on his adventure. He had been twenty the previous February and as he walked the length of the Avenue, to cut across the "Rec" into Delhi Road, he was aware of the suburb as he had not been since Eunice had brought him there when he was six. Lilac was flowering in the front garden of Number One Hundred and Twelve, laburnum in the garden of Number Ninety-Seven opposite, and dew gleamed on the swinging chains linking the gate-posts above the curving dwarf walls.

Every yard of the locality had some association with his childhood and with growing up. He passed the seat near the tennis-courts, where Elaine had told him of her father's desertion, and the trim allotments, with their eternal artichokes, that had always been for him the beanstalks of fairy-tales.

When he reached the Lower Road it was still very early, but the suburb was slowly coming to life. A milk-float clanked at the corner of Outram Crescent, and a sparsely-filled 'bus trundled by, its conductor lolling expertly against the stair rail as he pencilled his returns. All his memories, all those "little bonfires" Longjohn had talked about, began to smoulder, and although he still felt elated, he was conscious also of an undertow of fear. Dull this world might be, but it was safe, snug, and familiar, and he began to ask himself how long it would be before he felt the impulse to throw off this ridiculous knapsack, that was already making his shoulders ache, and come speeding back to the Avenue, where the warm smell of summer privet stood for safety and permanence.

Then the Croydon 'bus drew up, and he boarded it, and ran up the stairs and along to the front seat.

Sitting here he fought his panic. Longjohn was a romantic, and he had always thought of himself as one. Perhaps they were both wrong. Perhaps these people, who were boarding the 'bus on their way to their shops, and offices, had the right idea after all. As the 'bus swung along Old Orchard Road he admitted to himself that there was only one sure way of finding out.

Sane, comforting Harold, for insisting on that regular thirty shillings a week.

3

It would be unprofitable to accompany Esme on his wanderings. They occupied him the better part of three years, and carried him West as far as the Cornish coast, and over the Irish Sea to the stillness of Connemara; then North as far as Glencoe, and East as far as the Newcastle ship-building towns and the Norfolk Broads. He came back to the Avenue several times during the period, but the quest developed in him a restlessness that would not be denied. He was soon off again, stopping here and there, sometimes for a week, sometimes several weeks, and in Edinburgh, a city he came to love, a matter of six months, for it was there that he met the percipient Donald Shawe, who subsequently obtained for him the job that ultimately anchored him in London once again.

Many of his journeys were made on foot, as was the first, when he left the train at Salisbury, and walked, via the New Forest and the Dorset coast, as far as Honiton, and thence into the rich bracken and pine country of East and North Devon.

He followed Longjohn's instructions in most respects, but he soon tired of Norman churches, and castle ruins, avoiding almost by instinct the "quaint", and the "musts" of the holiday tourists, though he often used their charabancs and excursion trains. In this way he passed within yards of Wordsworth's Stone, at Grasmere, without turning aside to look at it.

Now and again he took temporary work to eke out his allowance, without which he must have returned home almost immediately. He sold a few articles to country newspapers. He spent three weeks in a West-country town doing clerical work for a timber-merchant. He was an undertaker's assistant in Central Wales, and a market-gardener's packer in Windermere. In the main, however, odd jobs were hard to find, and very poorly paid. In the Midlands the country was climbing out of the depression, but in the North, particularly in the Newcastle area, the apathy, and the visible distress of a vast army of unemployed, upset him so much that he almost fled across the border, heading for Edinburgh, where he found a more congenial job as a copyholder, and later proof-reader, on a small but lively newspaper, owned and edited by Donald Shawe.

Shawe took a mild liking to him. He was a hard-hitting, warm-hearted Scot, bitterly contemptuous of the failure of successive English parliaments to steer their own country and his, out of the economic slough, and extremely apprehensive of their blundering policies in the field of foreign affairs. It was Donald, and his son Keith, who introduced Esme to politics and political journalism, discovering to their surprise that the young man was woefully ignorant of what was brewing for him on the Continent.

Keith, who was sub-editor on *The Courier*, felt sorry for the lonely young man, and sometimes came into the readers' room when Esme was finishing a night shift, and invited him out for a glass of beer in a tavern frequented by journalists, off Princes Street. Like his father, Keith was shrewd, cool, and very much down-to-earth. He never quite got over the shock of learning there was an avowed deliberate purpose behind Esme's seemingly aimless wanderings.

"But d'ye mean to stand there and tell me it was your ain dominie who put the daft business into your head, man?" he exclaimed, running his fingers through his stiff, rust-red hair.

"In a way, yes," Esme told him, "but I daresay I'd have done it anyway. The point is, Mr. Shawe, I came into a small income when I was twenty-one, and I always knew the money was there. If I hadn't I suppose I should have found a job like anybody else, and settled for it. As it was, the only thing I really wanted to do was write, and this seemed to be the best way of doing it."

"And have ye written much since ye set out?" Keith wanted to know.

"Nothing except journalism, and odd jottings," admitted Esme.

"Then it doesna occur to you that you're not cast for a writer?" said Donald heartlessly.

"It does, very often," said Esme ruefully, "but I can't do anything else any better. At least I've found that out."

Keith emptied his tankard and ordered another. He was intrigued by Esme's story, but irritated by the boy's lack of design.

"Would you no' like me to speak to ma father aboot takin' you on here as a junior reporter?" he asked. "Maybe that's what you need most, something a wee bit more permanent."

"It's very kind of you," said Esme gratefully, "but I don't think I'd be much good as a reporter. I'm not nearly as observant as I thought I was, and I don't make friends easily enough."

"Och, we'll see aboot that," grunted Keith, who had scant sympathy with theory, and that was how Esme ultimately found a permanent post, not in Scotland, as a reporter, but in the small London Office that the Shawes had recently opened in Blackfriars.

Donald wanted someone who knew London well, yet was familiar with his paper, and its patriarchal background. Esme was offered the job of advertisement manager, at a starting salary of £300 a year, with a promise of steady increases if he made good.

He accepted gladly enough, for by this time he was heartily sick of an Odyssey that seemed profitless and, although he hardly realised it, he was homesick for the suburb.

For in one important respect he had been cheating Longjohn all the time. He had filled his notebooks, but not with impressions of people he met, and places he had visited.

There was nothing at all in his notebooks about factory-hands whose grandfathers had worked at village cottage-looms and through all his jottings ran a thread, that led him directly back to the Avenue, and this thread led only to Elaine, who had somehow become identified with the Avenue, even though she was no longer there, nor likely to be in the future.

Over and over again Esme argued with himself about this. Sydney Frith had left him in no doubt but that Elaine's ultimate return home was an extreme improbability, that she was now on the stage (what, in Heaven's name, thought Esme, could she be doing on the stage?) and that she had never once written to her mother since going off to join her father in Wales. Even her father had no sure knowledge of where she was, or what she did. The hotel people, for whom she had worked, had told him she had left Colwyn Bay with a conjurer, who had stayed there one week, but beyond one or two scrappy letters, from towns in the Midlands, Edgar Frith had received no word from her, and when Esme, passing through Wales, had called at their smart little antique shop the wanderer recorded:

Llandudno. July.

"Saw Elaine's father today, and met the 'other' woman Frances, the one Elaine told me about. They seem very happy. The woman's daughter lives with them, and they have an antique shop up here. I told him about Elaine and myself—he seemed to understand, so much better than I imagined he would, and so did Frances, whom I liked very much. They showed me two letters they had received from her, several months old. One was from Nottingham, and the other from Hereford, but neither said what she was doing. Both were about things she wanted sending on. I can't help feeling that old Harold was right that night—she seems absolutely incapable of feeling deeply about anyone or anything. You might almost say she never feels anything at all. . . ."

From this extract two things are obvious. One is that Esme had forgotten or ignored Longjohn's admonition to keep soul-searching out of his notebooks, and the other is that Elaine still occupied the central position in his thoughts.

Perhaps this was what was the matter with him and was the reason behind his hopeless inability to profit from his Odyssey. For the truth is there was little but Elaine in his notes. Thus, in his jottings on Exmoor:

Doone Valley. April.

"This is a wonderful country. It always seemed wonderful in 'Lorna Doone'. Elaine reminded me of Lorna in the old days, and I always had a picture, at the back of my mind, that I might bring her here, perhaps to Lynmouth, perhaps even to get married in Oare Church. I haven't much doubt that she would disappoint me like hell if I did, for she isn't really like Lorna. Lorna was small and gentle, and so grateful for being looked after. Elaine isn't like that at all, and sometimes I'm amazed at myself for feeling about her the way I do, for she isn't my type at all. Perhaps it's just that she was the first, or perhaps, its because she's so wonderfully pretty, and her hair is exciting to touch. . . ."

Poor Esme! It was just the same in the Lake District.

Derwentwater. October.

"I came out to Friar's Crag today, and looked out across the lake. This place has become even more famous than it was since Walpole's 'Herries' series was published. They say it's a great place for honeymooners. I wonder if Elaine would be bored here, or whether the colour of the woods on the far shore would touch her, as it does me. I imagine she would want to go to a gay place on her honeymoon, somewhere like Paris, or Cannes. But maybe she's already had her honeymoon. I wish to God I'd never met her. . . ."

And finally, when he was back in London, beginning his job, and living at Number Twenty-Two permanently once more:

"I saw Sydney Frith again today, and asked after Elaine. They still haven't heard. Nobody ever hears, least

of all me. I haven't mentioned her to Harold. He probably thinks I've forgotten all about her. As if one could? Or is it pure masochism on my part? Its years now since that night, and it should be abundantly clear, even to me, that she doesn't give a damn, and probably looks back on it all as I look back on a Grammar School crush. . . ."

After that, however, Elaine disappears from the diary. Indeed, the diary soon ceases, and it looks as though Esme is settling into his job at Blackfriars and adopting a more realistic attitude towards his dream of becoming a writer. About this time he sold his first feature programmes to the Empire Broadcast Section of the BBC, and earned some of his first, freelance guineas.

Perhaps it was this, his first gleam of success, that put Elaine out of mind for a time, or possibly a slightly earlier entry in his diary had a little to do with it, for the Christmas before he returned to the Avenue for good his path crossed Judith Carver's again, and he wrote.

London. Christmas.

"I ran into Judy Carver in The Lane today. She seems very grown up, and struck me as having an unusual kind of tranquillity. I had forgotten all about her, and how much fun we had as kids on this very spot. She is quite pretty in a way, tho' a bit open-airy, and blown about. This is odd, because she used to remind me of a Rossetti heroine, all pinched, and solemn-eyed. She was surprised to hear that I had been quite close to her place in Devon, where she helps run a riding-stable, and she told me I ought to have called in. I didn't like to explain that I didn't even know she was living down there, but I think she probably guessed it. She was a good, sporting kid, and seems so sane about everything. I quite like talking to her."

After that, nothing. It is to be regretted that Judy Carver no longer kept a diary, her last entry having been made years ago, the night before Esme came into her shop on the Lower Road to buy a powder-compact for Elaine. It was a pity also that she attributed Esme's friendly eagerness to naturally good manners, and failed to press her slight advantage that Christmas.

Had she done so, it is just possible that she might have saved Esme a great deal of heartache.

CHAPTER XXVI

Jim Closes The Door

BY the Spring of 1937, when the Spanish agony was at its height, and Munich was still more than a year away, Jim Carver, socialist-pacifist, had resigned himself to World War II, and had even rejected a chance to escape it by emigrating to Canada.

He chose, instead, to fold his arms and await Armageddon, freely admitting to himself that he was crazy, that none of his children, save possibly the younger set of twins, stood in the slightest need of him, and even these two had been included in Jacob Sokolski's offer.

The Russian Jew often discussed the news with his employee. Since their experience in the Hunger March scuffle they had become close friends, and although Jacob had no patience with Jim's gospel he was grieved when Jim rejected his offer to escape while there was still time.

The fact that he was a Jew made the old man nervous of the future awaiting Europe. He was in close touch with some of the refugee groups from the Continent, and had proved a generous subscriber to their resettlement funds. He did not like the look of things at all, and told Jim:

"That bloddy Hitler, he'll be over here before long, my frien'; you see if I'm not talking truth!"

And when Jim, who was not quite without insular arrogance, pooh-poohed this idea as monstrous, he added:

"All right, my frien', you just vait! Vot you got to stop the bloddy man, anyhows? The Pritisch Navy? Bah! There won't

be no navies, my frien', not in the vor that man is cooking
up for you over there! You listen to this bloddy rubbisch
about their cardboard tanks, and suchlike? You tink because
you beat them vonce you beat them twice, hey? Let me tell
you, my frien,' this time it is different! They fly here, and
knock pieces off you before you do your braces up! You tink
I stop to vatch? And me vid a nose like this? And name like I
got? Not Jacob Sokolski, my frien'! Vonce is enough for me,
and I get out. *Poof*—like that!"

And Jacob smote his fist on an open palm, and waddled
off to the Canadian Embassy, to make preliminary arrangements for the transfer of capital to his Quebec branch,
leaving Jim to grin at his fears, and tell him that he was
going to a great deal of trouble for nothing. War there might
be, but German occupation of Britain was unthinkable.

"All right," said Jacob, when he returned with an attaché
case full of papers, "you vait, my frien', and ven it happen
you tink on vot I tell you."

"Dammit, Mr. Sokolski," Jim argued, "we haven't been
invaded since 1066."

"No? But there's a first and second time for efferything,"
said Jacob, and then, with seriousness, "I tell you vot, Carver, I make a proposition, hey? I take you too, you and your
two youngest. It iss a goot country this Canada. There's big
futures there, even for you, at your age. We live in Quebec
first, and then go inland, avay from it all, to my wholesale
districts. Vot do you say to that, my frien'?"

"That I'm a damned sight too old to emigrate," said Jim,
"but thanks all the same, and I'm very grateful to you, Mr.
Sokolski."

"How about your children?" pursued Jacob; "vot is there
here for them?"

Jim had often asked himself this question and never yet
found a satisfactory answer. They all seemed settled enough,
Louise with her yokel husband, the twins roaring from job to
job on their infernal motor-cycles, Judith deep in the country, with her horses, Archie making money hand over fist
with his grocery chain, and the twins, Fetch and Carry, now
eighteen and still together, crooning *Little Old Lady* in harmony as they wiped tea-stains and picked up their threepenny

bits from their marble-topped tables in a Catford restaurant.

"I think they're all old enough to shift for themselves," he told Jacob, "and as for me, well, it's not just a question of age, it's something to do with seeing it out from the front-row. I never saw our chaps run from the bastards yet, not even when they smashed their way through in March, 1918, and I don't intend to start running at my time of life. It's different for you, Mr. Sokolski; you're already an exile, and you're much older than I am. I don't think I could live with myself if I wasn't here when we did stand up to the swine!"

"You tink they take you for a soldier, my frien'?" asked Jacob, incredulously.

"If they don't there'll be plenty of jobs for an active man when it does start," Jim told him.

Sokolski sighed. "Very well, my frien', but I tink you the fool just the same. These times a man looks for himself, and I stop here too long as it is."

They left it at that for the time being, but later, when Jacob was on the point of leaving, he made a final approach, but with like result. The old man did not know how near he came to persuading Jim to uproot himself, and whisk himself and his two youngest girls into the vast refuge that awaited them on the other side of the Atlantic. It was Munich that almost decided him, for Munich filled him with shame. He had never considered that the British lacked courage, and the spectacle of the nation's hysterical joy at Chamberlain's return, waving an umbrella and a piece of paper, made him sick with dismay. He found it almost impossible to believe that any sane person could regard such a document as an infallible talisman against aerial bombardment.

So angry was he, indeed, that he fell foul of his Socialist colleagues at a committee meeting that week.

Chamberlain had just returned from his final meeting with Hitler, and someone brought a portable radio into the headquarters, in order that they could all listen to the nine o'clock news bulletin.

"Herr Hitler has told me, *and* I believe him . . .," chanted the recorded voice of the Prime Minister, but at this point

Jim's patience snapped, and he leaned forward and slammed at the knob of the radio with the ball of his horny thumb, leaving Mr. Chamberlain on his pinnacle of optimism.

"Hi, hold on, some of us want to hear if you don't," protested Figgins, the little Branch Treasurer.

"You do? Then I'm going out," snorted Jim, "for it's a bloody sight more than I can stomach!"

Figgins decided that he preferred an argument to the tail-end of the news, which he had already heard in full at six o'clock that evening.

"That's an ostrich attitude, Carver, old man," he declared. "After all, look at it any way you like, he's at least gained us time, hasn't he?"

"Something in that," murmured Gates, the Area Chairman, but Jim spun round on them.

"*Is there?* What do you think the Tories will do with the time they've 'gained' as you say? What have they ever done with time since the last show-down?"

"I think it's nonsense to assume there'll be a war," argued Figgins. "Germany doesn't want war, not the German Socialists at all events!"

Jim was amazed at their blindness. "The German Socialists, you bloody fool," he shouted, "where do you imagine they are? Do you think they're holding a protest meeting in the compound of Dachau? Do you think *anyone* has any say in what goes on over there, since that maniac and his gang took over? This was our last chance to call his bluff, and this time we had the Russians behind us! What do you think'll happen now, in God's name? How do you think Russia will react to this blasted bit of paper that silly old baboon keeps drooling about?"

"The Russian is no friend of British Socialism," argued Chairman Gates; "never was, and never will be!"

"God help me," said Jim, in a strangled voice, "she's our only sizeable ally, isn't she?"

"I say, I say, what about the Popular Front in France?" protested Figgins.

"I'll give France six months if war is declared," snapped Jim, "and after that the Fascists will take over! You talk to some of the Spanish refugees about France, and see if that gives you any confidence in the Popular Front!"

He realised that he was losing his temper, and reached for his cap. Whenever he lost his temper he upset his digestion, which had never quite recovered from uninterrupted months on bully beef and biscuits in the trenches of 1917, and whenever he had a bout the wind packed into his stomach, and made it feel like a distended balloon. Nothing would move it but continual doses of bicarbonate of soda. Deciding that this apology for a committee was not worth a teaspoons-ful of bicarbonate, he strode out into the street, leaving them to shake their heads over his increasingly sour temper, so alien to the old Jim they remembered, in the campaigning days of the 'twenties. Sometimes they thought he was wandering off to the extreme left, and at other times he seemed more in line with the Tories, particularly when he had brazenly supported their rearmament programme. They did not quite know what to make of him these days.

Sometimes Jim did not know what to make of himself. He hated the torpor that seemed to paralyse thought among the people he met in the train, and at work. He was appalled by their collective lack of imagination, and the cynicism of the ordinary voter, people of his own Avenue, whose grasp of the situation seemed to be confined to clichés, like "Hitler is turning East", and "Hitler is doing good in Germany". He could never understand why everybody did not share his horror at what was going on over there, how they could listen, without howls of protest, to Tory M.P.s telling them it was "none of our business", any more than the crucifixion of the Spanish people had been "our business". To him it was all so clear, and so menacing, a simple case of a megalomaniac, in league with Continental capitalism, setting out to absorb the entire world, state by state, and put back the clock to somewhere around the time the first Saxon invasions had crept up the East coast estuaries, and taken possession of Roman Britain.

He went home and called the dog, and they went off into the woods, following the winding path along as far as the old Manor, where he sat on the terrace near the gazebo, and tossed sticks into the shallow water.

The stillness of the scene soothed him. He looked back into the crumbling forecourt and wondered, as Esme had often wondered, who had lived here, and how much it had cost to maintain such a vast, sprawling place. Built about 1780 he imagined, a year or two before the French Revolution, in an era of carriages pulled by matched greys, a time of doeskin top-boots, and Fencibles, and jokes about Napoleon, encouraged by the grotesque cartoons he had seen in the London Museum, an age as remote now as that of Agincourt, and the Armada. People would never live in houses like this again, not with present taxation, and the costs of staffing and heating. What would happen to this one? Would it fall down, or would it be cleared away to make room for a new housing estate? Not for a long time yet at any rate. There would be little enough home building for the next decade and perhaps, when it was all over, they would all be living in caves again. Perhaps he should have accepted Jacob's offer. These people weren't going to fight, so what was the sense of staying to watch them enslaved?

He got up, and called sharply to the dog. Over in the Avenue beyond the trees, a hundred wireless sets were tuned in to dance music, and people who had sat up to hear the midnight news for a week or more, were telling themselves that they would make an early night of it, and sleep safely tonight under Mr. Chamberlain's umbrella.

CHAPTER XXVII

Archie Under An Umbrella

MUNICH caused serious reflection elsewhere in the Avenue that September.

In the converted loft, above the store of his corner shop, Archie Carver had his own figuring to do and, in his own way, he was just as grateful for the temporary shelter of Mr. Chamberlain's umbrella as anyone along the crescent.

Although not the slightest bit concerned with the state of the world as such, Archie was nonetheless a keen observer of the effect the successive alarms of the 'thirties had had upon the Stock Market.

He was not an investor, owning no single stock or share. He was not that sort of gambler, preferring to gamble on absolute certainties, but he used the Stock Market as a weathercock, and his weathercock now told him that the steady drip of depressing events would stop in a year or so, and would be succeeded by a scorching wind liable to cause a severe drought in the suburb! Droughts meant shortages, all kinds of shortages, and shortages meant big profits for those with sufficient foresight to stock up against the day when it was impossible to replenish.

Archie had no need to go to the Book of Genesis to learn what happened when a drought caught a community on the hop. He had already engaged in the grocery trade during a big war, and had by no means forgotten the late Mr. Cole's closing-time zeal, at Coolridge's. If the war was coming, and by now Archie was quite convinced of the fact, then it behoved any intelligent tradesman who sold goods that suburbs could not do without, to buy, and buy, and buy, to stock, and stock, and stock, until every cellar, every odd corner of his premises, was full to overflowing with reserves.

Having finally made up his mind on this, Archie went to work with his customary thoroughness He closeted himself in his office for days on end, and compiled a list of every wholesaler with whom he had had dealings in the past fourteen years. Having completed the list, he made out his orders, and offered C O.D., in this way establishing confidence among suppliers, and also getting the benefit of their two-and-a-half per cent cash discounts. There was nothing niggardly about Archie. He went at the task wholeheartedly, laying out every penny he had to his credit at the bank, and sometimes dipping into the oil drums, that he kept in a padlocked cavity under the floor of his Avenue premises.

Not another living soul knew of the existence of these oil drums, not even Maria, or his eldest boy, Tony, now away at boarding school in the West. There were four oil drums now, and two, which were sealed, were chock full of silver (nothing under a florin), and far too heavy for one man to lift.

Archie was not a miser. He never gloated over the drums and bathed his hands in the coins like Silas Marner. He forgot the sealed drums for months together, for these held his iron rations, the fruit of systematic till abstractions over the years.

Archie consistently robbed his own tills, and had now perfected a system calculated to deprive the Department of Inland Revenue of a steady two to three thousand a year. Only now did Archie reap the full reward of his original planning, the tiny shops, the handy housing estates, particularly the small staffs, and carefully-screened branch managers, for his sort of husbandry would have been impossible in a large, busy shop, with half-a-dozen assistants on the lookout.

Nowadays Archie took his ease in the early afternoons, and went briskly back to work at four p.m. His system required split-second timing, based on his arrival, at his five busiest shops, round about closing time. As soon as the manager had gone, and the blinds were down, he went to work with devilish speed, making out a counterfeit till roll, and pocketing the difference between the old and new totals. Once a week, at each shop in the chain, he extracted thirty shillings from the petty-cash box. This was his levy, his fixed fee for the visit, and thus he began each week with a tax-free income of thirty shillings, multiplied by the number of shops he possessed. He never put his money into the oil-drums. They were fed by a number of tributaries, the chief being the till balances, supplemented by sale of damaged stock, sale of equipment charged against tax, and various other minor sources. This money went into the drums kept for notes, and this amount he did check from time to time, because he regarded it not as an emergency reserve, but as floating capital, with which he might want to acquire fresh premises at short notice.

One way and another Archie was doing pretty well, but he had his share of worries, and he made his small quota of mistakes. One mistake was the fire that broke out in the corner store, with all that money, largely in paper, directly underneath the blazing crates. No fireman ever worked more heroically to quench a fire and he put it out without even calling the Brigade, but the incident led to his purchase of fireproof cash-boxes, each small enough to go inside the oil-drums.

Another error was his sad misjudgment of character regarding Alf Blissaker, who got away with six cases of tinned goods. But by far his worst mistake, and one for which he could never really forgive himself, was that of trying to combine business with pleasure in the person of Gloria Hazelwood, a girl who graduated from counter-hand to concubine, and achieved the unique distinction of being the only person who ever got the better of Archie, and succeeded in laughing in his face.

Gloria was a cheerful, red-headed girl from Thornton Heath, where her father was a lamp-lighter, and there was something about her that lit lamps in the hearts of all the people she met, even on drizzling Mondays in November. This, and her habit of performing duties at a brisk, tireless trot, recommended her to Archie's attention, when he pulled up at a set of traffic lights, opposite her place of employment, that he happened to pass every day during his rounds. Once or twice he caught her eye, and she winked at him, not provocatively, but in the most friendly way imaginable, so that it was not long before she was installed as manageress of a little branch he had opened near the Addington estate, and was soon doing her trotting on his behalf, at first during the day, and later during occasional week-ends, when Archie, unable to earn money, was bored and lonely.

She was a lusty, open-hearted girl, with a strong sense of fun, and had she been less successful in the shop, Archie would probably have regularised the association by setting her up permanently in a little houseboat he had bought, and moored at Thames Ditton. Indeed, this is what Gloria hoped he would do, and when he did not, when it became painfully obvious to her that, notwithstanding her broadmindedness and pink curves, he valued her far more highly with her overall on than off, she made up her mind to settle for a cash bonus and try elsewhere.

Had she known about the oil-drums it is probable that Archie would have found her the most expensive frolic he had ever engaged upon, but fortunately she was unaware of the cache although, as events were to prove, she was extremely well-informed about the methods he used in building it up.

She knew, also, that Archie was in the habit of carrying large sums of money about with him. It was not always convenient for him to make deposits in his Avenue vault as soon as he had accumulated money, and so, at times, Archie's wallet was stuffed with the week's gleanings. She had seen the wallet often, during their week-ends at the houseboat, and its very thickness fascinated her, so much so that she was sometimes unable to take her eyes off his jacket when it was hanging on the chair beside the bed.

When he began talking of transferring her to the newest of his premises, and using her as a kind of new broom at each branch he opened, she began making her own plans She chose her time well, selecting the evening of Whit Monday, when Archie had been unable to complete his customary round the previous Saturday, and had something over a hundred pounds folded into his wallet.

It had been a sultry day, and Archie had gone off into the village for drinks, leaving her to lay out supper in the airless little cabin. Because it was so hot he had gone in his shirtsleeves, leaving his sport's-coat on the bed.

It was all done in less than five minutes. Gloria extracted the money from the inner flap of the wallet, and replaced it with wads of toilet paper. To be on the safe side she camouflaged the paper with one of the two five-pound notes she found. She did not touch the odd pound notes in the outer flap.

She knew that he was unlikely to require money until they parted the following morning, and that even if he did he was certain to have loose change in his trouser pockets.

Her plan was flawless. When he came back with the drinks she was waiting, with cold supper laid. They had their meal, bathed, listened to the radio, and went to bed as usual. He did not put his jacket on again until they climbed into his big, black Austin, and began their drive back to work the following morning.

He had intended dropping her off at her shop, for this was their usual practice, but as they were passing through Norbury she asked him to stop outside East Croydon Station. Her request irritated him. He liked his shops to open sharp on time.

"It's twenty to nine now," he warned her. "What the devil do you want to stop at the Station for?"

"I've got a train to look up," she told him.

He grunted, and pulled in outside the booking-hall.

"Hurry up then," he said, and began to light a cigarette.

But she did not hurry into the hall to make an enquiry, neither did she examine the trains advertised on the boards. Instead she stood looking at him from the pavement, with an expression of mild concentration, and when he glared back at her, all she said was:

"I'm going now, Archie."

"Going? Going where?"

"I don't know exactly," she said; "abroad, I think, for a little while. I've always wanted to go to the Riviera, but they say it's terribly expensive, and I'll have to leave myself enough to get back, and keep me going till I get another job. Perhaps it'll be somewhere nearer."

He stared at her, his unlit cigarette hanging on his lip.

"Are you out of your head?" he demanded.

"Archie," she said very softly, "you'd better look in your wallet before we say 'goodbye'."

He braced up on the word "wallet", and tore it from his inside pocket, plunging his hand into the silk folds, and bringing out a five-pound note and a fistful of toilet paper.

For a moment he said nothing, but simply stared and stared at the wallet on his knees, and then at Gloria, who still stood meekly alongside the car, now regarding him with mild amusement.

"Why you ... you bloody little fool," he shouted at length, "you'll never get away with this! There was more than a hundred in that wallet. Give me my money, you bitch!" And he jerked the handle of the car, so that the door swung open, and the breeze swept a few sheets of toilet paper into the gutter under the feet of people hurrying in and out of the hall.

She shook her head very slowly, and something in the unconcerned way in which she stood there, gently swinging the handbag he had given her last Christmas, stopped him from leaping out of the car.

"You won't miss that much, Archie," she said, speaking deliberately, "and if you try and get it back I'll explain how you got it, and then everything'll come out, won't it—you know . . . all that fiddling you do!"

"Fiddling?" was all he could manage.

"I kept some of the old till rolls," she explained. "You ought to have burned them. They always burn that kind of evidence in thrillers, but you didn't, you just screwed them up, and tossed them in the yard incinerator, before it was lit. You can make a hundred almost every week one way or another, with all the mugs there are about to make it for you. You wouldn't want all the fuss of a police court over one hundred, and anyway, it isn't a hundred, it's only ninety-odd. I put a fiver back, it isn't *all* toilet paper!"

He could say nothing to this. There was nothing one could say to such a monstrous confession. He could only sit there, with the car door swinging open, the wallet on his knee, and the toilet paper eddying about on the floor. After looking at him for a moment more she hitched her handbag higher up her arm, and smiled.

"Well, goodbye, Archie," she said, and, turning into the stream of travellers, disappeared almost immediately.

For a long time he sat there, hunched and brooding, like a glowering husband awaiting an overdue wife, but he was not thinking about Gloria. His thoughts concerned himself, and his monumental folly in laying himself open to such an ambush. He did not really blame Gloria for taking such an advantage of him. When he stood aside, and carefully reviewed his own errors, there was no blame left over for her, it was all used up on himself. Those till-rolls! Irrefutable evidence! Thrown into an unlit incinerator, for anyone to smooth out and keep, as a weapon against which there was no defence! And this wallet on his knee! How many times had he taken off his jacket, and flung it down on a crate, or a chair, when he had been working among men and women who counted their pocket money in sixpences? It was a miracle that he had not been blackmailed or robbed of thrice the sum years ago, and here was a devastating object lesson that had cost him a mere ninety-seven pounds. Damn it, he ought to be grateful to the little bitch!

As he thought this his face cleared, and slowly he let in his clutch, and moved off into the Upper Road. He discovered that he could close the door on Gloria and her ninety-seven pounds, not slam it perhaps, but close it. He was a man who was well accustomed to weighing profits against losses, and it seemed to him that this was a cheap enough price to pay for an invaluable lesson. And it was not all loss either, not when one took into account Gloria's company over several weekends.

By the time that he reached home he was grinning.

All that was behind him now. He never made out new till rolls, but simply erased the figures on old ones. He checked his expansion, and even contracted a little, by letting off two shops where private housing development had been halted on account of the international situation.

The ploughlands, and the woods between Shirley and Addington, were mostly filled in now, and all his premises were within five minutes' walk of the ever-increasing population. What was even better, he had got in first, well ahead of the company shops, and his staff had established themselves with their regular customers.

So he went on buying and buying stock, against the day when the rain would find its way through Mr. Chamberlain's umbrella.

CHAPTER XVIII

Elaine Comes In Out Of
The Rain

1

THAT season, early autumn 1938, saw someone else from the
Avenue come in out of the rain, for in August of that year
Elaine Frith returned to the Avenue. In the first week of October, before the beech leaves of Manor Wood had changed
colour again, she moved into a house of her own, on the
uneven side of the crescent, with a back bedroom window
looking out over the meadow to the trees. It was Number
Forty-Three, to be precise, a mere twelve houses along from
her mother and Sydney, and next door to the house occupied
by Ted Hartnell, and his wife Margy.

Elaine had seen much and travelled far since the night she
had decided to throw in her lot with the Great Eugene. That
partnership had lasted nearly two years, just long enough for
Elaine to grow thoroughly bored with her share of the act,
and for Eugene to wish he had never been born.

For Elaine, once she had found her feet, and donned her
tights (spangled ones they were, for she would have none of
his Hungarian pantaloons), had led him the merriest of
dances. It turned out just as he had feared, when his desire
for her had swept away his caution that night in her room, at
The Falconer, Colwyn Bay.

He had misjudged her in every respect. She had never
insisted on separate hotel rooms at the Number Two towns
they visited, and as a mistress and a stage assistant he could
make no serious complaints against her. He could have
wished, perhaps, for a little more enthusiasm in the first role,
and rather less in the second. Once she was utterly sure of
him her physical responses were no more than dutiful, where-

as, on the stage, she went out of her way to divert the audience's attention from his swinging cape and ironic patter, pirouetting when there was no real need to pirouette, and flashing a smile at boiled shirts in the stalls when she should have been flashing one at chokers in the gallery.

On the whole, however, it was in neither of these respects that she distressed him. What did was her generosity towards every footloose artist, and every middle-aged agent whom they met in the course of their travels—and they seemed always to be meeting lusty young acrobats, and spry young comics, while they ran into Benny Boy, Eugene's agent, at almost every turn of the road.

Poor Eugene soon began to wonder if Benny Boy had ever returned to his office, in Dolman Street, after the day he had first ushered Elaine into the room, when Benny Boy had carefully wiped his glasses, and then suggested that they all had lunch together, a courtesy he had never extended when Eugene had called on him in the old, carefree days.

He tried the hoary routine of seeking to make her jealous by paying marked attention to a soprano, who also recited excerpts from *Othello* and *Macbeth*, but Elaine showed her broadmindedness by actively encouraging both him and her. The result was that he was stuck with the talented lady for nearly a week in Leamington Spa, and only escaped from her by letting it be known that they were booked at Aberdeen the following week, when in reality they had a free week, followed by a week at Boscombe.

He had it out with Benny Boy, and threatened to change his agent, but Benny Boy called his bluff, and said that this might be quite an idea, providing he left Elaine behind him. He tried reasoning with her, threatening her, and even pleading with her, but in vain, for she did not seem to possess any of the finer feelings to which he could appeal, and as for being frightened of him, she was obviously frightened of nothing, not even a Saturday night house in Portsmouth when the Fleet was in.

At last he gave up the struggle, and drifted with the tide, grateful for the time she spent with him when all the other men in the company were travelling with their wives, or were otherwise engaged, and Benny Boy was on a rare visit to London, attending to his neglected clients.

She finally abandoned him in Morecambe, and went off with Benny Boy for good, leaving him to slip from the Number Two dates to the Number Three, and from thence to the "Die-the-Death" seaside towns, with very long names, and very short piers.

At one such town he collapsed, during a Thursday matinée, and was carried away to the nearest infirmary, where he died the following night. There was a small piece about him in *The Stage*, but Elaine did not read it, for by that time she was abroad, and driving down to Biarritz in Benny Boy's Daimler, the one that ultimately had to be shipped back to England, for the forced sale that preceded Benny Boy's bankruptcy.

Elaine seemed to have this effect on her men. It was not that she was particularly foolish with money, or extravagant in her tastes, but just that she seemed to disorganise them in some way, and prevent them earning the kind of money they were earning when they met her.

Benny Boy was a case in point. He had been making a steady two thousand a year when Eugene introduced him to his new assistant. But all those trips about the country sapped his authority over his London staff, and his junior partner suddenly grew big enough to gobble him up and did so, the moment he and Elaine left for the holiday on the Continent. The result was that Benny Boy flew home from Biarritz to find his name erased from the wooden plaque outside the Dolman Street offices, and from the doorstep of the office it was but a short step to Carey Street, and the loss of premises, goodwill and, within a few days of her return to England, of Elaine also.

After that Elaine joined up with a circus. She still had her spangled tights, and a circus seemed an appropriate place to use them. She had, by this time, a fairly wide range of experience within the world of variety, and considering her exceptionally strict upbringing, an even wider experience in the art of handling men.

The touring circus she joined was a small, seedy outfit, owned by a jovial little man, known throughout the profession as "Tom Tappertitt". Whether this was his real or an assumed name Elaine never discovered, and during her apprenticeship period she saw very little of him, for he no longer acted as ringmaster, but concerned himself with publicity and finance. He did not impress her during her brief initial interview and she recalled him as an undersized, red-faced man, with a long waxed moustache turned up Prussian fashion at the ends, lending a touch of fierceness to an otherwise bovine expression.

Her first duty was that of assisting "Captain" Roxley, the alligator man, and she soon overcame her repugnance to the squirming reptiles, and learned to pass them round among the ringside customers, and encourage hesitant customers to hold them for a few moments.

"Captain" Roxley, a South African, behaved towards her with rectitude, and in general she found the circus folk unexpectedly reserved in their dealings with her. She remembered, as a child, reading *A Peep Behind the Scenes*, one of the few books her mother had allowed into the house, and from her recollections of it circus people were a raucous, rackety lot, not at all like the rather sad, domesticated families, who trailed round the country behind Tom Tappertitt.

The acts, she discovered, were families within a family, and even when off duty they appeared to have little in common with one another. The high-wire group kept very much to themselves, and the clowns went about in a trio, drinking as much or more than they could afford and, despite this, sunk in contemplative gloom. The animal trainers were friendly, but they were dedicated to their work, and seemed to spend all their spare time rehearsing. Altogether it was a rather depressing life, and Elaine would have left, and tried to re-enter variety, had she not been discovered at length by Tom Tappertitt himself, the only man in the company who regarded the ring as a means of livelihood, rather than an almost dedicated vocation.

Tom had a reputation for gallantry, as Elaine was informed by Sonia, the girl Cossack, a day or two after she joined the show. If Sonia had ever visited the Steppes it must have been in earliest infancy, for she had since acquired a strong, nasal accent, which placed her somewhere between Aldgate and Bow.

"You wanner watch *'im*, dearie," she told Elaine, as they stood together in the changing tent after the show one night; "he's Tappertitt be name, an' 'Tap-a-tit' be naychure! Several girls left bekos of *'im*, but 'e don't try nothin' on when *she's* abaht. Wouldn't do fer 'im, to, *'er* being wot *she* is!"

Judicious questioning established that " *'Er'*" was Mrs. Tappertitt, the professional strong woman, billed as "Audrey the Amazon". She was capable of tearing encyclopædias in half edgeways, and gathering a squad of struggling marines to her vast bosom, by hauling them into the ring on the end of a steel cable. She weighed something over sixteen stones, and was reputed to eat raw beef by the pound.

"Ever ser gone on 'im, she is," explained Sonia, "tho' why I can't say, c'n you? I mean, 'e's sorter dresses neat, but 'e ain't all that to look at, is 'e? Like Kaiser Bill, cut down to a lit'l turkey-cock, wot wi' that turned-up moos-tash, an' that boiled lobster face of 'is! *She* is tho', and when she's around 'e don't look at no one, but you want to turn *facin'* 'im when 'e finds you on yer lonsesome. He's a bit like the sailor, ducks. You know, 'andy enough, so long as you watch 'is 'ands!"

It was not long before Elaine made the acquaintance of Mrs. Tappertitt, who returned that week-end from a date-booking tour in the North. She was a loud, motherly woman, with a tread like that of a placid hippopotamus, and an overall gentleness of spirit characteristic of elephantine women. When she was around everyone brightened up a little, and she showed kindness towards Elaine by going out of her way to ensure that the new girl had comfortable travelling quarters in the big trailer, attached to the aquarium.

It was easy to see who kept the show together. Members of the various troupes brought all their problems to Mrs. Tappertitt, who sorted them out firmly but tactfully, although it was understood by everyone that she liked to maintain the pretence of deferring to "My Tom", whom she treated with exaggerated respect.

It was through Mrs. Tappertitt that Elaine obtained a rise of a pound a week, paid to her for helping out, during the earlier part of the day, at one or other of the fun-fair booths, usually the miniature-rifle range.

For this part of her duties Elaine wore tight slacks, and an even tighter sweater, and it was here, loading the rifles with tufted darts, that she one day came face to face with her brother Sydney. He did not seem in the least surprised to see her, as indeed he was not, having recognised her the previous evening during the alligator act.

Sydney, who was on a week's cycling tour, happened to visit the circus with an office friend, and spent a most uncomfortable evening, not daring to inform Alec, his friend, that the girl carrying the alligators around the ring was his sister. Curiosity, however, drove him to the fairground the following afternoon, when Alec was safely out of the way, and he mooched about rather self-consciously until he spotted Elaine at the range, and sidled over, awaiting his chance to speak.

When there was a lull in the shooting he greeted her with a toothy grin.

"I say, this is a bit of a comedown, isn't it?"

Elaine looked at him blankly.

"Where have you come from?" she demanded, with a sharp edge to her voice.

She assumed, for the moment, that Esther must be in the offing, but he hurried to reassure her.

"It's all right. I was cycling through. A tour y'know. Mother's at home."

"Then what do you want?" demanded Elaine.

Sydney looked vague and uncomfortable. There had never been any affection between them, but he found it a little difficult to accept this remark as an adequate bridge for a separation of four years.

"I . . . er . . . I don't *want* anything," he replied lamely, "but I saw you last night, and I didn't like to move on without saying 'hello'."

Elaine gave a little snort. Having grown up with Sydney she was not in the slightest doubt as to his real reason for approaching her. He must have convinced himself that she was down on her luck, and feeling very sorry for herself, and was thus unable to forgo the pleasure of gloating. In this respect she was only partly correct; the main reason why Sydney had called at the ground was curiosity and as yet it was unsatisfied.

"What's it like, working in a dump like this?" he asked.

"It's a lot better than living with you and mother," said Elaine, shortly.

He shifted his weight from one foot to the other, and she saw him again, as a bare-kneed boy, pumping her for information that would be conveyed straight to Esther.

"How much do you make?" he wanted to know.

"Six pounds a week and keep," lied Elaine.

He whistled, not knowing whether to believe her. His own salary was less than five pounds a week, out of which he gave Esther thirty shillings.

"Well, it's okay if you can stick it, I suppose," he compromised, and then, after a pause, "Do you want to send Mother any message?"

"Not 'specially," said Elaine, and to a nearby loiterer, "Six shots for sixpence! Have a go, sir!"

Sydney blushed as the man grinned and moved on. He cast about for some means of retaliating.

"All I can say is you were a fool to throw over that young Fraser," he said finally, "he's got a good job in Fleet Street now, and makes over six hundred a year, I'm told! That's apart from what he earns writing for the radio. He came into money too! He's worth quite a bit now, they say."

Elaine made no reply to this, and her silence only increased his embarrassment. She had always emerged winner in this kind of duel.

"Well, I'll be moving on," he added. "Goodbye."

"Goodbye," she said flatly, as he drifted away, and was soon lost in the crowd watching the Dodg'ems.

She went on breaking and loading the rifles, but she worked listlessly, for under her studied uninterestedness she had been disturbed by Sydney's visit. The sight of his narrow, toothy face had stirred in her mind musty, unpleasant memories of Esther, and his news of Esme was as exasperating as the malice that had prompted him to impart it. Come into money, had he? How much, and when? She always knew that Esme's people were the wealthiest in the Avenue, that at twenty-one he would inherit something from his father's estate, but *how much?* That was what was important, how much? Hundreds, or thousands? And six hundred a year, besides what he made on the radio! Could this be true? How much *did* a person make writing for radio? Were they paid in odd guineas, or in hundreds of pounds?

At this point in her reflections, a voice close by said: "How you doing, ducks?"

She looked up, and saw Tom Tappertitt, leaning lightly on the frame of the booth.

He was dressed in well-cut sports clothes, and a diamond pin flashed below the knot of his tie. He looked very spry and dapper, and there was the familiar gleam in his eye, that Elaine had never once failed to recognise. She was feeling exceptionally depressed, for the circus, as a circus, was beginning to bore her. Its gaudiness was a transparent gaudiness, and it lacked the sparkle of the variety world. Having tasted her brief moment of high living with Benny Boy she was not very satisfied with her actual wage, three pounds a week, less insurance, and pondering these things, she decided that Tappertitt was worth a smile. He really was absurdly small, but he was the only person about who took any pains at all with his appearance; his fingernails were cared for, and he looked clean and wholesome.

"Not all that well, Mr. Tappertitt," she told him; "the people don't usually start coming here until early evening."

"I'm going to lunch," he said. "Have you had yours?"

"No, Mr. Tappertitt, I was going to ask Charlie to take over, while I popped out and got a sandwich at the canteen."

"There's no matinée. Why don't you lunch with me, and come to a flick?" he suggested.

Elaine hesitated. She was not seriously tempted. He did not appeal to her as a man, and she was not yet quite ready to exchange the circus for another job-hunt. Then she remembered that Mrs. Tappertitt had departed for the next town that morning. Surely it could do no harm to entrench herself a little more firmly with this outfit. After all, Tappertitt was well known in entertainment circles, and if she cultivated him he might put something better in her way, either here, or elsewhere.

"That's very kind of you and I'd like to very much, Mr. Tappertitt," she said demurely.

He called across to a youth, loafing beside the hoop-la.

"Take over for a bit, Charlie! Miss Frith's going to lunch."

Charlie mooched over, and winked to himself as Tom and Elaine moved off together. He had been with the Tappertitts since he was a child. Here was a little something for the boys—all the dope on the boss's new filly.

2

They lunched at "The Old George" in the market square, and Tom ordered burgundy with the pheasant, and liqueurs with the coffee. Later they drifted out into the town, and. after a brief look at the shops went into the cinema. The film was a Hollywood epic about a white hunter, who probed his way into the upper reaches of the Congo, accompanied by a mad trader, and the mad trader's sleek, blonde wife. The latter seemed to combine an ability to shoot crocodiles by the score, with the facility to keep her linen shorts spotlessly clean, and her eyelashes heavily mascaraed. It was a very bad film, and the supporting picture was even worse, but neither Tom nor Elaine was able to pay much attention to the screen, for Tom had his own exploring to do, and Elaine was fully occupied with the delicate task of limiting its extent.

She soon decided that Sonia's simile had been a just one. Tom Tappertitt certainly was a handy man, and was almost as enterprising with his feet and knees.

He began by interlocking the fingers of his right hand with hers during the newsreel, but by the time next week's attraction was being advertised he had brought his left hand into play, and was reconnoitring the upper part of her taut sweater. Gently repulsed in this direction he called up reinforcements from between the seats, where their locked hands were now resting. Lifting them both, he placed them firmly on her thighs, which she had had the forethought to cross the moment they had sat down!

At this manœuvre Elaine whispered a mild protest:

"Mr. Tappertitt, you mustn't!", but even as she said it she wanted to giggle, for both his name and his stealthy persistence struck her as comic, and the wine and liqueurs had induced in her a tolerant mood.

He desisted at last, settling for a rather cramped position of half-intimacy, with his right arm along the line of her shoulder and his left, still holding her hand, on the angle of her right knee. In this posture, which left a good deal to be desired, they watched the white hunter shoot the mad husband in the act of knifing the blonde, and enfold the widow in á long embrace beside a dead rhinoceros. Altogether it was a stimulating afternoon.

In the weeks that followed Elaine played Tom Tappertitt like a small, darting fish, while his stalking of her· was constantly interrupted by the abrupt comings and goings of his wife. When Audrey the Amazon was with the show he never went near her, but as soon as she had departed on one of her booking trips he picked up where he had left off, and made steady, if strictly regulated, progress.

The climax came when the circus set up its tent on a derelict brickyard, midway between Birmingham and Wolverhampton, and Mrs. Tappertitt went on to Nottingham to make arrangements for the latter half of the week.

By this time Elaine had been able to extract a number of material benefits from the association. She had a brand-new outfit, including several pairs of shoes, a wristlet watch to replace the one that Benny Boy had given her (an adornment that, like its donor, appeared to take small account of time when close to Elaine). She also acquired a smart vanity case, of American manufacture, and a modest credit balance in the Post Office Savings Account. This she was accumulating against the day when, as was inevitable, Mrs. Tappertitt would redirect her into an indifferent world.

Taken all round she had the better of the bargain, for these perquisites had cost her nothing more than a few visits to the cinema, a few brief intervals on the banks of canals and park seats, a hasty kiss or two, plus any amount of curve-patting and bottom-pinching as she passed close by Tom in unfrequented sections of the waste lands that the circus occupied week by week.

It was only when he began to show unmistakable signs of impatience, culminating in what amounted to a flat ultimatum on the day that Mrs. Tappertitt left for Nottingham, that she consented to stay a night at his hotel out of town. She capitulated on condition that "he would be good", although it is to be doubted whether even Elaine expected him to take this proviso very seriously, particularly as, all smiles again, he forthwith presented her with a pair of black silk pyjamas, as a token of his appreciation.

So it came about, the following evening, that Tom and Elaine installed themselves as Mr. and Mrs. T. Smith (Tom was not a very original man) in a blameless little hotel, situated in the main street of a small country town, about a dozen miles west of the site. And it was here, at the unlikely hour of two in the morning, that their bedroom door flew open, and the lights were switched on, revealing to the tousled Elaine and her still sleeping partner, the awful reality of a professional strong woman in the role of outraged wife.

Elaine had no time to do more than blink, rub her eyes, and sit up in bed, before Audrey the Amazon, not even bothering to shut the door behind her, plucked her from bed, and tucked her under her massive arm as though she were a runaway puppy.

Then Elaine knew real fear, and cried aloud, her protests rousing Tom, who sat up very suddenly, looking more like the Kaiser than ever, with his true stature concealed by the bedclothes. Neither was he given any time to exclaim, for his wife, moving with incredible speed for one so huge, whipped round the end of the bed, threw Elaine heavily to the floor, picked up her husband with even less effort than she had lifted Elaine, and tossed him casually into a shallow closet, smartly slamming the door, and blocking it with the end of the bed, which she hooked sideways with her foot.

Although Audrey's disposal of Tom occupied but a few seconds it presented Elaine with her sole chance to escape, and she took it.

Breathlessly she scrambled to her knees, and dived over

the bed towards the door. She had stopped shouting, but her cries were now taken up by Tom from the closet, and by other people, presumably guests, or the proprietor and his wife, who had gathered in the passage, and were now adding their protests to the general uproar.

Elaine did not get very far in her scramble towards this group. Audrey the Amazon turned, seized her by the hair, pressed her face into the pillow, jumped on to the disordered bed, and pinned her down with one knee.

Then, releasing Elaine's hair so that she could turn her head just enough to breathe, she tore down her new pyjama trousers, and commenced to administer a spanking that could be heard very clearly in the lobby downstairs.

Mrs. Tappertitt had huge, meaty hands, that were able to cover quite an area, and they were hands that were accustomed daily to tying reef knots in iron bars, and tearing encyclopædias in two. The wild cries of Elaine, squirming on the bed, were soon far louder than those of Tom, folded into the closet, and were certainly penetrating enough to drown the scattered protests of the group standing in the passage, and looking in upon the curious scene.

It was perhaps a full minute before Audrey the Amazon paused and, with a final flip of her wrist, again deposited Elaine on the floor, this time on the side nearest the door.

"That," said Audrey, wheezing a little, "is what your mother ought to have done more often! Now get dressed, get your things together, and clear out of here, but don't take nothing *he* gave you, or I'll start on you again the minute I get me breath back!"

She then seemed to dismiss Elaine, and turned to the closet, kicking back the bed, and pulling open the door, so that poor Tom fell out face foremost, and landed abjectly at her feet.

"You get dressed too, Tom," she said, "and I'll give you your rations the minute we get home!"

A man in a flannel dressing-gown stepped over the threshold, and began to say something, but Mrs. Tappertitt pushed him lightly in the chest, and he staggered back into the arms of the group in the passage.

"We'll all be out of here in five minutes, so you mind your own business," she said, and slammed the door on them.

Elaine never forgot the next half-hour.

With Mrs. Tappertitt sitting grimly on the bed the two of them dragged on their clothes, and made half-hearted attempts to collect their small amount of luggage, and pack it into the two suitcases they had brought with them.

Neither Tom nor Elaine said a word, but Mrs. Tappertitt watched every movement they made, her eyes following them over to the washbasin, and back again to the alcoves, where the suitcases rested. Once Tom began to say something, but before he had completed a word his wife said, "Shut up, and get on with it", so they continued to pad to and fro, Elaine choking back sobs of rage and shame, Tom sniffing and hawking from his side of the room, and looking rather pitiful in his long woollen pants and striped shirt.

At last it was done, and they opened the door. The hotelier, a spare, angular man with a faintly military aspect, was still standing in the passage, in his woollen dressing-gown.

"This is outrageous," he began. "I shall make it my business to ..."

"You won't make it your business to do nothing," said Mrs. Tappertitt tartly. "It won't do you any more good than it would us, so stop blowing so hard, and come to the point. How much does he owe you?"

The man's Adam's Apple quivered. "Two pounds for the room, and one-pound-six for the meal," he said.

"Pay it," said Audrey briefly, and Tom took out his wallet, and handed the man four pounds.

"You can keep the change to mend the bolt on the door," said Audrey thoughtfully, as they all three walked past him along the passage, and down the narrow stairs into the lobby.

The proprietor hurried after them, and unbolted the front door. Outside the youth Charlie was sitting at the wheel of a utility van, and when they emerged he jumped out and ran round to open the door.

"There's still some of my things in the trailer," wailed

Elaine, as Mrs. Tappertitt pushed her husband into the van, and climbed in after him.

"We'll send 'em on! Where to?"

"I don't know ... how could I ..." began Elaine, and then, inexplicably, Esme's number, "Twenty-Two," sprang into her mind, and she gave Esme's address, Charlie jotting it down on the back of an A.A. map.

"Here, you might as well have this, I got no use for it," said Mrs. Tappertitt suddenly, and she tossed the black vanity case in Elaine's direction, just as Charlie let in the clutch and the van shot off into the darkness.

Elaine caught the little box, and put it on top on her suitcase. Behind her the hotelier had re-locked the door, and was turning out the lights. Somewhere near at hand a clock struck three, and it began to drizzle. It was then that Elaine realised that she did not even know the name of the town she was in, or whether it possessed a railway station. She stood there, her back to the wall, fresh tears welling. For the first time in her life she felt defeated and helpless.

A burly figure loomed out of the slanting rain, and stopped in front of her.

"Anything the matter, Miss?"

It was a constable, his raincoat buttoned to his chin, his hands clasped behind him.

"I'm stranded," said Elaine, "the ... the people I worked for just sacked me, and left me here."

He regarded her curiously. "Have you got any money?"

"Yes, I've got money but ..."

Suddenly Elaine perked up. It was three a.m. It was drizzling. She did not even know where she was, much less where she was going. Her behind glowed like a brazier, and she had bruised her knee, when that crazy woman had dropped her on the floor. Her hair was in a mess, and her face tear-stained and unwashed. But things might have been worse. She had money in her handbag, more in the Post Office, and here was a man. A police officer, to be sure, but a man, and she could handle all men.

She raised her head, and studied him in the faint, yellow glow of the single lamp a few yards down the street. He was. quite young, and obviously interested, extra-professionally.

"Perhaps you could show me where the railway station is," she said; "I want to go to London by the first train."

He relaxed, and picked up her case.

"Certainly, Miss. But why don't we go along to the station first? I'm going off duty soon, and there'll be a nice cup of tea there. Then you can tell me all about it—if you want to, that is—and I'll look up the trains for you. All right?"

"I think that's a wonderful idea," said Elaine, and fell into step with him, as they moved off towards the centre of the town.

3

She had her cosy cup of tea and chat over the charge-room fire, and then caught the six-forty for Birmingham, for the connection to London at eight. In the station cloakroom she had a wash-and-brush-up, and had just sufficient time, before the main-line train arrived, to eat a cooked breakfast in the buffet.

During the journey south she took careful stock of her situation, much as a castaway might explore the contents of his pockets on the morning after the storm.

She had more than twenty pounds in her handbag, and another sixty in the Post Office. With a capital of eighty, and all the new clothes Tom Tappertitt had bought her, she was safe for a few weeks, and might even take a holiday, in order to map out the future. She was finished, she decided, with the stage, and with circuses. The life had its attractions but its uncertainty, and the type of man it presented held out no real prospects for the future. There was no one there, no one at least whom she was likely to meet, who would ever provide the terrace, the drinks, the hammock, and the hovering courtiers she had so often promised herself.

She would have to look elsewhere, abroad perhaps, or in the city, where men made real money, and often, she had heard, acquired fortunes overnight. She might go back to secretarial work. Secretaries were always marrying the bosses, wealthy bosses. Show her such a man, and she would go to work. Within months there would be a terrace, drinks, hammock, and courtiers, as well as a sleek limousine that was not second-hand, like Benny Boy's.

Despite her ups and downs of the past few years her experiences had given her unlimited confidence in one respect. She understood men, all men. Almost every one of them looked at her in that certain way, and by this time she had learned precisely how to respond, when to hold back, when to encourage, when to do both at once.

She had read in a Sunday newspaper article that the way to make a million was to find something people wanted, and then corner a supply of that product. Well, she had what men wanted, any amount of it, and surely all that was really necessary was to display it in the right market. What she badly needed, she decided, was a base, a haven from which she could sally forth from time to time, and retreat into when necessary. A London flat was out of the question on her limited capital. If she laid out her money in that way she would be forever watching it dwindle, and a sense of urgency would soon tempt her into making rash judgements.

Suddenly she thought of Esme again. She had been thinking of him, at frequent intervals, ever since Sydney had mentioned him at the fairground. Six hundred a year, what he made writing scripts for the radio, and his inheritance! It was more than enough for the sort of base she was looking for, and mercifully Esme was still unmarried, otherwise Sydney would certainly have mentioned the fact. She worked out his age. He must be twenty-six, and if he was unmarried, at twenty-six, with all that security, then it surely followed that he had not yet met anyone who had displaced her in his affections. They had, after all, been the right sort of affections. She had never come across anyone else who had his ideals, who assumed that marriage must inevitably follow a few kisses in the park, who had looked so tragic and despairing when she had spoken lightly of marriage. True, their association had been a mere boy-and-girl affair, and she could hardly believe that he had taken it as seriously as he appeared to do at the time, but all the books said that first-love of this kind was much more enduring than subsequent affairs, and perhaps Esme was worth a try.

Thinking it over she reflected how unerring her instinct

had been when it prompted her to give his home as a forwarding address, to that dreadful woman last night! At the memory of Audrey, and the shame and ignominy of her public spanking, she faltered a little, and had to thrust the recent past into the back of her mind, and return to a deliberate study of practicalities—i.e., the precise means of contacting Esme again, without first showing herself in the Avenue, where she must immediately come under the scrutiny of her mother, and Sydney.

She settled herself in the corner of her compartment, and lit a De Reszke ivory-tipped cigarette. Her mind began to experiment with phrases and artifices, and by the time she had reached King's Cross, Elaine was herself again. She was very good at thrusting unpleasant memories into the depths of her mind, where they were difficult to locate, and never found their way to the surface again without her help. She took from the past only that which was useful in the present.

CHAPTER XXIX

Esme And The Promised Land

1

ESME took the letter from his jacket pocket and read it for the fifth time, running his eye down the widely-spaced lines, and forgetting a cigarette that he had lit on entering the carriage, at Woodside. The cigarette burned away, unsmoked, as the train rattled through Clockhouse, Ladywell, and Sydenham.

He had recognised her handwriting immediately, although he had not seen it since Edgar Frith had showed him her two letters at Llandudno, years ago. He had not wanted to read it at breakfast, with Harold and Eunice looking on, and had "suddenly remembered" that he must catch the eight-twenty, instead of his usual eight-fifty-five.

He had not hurried to the station, but had gone, instead, along the crescent, and into the "Rec", to the seat he always associated with Elaine, the one near the tennis-courts. Here, with fingers that trembled a little, and with the familiar fluttering sensation halfway between breastbone and stomach, he had carefully slit the thick envelope, extracted three folded sheets of hotel notepaper, and smoothed them out on his knee, clearing his throat, as though he proposed reading the letter aloud to an audience of a park-keeper, and a pair of chaffinches, which hopped round his feet in search of yesterday's sandwich crumbs.

"My dear Esme," it began, *"I almost called you Launcelot, but decided that you would have forgotten my teasing after all this time, and imagined you were getting a letter intended for somebody else!"*

He shivered a little. Was it possible to forget a thing like that? The memory of it was as bright now as it had been eight years ago, the evening he had shown her a picture of Elaine in his illustrated *Myths,* and she had jested: "What a pity you aren't called Launcelot, Esme!" From then on, she had sometimes used the name in fun, and told him that he had been born centuries too late, when all the dragons were dead, and all the ladies rescued.

He read on:

"I expect you will be staggered to hear from me after all this time, but this really is the first chance I have had to write."

(Dear God, he thought, the first chance in eight years!)

"You will see I am now back in London, having left the stage for good, and lost touch with everybody during the last few years, after I was silly enough to try my luck on the road and turn my back on hotel work, which was

steady but so dull. The fact is, Esme, I want to get a good office job. I can still type, and I'm sure I can soon work up a shorthand speed. Sydney told me you were in a good job in London and I thought perhaps you knew of someone. Do you think we could meet and have a coffee somewhere? I've such heaps to tell you and knowing you I think a lot of it would make you laugh, and perhaps give you some stories to write about if you still write stories like you used to. Sydney did say you wrote stuff for the radio, and I was thrilled to hear it because I always knew you would if you kept on trying.

"I'm staying at this little hotel for a few days, as I still don't think I could stay at home and I'm still not sorry I left. You could ring up but the man who takes messages here is very deaf and would probably get the time and place wrong. Would you think me very silly if we met (providing you want to of course) under the dead poet picture in the Tate Gallery where we met once before? I've never forgotten that—his breeches were such a beautiful blue and it was romantic to meet there like that. In any case, I'll be there at one o'clock today (the day you get this)—and tomorrow as well, in case you can't make it. I was going to see the picture anyway, so even if you don't turn up it won't matter and I shall understand because it's a bit much for me to pop up suddenly like this and expect you to remember the same nice things I remember, you know —take everything for granted in this way.

"Goodbye for now, Esme dear. I'm terribly excited at the thought of seeing you again and wonder if you've changed as much as me,. not to look at I mean, but inside.

As ever,

Elaine.

P.S. Some things of mine in a parcel might arrive at your address. I had to give the number as I didn't want them to go home and there was nowhere else.

P.P.S. I meant to send a photo but haven't got a good one. I'm sure we'll be able to recognise one another."

The right-hand corner of the last sheet was turned back, and under it was a tiny cross.

He sat looking at the pages for so long that he had to run into Delhi Road, and most of the way to the station, in order to catch the later train.

He found it impossible to digest the letter, and all it implied, in spite of several readings, but as the train pulled into Charing Cross (he had an appointment in the West End that morning and did not leave at his usual terminus, London Bridge) one factor did emerge. That was the astonishing certainty that she had by no means dismissed him from her mind, as he had imagined himself to be dismissed all these years. Neither, it would seem, did she regard their immature courtship as a naïve milestone in the process of growing-up, but had seemingly kept it fresh and green, looking back on it with flattering warmth, and recalling moments of it that even he might have forgotten—that Launcelot business, for instance, and their trysting place, under *The Death of Chatterton*.

She even remembered the colour of Chatterton's breeches, and that kids' trick of putting a kiss under the turned-back corner of the page! Then there was the "Esme dear", slipped into the final paragraph. To judge by this letter, indeed, she might not have been absent and silent for years on end, but simply returning from a separation of a few months at most. Was it really possible that he had misjudged her to that extent?

He found that he could not concentrate on work, and stopped at a kiosk in Trafalgar Square to make a 'phone call to his office and ask the typist to ring up and cancel his appointment. It was then nearly ten o'clock, and he had three hours to waste until one.

He drifted into the Mall, and thence into St. James's Park, where he sat watching the ducks for a time, trying to rationalise the jumble of emotions her letter had stirred in him. He was only partially successful. Every now and again a cold douche of caution swamped down on his elation, and his reason warned him that a person could not change to this extent, that he was reading into her letter things that were not there. But as soon as he had convinced himself of this equally obvious points hurried to his rescue—the Launcelot joke, the "Esme dear", the tender memory that prompted her selection of the point of reunion, the turned-back corner for the kiss. Surely this last must mean that she would still like to be kissed by him, that she still remembered those eager kisses of years ago.

It did occur to him that she had purposely introduced the nostalgic note into the letter, purely in order to encourage him to help her find a job. She was quite capable of such a thing, or had once been. Was she still? Or might she not have grown up, and changed to the extent of completely disproving Harold's assertion that she would never feel deeply about anyone or anything? Then he found himself resenting Harold's estimate. After all, what did Harold know of her? What did her father, or anyone but himself, who had once loved her so desperately, and had been unable to forget her in almost a decade?

And here Esme began to lie to himself a little, for in truth, he *had* almost forgotten her, since returning home and settling happily at the office. The encouragement of his employers, and the pleasure of actually receiving money from such an august establishment as the BBC, had done a great deal to erase the memory of Elaine, and he was now old enough to ask himself whether his sustained longing for her was not a kind of crystallisation of all his adolescent ideas about love. He was still an incurable romantic, so much of one that he had so far been unable to attach himself to any of the young women he met in the course of his work or recreation. He found that their slang and banality irritated him, and encouraged him to isolate himself. He would have been hurt, but not much surprised, to learn the estimate of the typist, Mavis, who described him to her friend Marlene as "nice, but just-the-tiniest-bit-stuffy-if-you-know-what-I-mean-dear".

This was a fair estimate of Esme Fraser, at twenty-six. Nice, but stuffy; not stuffy in the accepted sense of the word, but stuffy in a way that made no appeal to the level-headed young women who had replaced the flappers of the 'twenties. In one way they found him naïve, and in another almost middle-aged. He was a highbrow, but without the sophistication that distinguished a highbrow, and made him pleasant to exhibit to one's girl friends at dances and staff socials. Other girls, Avenue girls, had assessed Esme in disparaging terms. Freda Geering, for instance, of Number Five, whom Esme had once taken to a dance, put it another way, when replying to a question put to her by an exasperated mother, who had heard exaggerated reports of Esme's inheritance "Why don't I go out with him again, Mum? Well, in the first place because he's never asked me, but even if he did, I'd think twice about going. He's odd, and kind of moody, and . . . well . . . unpredictable. That time we went to the Club dance, do you know. what he talked about? Some silly old revolution or other . . . no, he's not a Bolshie, Bolshies are often quite interesting; this revolution happened millions of years ago, in Rome, or somewhere, and was started by a lot of martyrs, or gladiators. I remember now, they were all crucified, like Jesus. I mean to say, who wants to hear about people being crucified when you're dancing a tango?"

There were, of course, plenty of girls available to Esme with whom it might have been possible to discuss crucified gladiators, and kindred subjects, but like most romantics under thirty, Esme wanted cake and ha'penny too. He wanted a girl who looked like Elaine, but was still able to provide him with a readily available audience of one, as Judy Carver had done so patiently in days gone by. He had, in fact, already made the depressing discovery that girls who were equipped to discuss Spartacus had a tendency to wear horn-rimmed glasses and lisle stockings, and a man did not always want to be talking about gladiators' revolts.

At eleven o'clock he left the Park, and climbed Clive Steps into King Charles' Street, walking thence to Parliament Square. At the corner of Whitehall he decided that he needed a drink, and went into a basement bar near Scotland Yard, ordering a double brandy, which he sipped slowly. As Big Ben struck twelve he climbed to the street again, and began to make his way towards the Tate, arriving at the Gallery at ten minutes past twelve.

It was some years since he had visited the Tate Gallery. His tastes in art, he was informed, were lamentable, for he demanded incident, rather than power, colour, or design. He did not much care "what the artist was getting at", and was obstinate in his defence of the Pre-Raphaelites. His preferences infuriated Aubrey Caseman, one of his Bloomsbury associates at the office. "If you want bloody stories with your pictures why the hell don't you go out and buy a magazine?" he demanded, when Esme chipped into discussions on modern art.

Esme was sorry about this. He would have liked to have gone all the way with Aubrey, and enthused over Picasso and Matisse, but he was a very honest young man, and found it impossible to pretend to enthusiasms he did not feel. It was the same with poetry. He still preferred Tennyson, Masefield, and Rupert Brooke, to the poets Aubrey was always trying to sell him, young men whose verses had alternately short and long lines, and who appeared to dispense with old-fashioned metre and rhymes.

He found *The Death of Chatterton*, and stared at it for five minutes, trying to discover the mystical link, if such link existed, between the vivid blue of the breeches and Elaine, and wondering what it was about the picture that had imprinted itself so firmly on her memory. Then it struck him that they did have one thing in common. Both the artists' colour and Elaine had magnetism. On entering the gallery it was Chatterton's breeches that caught and held the eye, to the exclusion of the pictures on either side, and, indeed, to the detraction of the subject as a whole. Elaine, as he remembered her, had always had the same effect on people when she entered a room. It was not that she was strikingly beautiful—simply vivid and exciting, in the way that this splash of colour was vivid and exciting.

He found the idea so fanciful that he smiled to himself, as he moved on to have another look at his favourite picture, *Derby Day*. He had been attracted by *Derby Day* ever since Eunice and Harold had first brought him there as a child, and he supposed that this was because people interested him so much more deeply than abstract ideas. Aubrey Caseman, of course, would snort at this; in *Derby Day* there was not one story, but a baker's dozen: the penniless young dupe, the card sharper, the girls in the phaeton, and so on. Studying it, section by section, he forgot Elaine, and after a few minutes drifted round under the begrimed dome, to a gallery where hung another old favourite, *April Love*. It was a picture that would have sent Aubrey Caseman groping for the brandy bottle, depicting as it did a young girl, awaiting her lover, in a conveniently rural setting. But Esme had always liked it, and it seemed to him an appropriate sort of picture to inspect that day, although he had to admit that Elaine and the principal subject had very little in common. He was, indeed, methodically comparing their differences, when a voice at his elbow said:

"Hullo, Esme!"

He spun round and saw her, standing less than a yard away, and at his first sight of her all the old enchantment invaded his senses, driving out uncertainty, and doubt, and fear, and lighting up his face with joy.

She had given a great deal of thought to her appearance when she dressed that morning. Despite her existing stock, half her small capital had been invested in yet more clothes, and she had purchased wisely, reminding herself that she was out to coax, rather than dazzle. She remembered that, despite Esme's habitual carelessness with his own appearance, he had always been quick to notice what she was wearing. Wasn't it that demure, slightly-outmoded dance-frock that had caught his eye in the first place, all those years ago at the Stafford-Fyffe's ball?

She remembered too that he liked women to look dainty and ultra-feminine, irrespective of fashion. They had even had talks about it, and she recalled how he had once deplored the passing of the crinoline. It was a pity, she thought, that crinolines were no longer in vogue, for this, if ever, was surely a crinoline occasion. So she chose the next best thing, a white linen blouse, and a simple blue pinafore frock, that matched her eyes. Over it she wore a brief, scalloped cape, of very light wool, and a little black straw hat, that sat back on her dark hair like a biretta, its small cluster of marguerites above the right eye.

Her concessions to the West End were her smartest Italian shoes (bought by Tom Tappertitt in Bournemouth, shortly before the debacle) and her crocodile handbag, the one substantial legacy of Benny Boy. Just before she left her room she had changed her mind about gloves, peeling off her long suede pair, and replacing them with short cotton ones, transparent, and frilled at the wrist.

Her instincts and her memories were reliable. The moment he saw her he made no attempt to conceal the wonder she stirred in him. She smiled to see it, not her old catlike smile, that had always seemed to him to murmur "Stroke me if you like, but I shall claw you if *I* like", but a warm, almost sisterly smile, that took no advantage of the fact that it was she who had surprised him, for once she realised that he had some difficulty in greeting her she dropped her eyes and said:

"You weren't ᵇby the picture, but I knew you'd be somewhere about. . . . I tried to remember the pictures you liked, but the man said they changed them around."

He began to apologise, abjectly. "I'm terribly sorry, Elaine. I got here early, and forgot the time. . . ."

She came to his rescue again. "No, no, Esme, it was my fault. It isn't one o'clock yet." She glanced at Tom Tappertitt's watch. "I think I'm a bit fast."

He calmed a little, but his heart continued to thump.

"You . . . you look quite wonderful, Elaine . . . it's been so long now, I'd almost forgotten."

"You too, Esme . . . you're so grown up and . . ." she smiled again, "so much taller, and even a little tidier."

He was able to smile at that. Eunice was always nagging him about his personal appearance. He was forever putting off having his hair cut, and he never once used the oak trouser-press that his mother and Harold had given him on his eighteenth birthday, but continued to fling his clothes on a chair beside the bed.

"I was never much of a one for dressing up, was I?" And then: "Could you eat a really good lunch . . . something a bit different?".

She looked surprised. "Lunch? I thought just a coffee. . . . What about your work, don't you have to be back at two?"

She *had* grown up, he decided. In the old days she would never have thought about a thing like that.

"I'll take the day off . . . I'll say I felt rotten, and went home again."

He felt reckless and carefree as he made the announcement. "Let's go to Soho; we've got so much to talk about!"

Soho? Was he so sophisticated? It used to be Lyons. And weren't Soho meals expensive? Perhaps Sydney had been right about the legacy.

He led the way to the main exit, and as they left the long gallery she put her gloved hand on his arm. He stole a cautious glance at her as they descended the steps, noting that her face was not quite as full as it had once been, but that her lashes were just as long, and her complexion still had the freshness and bloom of rose-petals.

In Parliament Square she had another slight shock. He hailed a taxi, and gave the name of a good restaurant in Old Compton Street. He handed her in, and when he sat down beside her she let her hand remain for a moment on his wrist, and then gently withdrew it. She was a far better tactician than Tom Tappertitt.

She was amazed by his apparent familiarity with the Soho menu. He seemed to speak French quite fluently, and, moreover, the head waiter recognised him, and came across, bowing.

"Sir ... madame ... will you have something to drink now?"

She watched him, smiling with pleasure, while he ordered sherry and the meal. As he discussed various dishes with the waiter he kept looking across at her, and each time she met his eye she tried to convey her admiration.

It was not a difficult thing to do. She was already beginning to suspect that she had made insufficient allowance for the passing years.

Yet, in his approach to her he remained shy, and she had to feel her way carefully. The one sure path was flattery.

"I can't get over it, Esme ... you're so different ... so sort of relaxed and experienced. I think I'm the tiniest bit frightened of you! Do you come to places like this very often?"

"Most of the work in my line of business is done in places like this, over meals," he told her.

"But what exactly *is* your line of business? Sydney didn't seem to know."

"I work for a newspaper, a Scottish newspaper, but I don't

exactly write for it; it's more of an office job, seeing people about advertisements and things."

"But Sydney said you wrote for the radio."

"Yes, I do, but that's nothing to do with my job. I write half-hour features for the Empire programmes, most historical stuff . . . you remember, like some of the stories I was always boring you with?"

"You didn't bore me!" She sounded almost indignant. "Why, some of them were very naughty stories!"

He laughed for the first time since they had met.

"I'll wager you can't remember any!"

"But I can. . . . I always liked that one about the widowed Queen who secretly married the Welsh soldier because he could dance, and who had all those children that everyone was so angry about!"

He was unreasonably delighted. "I say, but that's marvellous! Queen Katharine and Owen Tudor! I did that one a month ago, and picked up eighteen guineas for it. I shall get another nine if they repeat it!"

Twenty-seven guineas for a little play! Well, here was a promising source of pin-money!

She decided to risk further enquiries.

"But that's wonderful! Esme, you must be terribly clever! Sydney also said you only worked because you wanted to . . ."

"Sydney was talking out of the back of his head. My father left me a bit, but it's in trust, and I couldn't blue it if I wanted to! Still, it might come in handy one day, if things work out."

"What things, Esme?"

"Oh, I don't know. . . . I still want to write more than anything, and I've got some idea of living abroad when I do it."

"But you *are* writing . . . I mean . . . surely it's something to be writing for the BBC."

"It's a start, but I've found out so many things about writing since I was a kid, Elaine. It isn't just putting the stuff on paper, it's selling it, and for that you need contacts, a good agent, and a real knowledge of the market. You really shouldn't ever write anything until you've sold it first."

"But how on earth could you do that?"

"You get a commission and an advance. I've done a bit of that for newspapers, and it pays better than script-writing, but you have to have a new idea, and I'm not much good at ideas. I think I might be, if I travelled abroad. Everyone who's a success has done that."

"But surely . . ." she did not altogether approve of this overseas trend, reflecting that it might whisk him out of her reach . . . "surely, there must be heaps to write about in England . . . all the people you've met, places like this restaurant, and so on? Why, some of the places I've been . . ."

"Tell me about that, Elaine, tell me everything."

She told him, but by no means everything. She told him of her uneventful life as a hotel receptionist, and of the coming of the Great Eugene, and her ridiculous notion that life would be exciting on the stage. She told him a little of the variety circuits and how, when she despaired of getting anywhere, she had accepted the proposal of Benny Boy, and was silly enough to accompany him to the Continent on a promise of marriage.

"It may seem awful to you, Esme," she said, "but I was at the end of my tether after Eugene left me, and he seemed kind, and in a real position to help me. Then he went broke, and flew off home, and I had just enough money to get back. That was when I joined up with the circus!"

She made it sound as if she had suffered a great deal, but with dignity. She did not lie, but simply withheld portions of the truth, and was rather vague about dates, and the alternatives open to her during a succession of crises.

"Oh, I was a little fool all right!" she admitted readily, "but it isn't easy for a girl to keep going on her own, Esme. I suppose I believed everything Benny said simply because I wanted to, and because it was a way out. I didn't love him, of course, he was old enough to be my father, but he seemed more genuine than the people I toured with, and he did promise that we'd be married, as soon as he got his divorce. It wasn't until much later that I found out he'd been free all the time, and was divorced years before I met him."

He heard her in wonder and pity, grinding his teeth at the thought of the seedy Eugene, and the lascivious Benny Boy, who sounded like a cross between the wicked Levison, in his mother's well-thumbed *East Lynne,* and some scoundrel out of a Sunday newspaper feature.

"What happened to you in the circus?" he wanted to know.

"I don't want to talk about it," said Elaine, with truth. "I'll tell you sometime, but right now I've made up my mind to put it all behind me, and start afresh. That was why I wrote to you about the office job. I didn't know anyone else, and the employment agencies are hopeless."

He reflected for a moment, looking very serious indeed.

"Elaine dear," he said finally, "maybe this will shock you a bit but ... I've got to know something, I've got to know it right away."

"Yes, Esme?"

She could hardly believe that she was progressing at such a prodigious rate. It was still less than two hours since she had entered the gallery.

"I've got to know whether that was the only reason ... why you wrote, I mean. It may seem silly to you, but it happens to be terribly important to me."

She looked hard at the table-cloth. "I think you know the answer to that question, Esme," she said softly.

Her reply made his heart leap. "But I don't, Elaine ... it just isn't possible that you have felt the same way about me as I did about you all this time. This is something you've got to be absolutely honest about, not only honest with me, but with yourself! If you'd really cared you would have written at least once ... you'd have wanted to see me."

She raised her eyes, and he noticed how blue they were, as blue as the periwinkles that grew in Manor Wood. Her hair shone in the soft glow of the table lamp, and there was so much of it, even though it had been shorn since the night he had seen her glide from the back door of Number Seventeen, and pause for a moment in the path of moonlight, as he watched from the greenhouse at the end of her garden.

"Can't you understand that I was ashamed, Esme?"

Relief, and a great surge of possessive joy swept through him. He had thought, for a moment, that she was going to lie, if only to spare his feelings, that she would tell some unconvincing story about "not having appreciated his devotion until it was too late"—a speech straight from one of the true-story magazines she used to buy, something designed to explain away her ridiculous, novelettish entanglements with men like Eugene, and this old roué of an agent. Instead, here was the truth, freely and frankly admitted. She was ashamed, as any decently brought-up girl had a right to be ashamed of impulsive errors, and at long last she was accepting the role he had allotted her from the very beginning, that of a lady in a tower, awaiting rescue from dragons.

The wheel, incredibly, had swung full circle.

Instantly he began to extenuate for her.

"You made one initial mistake, and then got mixed up with a rotten crowd. That happens all the time, doesn't it? But at least you had the courage to make a break in the first place, and that's more than I did. I only pretended to, and kept coming back, wanting the safety and security of the Avenue, and a humdrum job to go with it! Suppose you had had some money behind you, even the little bit I had, you would have got somewhere, Elaine, but I'm glad you didn't, and I don't care how selfish that sounds, because I'm in love with you, and I've always been in love with you!"

He paused, trying to decide whether their present relationship could survive the final hurdle. Then he plunged on, determined to be done with all this hovering, done with it one way or the other.

"I don't just want to be standing around trying to get you a job, Elaine darling, I want you as much and more than I did in the old days. I want to look after you, and come home to you, and be with you all the time. I want us to go places together, and have fun together. I've never wanted anything else since the minute I set eyes on you, and the only mistake I ever made about you was to give up so easily, and leave all the deciding to you!"

Many, many times over the years Esme had rehearsed his proposal. He had begun phrasing it two or three days after the Stafford-Fyffe's dance, as long ago as 1930. Now it was 1938, and the world was slowly going mad, and people had already started digging air-raid shelters in their gardens, and old Mr. Forbes, his boss, was saying that this was a

Twilight of the Gods, and that everything would soon disappear in one vast cloud of cordite and brick-dust. But Esme did not care about these things any more, and the declaration tumbled from his lips without even a memory of the measured and stately sentiments of his oft-rehearsed proposal. He simply said what was in his heart, and what had been there, waiting to be said, for so long now that the very freshness of his utterance surprised him.

As for Elaine, for the second time that month she felt momentarily helpless, so much so that she all but lost her head. She had lived and moved among the Eugenes, the Benny Boys, and the Tappertitts, for so long now that it required an immense effort to adjust herself to a person like Esme, at once so astonishingly naïve, and so utterly sincere. She had remembered these aspects of him, of course, but had assumed that he would have outgrown them, that nobody in these days could remain so young, yet still be old enough to be yearning to kiss her.

Then a sense of reprieve shot out like a lifeline, and she clutched at it, frantically, and hauled herself back to reality, the changeless reality of three meals a day, money for good clothes, a soft bed at night, above all a base, and a breathing-space.

She reached across the table and caught his hand.

"Oh Esme, my dear, that's the most wonderful thing anyone's ever said to me, but you can't *know*, not like this, not so quickly. . . ."

For answer he stood up, and snapped his fingers at the waiter, who was hovering close to the street door, hoping against hope that the drivelling couple at No. 4 table would get up, and leave in time for him to get a bet on the three o'clock at Sandown. He hurried over, scribbling as he ran, and allowed his worried features to slip back into their habitual, rubbery smile.

"Thank you, sir! Delighted to see you again, sir! There was no coat was there, sir?"

"No," said Esme, "no coat," and to Elaine, "Let's go out to Hampton Court, and then come back here to celebrate with a show."

They moved out into the fruity smells and the sunshine,

and this time it was Esme who took her arm. Neither said anything until they reached Windmill Street, and then Esme suddenly excused himself, and skipped into a florist's, emerging a few moments later with an armful of yellow roses and pink and white carnations.

Then Elaine remembered that Hampton Court was a long way off, and that it was time that she did something as positive. So she leaned over the flowers as he thrust them towards her, and kissed him softly on the mouth.

An elderly prostitute, lazily swinging her bag, and enjoying the sunshine from a shuttered shop doorway, looked on with mild interest, and a street-vendor, in the act of rebuilding a pyramid of pears, paused to exclaim: "Say it wi' flahers, mate, say it wi' flahers," and winked in the direction of the prostitute.

Esme did not even see them, he was shouting at a passing taxi. It braked, and they climbed in, Elaine grasping the flowers.

"I must take these to the hotel first, Esme—it's the Leicester Court, just off Sloane Square."

"I know it," said the driver, and reached out to slam the door.

Once the taxi was moving Elaine laid down the flowers, and turned to him, wordlessly, but he was swifter even than she, and had already buried his lips in her hair.

2

Esme and Elaine were married on the first day of October, in the same registrar's office as that used by Louise and Jack Strawbridge, but the Avenue was not as well represented as on the former occasion. There were only three witnesses, Harold, Eunice, and Elaine's father, who was eventually summoned by Esme after opposition from Elaine.

He failed in his half-hearted attempt to persuade her to relent in respect of her mother and Sydney, but regarding Edgar, who had been kind and hospitable to him when he had called on him in Wales during his travels, Esme was insistent. It seemed to him a shabby trick to let the little man hear of the wedding of his only daughter from outside sources.

The preliminaries as a whole were not without their stresses. Eunice badly wanted a church wedding, however small, and Harold privately disapproved of what he described to Esme as "the rather indecent haste of it all, old man."

Esme's announcement, and his swift introduction of Elaine into Number Twenty-Two, was a shock to his mother and stepfather. Had he been a year or two younger, or less independent financially, they would probably have opposed the marriage tooth and nail, and this in spite of Elaine's extremely tactful handling of Harold.

Harold had by no means forgotten his long, midnight talk with Esme, on the subject of the bride, but although conventional in most respects Harold always loosened up a little when asked to pronounce upon the subject of love. His experiences as a solicitor had taught him the fatuity of looking for a logical reason in a particular man's desire to share life and income with a particular woman. He himself had been cosy enough in bachelor lodgings, and had been quite satisfied with life until Eunice had turned her china-blue eyes on him, and whispered: "But you have got such a *grasp* of things, Mr. Godbeer!" After that he had had no peace until they were married. He had little enough peace now, for when Eunice wasn't chattering she was usually badgering him to do some little job about the house. For all that he would never have returned voluntarily to bachelor lodgings, and he had never ceased to be proud of Eunice, particularly when he took her "Up West", and watched men far younger than himself turn their heads and note her prettiness.

Like a good many mild-mannered, conventional men, who have entered upon their forties with wild oats unsown, Harold was still very susceptible to a pretty face and a good figure, and Elaine, recognising this at a glance, soon overcame his initial opposition to an immediate wedding.

"After all," he told Eunice, when she wept intermittently on the night that Esme had come home with his news, "the boy's twenty-six, and he's been in love with the girl ever since he was an adolescent."

"How can you possibly *know* that, Harold?" she wailed,

brushing away at her soft hair, as she sat before the dressing-table mirror.

"I know it," Harold had replied, with pardonable smugness, "because Esme confided in me from the very first! I told you I'd be a father to the boy, and I have! He trusts me. He's always trusted me."

"But you never even *whispered* it to me," complained Eunice, laying down her silver-backed brush, and turning to him where he lay, his peaked face just showing above the sheets.

"There are occasions, my dear," he replied, "when matters between father and son must be regarded as strictly confidential, even to the exclusion of mothers! Esme has been faithful in essence, for many years, and it is now quite obvious that having had what it usually termed a "fling", this girl has brought herself to recognise the full merit of such fidelity."

"I simply don't understand you when you talk in that solicitor's way," grumbled Eunice. "I never have, and I believe that's why you do it! Why can't you say what you want to say in ordinary English?"

Harold sighed. Sometimes Eunice could be agonisingly stupid, and he was always more prone to notice it when he was sleepy, as now.

"I simply mean, my dear, that he's very much in love with her, and I think she has now appreciated the fact. I don't know how I can simplify it further, but I do wish you would turn out the light and get into bed!"

Within a matter of days, however, Eunice was reconciled to the loss of Esme, although by no means approving of the manner in which the wedding was to be carried out. She wanted a party, with everybody in smart, new clothes, and floppy hats, with plenty of champagne, and silly speeches, and a photographer to take group pictures in the garden. It is possible that, under other circumstances, Elaine might have accommodated her in this respect, but Esther lived just across the road, and, regarding her mother, Elaine was implacable. She therefore fell in readily with Esme's proposal for a register-office ceremony. Eunice made no attempt to conceal her disappointment.

"It's so . . . so *shabby*," she complained, "and it's only once

in a lifetime. I think you *owe* it to yourselves to have
something to remember. There's no need to make it a big
wedding, and you can go to the church early in the morning,
but for heaven's sake let's have *something*—not just a ... a
... '*bus-ride* into Croydon, and a lot of forms to fill in."

Harold again came to the young couple's rescue.

"It isn't quite so simple as that, my dear," he reasoned.
"Elaine was very unhappy with her mother, Eunice," and
turning to Elaine, "so unhappy that you ran away, didn't
you, my dear?"

"Yes, I did, Uncle Harold," said Elaine, contriving to look
as though, prior to her escape, Esther had kept her locked in
an attic, and had only disturbed her solitude at regular
intervals, with rations of bread, water, and birch-rod.

"There, you see," went on Harold persuasively, "it
wouldn't be very nice for Elaine to have to invite her mother, and of course she would have to invite her if the ceremony was public and we had any sort of reception here afterwards. I don't mind telling you, my dear, I've had some
professional experience with Elaine's mother, and under such
circumstances she might prove a difficult woman!"

So all was arranged to the general satisfaction, and even
the opposition from Eunice began to lessen under the stimu-
lus of a gigantic shopping spree, carried out along the entire
length of the Croydon High Street.

This expedition, or series of expeditions, began with the
avowed object of buying Eunice's wedding costume and Esme's present, but it ended in Eunice buying an entire house-
ful of new furniture and household fittings, down to the
shoe-scraper for the back door, a set of "humane" mouse-
traps, and the rustless, metal toilet-roll holder.

Elaine accompanied her prospective mother-in-law on the
first two of these expeditions, but subsequently excused herself, and went off to the pictures. When Eunice once entered
a large shop there was no knowing when she would emerge,
and it did not take Elaine very long to discover that she
herself had no instinct for home-making, whereas she thought
it best to conceal her boredom under a modest avowal that
"Eunice would make Esme's money go so much further."

Indeed, when it came to the point, neither Esme nor

Elaine had much to do with the setting up of their new home. This was not far distant—just across the road in fact, for Harold had persuaded Esme to buy Number Forty-Three, partly because it was going very cheap (Mr. Thorburne, the previous occupant, had just been declared a bankrupt), and partly as a concession to Eunice.

Esme himself had no wish to move away from the Avenue. Since returning to the suburb, after his cheerless wanderings up and down the country, he had recaptured some of the enchantment it had held for him in childhood. It gave him pleasure now to think that his "study" window, at the back, looked out on an uninterrupted view of the meadow and his beloved Manor Wood.

He had been very doubtful at first whether Elaine would agree to begin her married life so near to her mother and Sydney, and had expected considerable opposition to the proposal. In the event he encountered none. Elaine thought the house "very nice", and confessed that she was only too happy to be within such close call of Uncle Harold and Eunice. She called her "Eunice" now, having remarked, during one of their later meetings, "I can't very well call you 'Mum', or 'Mother', can I? You look too much like my little sister!"

This naturally delighted Harold, and it was "Eunice" from then on.

It was no wonder that Esme walked about in a trance these days! Had he had his wits about him he might have thought that Elaine's willingness to leave the entire planning of Number Forty-Three to her mother-in-law was a little strange in an ardent bride-to-be, but Esme was now infinitely removed from a state of mind where he could contemplate curtain-runners and kitchen linoleum, and even further removed from the somewhat weightier matters then engaging Mr. Chamberlain's attention at Berchtesgaden and Bad Godesberg. He drifted about, to and from his office, and in and out of Numbers Twenty-Two and Forty-Three, like a young saint anticipating swift transition to Paradise, and he only emerged from his daydream, and then but briefly, when he and Elaine were alone.

He had never imagined that dreams could be so quickly

and unexpectedly translated into ecstatic realities. Where Elaine had once been pert and mocking, she was now gentle and pliant. Instead of having to speculate on her mood, as in the days when she had stolen out of Number Seventeen to meet him at some prearranged place in the Lane or "Rec", he could now rely, with complete certainty, on laughing affability and impulsive embraces. At all times, and to all three of them, she was soft-spoken and dutiful, and to him, when they were alone, she was either tender or rapturous, according to the place where they happened to be. Sometimes, when he was holding her, he thought his heart would burst, and because he was bewitched he had no difficulty at all in reconciling the Elaine that was with the Elaine of the present, happily writing off the transformation as a by-product of her unhappy past, an exchange of uncertainty for security. For even now he could not really believe that she was in love with him as he understood love; but nonetheless felt that he could await the future with confidence.

He was probably about halfway towards the truth. For the moment, for a year or so at least, Elaine had had more than enough of insecurity. She had turned her back on the circus to look for a base. Miraculously she had found one almost at once, one that promised to be warm, cosy, and securely entrenched against the disasters that had overtaken her with Benny Boy and Tom Tappertitt. She was certainly not in love with Esme, nor ever likely to be, but his adoration pleased her, as it had always done, and gave her confidence in the future.

In her touring days she had never looked ahead for more than a week or two ". . . sufficient unto the day are the bookings thereof", Eugene used to say, and the liquidation of Benny Boy, and all he stood for, had been so sudden that all her powers of concentration were centred on providing for existence, without returning to Esther, or to the boredom of a nine-till-six occupation.

It was the sudden eruption of Audrey the Amazon, and the contemplation of her own utter loneliness when the circus party had left her standing in the rain, that brought her so sharply up against the facts as she now saw them. It seemed to her now that a woman could choose between a humdrum job, the capture of a man with money, or the compromise of a marriage such as the one she was about to make with Esme Fraser. The first alternative, a job like the one she had at The Falconer, was not to be thought of, for there was certainly no future in that. The second, a limited liability partnership, with an older man like Benny Boy, or Tom, was all very well in its way, but one could never be sure how and when it would end, leaving one penniless in a strange country, or face down on a hotel bed, having one's bottom tanned by an irate wife. Of course, few wives would be likely to possess Audrey's weight of muscle, but there were plenty of other forms of retaliation—divorce courts, damages for entice-ment, blackmail, and heaven knew what else. Even if she steered a course between these hazards, what could protect her from the whims of these experienced philanderers, who might pack their bags and be off at a moment's notice, leaving her to pay the hotel bill, as Eugene had done on at least two occasions.

There could be no doubt about it, marriage to a man who adored her was the safest bet, particularly when he was not nearly so short of money as most of the young men in the Avenue. Esme, she could manage, now and always. He was absurdly uncomplicated, at least as regards herself, and it was an additional stroke of luck that his mother and stepfather were equally manageable, and only too eager to shoulder the tiresome domestic responsibilities that seemed to attend this sort of compromise.

She would stay put for a year or so, and take careful stock of all the available possibilities. She knew the ground round here and, with all this war talk in the papers, who could say what fields might be opening up ahead?

Yet, for all that, Elaine was not wholly bogus. She was willing, up to a point, to give something in return for the tenancy of Number Forty-Three, and the respite it offered. Not lifelong fidelity, not wifely devotion as it was generally understood in the Avenue, but at any rate a strong, physical manifestation of gratitude, which was all that Esme was really interested in at the moment, notwithstanding his arm-fuls of flowers and pretty little avowals.

She would give him, she told herself, slightly more than his moneysworth for the time being, but how long she would continue to give it she was not prepared to promise, certainly not till death did them part. If, in the not-too-distant future, he could provide the terrace, and the hammock, and the courtiers, the sports car, and the clothes to go with them, then perhaps she might even be willing to continue giving him his moneysworth indefinitely.

In the meantime there were to be no children.

They were married at 10 a.m., and afterwards Harold, Eunice, and Edgar travelled to Victoria to see them off on the Golden Arrow, for their ten-day honeymoon in Paris.

Esme's guess had been a good one. Elaine had always wanted to honeymoon in Paris, for somehow Paris went along with terraces, hammocks, courtiers, sports cars, and advertisements in *Vogue*. Benny Boy, doubtless for reasons of his own, had by-passed Paris when they had driven across the Continent to Biarritz, and Esme, whose foreign travel was limited to a week in Ostend, and two steamer-trips to Dieppe, and the Channel Islands, was delighted with the idea. He had always looked forward to visiting Napoleon's tomb, the Louvre, the Conciergerie, and Montmartre, by night.

Edgar had been very generous to them and had given them fifty pounds, as well as a serpentine chest, said to be worth at least another fifty, "and more if you hang on to it, my boy." He had wrung Esme's hand with great feeling when the guard began to wave his flag, and Eunice had started to cry again, to be firmly patted by Harold, himself in a very emotional state.

Then their three wellwishers were out of sight, and Esme and Elaine were sitting beside one another at the table as the train rattled over points beyond Croydon. From the windows they fancied they could see the blurr of the wooded country south-east of the Avenue, but today the crescent was very remote from their world, and Esme said:

"I wish we'd had confetti. I'd like everyone on the train to know we're on our honeymoon, and that you really belong to me now, Elaine."

And Elaine had made a bewitching little grimace with her

red, red mouth, and replied, as she drew off her long, tan gloves:

"I don't think anyone on the train will have the slightest doubt about us, darling," and just to make sure had reached up, taken his face in her hands, and kissed him softly on the tip of his nose.

3

They had booked, through an Agency, at a hotel in the Avenue des Capuchins.

In the morning Elaine was the first to wake, and she lay still for a few moments, listening to the street noises, and wondering how Esme could continue to sleep through the defiant blare of horns and the agonising squeal of brakes.

As her eyes travelled slowly round the room, noting the old-fashioned brass bedstead, the wash-basin with the perished stopper, the heavy ormulu dressing-chest, and the print of Notre Dame in its heavy oak frame, they finally came to rest on Esme, lying on his back, his hair tousled, his breathing deep and regular.

She turned gently on her elbow, and regarded him objectively. He was, she decided, not bad-looking, with his short, straight nose, his small girlish mouth, and obstinate chin, that did not seem to belong to him, but to someone of far more determined character.

Apart from the chin he was very much like his mother, small-featured, and finely made. The chin, she thought, must have come from his father, the kilted officer, killed in the war, whose photograph still stood in the front-room of Number Twenty-Two, or perhaps from the grandmother, whose photograph stood on Eunice's what-not in the back room.

She wondered, still looking down on him, what he would think about it all this morning, and whether his recollections would be sufficiently clear to realise that he had had the benefit of her not inconsiderable experience. If they were then he would be very unlikely to comment on the matter. One of Esme's advantages, she decided, was that he would never probe her past. They had made a bargain about that, only a day or two after they had met in the Tate. She had been reasonably frank with him, a good deal more frank, she felt, than most prospective brides would have been, and now, if he did suffer on that account, he would have to suffer in silence. After all, he was good at suffering in silence, having done so, it seemed, ever since the night they had met at the Stafford-Fyffe's ball.

Remembering him there, in his prim little dinner-jacket, and recalling his pathetic eagerness to benefit by her earlier lesson, the lesson in dancing the Charleston, she felt genuine affection for him. He seemed so young, surely not one year, but twenty years younger than herself. Nevertheless, it was nice to be coveted, to the extent that he coveted her.

She leaned forward an inch or so, and let her heavy curls brush across his face. He stirred, and opened his eyes, looking straight up into hers, and even before sleep had faded from them a great light of happiness shone in his face.

"*Well?*" she said, with a teasing laugh.

He stretched, and then turned suddenly, catching up a handful of her hair, and stroking it very gently before press-. ing it to his lips.

"Have you been awake long?" he asked.

"Ages! Listen to those hooters! It must be wonderful to be able to sleep through that uproar."

"I was tired. You should know!" and he grinned, like the schoolboy he seemed.

"What's the time?" he wanted to know.

"It doesn't matter what time it is. We're on a honeymoon. You never wind clocks when you go on a honeymoon!"

He sat up, laughing, loosing her hair, and pulling her close to him.

"I love you, Elaine, more than anyone ever loved anyone, and more than you'll ever know! Marrying you is the most wonderful thing that ever happened to me, and if it all finished today I'd go on thinking the same about it, and about you. Do you believe that?"

She smiled, and slowly traced a finger-tip down the length of his face.

"It won't end today, Esme. Tomorrow, or the day after perhaps, but not today. This I promise."

He laughed again, and held her very close, rocking her

slightly, so that her curls fell away, and piled up on the pillow.

Below the tall windows the hooters honked and honked, reminding him of startled pheasants in the Manor Wood when they soared up from the bracken beside the path, squawking their raucous *Kark! Kark! Kark!*

It was strange, he thought, that they had never yet walked in Manor Wood together. In the Lane, in the copses, in the "Rec", and all over the West End, but never in the Wood, *his* wood. Well, that could be remedied now perhaps.

CHAPTER XXX

Carver Roundabout. III

1

CHRISTMAS WEEK, 1939. The decade had just over a week to run, and along the Avenue, a crescent at war yet not at war, the families waited and wondered.

The first snow had fallen, a heavy fall for the time of year. The drifts had piled up under the dwarf walls; and the open sky, between the backs of the odd numbers and the Manor Wood, was slate-grey with the certainty of more snow. The front gardens in the crescent looked pinched, and even smaller than usual, beyond their rows of looped chains, and at night the entire sweep of the Avenue was still and lifeless behind makeshift blackouts.

Only at Number Four, where Becky either could not or would not understand about the blackout, did an occasional beam of light flash from the porch-room, a beam strong enough to encourage Grandpa Barnmeade, of Number One Hundred and Two, to scurry along the pavement in his capacity as Air-raid Warden, and scream: *"Light! Light! Put out that light!"*, as though German aircraft were already hovering over the Avenue, awaiting Becky's signal to loose their avalanche of bombs.

Yet no bombs had fallen, despite Becky's carelessness. The Avenue was still intact, although many of its inhabitants were already scattered far and wide, a few never to return.

Christmas 1939, the last Christmas of the 'thirties, and here was Europe at war again. Nobody could really believe it, for there were more than a hundred people still living in the Avenue who could remember the Christmas of 1914, with its terrifying casualty lists, its marching songs, and saucy slogans. This present business was neither the war they remembered, nor the war they had expected. There were no casualty lists, and no air-raids, which was odd when one remembered how often the politicians had promised them death in generous measure, should war break out despite Mr. Chamberlain's efforts.

There had been that first terrifying warning, within minutes of the Prime Minister's solemn declaration on the radio. Nobody in the Avenue possessed a real shelter, so that on the first wailing note of the siren they had scrambled beneath tables, and into cupboards under the stairs. Only Mr. Baskerville, of Number Eighty-Four (he of the 1926 four-valve set, who always went one better than anyone else in the Avenue) had been able to shepherd his family into a "bomb-proof" shelter, at the bottom of his garden. There the Baskervilles had crouched, all six of them, praising father for his foresight and his energetic Saturday afternoons, until they heard wheeled traffic passing up and down the crescent. They had crept out, feeling rather foolish, as Mrs. Jarvis, of Eighty-Six, poked her turbanned head over the fence, and shouted:

"It's a false alarm! Mr. Harrison 'phoned from the Post, ten minutes ago!"

Some of the outward trappings of war could be seen in and around the suburb. There were plenty of posters, urging the Avenue to save, to dig, and, above all, to keep the closest possible counsel about troop movements and any military plans they found lying about. There were plenty of tin-hats to be seen. Grandpa Barnmeade had one, and almost everybody carried a little cardboard box, slung with string, containing a respirator. Grandpa Barnmeade did not have one of these, but strode about with a much more military-looking appliance that fitted into a khaki-coloured haversack. He also wore an armband, such as the Specials had worn during the General Strike, and he carried a torch almost as big as a mace.

There were fewer children about the Avenue. The two younger Carvers, Archie's children, had accompanied their mother down into Somerset, and several other young families had disappeared in groups into the remoter provinces, with identity labels pinned to their jackets and blouses. Other children had departed, more decorously, with a parent, or parents, just as though they were setting off for a holiday to the seaside.

Apart from these superficial changes, however, the Avenue was outwardly much the same. The menfolk, or by far the greater number of them, still hurried along towards Shirley Rise, to catch the eight-ten, and the eight forty-five at Woodside. The women still went down to the Lower Road to shop, but took rather longer to fill their string bags and baskets, and often shopped further afield, sometimes as far as High Street, Croydon. At eight, one, six, and nine o'clock they listened, half-heatedly, to the news bulletins, but these provided little or no war news to gossip about over the fences. There was only the sinking of the *Graf Spee* (a typical German scuttle), and the capture of the *Altmark*, with its vaguely comforting battle-cry of "The Navy's here!"

Nothing else had happened, or seemed likely to happen. The French were snug in their Maginot Line, and everyone in the Avenue had been told it was quite impregnable. The British Expeditionary Force had apparently settled down in the same villages as their fathers had occupied, when people were singing *Mademoiselle from Armentieres*, and *Hold Your Hand Out, Naughty Boy*. People talked of their sons being "somewhere in France", just as they had done in 1914. The people in the Avenue imagined they were all sitting it out in trenches and dugouts, waiting, like everyone eles at home, for someone to call off this ridiculous war that wasn't a war, or alternatively, to get busy, and put that idiotic little house-painter in his place, and stop him, once and for all, from being such a monumental bore.

The only real inconvenience the Avenue had suffered so far arose from the blackout, against which people were already beginning to murmur. The great, floppy frames, and the depressing curtains, were difficult to make, yet easy to overlook. One either had to fit them in every room in the house, or resign oneself to groping about in the gloom, barking shins, and smashing ornaments whenever there was occasion to move out of the back room or the kitchen.

As for Grandpa Barnmeade, someone must have waved a wand over him, for he changed overnight from a garrulous, old dodderer into a pettifogging, old tyrant, and was forever hammering at their front doors and theatening them with long terms of imprisonment. Some of the least charitable in the Avenue were beginning to wish that Hitler would drop at least one bomb, just a little one, powerful enough to eliminate Grandpa Barnmeade, together with his torch, armband, and respirator. It would be, they reasoned, a happy release, for surely the old fool could not last out the severe winter, trotting up and down at his age, climbing on to porches, and up trellisses, in order to smash windows and unmasked light-bulbs?

Christmas came and went, almost unnoticed in a general atmosphere of acute boredom and petty irritation. There were no Christmas trees in the front-room windows. Grandpa Barnmeade saw to that. There were no carol parties of children, to sing one verse of *Good King Wenceslas*, before ringing the bell and demanding money. There was nothing, nothing at all, beyond a sense of bewilderment and disappointment.

The Avenue hunched over its radio sets on Christmas Day, and heard news that was not news, and recordings of carols, and the King's slowly articulated speech.

The decade ended in a kind of universal yawn.

2

Of the men still residing in the Avenue in December, 1939, two at least had no occasion to share the many-mouthed yawn. One was too busy, and the other was too worried.

The months since Munich had been frantically busy ones

for Archie Carver, a period of consolidation, staff reorganisation, and relentless buying.

He worked, on an average, sixteen hours a day. There was so much to do, and so little time to do it. If war really was on the way, not only his stockrooms needed attention, he had to look both to premises and personnel, especially personnel.

He remembered, towards the end of the last war, that men of forty had been called up, and it was, therefore, not impossible that he himself, with his thirty-eighth birthday just behind him, might be gathered into the fold, if not as a soldier, then in some sort of civilian capacity. Perhaps, he reflected, it would be as well to put oneself down for something now, when there was still an element of choice open to volunteers, and on the day Maria had shouted down the stairs that Hitler had invaded Poland, and war was said to be certain, he was on the point of enlisting as a part-time ARP worker, or a Special.

It was Mr. Brockett, a knowing traveller from a wholesale firm, who prevented him from committing this folly, for Brockett had studied the situation very carefully, and because Archie was a good customer he was willing to give him the benefit of his enquiries.

"Don't do a thing, old man," Brockett cautioned him. "I've had inside information on this, and the thing to do is to lie doggo! You're in food aren't you, and someone's got to stay behind the counter. If you're thirty-eight now, and in a key position handling food, then you're sitting pretty, take it from me. Slap your name on some list, and you'll have a lot of trouble talking yourself out of it when something does happen. Now how about pilchards? There's bound to be a run on pilchards . . . !"

So Archie did not volunteer, and soon had occasion to be grateful to Brockett, for the discussion encouraged him to look into the age-groups of the people he employed, and to replace every man younger than himself with a woman over forty. Thus the outbreak of war found him with eleven branch managers, eight of whom were women, and a dozen or so fourteen-year-old boys, all of whom had been hand-picked by Archie from the local Council Schools.

Here again Archie showed good sense. He not only hand-picked the boys, after talks with their Headmasters, but he followed up the engagement of each one of them with a visit to the lad's parents. The object of this was to forestall mothers and fathers who might persuade their offspring to exchange the grocery trade for something more lucrative, or more spectacular. Labour, he told himself, was soon going to be as short as food, and he did not want his trained personnel giving him notice in the middle of a war.

He made each visit a quasi-avuncular occasion, taking the parents into his confidence, and giving them to understand that they had, all unknowingly, produced a future Thomas Lipton.

"You've got a good boy there, Mrs. Dutton," he would say to a flattered woman, on one of the Council estates that adjoined his premises; "a remarkably good boy in many ways, and I shall make it my business to watch him very carefully, with a view to his future, and mine!"

Having studied the effect of this introduction, he would continue: "I started in the grocery trade at about his age, and he reminds me of myself—willing, keen, and full of initiative! He's not simply using this job as a stop-gap, like most of them these days, so don't run away with the idea that I'm going to pay your lad an errand-boy's wage, Mrs. Dutton. That won't encourage him very much, and it's not fair to you! He'll go on to a qualified counterhand's rate in six months and, believe you me, he'll *get* somewhere; you see if he doesn't!"

He would usually stay and have a cup of tea with the mother, and he always saved a parting shot for the doorstep.

"There's one other thing, Mrs. Dutton! Times aren't any too good, are they, and it might pay to have a lad in the grocery trade if it comes to war! Well, nice to have met you, Mrs. Dutton, and my advice is keep young Arthur hard at it, no matter what else comes up."

These visits proved extremely fruitful in the strenuous days ahead, and Archie must have somehow convinced the boys themselves that they were on the way to becoming Liptons and Sainsburys, for not one of them left him for better-paid war work, and only one, Johnny Lewins, anticipated his call-up by volunteering for service with the Armed Forces. Lewins went down with the *Hood* in 1941, and Archie could not help feeling that it served him right.

The mass evacuation from the suburbs, in early September, was a means of solving yet another of Archie's problems. It presented him with a wide choice of empty premises, three of which he immediately bought, thus adding three more links to the chain. Others he was able to rent for storage purposes.

When war came he had bought so heavily that he had an overdraft at the bank, and he had also drawn extensively on his floating reserve in the oil-drums. But Archie never thought in sixpences, and shortage of ready cash did not bother him in the least. He was now stripped for action, with fourteen branches, each staffed by employees too old, or too young, to be called up, and with sufficient stocks to garrison a small town for a long siege. Hitler, he thought, could now do his worst, and if Archie yawned with the rest of the Avenue during the dragging months of the phoney war, it was not because he was bored but because he was tired. After all, he began work at six a.m., and seldom went to bed before midnight.

Maria, his wife, saw even less of him than usual these days. He had no time at all for family life, and since the Gloria Hazelwood episode, his private life had been cut to the barest minimum. When evacuation began he sent Maria and the two younger children to Somerset, finding them a cottage not far from the district where Tony, his elder boy, was at school. He had a woman in to clean the house over the corner shop and to prepare such meals as he had time to gobble, but he saw to it that his daily was a widow on the safer side of sixty, thus proving that even Gloria's ninety-seven pounds had been an investment.

3

Jim Carver was no longer yard-manager for Jacob Sokol-ski, the wholesale furrier of Bond Street, for Jacob had gone, more than a year before, and his firm closed down in October 1939, putting Jim out of work once again.

At this time, however, there was no sting in the word "unemployment", and one hardly ever heard the word "dole". There were so many jobs for men over forty that Jim could have found plenty of steady work within five minutes of the Avenue. He would even have been welcomed by his former employees, Burtol and Twyford, the removers in the Lower Road, but Jim did not care about starting all over again, on the brink of sixty. He was now better off than he had ever been, for he had his savings, plus a recently matured life-insurance, but this did not add up to retirement.

He had not been caught unawares by the closing down of Sokolski's, being one of the few people in the Avenue who had made an intelligent assessment of the situation from Munich onwards. Perhaps this had some connection with all the pamphlets he had read, or perhaps it was because he had once fought in the field against Germans. At all events, Jim did not regard Hitler and his cohorts as a bad joke, but as dangerous lunatics, capable, likely indeed, to bring the whole of Western civilisation crashing down whenever they felt so disposed, and therefore, the actual declaration of war brought him a certain amount of relief. His relief, however, proved momentary, for even now, with armies in the field, it did not look to him as if Fascism was being seriously challenged, and he had an uncomfortable suspicion that the "Old Gang" at Westminster were "up to something or other".

It had given him no satisfaction at all to see his prophecies regarding the fate of Czechoslovakia fulfilled to the letter, and that within six months of Munich. Throughout that final summer of peace he campaigned furiously for an alliance with Soviet Russia, as the one certain hope of national survival.

When, in August, the Russo-German Pact was trumpeted across the world, he almost despaired, and the actual declaration of war came as an anticlimax. What frightened him more than any one factor was the apathy of the Avenue as a whole. He found it very difficult to believe that sane men and women, people with access to the same sources of information as himself, could hunch their shoulders against the storm, and continue to plod to and from their work, and up and down their back-gardens behind lawn-mowers during the week-ends, without showing more than a casual interest in the situation.

He did not expect to witness a repetition of the 1914 fervour, with hysterical crowds howling for war (as later they howled for peace) outside Buckingham Palace, and in a way he was glad about this, for at least it proved that the Avenue had learned something from the past.

Something, but what? The power of German might? No, by God! Even in committee his colleagues were still drooling about cardboard tanks, and Luftwaffe paper squadrons. The strength of the Maginot Line possibly? But how long could France defend itself against Fascism, when it already had its own concentration camps for fugitive Spanish patriots in the South? The crass idiocy of war as a means of settling disputes then? Perhaps, but what good was that, when one was facing a bunch of neurotic gangsters?

He sat in the kitchen of Number Twenty biting his nails, as the long weeks dragged by, and at last he could stand it no longer, and marched round to a recruiting office, to sign on with his old regiment. A bored young regular sat doodling at a small card-table and when Jim stated his purpose the N.C.O. laughed in his face.

"You? How old are you, dad?"

"Forty-one!' lied Jim, wishing heartily that he could knock the cigarette stub from the man's mouth.

The man sniggered. "Well, let's say that you are ... er ... forty-one, *and* an ex-sergeant, with bow-and-arrow experience! Take a look out there, Dad!"

He pointed through the grimy window into an alley that ran alongside the office. Jim looked, and saw a stationary queue of young men. The queue was more than a hundred yards long.

"They're not forty-one, are they, Dad? But not one of 'em'll get taken on today, nor tomorrow either."

Jim passed a hand over his freshly-shaven chin.

"Then what the hell is the idea, man?" he demanded. "You've got a notice chalked up outside, and it says '*Drivers*

Urgently Wanted'. If you can't take any more on why don't you scrub the notice?"

The Sergeant half-rose from his broken-backed chair, and regarded Jim with an expression of dismay.

"Scrub the notice?" he echoed. "Scrub the bloody notice? And you an ex-sergeant, telling me to do that? Listen, cock, I'm here to obey orders, aren't'I? I was instructed to put that notice up, and so far I haven't been instructed to take the bloody thing down again. So don't throw your weight about in here, trying to teach me my job, Dad!"

Jim gave it up. It seemed to him that he was living in a vast lunatic asylum, but before he started for home he had a word with two or three of the young men at the head of the queue, and was afterwards glad he had done so, for their conversation cheered him a little.

"It's the same everywhere," one fresh-faced youngster complained. "Wait for the call-up, they say, but I got a pal of nineteen, who's had his papers seven weeks, and he hasn't heard a word since! What's it all in aid of? That's what I'd like to know. There's all these posters about—join this, join that, and when you show up all that happens is that you get your arse kicked, don't you, Charlie?"

Charlie, the young man beside him corroborated.

"Yerse, you do that. Take me, I been turfed out of four recruiting offices a'ready."

"This looks like being your fifth, son," said Jim, "but all the same I like your spirit. Just keep on trying."

"You know what they say," called the first boy, as Jim moved off, "we lose every battle but the last!"

Perhaps that was it, thought Jim, as he walked to the 'bus stop. Perhaps almost a thousand years of victory over all Continental armies had bred in the British a confidence that had become swollen to arrogance. Maybe Hitler was relying on that, and even more perhaps, on all the strident pacifist talk that had streamed across the Channel between the wars, and for which he himself must take part of the blame. For all that, he was sure that there was nothing basically wrong with the country. Those boys were keen enough; their fathers and uncles had once stood shoulder to shoulder with him in flooded ditches all the way from Switzerland to the sea, and had fought like lions, year after year. What they needed was direction, direction and inspiration from the top, but would they get it from Chamberlain and his gang? Did the people at the top really believe in this war?

He found a partial answer in the company of his old crony, Goreham, the former school inspector, whom he had met, and made a friend of, after the twins' escapade at Lucknow Road School in the early 'twenties. Like himself Goreham was a trench veteran, and a Socialist, who now found himself in a limbo of conflicting ideals.

"I don't know," said Goreham, as they discussed the news. "I imagine that little basket over the water will have to make the first move, and you can be dead sure he'll make it, as soon as the ground is dry enough for his tanks!"

"That's fine," argued Jim, "but suppose it's too late then? Damn it, man, we didn't sit about on our backsides, waiting for Jerry to move first in the old days, did we?"

Goreham chuckled. "Didn't we? How about the big breakthrough, in March '18? We knew he was transferring all his Eastern Front divisions to the West in front of Gough's mob, didn't we? And what did we do about it? I'll remind you, Jim: we put up a bit of bloody wire, and hoped for the best! No, Jim old man, there's nothing to do but wait, and the minute Jerry begins to make progress you might see a General Post over here. Might? I'll go further than that! You will! They won't even have time to put up the ruddy umbrella!"

"And who are we going to put in their place when that happens?" grumbled Jim. "Clem and Herbie Morrison couldn't handle it, could they?"

"Search me," said Goreham, "but I can promise you some rare scurrying around, once it looks like invasion."

"Invasion?" Jim's jaw dropped, "Lord, you don't think they'll get that far, do you?"

"Why not? Wouldn't you, once you'd bagged the Channel Ports?"

"But dammit, man, we've got the French, and the B.E.F. over there."

"So we have, so we have," said Goreham, "but we're going to need men over here too. So my advice to you, Jim—if you can't get stuck into a good book by the fire, that is—join one of the Auxiliary Services, and be sure of a front seat when it happens."

That week Jim took Goreham's advice, and joined the heavy rescue squad at the A.R.P. Centre. There was not much to do, but the conscientiousness that he brought to all his jobs soon recommended itself to his superiors and within weeks he was promoted, and taken on full-time.

If Goreham was right, Jim reflected, if Germany did break through in the Spring, then maybe he would be as useful here as anywhere. In the meantime, like the rest of the Avenue, he could only wait, and hope, and wonder what sort' of messages they were printing on the leaflets that the R.A.F. were forever dropping over the Rhineland. He knew what he would print on the leaflets: simple, a six-word message, reading "Just try it on, you bastard!", but something told him that the messages were probably couched in more diplomatic language.

They often saw him striding along the Avenue, as the frost held into the new year, a long, lean figure, with serious eyes, and large, swinging hands. Little Miss Baker, who had lived in the downstairs flat of Number One since 1915, and remembered him swinging along from Shirley Rise for the first time in the year of the great influenza epidemic that had carried off his wife, thought to herself how little he had changed in twenty years, and wondered whether he ever *would* marry that spinster at Number Four who seemed so attached to him.

The Avenue had been little Miss Baker's window on the world ever since she had been confined to a wheeled chair, with arthritis, a score of years ago, and she did not miss much that went on at her end of the crescent. That was why, in the summer before war broke out, she saw Judith Carver and a young man turn in from Shirley Rise, and walk the short distance to Number Twenty. Seeing Judy reminded Miss Baker of two inseparables long ago, a pair of whom this graceful girl was one, the other being young Esme Fraser, who had recently married the Frith girl.

Musing, Miss Baker wondered who this strange young man was, and if the Carver girl had heard about the Fraser wedding, which, to Miss Baker's intense disappointment, had been celebrated very quietly, so quietly indeed that there had been nothing to watch except the departure of a couple of taxis.

4

Judy had heard about the wedding by letter from Louise, and the news made her a little pensive, as she walked her hunter along the pinewood rides overlooking the Channel, at the head of her small cavalcade of chattering children.

Judy had lost touch with the Avenue years ago, and only came home at odd and widely-spaced intervals, to spend a week-end with Louise and her bull-necked husband, Jack.

Judy's dream of a semi-detached in the Wickham area had faded long ago, ironed out by new interests, in new localities, but not, until quite recently, by a new face. That was what had brought her home to Number Twenty again, in the summer of 1939, for she wanted to display Tim Ascham, the young man she intended to marry before he sailed for Kenya in the New Year.

Maud Somerton, her employer, had been quite right about the cure for love. The dream of Esme, and the semi-detached in Wickham, had survived a few months of tack-cleaning and pole-jumping at the riding school over beyond Keston, but it began losing ground rapidly once the Somerton stable moved into the West, and set up in business on the heathery plateau, between Exe and Otter. Then the tear-stained little girl, who had never so much as led a horse until that dismal afternoon when she met Maud beside the Roman Well, found a new dream, and began to study for her B.H.A., and enter gymkhanas that led on to hunter trials and county show-jumping events. A serious study of equitation, Miss Somerton had warned her, left little room in the mind for anything else, not even faithless lovers, and that was why it was so often prescribed by doctors as a cure for nervous disorders; the patient was so occupied with the business of keeping her seat that there was no opportunity to brood on anything else.

In general Judy found this to be the case, but her new occupation did much more for her than heal a bruised heart.

It provided her with a passport to a new world, that seemed a thousand miles from the suburb, a warm, hearty, open-air world, of sun, rain, and wind, of thrilling gallops across open country, and gentle jog-trots into the sunset, with every muscle aching, but pleasantly so, and the feeling of a day well spent in good company. Then, as darkness came, there was the prospect of boiled eggs, and an open hearth, and the comforting sound of tired horses, champing away in their loose-boxes across the yard.

On nights such as these, when she climbed the uncarpeted stairs to her little room, Judith sometimes did think of Esme, but she was able to smile at the solemn child of Number Twenty, whose life had been centred in the boy next door, yet who had, it seemed, cheerfully survived a broken heart.

She discovered too that Manor Wood was not the only wood where campion and cow-parsley grew, and where it was possible to smell the resin in the pines on lazy summer afternoons, or where the larches whispered like gossips in the evening breeze. Before her chance encounter with Maud Somerton, Judy had never been more than a few miles outside the suburb, but now she had travelled over wide stretches of English countryside, the Cotswolds, Cornwall, the West Midlands, and almost every part of Devon and Somerset.

She did not make friends easily, but she came to love the craggy, hoarse-voiced Miss Somerton. Maud Somerton loved her in return, and took pleasure in teaching her everything she knew, until there came a time, some five years after their association had begun, when the riding instructress led out a huge chestnut that she had bought (much to Judy's surprise) the previous day at the horse fair.

"There you are, me gel! See what you can make of this joker! He's all yours!"

"Mine?" exlaimed Judy, with wildly beating heart, "you mean . . . *my own?*"

"I always promised you something worth riding when you were good enough, didn't I?" Miss Somerton had replied, speaking even more harshly than usual, in order to conceal her emotion. "Well, you're as good now as I can ever make you, and you've worked harder than any gel I ever took in hand, so take him, and try him, and don't let me hear another word about it!"

Judy had to use the block to mount but, once up there, it was like sitting astride a warm, golden statue.

"What's he called?" called Judy breathlessly, as Miss Somerton released the bridle, and stood back against the wall.

"Jason," Miss Somerton shouted, "but if you don't like it change it. Take him across the Common, and I'll follow on, as soon as I've mucked out."

The chestnut moved beautifully, responding to the slightest movement of calf and finger, and once on the open common she gave him his head, and raced into the wind on huge, even strides, so that Judy felt she was flying, and would have ridden Jason to John-o'-Groats and back without drawing rein.

It was a glorious gallop, a glorious world, a glorious day. It was the day she was introduced to Jason, and the day she introduced herself to Tim.

Tim Ascham was a thin, lanky young man, with unruly, copper-coloured hair, a mass of freckles, and laughing eyes. That afternoon he was sitting on a low bank at the edge of Hayes Wood, and his horse, a fat, slow-munching skewbald, was cropping the long shoots a few yards away.

The young man stood up as Judy thundered into the mouth of the sunken lane, and called "Hi there!" as she sat back and wheeled, slowing to a trot, and bringing the chestnut smartly up alongside him.

"My, but you've got a beauty there," he said, reaching out to stroke Jason's sleek nose.

"It's my first time out on him," said Judy, smiling down. "Isn't it a wonderful day?"

"Any day would be wonderful from where you're sitting," he said. "Does he belong to the riding stables over at The Dene?"

"No," said Judy, unable to keep pride out of her voice, "he belongs to me! I'm Miss Somerton's assistant, and she's just given him to me."

The young man whistled. "Some boss!" he said, and then,

"I'm staying with the Applegates. I'm a sort of cousin to them."

Judy knew the Applegates, a rowdy, horsey family, who had recently moved south from the staghunting country round Dunkery Beacon. She looked at the young man with interest.

"Weren't you out with the hounds on Tuesday?" she asked.

"Yes, I was," he admitted ruefully. "but I got left behind, soon after you found. You killed over at Twelve Beeches, didn't you?"

"I believe so, but I was left behind too. I had someone on the leading rein. That's usually my trouble!"

They chatted about horses and hunting for a few minutes. Then Judy said:

"Aren't you going to ride?"

"Good Lord no," said Tim, jerking his head towards the skewbald, "nobody rides 'George'. He was at Waterloo, or Balaclava anyway! I'm just taking him for a quiet walk. Come on, George, old chap, we can't face this sort of competition," and he freed George's reins from the stirrup leathers, and pointed up the lane. "Show me what he can do."

She waved her goodbye, and cantered away between the high banks. A day or two later she met him again in the same place, but this time he was riding a young mare, and they circled the wood together.

After that, effortlessly, they drifted together, and he told her he was "killing time" until the New Year, unable to make up his mind whether to sit for Army Entrance, or emigrate to Kenya, and farm. He was inclined to the latter course, for he liked the prospect of an open-air life in a new country, but his father, a retired lieutenant-colonel, was trying to bully him into making a career of the army. He explained that the army was a tradition in the Ascham family. He already had two brothers in the Royal Engineers, and another in the Artillery.

"Our place at home looks like the Imperial War Museum," he told her, laughing. "Everywhere you look scarred old warriors scowl down from the walls, and all the spaces between their portraits are filled with loot, from Asian battlefields, and the implements we used to slaughter our wretched victims! I went for it in a big way when I was a kid, but now I'm not so sure; I mean, army life isn't like it used to be is it, you know, all lance pennants, and point-to-pointing, and 'Floreat Etona', and broken squares? Most of the time you seem to be sitting for exams, or wangling for a Staff job in town."

She liked his sense of fun, his lack of snobbery, and his unexacting companionship. She liked his loose, easy seat on a horse, and the way his snub and freckled nose wrinkled when he laughed, which he did every few moments. Falling in love with him was rather like catching up with a gay fellow-traveller on a lonely road, and agreeing to complete the remainder of the journey in his company. There were few kisses, and hardly any avowals, between the day she first saw him, sitting on Hayes Bank, and the day he suddenly said to her:

"Well, Judy, I've finally decided to sidestep the army, and try Kenya." And before she could exclaim, "On one condition tho'—that you come with me! Does that appeal to you at all, Judy?"

It appealed very strongly. He seemed to her the most gentle, engaging, and undemanding male she had ever met, and there was something about his quiet strength, and unhurried enthusiasm for open-air life, that told her he would make a first-class farmer, in Kenya, or anywhere else.

"I think I'd like that better than anything I can imagine, Tim," she told him quietly, and they kissed very softly, more like brother and sister than lovers, and then rode silently back to The Dene, to talk it over with Maud Somerton.

5

The twins, Boxer and Berni, did not waste their time in any recruiting queues.

As far back as the autumn of 1938 they had smelled noise and speed, and jolly companionship from afar, and had come speeding down from the Midlands, where they were testing for a firm of motor-cycle manufacturers, to join a London anti-aircraft unit as transport-drivers.

They need not have travelled south to enlist as Territorials, but they wanted to soldier with all their old Speedway mob, who had enlisted in a body. Within a fortnight of the Prime Minister's sombre challenge of "those evil things", they were lumbering along French roads, one behind the other, towing brand-new Bofors guns, and shouting "Allez à la bloody trot-whah!" to smiling civilians, whose plodding progress along the centre of the *pavé* caused them to apply brakes.

The twins took to France, and the French took to the twins. Whenever they had an off-duty spell they could be found in the nearest estaminet, tossing off beakers of rough, local wine, and roaring lewd songs into an admiring circle of villagers.

The patron of the estaminet took to them, the mountainous Madame Drouet, with whom they were billeted, took to them, and all the girls who moved in and out the depot, in short woollen stockings, and plain, serge skirts, took to them. By the New Year, when they were due for their first leave, they were known, and readily recognised, in a whole string of shabby villages and hamlets along several main roads that led to Lille, and Madame Drouet shook with emotion when they told her they were going home for nine days, and she implored them to accept a roll of Lille lace, as a gift for their mother, who must, she declared, be very desolate to be robbed of two such fine sons for the duration.

Boxer grinned his clownish grin, and nudged Berni, who said:

"Nous avons no mère, Madame! Elle mort, a long time ago!"

And then, improving somewhat: "Après le Quartorze guerre!"

This news reduced Madame Drouet to a flood of tears and she reached out, enfolding Bernard in a bolster-like embrace, so that Boxer, with the object of rescuing his twin, added:

"We've got a sister, Madame, and she'll jump at it!"

He disentangled the red-faced Bernard from Madame, and stuffed the lace into his haversack, and they climbed into their lorries, and drove off up the road towards the base.

Back in the Avenue, Jim showed more interest in them than he had ever done when they were small, sitting over the living-room fire long after Jack and Louise had gone up to bed, and asking them question after question about their life and conditions, and the general prospects of the B.E.F. He was comforted a little by their confident outlook, which did not seem to justify old Goreham's gloomy prophecies.

"You think then that we'll hold them if they do try and break through, son?" he asked earnestly, after Boxer, with loud guffaws, had described how unerringly their unit had shot down a French aircraft in error.

"I only hope they try," Boxer chuckled and then, as ever, "Whatd'ysay, Berni, whad'ysay?"

Berni threw his cigarette butt into the fire.

"I reckon we'll see 'em off, Pop," he said enigmatically.

CHAPTER XXXI

Heroics Strictly Rationed

1

HEROICS were strictly rationed at two of the houses along the Avenue during that first, wartime winter.

At Number Forty-Five, headquarters of the "Hartnell Eight", Margy and Ted had their first quarrel, and the cause of it was the discovery, deep in the cyncopating bosom of the bandleader, of a totally unexpected vein of patriotism. This seam had been laid bare by a refugee accordionist, who had joined the orchestra after a hairbreadth escape from Berlin, the previous Spring.

In the last few years Ted and Margy had progressed a long way towards realising the dream they shared. The "Hartnell Eight" had not only broadcast on a number of occasions, but was booked almost every night in the season, and had toured extensively throughout successive summers.

It had never multiplied itself into a Hartnell Dozen, or a

Hartnell Fourteen, remaining compact and self-contained, for it was Margy's theory that a well-paid eight played better than a moderately-paid twelve. In this way it attracted good musicians, and maintained its reputation for good taste and high-quality rhythm.

Of the original team only the tall, bespectacled violinist, who had inadvertently witnessed the final exit of Al Swinger, remained with them, and by now he was practically one of the family.

The outbreak of war did not result in the anticipated falling-off of business. On the contrary, the blackout increased the demands made upon them, for the theatres were closed that autumn, and there were a large number of local dances organised by clubs, on behalf of war charities.

Margy therefore decided to ignore the war. Ted was over military age anyway, and most of their musicians were unlikely military material. The years had slipped by smoothly and prosperously. They now had a comfortable bank balance and a cosy home, with a daily woman coming in to cook and clean, and could enjoy long, lazy mornings in bed, after late-night sessions.

They had plenty of friends, whom they provided with vast quantities of gin and vermouth (although they hardly touched liquor themselves), and they were in the habit of giving little parties on their rare free nights. On these occasions they filled the little house with Margy's sisters and brothers-in-law, and Edith Clegg, her sister Becky, and the artist lodger, Jean McInroy, were often asked over from Number Four to swell the uproar that these convivial gatherings inspired.

In short they were content, and just the tiniest big smug.

Then Nikki, the German accordionist, had to upset Ted with his terrible stories of the concentration camps in which his father and brothers had perished, and from which he had only just escaped through the courage and presence of mind of the music professor with whom he was staying, when the Storm Troopers had called for him in the middle of the night.

Now Ted was troubled, and seemed to have lost interest in what they were to play at the Chamber of Commerce dance.

He appeared to Margy to do little but mooch about the house, chain-smoking, or sitting hunched over the radio, listening, not to a swing session if you please, but to boring news-bulletin about leaflets, and fuel wastage, and digging for victory!

Finally Margy decided that something drastic must be done about it, and being a very practical woman she hit on something calculated to take her husband's mind right off the inmates of concentration camps and Storm Troopers who called in the night.

She tried reasoning first: "What can you *do* about it anyway? You're over forty, and they won't take you in the army, you silly great gawk!"

"There's the 'Pioneers'," he mumbled, "they'd have me in the 'Pioneers', wouldn't they?"

"*What?*" Mary was outraged. "Spend your time digging latrines, in some awful camp miles and miles from anywhere? Not if I know it, Ted Hartnell! You've got me to think of, as well as the band."

He looked at her obstinately. "Aw, you'd be okay, Margy. We've got money saved up, and you could run the band on your own, you know you could, and what's more, so do the boys!"

"I could, but I wouldn't want to," she said flatly, and then, in despair, "Oh, Ted, Ted, skip it, and let things take their course, can't you?"

But reasoning was no use. For years he had always listened to her, but now she did not seem to be able to get through to him at all. He continued to mooch, and mutter about the terrible things Nikki had told him, things that went on in places called Dachau and Sachenhausen. "They gas people," he told her, "and then make maps out of their skins! How do you like that? Maps out of people's skins! Then they take out their teeth, just to get at the gold fillings for more tanks and 'planes! You wouldn't think people could carry on like that, not nowadays!"

"I don't believe it," snapped Margy; "it's just a lot of propaganda to get more recruits!"

"Well, I *do* believe it," he growled, very ill-humouredly for him. "You talk to Nikki. He isn't the kind of chap to make things up like that, and he's lent me books about it."

"But what can you *do* about it?" wailed Margy wretchedly, "can you fly over there and wring Hitler's neck?"

"No," said Ted seriously, "I don't reckon I could do that, but I could do *something* to stop 'em, and I damn well will, the minute I figure out what, and nothing you can say is going to stop me, Margy! Nothing, you understand!"

But Margy did say something to stop him, at all events for an interval.

"Ted," she said one morning, a week or so after their last argument on the subject, "you're going to be a father."

He dropped the Spanish guitar he was tuning, and it crashed to the floor with a clang.

"What you say?" he muttered. *"What you say,* Margy?"

"I said I'm going to have a baby," said Margy, "and it's going to be born in June, or maybe a week or two before."

He instantly forgot Nikki and Dachau, and threw his arms around her, just like a husband in a Hollywood film, and then he released her and went leaping about the room uttering squeaks of delight, and she watched him tolerantly, as a mother might watch a small son showing off.

"It's about time," she said at length, when he had calmed a little, "another year or so and it might have been too late. Now call up our Oscar, Teddy, and tell him the rehearsal is at twelve sharp, and don't forget to stop into Murchison's before they close and order those extra parts of *There'll Always be an England* like I said. I tell you what, Teddy," she went on, as her mind switched from certainties to possibilities, "we might even have another later on. I don't like the idea of an only child. There were nine of us at home, and we always had a peck of fun together."

He picked up the guitar and twanged it, triumphantly.

"Margy," he said, "Margy, you're wonderful!"

Margy Hartnell was not all that wonderful, for her idea was not original. After all, she lived next door to the newly-weds, Esme and Elaine, and in the last summer of peace there had been unmistakable evidence that something had gone sadly awry with Elaine's autumnal resolutions.

Every time Margy went out of her back door she was

confronted with a row of nappies on the line of Number Forty-Three, and every time she left by the front door she passed the new pram, a gift from Number Twenty-Two. The pram was braked against the dwarf pillars of Esme's front-gate.

Sometimes, when the sun had climbed over the woods, and was beating on the front windows of the odd numbers, there was a baby in the pram, and Margy stopped for a moment to gurgle at it. In short, a month or so before Margy hit upon the means of deflecting Ted's mind from Dachau, Eunice Godbeer, of Number Twenty-Two opposite, was an ecstatic grandmother.

2

When Elaine Fraser was informed that she was pregnant her astonishment was so great that she at once began to argue with her doctor.

She had paid a call on Doctor Cheadle, in the Lower Road, before announcing her suspicions to Esme, and as Doctor Cheadle was over sixty, and grossly overworked, he was inclined to be very testy with incredulous patients.

"It's not the slightest use protesting to *me*, young woman," he snapped. "You came here for my opinion, and I've given it to you. Whether you like it, or whether you don't, you'll have a baby somewhere around the end of August. So go off home and tell your husband about it, and I hope he's better pleased with the idea than you seem to be!"

Elaine left him then, but she did not go straight home. Instead she cut up one of the shorter roads to the southerly entrance of the "Rec", and sat down on the familiar seat near the tennis-courts to study the situation.

The seat had no special significance for her. It was just a seat, somewhere to rest while she collected her scattered wits.

August, he had said. Then that must mean she had started it within a month of the honeymoon. She still couldn't believe it, no matter what the old fool had told her.

A baby! *Her!* And almost right away! It was not only astounding, it was humiliating!

She sat there, for nearly an hour, trying to come to terms with the news, and endeavouring to formulate some sort of plan, any sort of plan, that might result in extricating her from such a ridiculous situation.

There were ways and means, people said, but she discovered that she wasn't at all sure what they were. All the information she had on the subject related to the prevention, not cure. You could have some sort of operation she had heard, but that was illegal, wasn't it, and the cost was said to be prohibitive on that account? Esme could probably afford whatever it was, but would he? She decided not, almost at once. He was far more likely to go off into transports of delight, cluck like a hen, plan her diet, and insist on carrying her upstairs every night. She dismissed Esme from her mind, and tried hard to remember all the talk she must have heard on the subject at one time or another.

Some of the girls on the variety circuit had spoken of drinking bottles and bottles of neat gin, a treatment supplemented by frequent immersions in cold water. But she loathed the smell of gin, and hated cold water, and besides, her memory was probably faulty, and there was almost certainly something else one had to do, in addition to guzzling gin and climbing in and out of cold baths.

As the afternoon waned she began to feel chilled, and got up from the seat, leaving by the north entrance, and walking slowly back towards the Avenue. Esme would be home by now, and was probably wondering where she was, but she shrank from the prospect of meeting him, and passed the house, going on over Shirley Rise, and then down towards the Lower Road.

It was almost dusk now, and a thin stream of traffic was beating up from Elmers End. She stood at the front of the Rise, uncertain which way to go, and feeling desperately miserable. Suddenly she made up her mind to go home and drop the whole problem in Esme's lap, insisting that he do something at once. He would argue, but she would strike down his arguments, and she would win in the end, as she won every time, simply because he was enslaved, and freely admitted it.

She felt better immediately, as she always did when she

had once made a decision, and she turned to cross over to the Avenue side, stepping off the pavement without glancing to the right.

There was a flash of headlights and a screech of high-powered brakes, as she leapt back, turning her ankle, and falling sideways in the gutter. Before she coud struggle to her knees a man was stooping over her, helping her to her feet. Badly scared as she was, she instantly recognised him as Archie Carver, owner of the long, cream sports car that had knocked her down.

Archie was profuse in his apologises, but even so was careful to establish at once that her own jay-walking was to blame.

"I say, I'm terribly sorry! Are you much hurt? Did the wing hit you? My God, but that was a close one! You stepped clean off into the road, without looking! I stood on everything, the moment I saw you. Are you sure you're all right? It's Mrs. Fraser, isn't it?"

Elaine concluded that she was all right—more or less. She was badly shaken, and her ankle throbbed. Her handbag lay on the kerb, its contents scattered in the gutter, and there was a hole in her silk stocking, where one knee had scraped along the tarmac.

"I'm all right—at least, I think I am. I'm a bit shaken . . . my handbag . . . oh, God, everything's spilled out of it."

A baby in August! And this had to happen . . . now! If only it had happened a few months later . . . !

He was on his hands and knees at once, gathering up powder-compact, keys, lipstick, and coins, in the light of his headlamps. She noticed his smart new suit, a blue pin-stripe, and it crossed her mind that nobody else in the Avenue wore those kind of clothes, just as nobody else owned a long, cream sports-car, instead of an old Morris Cowley, or a baby Austin.

She had always been mildly interested in Archie, having been aware of him ever since he had gone into partnership with that funny old Italian, who had collapsed and died in the meadow not long ago. She had heard that he was making money hand over fist, and had little branch shops all over the place, as far away as Bromley and Chislehurst. Suddenly she began to feel less irritated with him, and his flashy sports car, reflecting that this might not be such an unlucky day after all.

He gave her the handbag.

"I think everything's there. Now what about me taking you home? You were on your way home, weren't you?"

"Yes, I was going home."

She spoke slowly, as though she had hardly heard him, and he looked hard at her, his forehead wrinkled with worry.

"It's Number Forty-Three, isn't it?"

She nodded. He knew the number. Why? She hardly ever went into his shop, preferring to go shopping in Croydon, and he had never delivered at Number Forty-Three. Her ankle was throbbing painfully now, but she ignored it. Away at the back of her mind a familiar picture was forming, and as he helped her into the car the picture began to merge into a series of pictures, like the slowly revolving cards of the peepshows she had seen, on seaside piers. She was on her terrace again, in the gently swinging hammock, with the courtiers standing round, and in the background, smiling complacently, was the Great Provider. She was interested to note that he no longer looked like Esme, but much more like this man, in a smart West End pin-stripe, and she knew somehow that this sports car of his was parked somewhere in the background.

As he leaned forward to release the handbrake his eye fell on her ruined stocking.

"I say, that's a pity! But I daresay we can soon replace that, Mrs. Fraser."

She smiled as the car shot forward. The peepshow faded, and she relaxed against the red leather cushions.

"It's nothing," she told him, "you mustn't bother. It was my fault . . . I was thinking, and not looking out."

She was even tempted, for a brief moment, to tell him her problem. He would know what to do about it all right. He was that sort of man, wise in the ways of the world. How else would he have acquired this car, and all those businesses? But she checked herself and said nothing more until he pulled up outside Number Forty-Three, and jumped out to open the door. Her mind was exploring all manner of interesting possibilities, and at times like this it was always best to say as little as possible.

"Hadn't I better carry you in?" he said, hovering on the kerb.

"Good heavens, no, Mr. Carver; I'm not crippled, just a bit shaken."

"Are you quite sure?"

He sounded as if he would very much like to carry her in, and her mind registered the fact.

"Quite sure, thanks."

She got out, and smiled at him again, "You've been very kind."

"Not a bit of it; you've been most sporting. Dammit, most pedestrians would have kicked up no end of a fuss."

"I hate fuss," she said simply, and went on up the short path, feeling in her bag for the key.

He stood by the gate while she opened the door and heard her call "Esme!", as she looked over her shoulder, and smiled back at him. Then the door closed very softly, and she was gone, but her perfume lingered on in the car.

Thoughtfully he reversed down the Avenue towards the double doors of his yard and for once he was not thinking about his businesses.

3

Elaine's baby, a girl, arrived with a dramatic sense of timing, being born at the St. Helen's Private Nursing Home in the Upper Road, on the morning of September 1st, 1939.

Esme had behaved about it all just as she had known he would, outdoing all his earlier performances in a non-stop display of tenderness and gratitude. The whole business had been far less worrying and irritating than she had feared. Somehow the encounter with Archie had steadied her, so that she had been content to prolong her performance of a dutiful Avenue bride throughout the period of pregnancy, even to the extent of pretending to learn to knit, and asking her mother-in-law to choose a name.

Eunice chose "Guy", of course, after the hero of the

Marne, but in the event it was Harold's choice, Barbara, that was used. Now they had all gone home, and the Nursing Home Staff was glued to the radio, or hanging about in the corridors discussing the news with the doctors, while Elaine had leisure to lean back on her pillows and let her mind range into a future that had nothing whatever to do with the wrinkled morsel asleep in the nursery across the passage.

As she mused she reflected what a great deal of nonsense people talked about motherhood and babies. To begin with they always gave one to understand that birth itself was an agonising experience, but that the moment one looked at one's child, all memory of the pain was submerged in wave after wave of joy, love, and fulfilment. They said that, no matter how ugly a child looked when first born, it was sure to seem radiantly beautiful to its mother, and then they drivelled on and on and on, about "the exquisite joy of holding and feeding the baby, for the very first time."

She knew now, as she had suspected long ago, that not a word of this was true. The birth had not been agonising. Uncomfortable perhaps, but, as far as she could recall, not nearly so bad as an abscessed tooth she had had in Edinburgh, when she was playing the Royal with poor old Eugene. Then again, not by any stretch of imagination could a sane person describe the mottled, puckered, brick-coloured thing they had held up to her as beautiful. To her it looked like a small piece of raw beef, and when they had given it to her to feed, she had derived no satisfaction in *that*, finding the process almost as uncomfortable as having the baby.

Now that she was alone, and everyone was chattering and chattering about something Germany was doing to Poland, and something we were going to do to Germany in return, her thoughts were occupied neither with the baby, nor the international situation. These did not interest her in the slightest, but what did was a huge basket of fruit the nurse had just brought in, fortunately after Esme, Harold, and Eunice had beamed their way out of the ward, looking, she thought, like a trio of Chinese coolies, bowing themselves out of an ancestral shrine.

It was the largest basket of fruit she had ever seen, a towering pyramid of rosy apples, oranges, tangerines, bananas, peaches, and pineapple, gathered into an enormous yellow basket, with huge curved handles, all twined about with evergreen, and finished off at the top with a vast bow of broad, pink ribbon. It stood by the window, dwarfing the pitiful little bouquets that Harold and Esme had brought in, and she looked again at the card that had accompanied it, propped up against a vase on her bedside table.

The card read: *"Congratulations—Archie Carver,"* and on the back, in his bold, flowing handwriting: *"May I pop in and see you one day next week? I'll 'phone first."*

She looked at the basket for a long time. It was, she decided, the sort of basket that went with cream sports cars and chains of grocery shops, and it might go very well with a lot of other things, a terrace, perhaps, and a hammock, and a cloud of courtiers, all standing by with iced drinks and bushels of flattery.

4

Not everyone along the Avenue was cast down by Hitler's activities that September morning.

Over at Number Seventeen, where Sydney Frith and his mother had lived so quietly all these years, there was unaccustomed bustle, and a great deal of running up and down stairs, as Sydney emerged on to the landing and called imperiously for shirts, and studs, and clean underwear, using the authoritative voice he had acquired since Edgar had abdicated in his favour.

Sydney was very excited that morning, as he tugged at the straps of his new valise, and glanced at himself sideways in the mirror of his wardrobe door, excited and extremely pleased with himself for being so clever as to anticipate events. So accurately had he anticipated them that he was the very first man in the Avenue to don a uniform and, at the same time, insure himself against the risks of an uncomfortable war.

For Sydney was already an officer, with the expectation of receiving smart salutes from any rankers who crossed his path, even such bounders as those motor-cycling maniacs over at Number Twenty, and all the chaps at the office, who (lacking his foresight) were now liable to be thrust into uniforms for which they had not been measured at Simpson's, in the Strand.

It had been a bit of a gamble, of course. If there had been no war he might have been faced with the prospect of sitting in a draughty Nissen hut two nights a week, and throughout occasional week-ends. That was the risk Alec Cartwright, his friend, had foreseen, and explained to him, during the uncertain weeks that followed the Munich crisis, and every young man at Claxton and Wragg's, Holborn Way, was looking over his shoulder at the headlines.

"Get on a Squadron now," Alec had advised, "and keep on putting in regular appearances at H.Q. until something definitely happens. If it doesn't, then you're stuck with it for a spell, but if it does you'll be commissioned, and you'll have fixed yourself nicely for the duration!"

It had been good advice, and Sydney was very glad indeed that he had taken it, and signed on as a volunteer clerk (accounts) at the Lucknow Park depot of a Balloon Squadron. He had, it could now be admitted, been very doubtful at first, for he had had a strong aversion to all uniforms since his career with the Blackshirts had ended in a brick kiln. But Alec's information had been sound, for here he was, after only a few months as a volunteer, credited with thirty-five pounds to spend on kitting himself out as an Acting Pilot Officer, and with the virtual certainty of quick promotion as war-time expansion got under way. In addition he had authority, authority over all latecomers, both volunteers and Grade II men, pulled in by the call-up.

In the meantime he had steered clear of heroics. The ante-room at Lucknow Park was already crammed with eager young men, shouting for "cans-o'-wallop", and exchanging information on "Spits", and "Hurrys", "prangs" and "wizard shows". Sydney listened to them attentively enough to learn the new slang, but he did not experience the slightest desire to change places with the most splendid of them, having learned his lesson in heroics long ago. They were anxious to become "flying types", and he was quite content to remain a "wingless-wonder". They could have their Spits, and their Hurrys, by the hangar-full. He was happy enough with his loose-leaf ledgers, his trestle tables, and his bespectacled L.A.C. assistant.

Now the future was bright indeed. If they were going to have trenches in this war he wouldn't be expected to stand in one, and if they bombed the Balloon Centre he could always carry his ledgers down to the bomb-proof shelter, and put a "Business-As-Usual" card on the door.

In the meantime, he could walk about the suburb with his chin up, watching, out of the corner of his eye, for any unsuspecting "brown jobs" and "erks", with their hands in their trouser pockets.

Before he kissed Esther's cold cheek, and humped his new valise to the 'bus stop in the Lower Road, he had just sufficient time to send one of his infrequent letter-cards to his father, up in Llandudno, informing him that Edgar could continue to direct his monthly remittances to Number Seventeen, but that henceforth they must be addressed to *Pilot Officer Frith, S. RAF. V.R.*

5

Edgar Frith pursed his lips over Sydney's letter-card, received the Monday after war had been declared. He knew nothing about the different branches of the R.A.F., and to him a Pilot-Officer was an officer who piloted an aeroplane. He could not help wondering when, where, and how Sydney, whom he recalled as an excessively timid boy, had mastered the technique of such a hazardous calling.

The war news had given Edgar a severe bout of indigestion, and throughout the week-end Frances had been mixing him frequent draughts of his special bismuth medicine, so frequent indeed that he was quite unequal to attending a sale, at Menai Bridge, for he feared that he would burp too often and too obviously during the bidding.

All that week Edgar was in very low spirits. They said that a war would paralyse the antique trade, and they were probably right, for it was a luxury business, and people didn't go in for luxuries in war-time, but made do until it was over, and then prices soared and it became almost impossible to acquire fresh stock.

It was a great pity that things should come to this after all. These had been smooth, prosperous years, and very happy ones indeed for Frances, Pippa, and himself.

Pippa had just come into the business, and now helped Frances look after the shop, giving Edgar ample time to go further afield to auctions and private sales. In the mid-thirties he had made three or four lucky purchases, and sent them to Christie's. He had also bought, and held back, thirty to forty choice little pieces to furnish the house they had intended buying, before it had been requisitioned by the Council for evacuees and migrating Government clerks.

Now every plan they had was suspended for the duration, and Glyn Davies, the kindly auctioneer, told him that there would be very few sales until things sorted themselves out a bit. By the time they did, he reflected, he would probably be too old to get about and compete with younger dealers who were beginning to drive up from town in their dozens, and assist in the search for "genuine bits" for the American market.

Frances said he wasn't to worry but he did worry. He couldn't help worrying, for he was getting on in years, and if anything happened to him what was to become of Frances and Pippa?

He passed the letter-card to Frances, and watched her eyebrows lift.

"Sydney? Did you know he had joined the Air Force?"

"No," said Edgar, "but I suppose he'd have had to join something, sooner or later. They all will, won't they?"

She glanced at him, trying to think of some way to cheer him up. It was not like Edgar to be so depressed and fidgety. For years now he had been so relaxed, even when he had come home from a sale shaking his head, and admitting that he had paid too much for a piece, and that it would probably hang around in the back room for years.

For all that she knew him so well she misjudged the true cause of his gloom.

"Wouldn't you like to go up to town and see Sydney, Edgar?" she suggested. "He might be going overseas, and it might be for years."

Edgar considered, and then shook his head.

"Sydney wouldn't want to see me after all this time, Francie, and I don't think I want to see him. I suppose I ought to be proud of him, doing a thing like this so quickly, but I'm not. You see, Francie, I never really liked him, not even when he was a little chap. I always felt he was watching me, but in a nasty way, if you know what I mean."

Frances laughed, and at the sound of her laugh he smiled again.

"Ah, I know what you're thinking, Francie," he said.

He seemed to have aged ten years over the week-end, and the relationship between them today was more like that of an uncle and niece than a man and his wife. "That was before I met you, and in those days I didn't need watching!"

She kissed him lightly on his bald spot, and went out into the kitchen, where Pippa was making coffee on the gas stove. Pippa had grown into a tall, graceful girl, with a long, and rather serious face.

"He's terribly down in the mouth today," Frances told her. "Do you think he's still worrying about the war?"

"Isn't everybody?" asked Pippa.

Mother and daughter had long since discussed Edgar in this way, as if he was a special kind of relative they shared with one another.

"I don't see why he should let it upset him so much," said Frances, doubtfully; "they aren't likely to call on us, are they?"

She took over Pippa's task, and the girl stood looking down from the window on the slow-moving holiday crowds, that were threading their way through the narrow street towards the Esplanade. She was a thoughtful girl, who sometimes surprised them when she put her thoughts into hesitant words.

"It isn't a *personal* thing, mummy," she said presently, and Frances thought she had never seen her look so solemn. "I think it's more the feeling of nothing mattering any more!"

So, thought Frances, now I've got two of them in this silly mood!

"That's quite ridiculous, Pippa," she said impatiently; "there have been plenty of wars before, and the last one was terrible enough. This one certainly couldn't be any worse!"

Pippa looked at her, and decided that she was convincing herself, remembering, perhaps, a young man of long ago, who had come to her in the night, and wept because he had to go back and die in the slime. She knew all about her father now, for since coming up here, and since Pippa had grown up, Frances had made it her business to ensure that there were no secrets between them, not even trivial ones.

The girl said: "All the people you talk to are most afraid of air-raids, and gas, and things like that. I don't think those things are really important. What *is* important is that people have let it happen again, so soon after your war. That means that they always will let it happen, even after this is over and done with. You see, a war like this makes everything else useless, doesn't it? I mean, planning things, and looking forward to things."

"What sort of things?" asked her mother, and it occurred to her that Pippa might have a secret or two after all.

"The sort of things," said Pippa, "that you dream about, but without meaning to."

Frances suddenly discovered that she was crying, and wondered if it was simply because Pippa had grown up, and she hadn't noticed it before. She put down the coffee-pot, and half-turned, dabbing her eyes, and if Pippa saw the tears she was sufficiently adult not to comment on them, and Frances was duly grateful.

"I don't think you're the one for Edgar today," she said, as soon as she had recovered herself. "There is one thing though, a thing like this is never as bad as one imagines, not for you, not at your age! You can take it from me, Pip, war or no war, there'll always be plenty to dream about."

Pippa shook her head slowly. "I don't think you understand what I'm trying to say, Mummy." She pointed down into the street below. "All those people ... they've all got plans—coming here for the summer holiday was just one of them. But I don't really mean that sort of plan, I mean big plans, big for them anyway. They were all saving, or working, or falling in love, or studying for something; and now this thing's happened, and they might just as well have not made any plan, because at any moment now all the young ones will be given a railway ticket to go somewhere they've never wanted to go, and when they get there they'll be pushed into something that isn't part of their plan. Then all the old ones, like poor Edgar out there, won't count any more, just because they *are* old, and when it's all over they really will be old, and they'll just go on living on things they remember before it happened. That's what's so awful about a thing like war—it stops people dreaming."

"Maybe they just mark time for a bit, and make do with dreaming about what they'll do when it's all over," said Frances, but without much conviction, for Pippa had never talked like this before, and her words had a peculiar chilling effect on the older woman, as though Pippa was saying them to her over a telephone from a long way off.

"Yes, there is that, I suppose," said Pippa, after a long pause, "but that isn't really dreaming, is it? Not the sort of dreams that make up the nice part of life. That's just like a prisoner in a cell, waiting for the years to pass until they let him out. Take today, for instance—it's the second day of the war, and nobody, not even Hitler, could possibly say how long it'll go on. So from yesterday we start counting the hours, all of us, the Germans as well, and we've all got to stop what we're doing, and just count, without even knowing whether we've got to go on up to a thousand, or a million, or a million millions. We've got to start without ever knowing when we shall stop."

But neither Pippa, nor Frances, nor Edgar really began counting that day, any more than the people in the Avenue, two hundred miles away, began on that day, or that month, or in that year even. They had first to live through a prelude unique in the history of wars, and then begin counting when the winter was gone, and the sun that was to shine so brilliantly week after week beat down on scenes and events that were now just around the corner of time, waiting to be born, like Margy Hartnell's baby.

CHAPTER XXXII

A Last Look At The Avenue

IN one sense Pippa was right. Most of the Avenue dreams were soon to go into cold storage for five years, but in another sense she was wrong, for the years ahead were prolific in new dreams.

It was during the Spring, and the early summer of 1940, that old dreams fell away,. and the new ones began to germinate along the Avenue. But first, for most dreamers, there was an interval, during which day-dreaming was altogether suspended, and they stumbled about like the people of some ancient city, overwhelmed by a catastrophe, the dimensions of which made the lives they had been leading up to that moment seem plodding and insignificant.

It began that April, when the long frosts had passed and the buds were bursting beside the tangled tracks of Manor Wood, but the rumblings of early Spring were faint and far away to the north, and they were not heard very clearly in the Avenue.

In after years, when somebody mentioned the rape of Norway, all that the Avenue could remember about it was the Prime Minister's comment about Hitler missing a 'bus. The invasions of Norway and Denmark were thus a mere stretch after the long yawn of winter.

Jim Carver heard the rumbling more distinctly, and sensed panic afar off, but then Jim was a trained soldier, and Jim read lots of books and pamphlets, and more than one daily newspaper.

Once the rumblings began to be heard generally there was no mistaking them for other than what they were. As the Maytime sun swung over the meadow, and began to warm odd and even numbers alike, and shine on with an intensity and permanence reminiscent of 1919, the news from across the Channel grew more alarming day by day, almost hour by hour. It was this that finally peeled away the reticence of the most isolated Avenue train-catcher, and prompted him to address neighbours he hardly recognised whilst en route for Woodside Station each weekday morning.

"Doesn't look so good, does it?"

"What do you make of this chap Weygand?"

"What possessed those French to build a Maginot Line only half way along their frontier?"

Always that Maginot Line figured in these anxious conversations, perhaps because everybody in the Avenue lived on a modest budget, and to them it must have seemed very careless housekeeping to pour the greater part of one's annual income into the building of a boundary wall that enclosed only half the back garden.

The sun went on shining, and the news went on getting worse.

"Fancy the King of the Belgians packing it in. A bit much, don't you think?"

"They'll probably hold them outside Paris, like they did last time!"

"Nuns they were, coming down by parachute! It makes you think, doesn't it, old man?"

But soon even these conversations dried up, and the train-catchers took to spacing themselves out along the platform, and awaiting their trains in gloomy silence. Some mornings they could hardly bear to meet one another's eyes. There were still the old perky ones, like Mr. Westerman of Number Ninety-Eight, who was ready to crack a joke or two at the expense of the situation, but these jokes usually fell rather flat. Here were possibilities that didn't bear thinking about, much less joking about, things like utter defeat, and the sack of London, things that had hitherto belonged in history books, not in newspapers, and when the call came for amateur yachtsmen to extricate British soldiers from a town called Dunkirk the perky comments of Mr. Westerman were received in frigid silence.

By the end of May the very word "Dunkirk" came to have a kind of finality about it. To the Avenue folk it suggested an iron safety-curtain, slamming on an epoch, and cutting them off once and for all from the ragtime that Ted Hartnell used to play, the cloche hats that Eunice used to wear, the Charleston steps that Elaine tried to teach Esme, and everything they knew, or remembered, during the interval that they had always thought of as a peace. Even this they were now told, by knowing leader-writers, hadn't been a peace at all, only a kind of truce.

Then the word "invasion" came to be used quite freely, along with new words like "blitz" and "Panzer", and evacuation began all over again among families that had crept back to the Avenue after an uncomfortable Christmas in the provinces. They now set about packing again, sometimes leaving in a body, with "for sale" notices lashed to their front gates.

Dreams were going very cheap in the Avenue that season, and among the bargains was Jim Carver's twenty-one-year-old dream of the Brotherhood of Man. Jim hardly noticed its flight, for in its place he already had a new dream, the dream of Militant Democracy, of the gathering together of free men the world over for one frantic, pulverising assault on the active forces of Fascism, and on the maddeningly supine Government of his own country, which he now regarded as aiders and abettors in the murder of civilisation. For had he not read, in a pamphlet on Ghandi's India long ago, that sloth was the worst crime of all?

Jim was a difficult man to live with these days. His impotent wrath did not spend itself at committee meetings, as in the Depression and the Munich days, but spilled all over the kitchen of Number Twenty, sometimes reducing poor, bewildered Louise to tears.

"Bloody treachery," he would roar, crashing his huge, freckled fist on the table, and making the breakfast china dance, and the flies skim away from the decoy jam-pot that Jack Strawbridge had placed on the window-ledge. "Bloody treachery in high places! That's what it is! Open your mouth to protest at the muddle and what do they do? Slap you in jug, for talking alarm and despondency! My God, I'm alarmed all right! I'm alarmed and despondent right down in my belly, and I'll go on being alarmed and despondent, until there's a clean sweep of those fumbling bastards, and somebody takes over who really intends to fight Fascism. . . ."

And so we leave Jim for a moment, roaring up and down the Avenue at anyone who would listen to him, feeling round for a rifle, or a stick-grenade, that he did not possess, and then cursing the Government for failing to provide one. He was a man who had once seen a vision, of a sacrificed boy on a bank, but he now clamoured for a million such sacrifices, and the means to provide them. He was a man who had run the whole gamut of the "isms" during the peace that they now called a truce, all the way from pacifism to jingoism, with brief stops at every station in between.

And he was not such a rare bird at that. You could have matched him almost anywhere in the suburb that summer.

Eunice Godbeer, of Number Twenty, had been packed off to the country on May Day.

She had gone willingly enough, for all along the Lower Road the shop-windows were emptying, and there was nothing much to look at except shapeless, utility clothes, and Harold seemed to be acting very queerly these days, entrenching himself behind his *Times*, and poring over maps scored with lines and splashed with arrows, that he cut from papers, and held balanced on his knees, when the news-bulletins came over the air. He was gloomy too, gloomier than she ever remembered, and even talked about persuading Esme to let him arrange to send little Barbara, the baby, all the way to America, as if the poor mite wouldn't die of seasickness on the way, seeing that she found it difficult enough to keep down her spinach after a feed on dry land.

So Eunice took herself off to the hotel in Torquay, where they had spent their honeymoon, and from here she was able to rent a cottage on the Totnes Road, and send for the baby and Elaine, as soon as she had found a woman to clean the place.

She liked it down here, for Torquay was only a fourpenny 'bus ride away, and there were still well-stocked shop windows in the town. In the evenings, when the baby was in bed, she sat in the window-seat looking out on a network of forsythia and clematis, and re-read all her old favourites, *East*

Lynne, The Channings, Under Two Flags, and *The Way of an Eagle,* while the Luftwaffe squadrons began to weave vapour trails over the half-empty Avenue, and Harold trudged home to boil himself an egg, and climb into the big double bed, missing her very much, and wishing he hadn't been so irritable with her when she had taken such an interminable time undressing, and brushing her long, golden hair.

Elaine remained at the cottage no longer than was necessary to settle in Eunice and the baby. Elaine's dream had wavered somewhat under the stress of events, but in essentials it was still much the same. The terrace, and the hammock, and the courtiers were still there, but they had acquired a more ambitious setting, and several new props, a Casino for instance, and a private aeroplane, and a sleek white yacht that dropped anchor in places like Majorca and Monte Carlo.

She was secretly delighted with the way things had turned out. The baby was off her hands, perhaps for the duration, and Esme, whose excessive devotion was beginning to cloy a little, had done something sensible at last, and joined the R.A.F., so that she now had the house to herself. Her appointments with Archie, and the handsome broad-shouldered Pole that neither Archie nor Esme had heard about, were therefore much less complicated than they might have been.

For Elaine, in these hectic days, had worked out a simple compromise between love, duty, and pure advancement, and it appeared to be working out very well so far. Stefan, the big Pole whom she called "Stevie", could speak no English as yet, but whenever they met they had no occasion to talk, for Stefan's time was very limited. As soon as he had completed his course at Biggin Hill he was to be posted to a Polish Fighter Squadron in Scotland, and did not expect to live very long. It was fortunate, from his point of view, that there was a wide, unkempt meadow immediately behind the house in which the Polish-looking English woman lived, and that the grass in that meadow was so tall and so dry that summer.

Over at the corner shop Archie's dream had also undergone certain modifications. Just as a ship of war alters its appearance when it ends a courtesy visit to a seaside town and steams out to engage an enemy fleet, so Archie's dream had been cleared and trimmed to meet the new emergencies. He no longer thought only in terms of cash, for his enterprises were not merely stripped for action, but geared for rapid expansion. He no longer confined himself to traffic in food, but was already feeling his way into new, unexplored territories—house-property, building sites, second-hand cars, and even nylons.

Archie had always looked further ahead than anyone else in the Avenue, and now his horizons were not, as were most people's, obscured by tank-traps and wire barricades, from reaching out into the mid 'forties, and the early 'fifties, by which time, he supposed, the Boys-on-Top would have had enough of all this nonsense, and called "finish". Then all the people who were now living in Nissen huts would come streaming home, demanding houses, and sites, and pre-war cars with only a few thousand on the clock, all of which could now be bought, by certain far-seeing gentlemen, for a mere handful of notes, extracted from oil-drums.

In the meantime there was Elaine to play with, for a man must have some fun sometimes, Elaine, whose ripeness and realism fascinated him. It was strange, he reflected, that such fruit had been hanging over his garden wall all these years without his noticing it. They had to meet far afield, of course, and at irregular intervals, but it ought to be easier now that young Fraser had joined up (and not before time, thought Archie! Dammit, somebody had to man the guns, didn't they?). The great attraction about Elaine was her complete lack of humbug, the kind of humbug that had hitherto cluttered all his extra-professional relationships with women. She sold her time to him just as he sold packets of Rinso, and pounds of self-raising flour over the counter, and he liked it that way; there were no arguments, no complications, and no danger of domestic boomerangs.

He still had his worries, of course. Maria and the two younger children whined from the distance, and Maria, who did not seem to like Somerset, had developed a distressing habit of popping up when he least expected her, and of ferreting about the corner premises, as though she was looking for something, he knew not what. Tony, his elder boy, was due to leave school next year, and talked a lot of hot air about going into the Tank Corps, which was something he would have to deal with when the time came, and he could snatch a day or two from his crowded life to run down to the school and discuss the matter with Tony's headmaster.

So we leave Archie, the ex-errand boy of the multiple store, who had learned his way around so much more expertly than his neighbours in the Avenue. He was rich now, rich in money, and rich in the promise of power. The only real problem confronting him was which he was to choose in the immediate future? More money, or more power? Possibly a judicious combination of both?

Along at Number Forty-Five, Margy Hartnell was facing a personal problem that obscured much of what was happening all around. Her smokescreen had dispersed, and her dream had gone into a deeper freeze than most, for the Hartnell eight was no longer an eight. It wasn't even a six or a five. Four of its musicians had been swept away by the Enemy Aliens Act, and were now playing patience in the Isle of Man, with the prospect of a trip across the Atlantic in the offing. As if this wasn't enough, Ted, the Eight's Kingpin, was almost out of her reach, baby notwithstanding, for the hurly-burly of Dunkirk had coaxed his conscience out of its winter sleep, and persuaded him to sign on with the Royal Ordnance Corps for the duration of the present emergency. He was now hanging about the house, blowing odd, inconsequent notes on an old saxophone, or strumming stray choruses of hoary old numbers like *Always, Souvenirs,* and even *Red Red, Robin,* whilst awaiting his papers. Margy could do little or nothing with him, and because they seemed to have lost touch with each other the prospect of the baby, due at any moment, did not seem nearly so important as it had seemed a few short months ago.

He still loved her, of course, but not in the personal sense any more, at least, so it seemed to her at the moment. She wondered rather dismally what would become of them all, now that the number that had been so popular last autumn, the one about hanging washing on the Siegfried Line, was so hideously dated.

Then, at times like these, her natural cheerfulness of disposition would fly to her rescue, and she would say to herself: "It isn't for ever, Margy. The last war lasted four years, and we've already had nearly a year of this one. People will always want rhythm. People will always want to dance. And the Ordnance Corps is a sort of packing department, isn't it, where the men aren't expected to fix bayonets and charge anyone?" Then she would force herself to smile, and call from the bedroom where she was resting:

"Ted, *Ted*! Play something more up to date for the love of God, and then make us some tea!"

Thank God there was always tea; tea, Ted, and rhythm.

Over at Number Four Becky was having her spells again.

Edith thought it must be the worry, and the noise, and the tiresomeness of it all. She had been for many years now without a real spell, so long indeed that Edith had almost forgotten how to cope with them. Then, one day in May, when everyone was talking and talking about something that was happening at a place called Dunkirk (was it the same, Edith wondered, as the town she remembered from history books that was spelled with a "q"?), Becky came home, and set about mixing things in a bowl on the kitchen table. When Edith asked her what she was doing she had said, quite quietly: "I saw Saul today, and he'll be in directly! I must start his supper. Saul will have everything fried!"

Poor Edith had wept when she realised that it might be beginning all over again, and she had gone straight upstairs to jubilant Jean McInroy, the lodger, who was still drawing the ideal British male, now in an A.R.P. outfit, like the Chief of the Auxiliary Fire Service at the Upper Road depot, where she was working part-time.

For Jean had at last located her Ideal British Male, or his nearest approximate, and she scuttled off to fire-drill three nights a week like a 'teenager going to her first dance. Once arrived at the station, in her neat navy-blue uniform and tin-hat, she would sit watching First-Officer Hargreaves demonstrate the use of a stirrup pump, and memorise, not his instructions, but the long, sweeping lines of his jaw, so that she could transform him, on her return to Number Twenty, into an Infantry officer in the magazine story she was illustrating. The agency had sent along the story and captions for the drawings and today's read: "*Anthony had no faith in seeing Madeline again, but he wanted to remember her as she looked then, adorable, enchanting, and with the promise of everlasting love in her eyes.*"

Poor Edith had no such dream to escape into. In the old days she had wished only for life to remain the same, with Becky and Ted to look after, and Lickapaw to see to when he came home from his wife-hunts in the Nursery. But life never did remain the same for long. Becky was still with her, but Ted was married, and would soon be off to the war, dear Lickapaw was dead, and all the little music pupils had gone into the country to escape the bombs everybody said would come if Britain didn't give in. Jean McInroy was well enough as a substitute lodger, but she was not going to be much good if Becky began having real spells again. All the nice people in the Avenue seemed to be splitting up, and moving out, and one could hardly expect the new ones to be as quiet and respectable, even if there were any new ones to move into the empty houses.

It was a relief indeed that dear, worried Mr. Carver was still about. She trotted along to Number Twenty almost every day now, to enquire whether he had had word of the twins, who had not come home with the other young men after that awful Dunkirk or Dunquerque business.

No, he told her each day, he had received no word beyond the official notification that they were missing, believed prisoners, but one day he had other news, very sad news. The tall, young man that his girl Judith had brought home the year before was dead, torpedoed, they thought, on his way to Egypt in a troopship. Edith wept to think of it, remembering now that Judith had told her only last summer that they planned to be married on New Year's Day, and were then going out to Kenya, where her fiancé—what was he called, Ted, or Tom, or Timothy?—intended buying a farm.

That Frith boy, from Number Seventeen, had gone too,

leaving his poor mother all alone. First her husband left, then her daughter, now her son. Edith had felt sorry for her too, and seeing Sydney depart, in his smart, new uniform, she had nerved herself to cross the road and knock timidly at the door. But Mrs. Frith did not come out to answer it, although Edith knew that she was inside, and after knocking twice Edith had gone home feeling hurt and disappointed, but telling herself that the poor woman was probably far too upset to receive anyone, however sympathetic they might be.

So it went on, with people leaving all the time, and more and more *For Sale*, and *To Let* notices going up along the sweep of the crescent. Would it end by Number Four being the only occupied house in the Avenue?

The prospect so distressed Edith that she had to leave Becky in the charge of Jean for an afternoon, and go down to the Lower Road among people, and traffic, and shops. Here, as the sun sometimes breaks through a cloud-bank when least expected, she was caught up in her old and comforting dream again, for she happened to pass the old Granada, now an Odeon, and pause for a moment to inspect the front-of-house publicity.

They were showing the much-advertised epic, *Gone With the Wind*, a book that Edith had always been meaning to read, but had somehow never found time to borrow from Carter's Twopenny Library, at the corner of Cawnpore Road. The stills in the gilded frame fascinated her, taking her back more than ten years, when the display frame, a mere plywood affair, had enclosed similar stills of Gloria Swanson, and Alice Terry, and poor, dear Rudi, whose occult eyes still gleamed out from her scrapbook.

She had not been inside the Granada, or any other cinema, since the boom of *Sonny Boy*, and she found herself wondering what films were like nowadays. A sleek young man, wearing a dinner-jacket, was standing at the top of the steps, and he smiled down at her.

"Wonderful picture," he said; "takes over three hours. Starting now."

Edith hovered a moment, heart in mouth, and then suddenly made up her mind, and climbed the once-familiar steps to the greatly enlarged foyer. She bought her ticket, and went on through the double doors as far as a new brass rail, where a childlike usherette took charge of her, and piloted her down the centre aisle into what had once been the nine-pennies.

The music rolled as Edith looked about her in wonder. It was all so much bigger and more majestic than it used to be in her day, and the film, when it began, was actually in colour. As she watched she felt the old magic returning, though it was strange not to recognise any of the actors or actresses. Within minutes, however, Edith had stopped making comparisons, and allowed herself to be carried along breathlessly on the tide of the narrative. Soon she was groping for her handkerchief, and weeping silently, and ecstatically, for poor dear Melanie, poor dear Ashley, poor, headstrong Scarlett O'Hara, and the poor ravaged South.

When at last the lights went up she was converted. She tottered blinking into the sunshine, serene and uplifted, just as though, by some wonderful miracle, poor dear Rudi had been restored to her, and she had been watching *The Son of the Sheik* in Technicolour.

She almost bubbled as she tripped up Shirley Rise, and then she recalled, a little guiltily, that it must be long past Becky's and Jean's tea-time, but as she turned into the Avenue the reprieve caught up with her, as it were, and fell into step as far as the gate of Number Four.

"Well now," she thought, "things seem to be in a terrible muddle, but there are always the pictures. Whenever things get unbearable I'll slip down to the Odeon, even if I have to come home before the supporting picture and the news."

Judith returned to the Avenue when she had official confirmation of Tim's death.

She would have returned soon enough in any case, for Maud Somerton engaged a new assistant when Judy put her wedding forward from New Year's Day to September, on account of the war, and Tim's enlistment. But now, like everything else, the riding-school business was in the doldrums, and Maud was talking of selling off horses, and economising all round.

When she was told that Tim had been drowned in a

troopship off the Western Approaches, Judy had been unable to cry. Instead she had saddled up Jason, the big chestnut, and ridden out to the corner of Hayes Wood, tethering the horse to a tree, and sitting on the bank where she had first met Tim, such a little time ago.

It was early November by then, barely two months after their wedding and their three-day honeymoon. The beeches at the extreme edge of the wood were still in leaf, for autumn idled along down here, and the leaves were still green when they were brown and sere in the Manor Wood, at home.

It was very still at the corner of the wood. Sometimes the dead bracken rustled, and the feathered larches continued to gossip, although there was hardly any breeze. Here Judy found that she could think, if not clearly, at least with some hope of getting her future into some sort of perspective.

Their plan had seemed such a modest plan to begin with, but as crisis succeeded crisis it had been subjected to all manner of shifts and adjustments, even before they worked out its main details. If everything had gone as planned she would now be buying new cabin trunks and ordering wedding cards. Instead she was still using her old brown trunk, the one salvaged from the cistern loft of Number Twenty years ago, and she was not a bride-to-be but already a widow.

There had been the quick change of plan. Tim's enlistment, the wedding in the village church, attended by her father, her sister, and Maud (a mere three against the horde of Tim's relatives who drove gaily into the West for the occasion) and then three wonderful days in Cornwall, wonderful, but overshadowed, hour by hour, by impending separation.

Then he had sailed, not to Kenya, and not with her, but to Egypt, with hundreds of other young men, and a few days later she received the 'phone call, and a visit from the scarred old Colonel, his father, who had sat holding her hand in Maud's tackroom, and said, gruffly, but very gently:

"I suppose a father shouldn't have favourites, my dear, but Tim was mine, and his mother's too. Something about him, I suppose, always laughing, young devil, even at the things I brought him up not to laugh at!"

That was it. Tim was always laughing, and she could hear his laughter yet, ringing through the beeches on the edge of the wood, and as she listened she seemed to hear a message behind his laughter, telling her to snap out of it for God's sake, and to mount Jason and gallop off up the sunken lane, and into the future. For it was unreasonable to think of there being no future for a pretty woman of twenty-six.

Because she had loved Tim she listened to him, and presently, no longer dry-eyed, she got up, and did as he bid, feeling a great deal better for the hour she had sat there.

A week later she was back in the Avenue, and a month after that, during the endless frost, she joined the W.A.A.F. as a trainee plotter, and was sent off to a Training Centre in Gloucestershire.

When the summer came, with all its alarms, she had no reason to regret the impulse that had stampeded her into uniform, for she was posted to a South Coast Fighter Station, and down there it was difficult to mourn one death among so many.

Perhaps this was a contributory factor towards the mastery of her grief, or perhaps she had learned something important as she walked her horses along the high-banked lanes and over the windy commons of the West country, or maybe she had always had a generous share of Jim's sound common-sense and, what was more to the point, his capacity to pity. At all events, she was soon able to distinguish herself at her work, and to earn commendation, and with it the promise of rapid promotion, and here we leave Judy, with her memories, good and bad, well under control. As yet no new dreams had invaded the vacuum left by the one she had lost, a dream that had, after all, led by a somewhat roundabout route to a wedding in a village church, even though the fairies had let her down rather badly in the matter of the semi-detached at Wickham.

Esme was on a Southern R.A.F. Training Station most of that summer, and he and Judy might have met but did not, for a slight defect in his vision resulted in Esme being rejected for air-crew. At the moment he was in an orderly-

room, fighting the war with an ancient Oliver typewriter and
a set of stencils.

He had not yet recovered from his surprise at finding
himself in uniform. His interest in political events over the
years had been very lukewarm despite his association with
the Shawe family, who had succeeded in converting him to
their own particular brand of Celtic Liberalism.

The invasion of Poland had caught him off guard, but after
the first shock he too had yawned his way through the
phoney war, waking up with a start when Fleet Street
seemed to go raving mad, in the last days of May. Then, at
last, he saw things as they were, and did his best to make
amends. It was not his fault that he acted with an impul-
siveness that startled old Shawe, his employer, and threw up
his job overnight to enlist. Old Mr. Shawe had been sceptical
of his chances of coming to grips with Hitler.

"Och, Laddie," he said, "do ye not know they've more men
than they can handle? Ye'll be kicking your heels in some
hole-in-corner this time next year, and how am I to replace
ye?"

But Esme was lucky, or unlucky, depending on how you
regard it, for on the strength of fast typing, and his knowledge of shorthand, he was spared the long period of defer-
ment that attended most enlistments in these days, and was
summoned within a fortnight to the R.A.F. Recruiting Centre
at Uxbridge.

Elaine seemed to take it all as a matter of course, and
Esme was vastly relieved when Eunice offered to look after
the baby in Devon. Once this was arranged everything
seemed to happen in a flash. One day he was catching one
train for the office, and the next he was catching another for
the Reception Centre at Cardington, and sharing a bell-tent
with nine other young men, in the shadow of the huge hangar
that they told him had once housed the ill-fated R.101.

In these early days, before he became bogged down in
paper work, he found the community life far more to his
liking than he had imagined possible. He discovered that he
could laugh at the hoary army jokes about parades, and
ill-fitting kit, and hoarse-voiced corporals, who darted about
among them like sheep-dogs, yet who were, he discovered,

far more patient and far less aggressive than they appeared to be in their handling of thousands of volunteers, whose qualifications as airmen were limited to good health and enthusiasm.

He missed Elaine, of couse, and little Barbara, whom he had recently taken to bathing, and who looked at him gravely, with huge, grey eyes, when he lifted her from her cot, or tried to amuse her by making a noise like a train, but he was by no means sure that Elaine would miss him as much as he felt himself entitled to be missed.

During twenty months of married life he seemed to have learned almost nothing new about her, neither had he been able to inspire in her anything more rewarding than a purely physical response to his devotion. She was still the Elaine she had always been, despite that brief glimpse he had had of her as the tender, submissive, dutiful creature during the interval between their reunion under "The Death of Chatterton" and their return from the Paris honeymoon. He never once knew, or could guess, the pattern of her thoughts, when they were alone at meals, or sitting by their fireside. She never nagged him, and such tiffs as they had were trivial, even for newly-weds. But if there were no quarrels, neither was there any real accord between them, and although he was conscious of this, he was helpless to alter it in the smallest degree. When he made love to her she was all and more than one could expect of a wife who had never pretended that she was in love with him, and if her preparation of his meals and the care of the house left something to be desired, then that too was something he had half-expected, and had settled for in advance.

As time wore on, and there were so many external things to worry about, he was able to adjust himself to her aloofness, and if it worried him at odd moments he was always able to thrust it into the back of his mind, where he kept all his disappointments, and they were many.

His dreams were mostly ghosts now, keeping silent company with the cohorts of childhood, the cavaliers in their feathered hats, and the Arthurians in their plate-armour. He was not, and was aware now that he never would be, a great and popular writer of fiction, but he had earned good money by freelance writing and that, he decided, would have to suffice for the time being, at any rate until sanity had been re-established in the world.

Of all the dreamers in the Avenue, it is probable that Esme alone was conscious of putting his dreams into cold storage; this was because his dream was fundamentally unchanged.

By what still seemed to him a miracle he had accomplished the rescue of his lady-in-a-tower, and he was not prepared to see her exchange her wimple and stomacher for a siren-suit or a battle-dress, no matter how alarmingly the sanctuary rocked and shuddered.

In his limited free time, during his six weeks recruit training, he sat down in the N.A.A.F.I. and billet to write her long and passionate letters. But married life with Elaine had brought him closer to realism than all his wanderings, and he was aware by this time that tender words meant nothing at all to her, and that the purely physical manifestations of tenderness were all that she was prepared to give, or to receive. So that letters beginning *My Own Darling Wife* seldom continued in this strain, but trailed off into animated descriptions of the men around him and the life he was leading, and the love letters that he intended should rival Napoleon's outpourings to Josephine never got written after all.

He carried her photograph about with him in his pay-book, a favourite studio portrait, taken just before their marriage, showing her with her hair in a pageboy bob, curled at the ends, her oval face, half-smiling, looking over her bare shoulder. It was an impressive likeness, and his tent-mates whistled when he showed it to them. He made no attempt to conceal his pride in her, but he was beginning to ask himself if this was sufficient to sustain him for a lifetime, and whether or not he had a right to expect something more from her in the years ahead.

Then it struck him that perhaps there were no years ahead, for any one of them. It was strange that a thought like this did not worry him as much as it seemed to worry everybody else.

There was a minor event in the Avenue towards the end of June that succeeded in bringing the people of the crescent together in a way that nothing had done since the war commenced.

The twins, Boxer and Bernard turned up, more than a month after all the other Dunkirk survivors of the suburb had spent their leaves, told their stories, and gone into fresh training for another challenge.

The reappearance of the twins was celebrated in the Avenue like a local Mafeking.

They dropped off the 'bus one day at the bottom of Shirley Rise, and wandered slowly up the hill in stained and bulging battle-dresses, each with a haversack stuffed full of N.A.A.-F.I. chocolate and battered packets of cigarettes.

They did not think of themselves as heroes, and they certainly did not regard their escape across some three hundred miles of enemy-occupied territory as in any way miraculous, or even extraordinary.

To them, so long as they were together, it had been more like a prolonged, pastoral ramble, punctuated with occasional games of string-and-parcel with the Panzers. They came across a dump of antique French mines in an abandoned village, and laid some in front of German tanks, concealing themselves close by, and watching the first tank explode with the same glee as they had once watched an unsuspecting pedestrian stoop and grab at a half-brick, neatly tied up in brown paper.

It was exhilarating to crouch behind the burned-out frontier post, and watch the tank soar into the air, like an exploding Chinese cracker. Boxer nearly had hysterics.

"Let's nip across that field, and lay some more where the road forks," he gurgled, through his laughter. "Whatd'ysay, Berni, whadysay?"

Berni had looked quickly at the rapidly-reversing Number Two tank, before nodding his blond head.

"Okay, Boxer, but look lively, before the silly sods come out and see what's hit 'em!"

They laid another mine, and narrowly avoided a stream of machine-gun bullets. Then they moved on, crossing mile after mile of parched countryside, stopping to pass bits of news to distraught refugees, and unarmed poilus, whom they met in shattered villages, and whooping with delight when they came upon an abandoned N.A.A.F.I., with its stores and even its till intact.

Boxer disliked the N.A.A.F.I. "Let's set it on fire, and watch it burn," he suggested, after they had helped themselves to everything they could carry. "Whatd'ysay, Berni, whadysay?"

But Berni had sympathy for the hundreds of civilians who were now well behind them, and had slowly shaken his head.

"No, Boxer, let's leave it for the Frogs. The poor baskets can do with it, I reckon!"

And so they rambled their way along the coast, heading due west into Brittany, where their astonishing luck held, and they were able to jump a coal-barge on the point of putting out for Falmouth.

Jim gasped when he came in and saw them wolfing food in the kitchen that night. Then, with a great bound, he jumped to embrace them, thumping their backs, and pummelling them as he had never done when they were children. After he had coaxed some of the details of their escape from them, he refused their invitation to go down to the local and celebrate, but went instead, across the meadow, and into Manor Wood, taking the winding path to the lake in front of the old house.

Strike, the retriever, pottered along in his wake, too old now, and too blind, to chase sticks and imaginary rabbits.

It was dusk when man and dog returned, and as he crossed the Avenue, Jim saw a pipe glowing at the gate of Number Twenty-Two, and paused to exchange a word with Harold Godbeer, who was standing there in his shirtsleeves, looking down into the crescent.

The two men had never been intimate, in spite of living next-door to one another for more than twenty years.

In the past Jim had always thought of Harold as a "typical bourgeois", but that was in his agitating days, before he really understood the word. Now he thought of him as a little dull and stuffy, and would have written him down in committee-meeting jargon as "typically white-collar".

For his part Harold had always thought of Jim as a rather dangerous fellow. Ten years ago he too would have had his labels ready, and would have classified him "Red", or "Bolshie". But ready-made labels were not as reliable as they had once been, and now he would have preferred to describe his neighbour merely as "a steady chap, but Left Wing".

"I just wanted to say how delighted I was about your boys," he told Jim. "My word, but they must have had some terrible experiences over there!"

Yes, said Jim, they had, and were probably a great deal luckier than they realised. It was an obvious, and a civil reply, but as he said it Jim found himself drawn towards this peaky-faced little man, who had been such an inoffensive neighbour for so long, and because he was feeling uplifted by the miraculous return of the twins his natural reserve lost its topmost crust, and he felt closer to Harold than he had ever felt over the years.

Leaning on his front gate he showed a disposition to chat.

"What do you make of it all, Godbeer?" he began. "Pretty frightening, isn't it?"

Harold said nothing for a moment, but sucked his pipe, while he endeavoured to adjust himself to Jim's unexpected cordiality.

"Well, I'm not as worried as I *was*, old man," he said at length. "No, I'm not *nearly* as worried as I was!"

Jim was mildly surprised. He would have imagined Harold Godbeer to be the type of man who had helped to keep the muddlers in power for so long between the wars, and who was therefore quite incapable of facing up to the liquidation of the British Empire, and the collapse of civilisation as they both knew it. He would have wagered a pound note that, throughout the past winter, his neighbour had slept serenely on the ramparts of the Maginot Line, and was now floudering hopelessly in a welter of terrifying possibilities. Nevertheless he recognised, from Harold's tone, that this was not so.

"Do you think they'll have a shot at invasion?" he asked.

"No, old chap," replied Harold very levelly, "I certainly don't! I think they'll try hard to make us believe that they're going to, but their nerve will fail 'em at the last minute. As a matter of fact, I think that chap Hitler is in for one hell of a shock!"

Jim was impressed by the man's quiet, forceful confidence. It wasn't the brand of confidence he had encountered in pubs and committee rooms recently, rehashes of hastily written leader-articles, or echoes of the bombast of bewildered politicians. It was a confidence that had obviously grown up inside the man while he was living *here*, in this Avenue, among millions of people almost exactly like him, it was a distillation of centuries of security and national triumph, with its roots deep down in Trafalgar and Waterloo, and the assault on the Hindenburg Line. It drew its strength from the dry bones of men like Palmerston, and Gladstone, and Sir Edward Grey, and its inspiration from the Chartist movement, and the Education Act, and Lloyd George's campaign against the House of Lords. It was born and belonged here, among the small, neatly-kept front gardens of the terrace, with their rough-cast fronts, little gatepost pillars, and looped chains, that seemed at this moment of history to make each little block of brick and slate a fortified castle, manned by a garrison who would count it a privilege to die where they stood, with or without some reserve ammunition in the back bedroom.

Looking at Harold's pale, narrow face, in the soft glow of the pipe-bowl, Jim's doubts and fears of the last few weeks fell away from him. He felt immensely braced and refreshed by the contact, and intensely curious to hear more.

"Go on, Godbeer," he said earnestly, "tell me *why* you think that, please—it's important to me . . . I don't mind admitting, I've been in a fog up to now!"

Harold smiled into the gathering dusk, vaguely flattered by his neighbour's invitation.

"Well now, I don't pretend to be a strategist, old man," he went on, "but I've always thought of myself as a man of average intelligence, and I like to think about what I read, and what I see. Now here are those two boys of yours, I watched them grow up, and it always fascinated me to note how they always did everything together. Well, you see how it paid off in the end? Someone turned them loose over there, weaponless, as far as I can see, and with every card stacked against them. Just turned 'em loose, with the entire country-side in chaos, and what did they do? They just set out for home, using their heads, I imagine, and absolutely refusing to panic. But what struck me about it all when I talked to them earlier this evening was that they did it *together*, the same as they've always done everything together, and it seems to me—this is a bit far-fetched, no doubt—that this is what we've all got to do from now on. We've got to stop nagging at one another, and face up to things as *a people* again, the way we did last time, and I don't doubt every time before that! Once we do that no one can beat us. We'll get hurt all right, and it wouldn't surprise me if a lot of us didn't live to see the end of it, but plenty will, enough to put paid to that mob of scoundrels. The point is, if we once *do* this, if we once show the rest of the world that we're not going to stand for the sort of thing that's been going on long enough over there, then we'll be a sort of front-line of our own, and everyone else in the world who thinks like us will come bustling up to lend a hand. When that happens it can't last very long, can it, old chap? Nobody's going to convince me that there aren't a damned sight more decent people about than there are bullies and perverts, who get a kick out of stamping on other people's corns. Does that seem sense to you, Carver?"

Jim took a deep breath, inhaling the scent of baking grass, that blew in from the meadow on the light breeze. He felt better, and more at peace with himself, than at any time since Munich.

"It makes a dam' sight more sense than anything I've read in the papers since the last Armistice, Godbeer," he said emphatically, "and if my guess is right, and all the people round here think even roughly as you do, then I'd say you're on a good wicket, old chap, and that that little bastard is in for the biggest surprise of his life! I'd better go in now, the twins'll be back from the pub. Goodnight, old man!"

"Goodnight," said Harold, methodically knocking out his pipe on the pillar of Number Twenty-Two.

They went in, closing their doors after them.

The moon rose slowly over the beeches of Manor Wood, and its white light crept over the blacked-out façade of the even numbers. Presently, far away to the south-east, beyond the wood and the open ploughland of the Kent border, came the faint, intermittent throb of heavy aero-engines, and a moment later, from the direction of Shirley Rise, the long, banshee note of the siren.

People began to move inside the silent houses, making their preparations.

In the store at the corner Archie Carver came out of the back door, and carried a fire-extinguisher inside, placing it immediately above the trap that covered his oil-drum vault.

At Number Four, Jean McInroy buttoned her navy battle-dress blouse, and groped for her tin-helmet, reflecting, with a glow of pleasure, that it was her night on, and that she would soon be sharing a mug of tea with Chief Officer Hargreaves, the Ideal British Male, lean-jawed, silent, and superbly cool in a crisis.

At Number Seventeen, Esther Frith climbed stiffly out of bed, and fell upon her knees. Whenever the siren sounded she made a point of asking Jehovah to deflect all high-explosive and phosphorous from Pilot-Officer Frith, S. (Accounts Branch), wherever he might be. Her greying hair fell forward over her clasped hands, and her pale lips moved soundlessly. "Oh Lord, keep Sydney safe, keep Sydney away from the bombs."

It was not exactly a prayer. It was more like a politely expressed command.

At Number Four, Edith lit a candle, and gently woke Becky. "Come along, Becky dear, the si-*reen's* going! I've put the thermos under the stairs. We'll make ourselves comfy, and have a nice cup of tea. Come along now, there's a dear."

At Number One, little Miss Baker turned stiffly in her specially-constructed bed, flicked on her bedside light, opened her leather-bound volume of Rupert Brooke at the turned-down page, and began reading, *Blow Out You Bugles*. In the winter ahead this poem was to become a talisman against sirens, crumps, and the cough of aircraft-engines overhead.

At Number Twenty, Jim Carver made cocoa for Louise, Jack Strawbridge, and the faintly amused twins, as they all sat smoking in the kitchen. Boxer, grinning his medieval clown's grin, pulled back the blackout curtain an inch or so, and said: "Let's go out and have a looksee! Whatd'ysay, Berni, whad'ysay?" Bernard peeped too, and then winked at his father, where he stood pouring cocoa.

"Nope, Box! You go if you like. Me? I've had a bellyfull of bombs for the time being."

But Boxer, of course, did not go.

At Number Twenty-Two, next door, Harold finished screwing his striped trousers into Esme's abandoned trouser-press, and then went downstairs to mix himself a strong dose of bicarbonate.

His indigestion was very troublesome these days, and he was yearning for Eunice. When he heard the first far-away crump he kissed her photograph, and then gathered his flannel dressing-gown around him, turned off the light, and opened the kitchen door to look out into the clear sky. He was not afraid to die, but if he had to he would have much preferred to die with his pretty, silly wife close at hand.

Over at Number Forty-Three, Elaine Fraser was whispering to the Pole, "Stevie", as they stood, with his push-cycle held between them, in the deep shadow where the back gate of Number Forty-Three opened on to the meadow. "Not *now*, Stevie, there are too many people about! *No*, Stevie darling, you mustn't come in, Stevie. Thursday then— Thursday, I promise!"

She leaned over the 'cycle, and kissed him as lightly as it is possible to kiss a Pole. He tried to grab her, but she escaped from him with a little giggle, and ran up the path and into the kitchen, locking the door after her. When she was sure he had gone she shook the grass from the plaid rug she was carrying, and poured herself a large gin, sipping it slowly, and looking at herself in the mirror over the sideboard. She felt a little breathless and battered, and wondered whether she should answer the 'phone when he rang on Thursday. Then she felt sorry for him as, in a sense, she felt sorry for all men, all over the world. It must be terribly lonesome, she thought, to be hounded and hounded by such insatiable appetites, appetites urgent enough to induce Stefan to break camp, and push-bike all the way over from Biggin Hill night after night, urgent enough to induce Esme to hitch-hike two hundred miles last week, for a single night in her arms, and strong enough to persuade Archie Carver, who worshipped money, to part with it by the handful simply for the pleasure of an hour or so in her company. Tiresome for them, lucky for her.

She finished her gin and went slowly upstairs. She was not afraid of bombs and sirens, or of being alone in the house. She was afraid of nothing, except perhaps that awful water-dream, that still came back to her at irregular intervals.

Next door, at Number Forty-Five, Margy Hartnell sighed when she heard the long, wailing note, and felt the child kick inside her. What a hell of a time to have a baby! And Ted's papers had arrived that day, which meant that he would be leaving on Monday. He called up from below: "I've made the tea, Margy. Shall I bring it up, or will you come down?"

"I'll come down," she called back, rolling out of bed, and prodding about for her quilted slippers.

At Number One Hundred-and Two, Grandpa Barnmeade emerged in his full regalia—tin-hat, armband, and mace-like torch.

He stood looking up into the clear sky for a moment, muttering to himself, and then he saw a pinpoint of light, over on the odd side, where the crescent's curve was sharp-est. He began to run towards it, very nimbly considering his age. "Put that light out," he roared, while still fifty yards away, "put that flaming light out, you bloody fool."

There were a few people of the Avenue who were too far away to hear the siren that night, but they had read about the early raids in the papers, and their thoughts went back to the Avenue as soon as the moon rose.

Up in Llandudno, Edgar Frith lay staring at the ceiling. Frances and Pippa were already asleep, for they all went to bed much earlier these days, and he was wondering whether Esther's frigid, religious faith would help her through a bad air-raid. He hoped it would, but whether it did or did not he had made up his mind to write to Sydney in the morning, and instruct him to find his mother a place in the country. He should have done that before, long before. If he didn't drop